Polish Troops in the Middle East 1942-1943

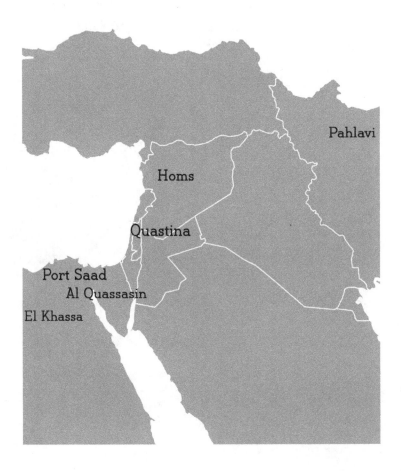

Pahlavi

Homs

Quastina

Port Saad
Al Quassasin

El Khassa

Polish II Corps in Italy
1943-1945

Bologna

Ancona

Rome

Monte
Cassino

Sangro River
Bari

Michael Pawlowski, after graduating from the University of Toronto, served the community in the insurance and legal professions. His memberships have included the Canadian Authors' Association, Brave New Works, Niagara Historical Society, Insurance Institute, Arbitration and Mediation Institute of Ontario, and the Law Society of Upper Canada. The obligation to tell 'the rest of the story' has motivated all of his literary endeavours. Michael is absolutely delighted with the publication of his novel: *Cassino, Conquest of the Mountain.*

To my father, Bernard Pawlowski and to all of the soldiers of the Polish II Corps who gave their lives and lost their country.

Michael Pawlowski

CASSINO, CONQUEST OF THE MOUNTAIN

AUSTIN MACAULEY
PUBLISHERS LTD.

A CIP catalogue record for this title is available from the British Library.

ISBN 9781786293190 (Paperback)
ISBN 9781786293206 (Hardback)
ISBN 9781786293213 (E-Book)
www.austinmacauley.com

First Published (2017)
Austin Macauley Publishers Ltd.
25 Canada Square
Canary Wharf
London
E14 5LQ

CONTENTS

PROLOGUE

Cassino, Conquest of the Mountain is the biography of Bernard Pawlowski, a soldier in the Polish 3rd Carpathian Rifle Division: from the first day of World War II, to the successful campaign in Italy.

Bernard was fourteen years old, living on a farm near Poznan, when he was seized by the Wehrmacht. After being transferred from one concentration camp to another, Bernard escaped from a moving train. With the assistance of the Polish Underground, he fled to Czechoslovakia, and then through Hungary to Italy. From Bari, he sailed to the Levant where he was adopted by the Polish force in Syria. After training in Egypt, the Polish troops were triumphant in capturing Monte Cassino. Bernard was one of the first to ascend the summit. Following successful campaigns in Italy, the Polish II Corps was disbanded. The troops had nowhere to go.

During this narrative of Bernard's torment, liberation and military combat, the dire events in Europe, particularly in Poland, are recounted: the occupations and tyranny, the mass murders and annihilation of races, the appeasement of nations, and the many factors and decisions that prompted the Allies to surrender the independence of the Polish nation to the Soviet Union. For one moment, none of us can imagine what it is like to fight for your country when it no longer exists, or to be successful in war and not have a home to which to return.

Cassino, Conquest of the Mountain is this tale of dreams buried in torment, of freedom fractured by tyranny, of national pride succumbed to abandonment, and of victory without recognition.

CAST OF CHARACTERS
(All persons listed are actual persons)

POLAND
Bernard Pawlowski - 14 yr old in September, 1939
Leon Pawlowski - Father of Bernard, Ryszard, Elzbieta
Teresa Pawlowski - Mother of Bernard, Ryszard, Elzbieta
Ryszard Pawlowski - 11 yr old Brother of Bernard
Elzbieta Pawlowski - 9 yr old Sister of Bernard
Andrzej Pawlowski - Brother of Bernard, born in 1940
Michal Pawlowski - Uncle of Bernard
Ignacy Moscicki - President of Poland
August Hlond - Archbishop of Poznan
Yacob Yossef - Rabbi of Poznan
Wladyslaw Anders - General of Polish II Corps
Zygmunt Bohusz-Szyszko - General of Polish II Corps
April 1945
Wilhelm Orlik-Ruckermann - Polish General in Kresy
Walerian Czuma - Polish General of Warsaw Army
Franciszek Kleeberg - Polish General at Battle of Kock
General Stanislaw Kopanski - Polish Independent
Carpathian Rifle Brigade
Josef Zajac - Chief of Polish Forces in the Middle East
Ivan - Prisoner
Iwan - Prisoner
Tomasz - Prisoner
Bartosz - Prisoner
Jarek - Prisoner
Stanislaw Wadja - farmer
Aniela Wadja - farmer's wife

Maciej - member of Resistance Movement
Radomil - Polish Underground
Czlowiek (The man) - Polish Underground
Bronislaw Duch - Commander of 3rd Carpathian Rifle Division
Hendryk - Member of 3rd Carpathian Rifle Division
Franck - Member of 3rd Carpathian Rifle Division
Franciszek - Member of 3rd Carpathian Rifle Division
Piotr - Member of 3rd Carpathian Rifle Division
Dawid - Member of 3rd Carpathian Rifle Division
Jerzy - Member of 3rd Carpathian Rifle Division
Wiktor - Member of 3rd Carpathian Rifle Division
Tomasz - Member of 3rd Carpathian Rifle Division
Nikodem Sulik - Commander of 5th Kresowa Division
Lieutenant Gurbiel - Lieutenant of the 12th Uhlan Regiment

BRITAIN
Neville Chamberlain - Prime Minister
Winston Churchill - Prime Minister
Sir Harold Alexander - Commander-In-Chief
Sir Bernard Montgomery - General of British 8th Army Aug.1942-Dec.1943
Oliver Leece - General of British 8th Army Dec.1943-Oct.1944
Richard McCreery - General of British 8th Army Oct.1944-May. 1945
Mary Saunders - Student at Holy Cross School
Reverend Jozef Madeja - Chaplain at Hodgemoor Woods Camp

UNITED STATES
Dwight Eisenhower - Five Star General
Mark Clark - Major General of US 5th Army
John Lucas - General of US 6th Corps.
Lucian Truscott - General of US 6th Corps

THIRD REICH

Adolf Hitler - Fuhrer

Rudolph Hess - Deputy Fuhrer

Martin Bormann - Gruppenfuhrer, Hitler's Private Secretary

Heinrich Himmler - Reichsfuhrer of Schutzstaffel S.S.

Joseph Goebbels - Propaganda Minister

Reinhard Heydrich - Architect of Final Solution

Adolf Eichmann - Director of Holocaust

Joachim von Ribbentrop - German diplomat

Hermann Goering - Commander of Luftwaffe

Gustaf Kleikamp - Captain of SMS Acheswig-Holstein

Karl Reimers - Luftwaffe Command Bomber Pilot

Abel Russman - Stuka Pilot

Heinz Guderian - General of XIX Panzer Corps

Konrad Werner - Sergeant Major of 8th German Army

Arthur Greiser - Gauleiter (Governor) of Poznan

Ernst Werner - Commandant, Fort VII Concentration Camp

Amon Goethe - Commandant, Plaszow Concentration Camp

Odilo Globocnik - Commander of Operation Reinhard

Pawel Degenhardt - Commandant of Czestochowa Ghetto

Eugene Mittelhauser - General in Vichy France

Erwin Rommel - Field Commander

Albert Kesselrig - Field Marshal, Commander in Chief

Heinrich von Vietinghoff - General in 10th Army

Friedrich Paulus - General of 6th Army

SOVIET UNION

Iosif Stalin - General Secretary of Central Committee

Vyacheslav Molotov - First Deputy Chairman/Premier Diplomat

Sergei Ulanov - Soviet assistant to diplomat

Lavrentiy Beria - Chairman of Soviet Secret Police

Grigoriy Litvinov - Member of Soviet Secret Police

Georgy Zhukov Chief of Staff, Deputy Minister of Defence
Mikhail Kovalyov Soviet Commander of Belarusian Front
Simon Timoshenko - Commander of Ukrainian Front,
Minister of Defence
Igor Kurchatov - Nuclear Weapons Program Director

AUSTRALIA
John Curtin - Prime Minister

CANADA
W. L. MacKenzie King - Prime Minister

CZECHOSLOVAKIA
Emil Beier - Nazi Governor of Ostrava
Pavol Tesar - Factory manager
Karina Tesar - Daughter of factory manager

INDIA
Hari Singh - Maharaja of Jammu and Kashmir
Harry Dimoline - Brigadier Officer in British Indian Army

IRAN
Reza Pahlavi - Shah of Iran
Aminollah Jahanbani - Minister of War

ITALY
Guglio - worker at shipbuilding yards
Reverend Pawel - Priest at St. Nicholas Church

NEW ZEALAND
Peter Fraser - Prime Minister
Bernard Freyburg - Commander of New Zealand Divisions

Chapter One
September 1, 1939

Rain from heaven did not fall that September morn; nor had it rained throughout all of August. Crops were picked, many were already shrivelled or rotted. Streams were drying. Animals were thirsty.

Fear and anxiety poured upon the population of western Poland. There had been so many threats. The Soviet-Nazi Pact affirmed the inevitable. Rhineland, Austria, and Czechoslovakia proved their capability. Dachau – the world knew. The terror of a raving lunatic – no one was stopping him. The horror of invasion consumed family life.

To run – they could. But, to where?

The young man dashed across the dusty yard. Farm duties were his chore. Many of his age would do anything possible to avoid them, but Bernard was different. Taking care of God's creation was his delight.

Expectant expressions greeted him every morning. Two horses, four pigs and several cows heralded the opening door with throaty sounds and brushing hooves. Even the chickens and rabbits reacted with instinctive joy. Bernard envied them. They had no fears, only assurance that every morning that young man with a plaid shirt and brown pants would be there to feed them.

Bernard was 14 years old on that September 1st of 1939. He had just celebrated his birthday thirty-one days before.

His mother was a dutiful loving housewife. Teresa provided for her children. She was like the perfect swan, guarding her cygnets in every way possible. Farm produce was always available. There was no day in which the family did not have a wonderful meal in spite of any restrictions on fuel. Many came to her from the community. Teresa was always there to answer their needs.

Bernard's father, Leon, operated a clothing store in Poznan. He designed clothes hiring two women to complete the task. Leon also worked with leather making shoes, hats, saddles and farm accessories. When the sale of dresses and shirts did not prove profitable, Leon switched to coats and shawls. His customers were appreciative, increasing in number with the coming winter.

Bernard had younger siblings: a brother Ryszard and a sister Elzbieta. Every day their mom took them to school and would accompany them home. Breakfast, like supper, was always a family gathering. There were normal disagreements, but always caring affection for each other. He often wondered how much he should thank God for his family life.

The young man looked forward to starting high school the following week. It wasn't just school, or a new school; but it was his friends. Summers always separated classmates with each having so many other chores, especially this year with the harvest starting in late July due to the drought. How many would return to school? There were rumours about several joining the army. Bernard knew he could do that because he was good with machinery and could ride a horse well. However he was well aware that a cavalry could never stop tanks.

Bernard loved history. It was so romantic with all of the personal tales and national struggles. Poland was at long last independent for these last twenty years, twenty-one in November. He was proud of his country being able to stop the Soviet attacks. The Treaty of Riga gave him confidence. There had been four elections since independence. Bernard loved democracy. So many more could read now. He couldn't believe the good fortune since Versailles.

Several students, he knew, would not be back. Audrea had been emphatic about her family and her heritage. She had vowed they would move west believing Poland had no right to occupy German land. Bernard, prone to anxious outbursts, had told her she could leave any time she wished. The teachers did not object to any patriotic fervour.

Jacob was also to be leaving – for America. He was a gentle sort, kind, but always a follower. Jewish? Many never understood why a Catholic school accepted such a student. But to Bernard, Jacob was a boy, a friend, a companion. He learned more of Hebrew practice than could ever be taught in any school. These were good people. Jacob's family conveyed kindness and a conciliatory acceptance. Yet in those summer months Bernard never heard any more about his friend.

Dariusz could be a volatile youth. Fellow classmates concluded this about him from his views supporting authoritarian leadership. Some presumed Dariusz supported the Bolsheviks. Bernard instead appreciated the opportunities to exchange thoughts on ideological issues.

Dariusz had no interest in the Stalin's Soviet Union. He espoused a benevolent dictatorship, a concept not so foreign to young aspiring minds. His family left for Hungary in early August. It was said that their farm sold for a pittance.

Many teachers would not be back having vowed to enlist. Bernard had heard that the total force in Poland was now numbering close to one million. He knew that from the last census, Poland had almost twenty-two million people, and that almost a quarter million of these lived in Poznan itself. History and figures were good to Bernard. It gave him understanding of life, and the occasional nightmare of the future.

The cows were fed. The pigs relished the Courtland apples. Raking the stalls was his least favourable chore. Yet like all others it had to be done. After that, as he did every morning, he looked up to the roof boards searching for any glimmer of light, ensuring there were no leaks. Bernard then checked the stability of the corrals, noting them to be in sound condition. The two horses were led to their hitching post outside. They bounced elatedly knowing their destination. Outside they eagerly chomped on the hay. Everything about their manner conveyed a sense of appreciation that was more than instinctive. Bernard often wondered if there was a place in heaven for such thankful animals.

The chickens too had a field day with all of the seed. Bernard hoped that his father would sell a couple of coats this week so they could have extra to buy more feed. There was only enough for one more week.

The rabbits also welcomed his presence, scurrying to the one side of massive cage. They were a godsend especially in the winter and rainy months. Chops or stew, even legs were wonderful tasty meals. Mother always had the right seasoning.

Bernard stood outside the barn looking into the fields. The corn and grain had been picked. A family friend had silos, so the goods were stored there. Bernard always marvelled at how well everyone got along with everyone else in this village outside Poznan's city limits. Then he quickly added to that thought noting in his mind that it was no longer just a village. If Poznan's expansion grew west anymore, there would be no farm. "But then," he concluded, "that will never happen. God will provide."

Turning around he looked toward the distant hill. Fields of sunflowers floated toward the horizon. "So beautiful," he whispered. His gaze then returned to the two horses. Bernard moved in their direction. It was a habit that prompted him to pray, he always prayed The Our Father standing in the yard looking out over God's benefice.

Ojcze Nasz, któryś jest w niebiesiech,

święć się imię twoje; przyjdż królestwo

twoje, bądż wola twoja, jako w niebie tak

i na ziemi. Chleba naszego powszedniego

daj nam dzisiaj, i odpuść nam nasze winy,

jako i my odpuszczamy naszym winowajcom.

During the prayer Bernard was prompted by some unexplained force to peer to his left. His prayer did not continue. There was a dark film on the horizon. Uncertainty became perplexity. The unknown was always foreboding. He stared intently. The ebony film became a dark thick band. Motion was definite, descending the incline. Bernard ran to his horses, not knowing exactly what, but starting to fear the worst. He whinnied to the steeds getting them inside their stalls. Moving down the centre of the barn he spoke to the cows offering assurance.

From the rear door, Bernard tried to get the chickens inside but they had no interest. Dropping some seed on the barn floor, he was able to entice several to return to shelter. Then Bernard returned to the horses, his favourites, stroking each one and patting their foreheads. For whatever reason, not just instinct, they were not jealous of each other. They always knew the young man would have enough time for both.

"Bernard!" his mother yelled from the house.

He turned, shocked by the demanding tone. "Na zdrowie," he whispered to the horses, giving each a final pat on the nose.

"Bernard!" his mother repeated.

He slammed the barn door, flipping the wooden latch; then ran across the yard.

"I must go right away."

"Where?" the son exhaustively enquired.

"Get the children. Knew this would happen. God, spare us."

His mother grabbed her shawl and ran out of the house. Bernard followed her passage onto the dirt road toward the school. Then he looked back toward the horizon. The black stream was now thicker, more ominous, frightening to the young teenager. Prayers were hastily repeated. "Dad?" he whispered. Motion on the horizon was discernible. He stepped onto the side porch for a better view, but most of that was obscured by dense growth of trees. "Dad?" he whispered from his heart.

(I I)

Karl Reimers was overly proud of his appointment, Luftwaffe Command Pilot. Everyone had a title. Such prestige made every German part of the Nazi dream. There were some issues not agreeing with his Christian morals. However those all belonged to a past generation, to a world dominated by the revenge of European nations who considered Germany a vile rodent, a vermin to be stamped out.

The Jews? That was an issue Karl would leave to the experts.

His bomber, Heinkel HE 111, would complete the task. His sights were set. Poland, whatever would be left of it, would be German once more. The co-pilot was quiet. He knew his position.

Heinz Guderian felt self-righteously superior in his position, as the Commander of XIX Panzer Corps. The assignment was simple: nothing was to stand in his way. He guaranteed that to his brother, the Chief of General Staff. To Heinz, the specifics of nineteenth century history really didn't matter. Poland had no right to exist as an independent state. It had usurped German land after the most hated treaty, and now Poland must pay the price. Heinz had one truth, one goal. If anything got in his way, well, it wouldn't.

Konrad Werner was an arrogant German. He conveyed every trait of bloodlust that history would ascribe to the aggressive nature of the Nazi war machine. His surname, too, echoed the belligerent contempt he bore to others. His name meant war.

Werner was a Sergeant Major, by an order recognizing his service with the Prussian Gestapo and in the acquisition of Bohemia and Czechoslovakia's remaining lands. His brother was presently influential in Berlin with a post considering the Jewish Question.

To Werner, there was no question. Konrad Werner was a devout participant in the Thule Society. German Supremacy was its fundamental precept. The principles were the foundation of Hitler's Mein Kampf – a book Werner had read many times. Belonging to the same society that embraced Adolf Hitler was obviously a benefit. The Thule Society justified any means to its essential end. The Jews, the Gypsies, degenerate men of effeminate nature, black persons, communists, and even Christians were the enemy. When you remove the enemies from Germany, you achieve the Supreme Arian Society. It was not just a concept to Konrad. It was real, the principle that directed his villainy.

Konrad Werner led his battalion of the German 8th Reichsheer into the valley west of Poznan. They had left

Trebnitz, Germany hours before. Hunger for battle had become bloodlust. The major thrust of the 8th Army was Lotz. Its final goal was Warsaw. Werner himself was commissioned to bring Poznan to its knees – burn its farmland, decimate its population, murder its Jews, and destroy the Polish army stationed at Poznan's citadel. Werner led the seventy-two vehicles providing rapid transport for essential soldiers and ammunition. The sergeant major vowed the Wehrmacht would complete the annihilation and assert German authority over territory destined to be theirs for the next one thousand years. There was to be no pity.

(III)

President Ignacy Moscicki panicked. He had done so for a week. Before August 23, 1939 he had feared Hitler's territorial plans, but thought he might have maybe two to five years before any confrontation. Still, there were fears.

Poland already had a security agreement with France. Such pacts had been necessary after Germany entered the Spanish Civil War. However, in the Spring of 1939 that pact with France became tenuous. France no longer wanted any part of Eastern Europe.

Hitler, too, became busy arranging his own accord with the Ukrainian Nationalists, wedging Poland between two extremes. The Nazis had also issued its demand to Lithuania, wishing to ensure the Baltic Corridor in German hands. The Axis alliance, vowing to destroy freedom, was the nightmare of European nations.

Then on that fateful fourth Wednesday of August, not only Hitler but Stalin too determined the fate of

Moscicki's beloved country. He had one million troops and over six hundred aircraft. However this was nothing compared to the combined force of eleven million Nazi and Soviet Troops.

The Prime Minister worked fast, and in two days had achieved an agreement with Great Britain. He was somewhat relieved, but his apprehensions remained. He was relying on a British government that had believed Hitler's every word at Munich.

Then the Gleiwitz Incident occurred, the only provocation Hitler needed to invade. All attempts at any negotiation in that last week failed.

After August 23, 1939, Warsaw prayed.

(I V)

In spite of any agreement with the Nazis, Iosif Stalin could never forget that the Dachau Concentration Camp had been established six years earlier to accommodate Jews, Slavs and his Communists. Hitler had happily proclaimed to the world that that detention centre would stop the spread of Bolshevism; and the world agreed.

But it wasn't just Dachau that prompted Stalin to carefully consider his alliance with the Nazis. Hitler had already attempted a pact with the Ukrainian Nationalists. Germany's intention was to surround Poland like a vice grip. However, Ribbentrop seemed to be forgetting that the Ukraine was part of the Soviet Union, and that the USSR would never tolerate any support for any independence movement.

Hitler, too, had previously declared his interest in Scandinavia and the Balkans. Specifically from Sweden, Hitler was obtaining more than sixty per cent of the iron ore necessary for remilitarisation. The Balkans provided Hitler with a wedge dividing Europe from the Baltic to the Adriatic. Stalin would never allow Germany to have unilateral control of those states.

In Spain, Germany was at war against the communists. Hitler's aim was to establish the Fascist rule of Francisco Franco. The Soviet force supported the deposed communist government. For both Hitler and Stalin, Spain had become the opportunity to experiment with their weapons. Would Germany then turn east and invade the USSR?

Stalin, too, remained wary of Hitler's intent with the Jews. The Soviet Union had no intention of opening its borders to any Jew fleeing Europe, especially from Poland. The Tsar had got rid of them more than thirty years ago. Stalin refused to have to confront that problem again.

In spite of everything, Poland was the key. Iosif Stalin realized he had to achieve an agreement with Germany primarily to thwart further expansion that the lunatic Hitler might later explore. More importantly, all land to the east of the Vistula River would now belong to the Soviet Union.

Stalin may have displayed the image of a tyrant, but he was a proud tyrant. USSR had a thriving industrial economy. Preparations for war had put so many to work. Employed peasants were happy workers. Factories flourished. Rail lines expanded. Cities grew. The Soviet five-year agricultural plan assured the necessary produce. War was incredibly beneficial.

(V)

For Arch Bishop August Hlond it was easy to read the minds of his parishioners. They were all terrified. Fear had no religious boundaries. For thirteen years, he had been the Prelate of Katedra Swiety Piotr i Pawel in Poznan. His knees were sore. The bishop could not say enough prayers. His voice was fading. Words were faltering. The Vatican Pact had given him some assurance, but he knew it meant nothing to Hitler. The priests were scared. Most nuns were ready to flee. However, the people were in need of their pastor. Farmers, shopkeepers, teachers, government workers, the unemployed, homeless, widows, grandparents and children – these were his flock. The clergy would remain. The Church would be there to do what it could to fight and to reassure.

(V I)

Rabbi Yossef visited a baker that morning. His congregation was the largest in Poznan. Out of the two thousand Jews in the city, more than half attended his synagogue. The purpose of his meeting with the Harel family would be most trying. How could he provide any comfort when the world was closing doors to the Jewish community? The horror of Kristallnacht still echoed beyond German borders. The certainty of destruction and death forced many to flee. Like the Harel family, being aboard a ship destined for North America was beyond a dream. Then they were turned away. For nine centuries England had proclaimed, "There are no Jews in England!" From Spain, the Jews had already been expelled. In southern Europe, they were not wanted; and in the Slavic countries they were despised. On that morning, Rabbi Yossef had run out of consoling expressions as there were none left.

Others in the Jewish community grasped at an improbable reality. The pacts with France and the United Kingdom would protect them, many thought. "War will never happen," others ventured. Throughout Europe, the destruction of synagogues and property had begun. But, Poland was different. In 1864, it had been one of the first nations to enshrine civic liberties of all persons regardless of race, ethnicity or religion. Some Jews were thankful for their good fortune. They had thriving businesses, and good family lives. Many believed such blessings could not be found elsewhere. And, there were still others who thought that if war did ever happen then the Poland, who had thwarted the Soviet Union in 1921, could stop any Nazi invasion.

Was the end near? Outside communications had been disrupted for a week now.

Rabbi Yossef did not realize that when he led his congregation on August 26th in the hymn Lecha Dodi Likrat Kallah (Come my beloved to meet the Sabbath bride), it would be his last opportunity to pray with his family.

(VII)

Leon Pawlowski was ever so thankful for his family. His wife – there could be no one kinder. That sense of generosity did him well in business, for it taught him that the most insignificant act of kindness may never be forgotten. Repeat customers meant a future. The farm provided food, and always the means to again be generous to others. Lately, he had been thinking of Christmas and the need to provide the church with food donations for those less fortunate. His sons and daughter were smart academically, and intuitive in so many aspects of life. They shared chores, participated in sports and school activities, and always smiled at their success.

Enterprise in Poznan flourished. However there were too many businesses conducting the same transactions, selling the same goods, looking for the same customers. Leon's friends were many, among them several in the Jewish community. He accommodated their needs, their dress and customs as much as he could. There were so many to consider who felt compromised by so many multi-linguistic cultures. In the city, not all were receptive to others. "It is very hard to be humble when you're waving your fist at someone." Leon was always philosophical; and his son adored him for that.

(V I I I)

The German SMS Acheswig-Holstein had been moored in Danzig harbour for a week. This was in appearance a courtesy visit, to honour the German seamen buried in Danzig. Danzig too was predominantly German-speaking in a Polish state. Situated at the mouth of the Vistula River on the coast of the Baltic Sea, Danzig became a focal point in Hitler's Plan Z, declared in January 1939. The aim of the program was to restore German naval supremacy.

When Britain objected based on the terms of the Treaty of Versailles, Germany renounced the Anglo-

German Naval Agreement and its Non Aggression Pact with Poland.

The battleship, SMS Acheswig-Holstein, was a coal powered pre-dreadnought vessel, commissioned in 1908 by the Kaiser. It had seen World War One action at the Battle of Jutland in 1916. That victory was still well revered by the German Navy. The ship was refitted with extensive firepower, an issue that European nations also claimed was a violation of the Treaty. It was ready for battle.

Its ultimate intention and presence were not peace. That which Versailles had given, the German Navy would take away.

Captain Gustaf Kleikamp fired the first shots at 4:47am on September 1, 1939. Harbour walls crumbled. The Free City of Danzig was ablaze. The Polish Military Transit Depot on the peninsula of Westerplatte was destroyed. German ground forces came ashore.

Leon's brother, Michal, died in the conflict. There would be no grave.

(I X)

Abel Russman guided his Junkers dive-bomber with immaculate precision. Together they were a team: decisive in Spain, and destructive in Poland. The thirty-seven foot aircraft with a forty-five foot wingspan was an ominous vulture having the malice of a pre-historic bloodthirsty Titanis. The range of over five hundred miles made the ultimate target easily accessible. The two-man crew could climb to almost three miles while maintaining a speed in excess of two hundred and fifty miles per hour. The Sturzkampfflugzeug, German dive-bomber, did not have to slow to aim. Precision was its forte.

His Stuka had two forward machine guns and another machine gun in the rear cockpit. Other dive-bombers were equipped with 20mm cannons. Abel preferred the machine guns. They were far more precise and deadly. The Stuka was also equipped with five bombs – the largest under the fuselage, with two under each wing. The destructive power was total. The scream of the soaring eagle was terrifying.

Villages east of the German-Prussian border were a memory. Rail lines became metallic splinters. Roads were craters. Polish aircraft were ineffective. Communication networks were severed. Farmhouses were ablaze. Markets were destroyed. Any moving vehicle was no more. The accompanying Heinkel bombers completed the devastation of land and any defence.

Russman and his co-pilot then flew to the north-east with their squadron over the valley toward Poznan. The city was in sight. But before that goal, there was still the farmland west of the city to obliterate.

There was no defence to Blitzkrieg.

(X)

Bernard ran to the road. There was no exhaustion, just total apprehension. The porch had given him no view beyond the trees. To his right, looking down the road he couldn't see his mother. "She must still be at the school," he thought. There was an opening in the dense foliage as the road turned to his left, but little was discernible. A quick thought, and then he chased his shadow back to the house. Inside, he scaled the wooden ladder beyond the closet leading to the attic. Bernard could barely squeeze through the opening.

Stagnant air made breathing difficult. The only light came from rays between the slats in the attic window. Bernard crawled upon the ceiling beams toward the dormer. They creaked precariously. The window's metal fixture was rusted shut. Wood trim was covered with black rot. Minutes of struggling and his bloodied hand broke the latch. Bernard pushed the window open; then his heart collapsed. "Tanks! Trucks! Troops!"

"My God!" his shock exclaimed. His heart raced. Then in that same instant his mind was silenced by the screech of German Stukas screaming overhead.

Bernard raced on his knees as fast as he could crawl. After banging through the opening his extended toes reached for the ladder. The descent was quick, as the sinister scream shook the house once more. Falling off the ladder he found himself on his back. Barely able to stand he limped to the bottom stairs. It was again a quick descent. Getting into the basement, he did everything his father told him. Hiding in the corner Bernard was petrified.

Prayers were instantly muddled with fears for his family. Bernard trembled, absolutely terrifying. Still barely able to stand, he made his way up the stairs returning to the kitchen. Picking up the phone he confirmed his peril. The line was dead.

Bernard returned to the basement and thought once more of his alternatives. "Should I let the animals free?" Before he could think further, an explosion shook the entire building. More bombs followed with heart-shaking tremors. The foundation shook. Bricks cracked. Boxes of family keepsakes fell. Before he could even think again, there were more bombs. Then there were distant screams, followed by an eerie silence. Bernard thought they were hopefully moving away. He wasn't certain. He had never experienced anything so horrifying. "The school," he prayed, "not the school." Then more bombs dropped, somewhere in the distance, with annihilating blasts. "Away," he gasped, barely able to breathe. "Where's the cat?" His mind was wild. Then all idiocy was silenced by the shriek of the Stuka squadron.

(XI)

Heinz Guderian led his panzer unit down the abandoned dirt road. The morning sun was guiding the battalion like the Magi following the Christmas Star. However, this was not a nativity. Poplar trees, bordering each side of the road, already lay in splinters. The hard clay road was pot-marked by craters. Trucks following the tanks encountered difficulty. Many with the invading troops swarmed the fields for quick advance. Farm houses and barns no longer conveyed a pastoral affluence. Bombers had destroyed the buildings. There were no survivors to be seen.

The panzer unit had already travelled one hundred and thirty kilometres from the German border that morning. The tank could attain a speed of about thirty kilometres an hour, and had to refuel after five hours. Destination Poznan was essential.

Guderian's tank was equipped with radio transmission. Upon receiving orders he would rise to alert others with specific semaphore. The flags usually consisted of a white square on a red background. He chose rather to display his commitment to the Reich by waving flags bearing the Swastika.

Instructions were always quickly carried out. Delays could mean, would mean, court-marshal. Guderian, proudly in his black uniform, rose to look around. The flags were extended. Simultaneously he ordered his driver to stop.

"Links!" he ordered. The turret rotated pointing the fifty-millimetre cannon at the grey barn.

(XII)

Parents were still rushing to the school as Teresa ran home with her two children. Every fear imaginable was driving her maternal instinct. Her racing heart pumped her feet faster. The kids could run quicker, and she let them. They knew something was terribly wrong. Mother had never taken them out of school before. Then Ryszard abruptly stopped. The crater before him was terrifying. His younger sister grabbed his hand and motioned her stunned brother away from the devastation. Teresa caught up with them. "Spieszyc sie!" she pleaded, out of breath. "Hurry!" she repeated. They ran onward, away from the craters and debris, staying to the side of the road. There were no more parents or children to be seen.

Then the bombs fell.

Teresa grabbed her children and hurled them into the ditch. Her heart was ready to explode. Her mind could not hide the horror. The mother whimpered covering her children. More bombs fell, farther down the road; and the school was no more!

(XIII)

Guderian directed his tank further down the road to acquire a more direct hit. "Destroy their will to live," he thought. "Might have to destroy their lives to do it," his wry humour projected. The tank commander had no difficulty justifying his need to destroy. The principles of the Thule with its devotion to the Arian race made any destruction of Polish property and life an obligation.

The panzer unit stopped.

In the basement Bernard had shifted to the far corner feeling safe. Boxes were assembled to partially obscure his view from a small window. He couldn't be seen; however there was enough for him to see daylight in the yard.

The rolling thunder of tanks tore his heart once more. Bernard couldn't fathom which hurt more: his head, his chest or his leg. Headaches, he rarely had one; but now his mind raced, his head pounded, his ears were ready to burst. His senses were pummelled as he trembled in the corner. The boy covered his ears to cushion the grinding cacophony of rolling machinery. Tears drowned his cheeks.

The panzer driver was just obeying orders, after all this was war. The gunner too had his job. There were no scruples. The turret was fixed.

"Feuer!"

The barn was no more.

Bernard was looking out the window the very moment of the blast. His entire being exploded with the devastation. Tears were immediate. His mind wailed. Bernard screamed but no one heard him. The animals, his closest friends; everything inside him screamed. Ben rubbed his eyes trying to stop the tears, wanting to clear his vision, hoping beyond all hope that the barn was still there, home to his friends. But such prayers are not answered. He could hardly breathe, not being able to imagine such destruction. Anger became the immediate consequence. How many times had he befriended the German children? How often had he extended care to the others? He considered himself always to be everybody's friend – and now this! Everything he lived for, every morning, each night, knowing the instinctive love animals could have for humans – all that was gone. He shuddered. Exclamations to a God who chose not to hear were obscured in his continuing sobs. He pressed his back against the bricks as if there was a comforting force in their damp porous nature. Ben trembled, unable to control himself. He wiped the blood from his nose.

Guderian celebrated. "Ziel!" he ordered. He had a need for more.

Bernard could barely hear the turret rotate. Every sense was muffled. There were further instructions telling others units to move on. The ground again shook as the panzer units motored down the road. Ben did not want to hear the terrifying pitch of invading armaments, but he didn't have a choice. His eyes were shut, his mind devastated.

Guderian's tank remained, fixed for the kill. The driver asked if they should move on. Abruptly Handel repeated his order, "Ziel!"

The cannon fired. The upper floor of their home was no more.

From a ditch covered in leaves, Teresa peered down the road. Hearing the blast, aware of the direction, she screamed in horror. God was not listening.

(X I V)

The bombers and dive-bombers hit Poznan simultaneously just after 7 a.m. that morning. Poznan was an affluent city. Situated on the Warta River, it is approximately the mid-point between Berlin and Warsaw. The city was founded in the tenth century and had been the capital of Poland. The commercial centre produced exports south to the Eastern European Nations, and north to the Baltic Sea and on to Britain, France, and Scandinavia. The Carpathian Mountains provided the raw materials. Many residents were tri-lingual. Business was conducted in the native Polish. German was the common second language. A considerable number also spoke Russian or other Slavic tongues. Its university was renowned. The Citadel provided military protection. The market was the focal point for rural produce and urban trade. The Baroque buildings were well maintained, conveying civic pride.

Hungary Habel Russman's first attack was determined to end any complacency. The day of Polish tribulation had arrived! Hitler's forceful tirade had been drilled into the mindset of each pilot – all two thousand of them.

Kill without pity or mercy all men, women and children of Polish descent or language.

Russman was well acquainted with the landmarks of Poland. Many times he had flown over the territory to East Prussia – an opportunity guaranteed by the Treaty. As to whether it was actually supported by the Treaty of Versailles really didn't matter. His Generals would argue that it was and that would be sufficient.

There had been little to no opposition once he crossed the Polish border. This absolutely surprised him as he expected a similar land and air defence that Poland had used to confront the Bolsheviks almost two decades ago.

Russman led his force of fifteen dive-bombers into the heart of the city. The Market naturally was busy that Friday morning. The stalls were packed with foreign goods and local autumn produce. Women were there searching for the best quality, the ripest fruit, the freshest meat, or the warmest bread. In less than two minutes the Market became rubble, strewn with the bullet-ridden corpses of customers and merchants. The bleeding who survived the initial onslaught begged for treatment. The nearby university was in flames. The access to the hospital was impossible.

In St. Mark the Evangelist Church many were attending the First Friday Morning Mass. They were standing for the Gospel, the compassionate words of their evangelist.

Everywhere Jesus went, to the towns, villages, and markets, people would beg Him to let them touch the hem of his cloak. And, all who touched it were healed.

But God was not to be found.

Sirens blared throughout the city declaring the inescapable horror. The city was in flames. Buildings were crumbling.

Russman's next goal was the city hall. As he approached, he could see that the bombers had already achieved their objective.

Karl Reimers directed his bombers toward the Citadel. These Polish troops, were the 8th Army's last target before Warsaw. Anti-aircraft fire initially provided a startling defence. Polish aircraft too were thwarting the attack. Reimers directed his convoy to make an abrupt right and circle once more over the city, dropping its deluge of bombs. The destruction of the Polish aircraft followed.

Russman's stukas then directed their attack toward the Citadel. The Polish defence had been weakened, and the opportunity to inflict major damage was there to be had.

By the end of that first day, the bombing of the Citadel made it critically incapable of providing further defence. Most of the city was in ruins. Politicians and leaders ran. German air forces were on their way to Warsaw.

(XV)

Teresa tried to comfort her children, but had little clothing to keep them warm. There were no blankets, and no sweaters. A neighbour's farmhouse had seemingly survived the cannon blast. Perhaps the abandoned dwelling could at least provide momentary shelter. Considering its distance from the road, "Perhaps they will not be back," Teresa reckoned. Hope came only in minute rays.

The children's tears would not end even after she returned. Teresa had left her two children in the derelict shelter to look for her elder son. Running in the dark she hoped beyond all hope to find what she did not want to see. Her heart collapsed with the devastation upon seeing the top floor collapsed. She called, but there was no answer. And again, but there was only silence. The barn was no more. The animals would be dead. What happened to her son? She did not know.

Her prayers were many. Trembling would not stop. "My husband?" she thought, and the prayers continued.

"Did he return? Where is he? Why haven't I heard? I would have seen him."

Panic quickly becomes anger when the benevolent deity is silent.

Teresa tried to grab what she could, but all edible items were inside the collapsed dwelling. Remembering the animal feed, she searched the barrels for the shrivelled apples. A cloak was lying in the yard. She picked that up and used it to carry the produce back to her children. Teresa planned to scurry around for more, thinking perhaps of even going to the next farmhouse.

Then the voices were heard. "Are they Germans?" She hid, and then scurried away.

Ryszard and Elzbieta had many questions among the many tears. They trembled with cold and fear. There was no comfort. Mother was there, but not their father, not their brother, not their home or their farm. The finality of horror was not complete.

(X V I)

Bernard awoke, but when he didn't know. It was dark. Was it a day, or two? He could barely see, but could perceive his dire plight. The mangled timbers prevented almost all mobility. He could crawl a few feet but the pain in his hip remained intense. Any movement caused him to cringe. The blood from his nose had stopped. When? He had no idea. He even forgot he had been bleeding profusely. The basement was cold and damp in the autumn night. He shook more from fear than from cold. Trembling obscured any sense.

Hope is just an obscure passing when not needed, and vital when required. Vanishing prospects were his reality, being buried in the ruins of his family home.

Bernard rubbed his thigh and hip to ease the pain; then tried to close his eyes and sleep till morning. If there was any mercy, God would at least give him that blessing.

Chapter Two
September 3, 1939

The Einsatzgruppen – the mobile killing forces – followed the bombing. In Poznan, businessmen were forced to their knees and shot. Gangs surrounded homes dragging residents outside and mercilessly ending their lives. The barrage of brutality knew no limits. Women were shot running away. Crying children were silenced. Hospitals were cleansed of their infirm. The disabled who couldn't run were no longer disabled. Armageddon had begun.

Catholics and Protestants alike huddled in churches for sanctuary; but God did not seem to care.

The dead in the market square and the bodies on the streets lay unburied until the killing squads ordered Poles to bury their own. There was no solemnity and no prayers. Open pits awaited the dead.

Bombing would return to Poznan; and by the third of September the city would be totally German.

(II)

Sable's persistent meow woke Ben that Sunday morning. The distant thunder of exploding bombs had become a drone putting him to sleep. Perhaps they would draw near again, drive down the street, or maybe the next bomb might even have his name on it. It was difficult not to be fatalistic in spite of pleas from the hungry feline.

The black longhaired cat was his favourite. Of course Sable had worked the family. She was good at that, guaranteeing her next meal or the available warm lap. But now she wanted him, and he couldn't help her.

Even the most non-believing can be amazed how human instincts are aroused by an animal. The pet would not leave. The meows became cries, and Bernard reacted.

Could he move the beam lying diagonally against the wall without abruptly causing the rest to fall on him? Could he break the panel and crawl over the broken glass and studs that blocked the stairway? The window was perhaps an escape? How would he get beyond the glass? His right leg started to kick the slanting stud to the side. If the rest of the debris collapsed Ben would be no worse off. The wooden beam moved to the side. Sable hearing the motion inside called even more. That intensified Bernard's action.

Was it an hour or two – perhaps three? Sable left and then returned. More timber and dust was pushed to the side. He found that the boxes he had stacked to obscure the view inside had actually prevented the debris from falling directly onto him. He got an area cleared. The next objective was the window.

The thick glass window measured sixty centimetres by a meter. He considered the alternatives, then all activity quickly stopped.

Deutschland, Deutschland uber alles

Uber alles in der Welt...

Troops somewhere outside were singing loudly. Ben instantly leaned back against the wall hiding himself from anyone who might look inside.

The anthem ended, and Bernard slid to the side to inspect the boxes. A cloth, a shirt, a sweater, or even a pair of pants, anything to blunt the sound of breaking glass, or to clean the chards: these were his meticulous searches. It was his father's winter sweater. Ben gingerly banged the glass. It broke. Then an hour later the frame was relatively clean.

He could barely fit. Stupidly he thought it must have been a godsend to have not eaten for three days. Bernard struggled, but he got out with much difficulty. Regardless of his prior efforts, or how careful he was, his hands were cut. His shirt was shredded near the left elbow. Glass particles tore his slacks. But he was out. He sat there relieved. He had passed the first test. The first guest was Sable.

Forever she purred cuddling up to him, the only human in her life. Bernard paused in those moments, thankful for what little he had. Exhaustion, hunger, and every extreme of torrid emotions still churned inside. Across the yard he walked carrying his friend. He never called the animals. He knew their fate. Beyond the shattered barn he stood staring at the burnt timbers, the collapsed roof, and the ashes where once there were stalls. Tears once again welled in his eyes.

Like his mother, he reached into the barrel. There was no concern as to whether the apples were rotten. If the pigs would eat them, they were edible. There was still water in the other barrel near the tractor. For whatever reason, the farm machinery had missed the brunt of the attack. Sable was gratified to drink … even water.

The ominous sound of rifle fire caused him to run immediately to rear of the remaining house. With his back to the wall, he viewed both sides and out beyond the fields. "Must be down the road," he concluded. Then his thoughts and fears turned to his parents. The questions were many. The tears were no less.

After seeing no one and not hearing anymore, he returned to being seated along the wall. It was warm outside. Sable was in heaven, her face buried against his neck. Bernard closed his eyes; but his mind would not rest. "What next?"

(I I I)

Teresa and her children never made it home. She did not look further for her son in the rubble. They stayed long enough in the derelict remains of the neighbour's dwelling, until she thought it was safe to leave. Decisions are made, and not always to one's benefit. They journeyed days. They begged and stole food. Ditches were hiding places. Fields, though barren, became temporary abodes. Teresa remembered the convent, and promised her children food and shelter there. It would be another treacherous five miles, but that was her last hope. Battered bodies, bullet-ridden corpses, murdered children – she could no longer hide these from her children. She always pledged good, with positive remarks, and promises of beneficial consequences. But with all that happened in these last three days, her empty soul was now filled with anger and hatred. Vengeance was not out of the question. If she could repay these villains, she would leap at the opportunity. Yet her primarily goal was her children, and in that end Teresa had to be the guiding influence in the midst of such tribulation.

(I V)

Leon remained in the bunker. Now only three others remained. With the first bombing, he directed many to the lower floor, beneath his shop. At the end of the corridor was a false wall that opened to a further tunnel that provided shelter. There was even food and electricity. As much as he portrayed the influence of a positive person, Leon was well acquainted with the reality of vengeance and hatred and how these two ills had in the past and would now and always unite factions in the hatred of a common cause. It was human nature, and that at times revolted him. All of the attempts in the last ten years to remove the German tongue from western Poland, there were going to be consequences. And now these threats had become war.

There were seventeen originally in the bunker. Within hours, five fled believing the invasion had passed. Others became claustrophobic and left with much anxiety amid forceful yelling. Others, too, stayed no longer than a day.

If Leon could see the consequences of their decisions, he would have seen women murdered on the street, men returning to their businesses being led away before firing squads, and families with their children not having time to say goodbye to the world.

For those who remained in the bunker, knowing the consequences was not difficult. They could hear the rifle fire, the blaze of aircraft ammunition, and feel the tremors of dropping bombs. That they were still alive that alone gave them hope.

There was no more time to quiver. He had to be resolute. He prayed only for his family. No prayers for Poland were said, for he knew that by the end of the week Poland would be no more.

(V)

Hunger woke him up, not his hunger but Sable's. The affectionate mew, cuddled against his neck became a rumbling purr. Patting did not stop the need for food. Kind words tried to comfort the pet, but the pause was only temporary. Bernard ventured there may be something in the destroyed barn. That was one prospect, so was journeying on to other properties. He couldn't wait forever. They weren't coming back. Now the only one who mattered was in his arms. Sable rubbed the side of her face against his chin. A few tears touched his eyes marvelling at the affection. Perhaps he should follow the train tracks west toward Germany. The Nazi forces had already gone that way. They wouldn't be back. "Gerta," he again thought. She was his mother's friend. She spoke German fluently. "Maybe they spared her. Maybe she could help." The options were again becoming endless.

Then a little rodent appeared, running in the sun light between the derelict home and the destroyed barn. The mouse suddenly became the main course. Sable spotted her supper immediately and was off in a flash. Several strides and less than two seconds, that's all it took. There was no game, just instant death. Sable sat in the sunlight, aglow with the catch between her paws. Ben viewed the delightful repast. Normally she would bring the half-chewed remains to his feet as if to proclaim, "Look what I've done.", but that did not happen. A noise startled her, and Sable fled toward the field carrying her prey.

Bernard looked to his right toward the barn, and then suddenly back to his left. The soldier stood there, his revolver pointed. Shock and terror were immediate. Ben tried to stand, but a strong hand upon his shoulder forced him to remain seated. The revolver moved in front of him, directly in front of him. Bernard couldn't see beyond the hand gripping the weapon.

His heart seized. His chest was exploding. When he tried again to stand, he was pushed to the side. They laughed.

"Put it away. We won't waste another bullet." It was Konrad Werner.

The Sergeant Major pulled the boy to his feet. His legs were limp. There was no opposition.

In German, the demands continued, "What is your name? Where are your parents?"

Bernard understood the German, but refused to answer.

The butt of a rifle struck his back causing him to stumble forward in pain. Ben was struck again, this time in the lower abdomen. He doubled forward. To inflict more pain, they held him erect. Then after a third blow they let him collapse. His gasping was intense. Lacking

49

control, urinary discharge flowed. They laughed in derision. Blood stained the dirt around his face.

Werner took out his luger to enhance the terror. The motion was quick. The shot intentionally missed the fallen youth. He was petrified, whimpering uncontrollably.

Between the corn stalks, Sable viewed the terror. Realizing there was no good to be had, she scampered away into the field.

The questions explored any potential for Jewish heritage. Werner referred to his mother as a whore, and his father as a pimp. He deceitfully told the youth that his silence didn't matter as his family was no more.

The attack on his family ignited his ire. As limited as he was, Bernard would never accept any such insult. Rolling over he eyed Werner with a venomous glare. The Sergeant Major derided him with a laugh.

"Zigeuner?" Werner prompted his cohorts to continue the scathing assault.

Bernard was pulled up and then forced immediately down onto his stomach. One guard with Werner's continued prompting applying his bayonet to the victim's hind quarters. They all laughed at the youth inflicted with pain and abuse. The intrusion was completed several times until Werner bade them to stop.

"Not a Gypsy!" the guard laughed. In the same moment, Werner pulled Bernard to his feet, and in that instant the youth was struck on the head from behind.

They stood there looking down at the comatose victim. The assailant laughed and then the others.

Werner looked beyond the remains of the house to the cart waiting on the street. "Here!" he called.

Two men came. They were dressed in khaki pants and cloaks. Their gloves and uniforms were already blood stained.

"This one, too," Werner ordered.

Onto the wooden cart, they threw Bernard's lifeless body to find comfort among the dead.

(V I)

The government of Poland was in flight: the President, Prime Minister, Members of the Parliament, Army Commanders, Air Force Personnel, and Mayors with their city politicians. Most fled south to the Carpathians. Others left the country to rule in exile. Still others never completed a journey to anywhere.

(V I I)

Some men find it most difficult to admit mistakes. If they are ever called upon to make such admissions, they tend to be incapable of being brief.

So it was with Prime Minister Neville Chamberlain on that Sunday afternoon.

This morning the British Ambassador in Berlin

handed the German Government a final note

stating that, unless we heard from them by

eleven o'clock that they were prepared at once

51

to withdraw their troops from Poland, a state of war would exist between us. I have to tell you now that no such undertaking has been received, and that consequently this country is at war with Germany.

You can imagine what a bitter blow it is to me that all my long struggle to win peace has failed. Yet I cannot believe that there is anything more or anything different that I could have done and that would have been more successful.

Up to the very last it would have been quite possible to have arranged a peaceful and honourable settlement between Germany and Poland, but Hitler would not have it. He had evidently made up his mind to attack Poland whatever happened, and although he now says he put forward reasonable proposals that were rejected by the Poles, that is not a true statement. The proposals were never shown to the Poles, nor to us, and, although they were announced in a German broadcast on Thursday night, Hitler did not wait to hear comments on them, but ordered his troops to cross the

Polish frontier. His action shows convincingly that there is no chance of expecting that this man will ever give up his practice of using force to gain his will. He can only be stopped by force.

We and France are today, in fulfilment of our obligations, going to the aid of Poland, who is so bravely resisting this wicked and unprovoked attack on her people. We have a clear conscience. We have done all that any country could do to establish peace. The situation in which no word given by Germany's ruler could be trusted and no people or country could feel themselves safe has become intolerable.

And now that we have resolved to finish it, I know that you will all play your part with calmness and courage.

With further words guaranteeing victory, the British Prime Minister completed his broadcast. However the dead do not hear.

On that same afternoon, Ernst Werner boarded a train in Berlin. His destination was Poznan, specifically an unoccupied fortress on the outskirts of the city. He carried with him Herr Himmler's personal letter with specific orders. Ernst Werner vowed he would never have any scruples that would get in his way.

Chapter Three
September, 1939

The forty-nine year old diplomat stared at the portrait on the far wall. Stalin looked imperial. Every thought, each act, and all decisions were designed to guarantee his success and the future of the Soviet dictatorship.

Vyacheslav Molotov knew his place, his limits, and the appreciation Stalin bestowed on him. Yet he acknowledged nothing was certain. As a diplomat and emissary, he excelled. The pact with Ribbentrop was just one agreement. There were so many others controlling so many other factions in the Soviet Empire.

Outside, the children's choir sang the National Anthem. The anthem was a daily ritual, but that day it had additional importance. That morning, eight days after Germany commenced its invasion of Poland, Molotov met with the German Ambassador Friedrich Werner von der Schulenburg. The Soviet message was concise, "We are preparing to invade Poland."

All such meetings were brief. There was never any opportunity for discussion. The message preceded swift final salutations.

Schulenburg, on his way to his Embassy, would have heard the anthem proclaiming the praise of the Soviet Union. That was well planned.

However, it didn't matter how often Molotov heard the anthem, the images of impoverished Russian soldiers returning to their Motherland still roused his emotions. "How much they sacrificed? Without them, where would we be?"

Rising from behind the mahogany desk, he attended the ewer on the side table. Clean hands were essential after ever meeting. He wasn't just finicky; he was cautious. No one could be trusted. Germs could kill faster than any weapon.

Trust – that was rarely considered a virtue, more a necessity. As long as Beria had the confidence of Iosif Stalin, and with Beria's position as People's Commissariat for Internal Affairs, there was no certainty. Everything had changed in 1932 when Stalin's wife died. The dictator swore, "Since I lost you, I have no love for mankind." Beria was his man to make that prophecy come true. Many millions, who were only thinkers or family men, had already died. Vyacheslav had no intention of being the next.

Sergei Ulanov entered the room. As the diplomat's assistant in a realm where common courtesy did not exist, Ulanov came and went as he wished. Molotov did not trust him. Conversations involving Ulanov were always without embellishment. Everything had to be as Stalin wished. Molotov knew that, and he wanted Ulanov to conclude Molotov thought only that.

The Soviet diplomat pondered the Reich's invasion of Poland. "Where was the Polish defence?" This was his primary interest. Surprised? He certainly was. Then he conjectured that so little that is heard in diplomatic circles rarely proves to be true.

Molotov unfurled a map of Europe while calling to Ulanov. "Do you understand this?" Molotov asked his assistant directing his attention to the border between France and Germany. "They have five million troops. They had the opportunity. Where are the French? The English?"

Ulanov shook his head, wondering too about Allied silence. The gesture was well received.

"Do you know why we must invade Poland?" Ulanov looked at Molotov wondering why he would be asked if the decision was already made.

"Don't worry. It's between us. It's good for us to talk. One day you will be advising others."

Ulanov spoke candidly. "I do not trust the Germans. Twenty-five years ago they were our enemy. They made sure they were the first to attack. Will they go further? Will they take over all of Poland? Can we say they won't?"

"You're astute." Molotov praised his assistant for being wise enough to agree with Stalin. "But there is more. You say you can't trust them. Sergei, I despise them. Hitler's pact with the Ukrainian Nationalists, he wants them to turn against us. Remember, the Poland near our border, more than half is not Polish. Ukrainians! Belarussians! These are our Soviet people."

Molotov rolled up his map, and then continued. "We will not obliterate the Polish nation as Germany will. Commissars, yes we will have them, to work toward the one goal, a Soviet Polish nation.

"And those that would disagree?" Ulanov prompted the expected answer with his question.

"Our Labour Camps are not full. Beria, if he has his say, will not even allow time to transport those who disagree. Yet, I tell you there would also be merit in that. My friend, Poland presents a danger to us. Food, buildings, production, trade – all these in Poland our own troops will find alarming. We want no opposition, and will not tolerate resistance. Now as to our division with the Nazis, we can rightfully claim that the land that was ours must be ours now, the land occupied by peoples belonging to the Soviet Union."

"When?"

"Sunday next."

"The seventeenth?"

"Stalin agrees."

(I I)

Bernard lay prone upon the wiry cot. His bruises and dried blood covered a blazing furnace of excessive pain. For three days now he realized his dire predicament. He had been unconscious at least two days he was told; but no one would say any more. He knew he was alive solely at the whim of those who vowed to eradicate the Polish race. For reasons that were void of common sense, he was still alive. Realisation was an inferno born of fear. Each creak of the metal springs could bring guards into the hall. A torn blanket doubled beneath him provided the mattress. The sheet was a piece of someone's night coat. Ben could not mention the cold or the damp, unless those may be his last words. He was hungry but that mattered only to him. His headaches would not stop. His mind was a constant whirlpool. His ears rung His vision was blurred. That which he could perceive caused him even more dread. Others in the brick building were all German. Bernard recognized no one.

(I I I)

Arthur Greiser, the Reichsstatthalter for Poznan, stood in the front of the nineteenth century fort, observing its grand archway and dark metal gates. Greiser was proud of his decisions, not only the project but also the location and the assignment. Ernst Werner knew how to play the game of Nazi tact. Berlin had taught him well. Agreement was always necessary. Over enthusiasm was definitely questioned as a sign of insecurity. Honest, abrupt, diligent – these were the attributes that presented him with this opportunity. Their chauffeur waited patiently. The streets were empty of vehicles, but not of the decaying bodies. The driver was astute, keenly knowledgeable of preferable routes so as to avoid the images and scent of death.

"Konzentrationslager Posen," Greiser suggested.

Werner's agreement was immediate.

"You will do well here. Himmler himself suggested you."

Ernst could only agree. "How many?" he repeated a question asked several times to others.

"One guard for every five pieces of scum." Greiser was direct. "Don't worry. They are to be here only six months. By then they will be dead by starvation or firing squad."

That part Werner had not heard before. Greiser sensed the silence and continued. "Those who resist: the students, Slavs, and of course the Jews. But, there will be others."

There was a finality to imprisonment that Werner accepted. Dachau was celebrated. This concentration camp would be no different. He would guarantee that.

Fort VII had been one of many surrounding Poznan built by the Prussians more than fifty years before. During Poland's Second Republic it had become only a storage facility. The plan, even before the invasion, was to use such facilities as Prisoner of War camps. However, with the desire to obliterate the Polish population, there were limits on how many Poles could be kept alive. The Nazi goal meant many would die on a regular basis just to make room for others.

Werner approached the metal gates pulling one open. "Allow me," he imparted his request to Greiser.

The Reichsstatthalter agreed, motioning to two guards to accompany the new commandant. "I will return to the Citadel. He will be back in an hour."

Werner saluted Greiser and watched the chauffeur-driven limousine with its Nazi flags blowing proudly in the breeze.

Fort VII reeked of death even before the first prisoner arrived. Debris may have been cleaned, but the stale odor of damp bricks, mildew, and the vile stench of the neighbouring chemical factories all created a caustic nightmare. He had heard of Dracula and Transylvania. The horror of the Slavs in Romania would be a gentle bath compared to the terror to be inflicted here.

Werner had no qualms. The passageway to the left drew his attention to several rooms, each about thirty feet by fifty feet. "Home to forty persons in each cell," he ventured. "Death will be a pleasant alternative," he concluded. Werner had already made that statement to Herr Himmler before his appointment.

Rationalizing the entire program was easy. Ernst Werner was a Lutheran. He despised Catholics. Poles were Catholic. But it wasn't just that, Lutheran beliefs had given him freedom from evil. He could confess his sins directly to God, if sin was to ever enter his life. In addition, he used Lutheran practice to assure himself of freedom of conscience. It was an incredibly astute belief as it justified any action as well as the result. If you can't be in error, you cannot sin, and in that case there was no need for God, and thus for the Church. Priests, they would die too.

Werner was hard pressed to locate the storage facility for food supplies. It was a concrete bunker in the middle of the court yard, to the far right, overlooking the city. There were other storage facilities. These were reserved for more important supplies like the munitions and uniforms, and food for the guards.

Lighting was limited to the German quarters. The courtyard too had spotlights to prevent any thought of unscrupulous activity late at night.

Against the outer wall to the right, a garden was already planted. There were no flowering shrubs. Roses would bloom in the spring, but not now. Forsythia bushes and Lilacs presented such a warm serene invitation. Beyond these, there were posts against the limestone wall. Werner had no immediate interest in that but knew he didn't have a choice.

In two weeks, on the twenty-seventh, the gates would open. The cells would be filled, and the firing squads would be ready.

(IV)

Molotov kept his promise. Just after midnight on the seventeen, in spite of there never being a declaration of war, Soviet tanks rumbled across the border into the Polish borderlands. The grasslands and low hills were an invitation to the rolling thunder. The Vickers T26 Tank with its 45mm gun was capable of destroying any defence at normal combat range. The Soviet BT Tank had greater mobility with its higher suspension and was well suited for any mountainous territory. Stalin's factories had been busy.

The Kresy was the principle aim of the Soviet forces. This was land awarded to Poland by the Treaty of Versailles as if Russia should have been punished for its peace agreement with the Kaiser's Germany in 1917. These acquired lands included portions of Lithuania, Belarus, and the Ukraine. Nearly half of the population in the Kresy did not consider Polish to be their principal language. Thus, when the Soviet forces attacked, they had the support of the residents. Molotov's timely promises had assured these states that they would re-acquire the lands taken by Poland's Second Republic.

In accord with the Soviet-German agreement three weeks earlier, the Soviet Union was to grab more land than Versailles awarded Poland.

The Soviet force was massive on two fronts. Comandarm 1st Rank Semyon Timoshenko commanded the Ukrainian Front. Comandarm 2nd Rank Mikhail Kovalyov led the Belarusian Front. These two forces directed a half-million troops belonging to seven Field Armies with thirty-three divisions. These were equipped with almost five thousand large guns. To eradicate the Polish air defence, the Soviet Union employed more than three thousand aircraft. The tanks numbered four thousand, seven hundred.

The Polish opposition was pathetically weak. Erroneous assumptions were made that left the nation extremely vulnerable. Most of the Polish force was in the west fighting the Wehrmacht. There was also the presumption that the Soviet Union would not attack. Further there was every expectation that in accord with mutual defence agreements that France and Britain would actively engage the Germans immediately. Some Polish forces had already fled toward the south forming the Romanian Brigade. The Polish force on the day the Soviet attack was about a quarter-million fighting on two fronts. More than this figure was available, but not ready to fight. All of the Polish force was limited to twenty battalions.

Molotov's information was accurate. The diplomat clearly understood the limitations in the Polish Protection Corp. These restrictions became grave with the achievement of the initial Soviet goal: the destruction of the communication systems. Thus, when Poland's President ordered a retreat to the Romanian Brigade and not to engage the Soviets except for absolute survival; the Polish troops did not hear nor heed the directive. As a result, Polish General Wilhelm Orlik-Ruckermann continued to fight the USSR incurring heavy casualties.

The result of the invasion was a foregone conclusion, but the Soviet forces could not rest. The German Wehrmacht had already driven east of the line established in the Ribbentrop-Molotov pact. Stalin's interest had become: stop the Nazi advance, enforce the demarcation established by the Ribbentrop-Molotov Pact, and restore the borderlands to Ukraine and Belarus. This required the annihilation of Poland.

Two days after the start of the invasion the Soviet force captured Vilnius. Wilna was the Polish name for that city. Three weeks later, the Soviet Union declared Lithuania free from all Polish influence. Then three weeks after that, the Soviet Union surrendered Vilnius to the Lithuanian Soviet Socialist Republic.

Simon Timoshenko's Ukrainian Front engaged both the Polish and German forces in the capture of two major cities: Brest, and Lviv.

Brest was an industrial centre on the Bug River. The city had been captured by Germany's Heinz Guderian's XIX Panzer Corps. On the twenty-second of September, the Soviet Union arrived with its 29th Tank Brigade. There was a Soviet-Nazi joint celebration parade handing over authority to the USSR. The Germans left, and the Soviets made themselves feel at home.

The Wehrmacht had already surrounded Lviv on September 14th. The city and commercial area were being starved into submission. The main fortress, Vysokyi Zamok, was under attack. Transportation on the Poltva River had been stopped. The Soviet Union seized the city on September 22nd. As it was in Soviet territory determined by the Ribbentrop-Molotov Pact, the Germans left without incident.

For ten days, from the morning of the seventeenth of September to the twenty-sixth, the German invading force was engaging the Polish Armies of Krakow and Lublin in a prolonged and deadly battle. The city of Tomaszow Lubelski, from which the battle would take its name, was situated near the commercial metropolis of Lublin. Lublin was in the Soviet territory determined by the agreement with Ribbentrop. This battle was a second largest confrontation involving the Wehrmacht and Polish troops. The Soviet commander let it happen. As a result of the battle, the German forces destroyed the two Polish armies, eliminating any further defence to invading foes. The Red Army claimed its territory and the Germans returned to their prior position.

Poland then ordered its remaining troops to evacuate into Romania. Many of these were in turn decimated by the Nazi and Soviet troops on either side.

By September 28th, eleven days after the start of the invasion, the Red Army achieved its goal of reaching the demarcation formed by the Narew, Vistula, Bug, and San Rivers.

On that very same day, Polish General Walerian Czuma surrendered to the German Wehrmacht. Warsaw was conquered.

(V)

Bernard awoke; he would do so every two hours. There was no comfort, nor rest to be had on the metal cot. He knew the situation. His mind had returned albeit slowly, but enough to make the aides think he was at least somewhat valuable. The hall in the Citadel was dank with all celebratory plaques removed. The Polish flags and troop colours no longer hung on the near wall. The stage at the far left was a reservoir for medical supplies and rations.

They were all strangers except for the one person. Ben envied him, but only for a moment. Rudolph was actually Reuben. He knew the lad, the son of the farmer about two miles west down the road. Reuben had in their infant years professed alliance with the German minority, a view obviously held by his parents. Many in the community suspected his heritage, but few spoke of it. There were always spies, and no one really knew who was with whom. It was always best to be still, say nothing and accept the reality. Playing together in their childhood, they did just that.

With the Enabling Act in 1933, Reuben's family acted quickly. His father moved west to work for pittance inside the German border. He joined the police. Reuben's mother was Jewish, a descendant of her grandfather who had left the Czarist pogrom. Though it had suddenly become a major issue, Reuben's father would not abandon her, or his son. As a German officer, he was able to have papers altered. Suddenly the family's Jewish faith was no more. Prayers could be said, but silently. The menorah was buried. Their passports declared the desired truth.

Reuben always had the marvellous capacity to say the right thing. He repaid Bernard's friendship handsomely by instructing the accompanying guards that Bernard had been a supporter of the Reich. He even said he had documents to prove that; but he was never tested to produce them.

As Bernard lay upon the cot, he thanked his God that his leg and hip were healing. Scars had become small scabs. Bruises were disappearing. However, the heart still ached immensely. Often his chest would grip and he would silently gasp, "Is this it?" The mind became more active, and he loathed that reality. His mom? His dad? His brother? His sister? The animals? The farm? And, with each question there was a multiplicity of anguishing enquiries.

Every so often Rudolph would lean over and briefly clutch Ben's hand. It was so reassuring. Rudolph had the sense to repeat the same encouragement to all of those recovering.

"What day?" Bernard asked in German. He knew enough the importance of mixing in. One word in Polish could mean his death.

"The twenty-ninth," Rudolph advised.

"The feast of St. Michael." Bernard thought of his uncle. Rudolph, too, held the Archangel sacred.

"I would like to walk."

Rudolph cautioned him, and then provided the necessary assistance.

The steps were timid, weak, unstable. Bernard held the guard's arm for the moment, then the thought directed him to be independent if he wanted to stay alive.

Bernard made it to the cot, two away from his. He smiled at the German lying there who was barely able to see through the bandages. Though difficult to discern there was a glimmer of appreciation. Then onward Bernard slid, his feet stumbling forward carrying his legs. Four more beds met further smiles. Then Rudolph helped him return to his cot. The bed was made with an extra blanket for the mattress.

Ben smiled in bed that night and said another prayer. There is no assurance a good day will follow another; but for whatever reason, that started to happen. He was walking better, without assistance, greeting many more people, and being accepted. His German came naturally. Thoughts of his family would always be there – silently – in Polish.

That September had been the realm of Satan. To survive Hades, Bernard knew he had to smile in Hell.

Chapter Four
October, 1939

In the first week of October, Polish forces continued their battle against the Red Army. Remaining troops were surrounded. Those who fled lacked communications. Behind them they left a silent hell.

On October 6, 1939, the end arrived. Polish General Kleeberg capitulated to the Soviet Union after four days of heavy fighting. Poland was no more.

Germany on October 8th formally declared the annexation of western Poland and Danzig. Hitler's dream of the destruction of Poland was complete.

Concentration Camps were immediately being established. Nazi tyranny reigned. There would be no dispute to the Aryan claim that all land west of the Vistula would be theirs. To assure this reality, there would be no opposition. Before October 8, 1939 the Nazis were mistreating Polish citizens. After October 8th, Germany was mistreating its own citizens in the territory it now called its own.

On October 17, 1939 Hitler witnesses the German parade in Warsaw celebrating the Nazi triumph.

Many Poles preferred surrendering to the Soviet Union having already witnessed the atrocities of the Nazis. The USSR initially established a program of

Sovietisation. Soviet officials governed the regions, counties and municipalities. Lithuania, Belarus and Ukraine were Soviet Social Republics enlarged by the lands re-claimed from Poland. Poland was a communist state with rules that were stringent. Whatever may have been thought, there were rules and civic expectations. No matter how unfavourable they may have been, at least Poles in those first months could breathe. Some had life.

Although Lenin and Stalin had promised much to the Soviet people, their standard of living was clearly inferior to the Polish way of life. Sovietisation of Poland hastily became a program of diminishing Poland's standard to the lowest common denominator of Bolshevik life. Dining became starvation. Clothes became rags. Homes became hovels. Those who spoke against change were imprisoned, murdered in cold blood, or taken for a walk and seen no more.

Any leniency ended with the decrees of Iosif Stalin. Beria's Secret Police became the tyranny of the regime. Jews were murdered in their homes, shot while fleeing on the streets, or marched together to their deaths. Ditches with decaying corpses became cavernous pits. Approximately two million Poles were deported to Soviet slave labour camps and gulags. Hypothermia, starvation, typhoid and disease were their fate. In the occupied lands of the Ukraine, Belarus, and Lithuania, the Polish minority was terrorized. Houses were burnt. Firing squads controlled the terror. Many fled to the forests, and there many met their deaths. Mercy was a word not to be found in the Soviet dictionary.

In the first month of the war, approximately 65,000 Poles were killed, and about 660,000 were taken captive by the German and Soviet forces. Subsequent to that, the deportation of about two million persons occurred, together with deaths attributed to the killing squads.

Up to 120,000 Polish troops escaped to Romania and Hungary, and approximately another 20,000 troops made it to Latvia. France also became a home for many who could escape to the west. The Polish Government in Exile established a home in Britain. The Polish Navy sailed west to Britain.

(I I)

Bernard was roused from his sleep early that Saturday morning. The entire hall was raucous with celebration. Rudolph's hand continued to rest on Ben's shoulder.

"Pani, Poland is no more."

Instantly the patient closed his eyes. Absolute vulnerability gripped his chest. Bernard said nothing.

"I, too, was hoping," Rudolph whispered.

The celebratory yells grew louder. Shrieks defaming Poland inflamed further howls of those hungry for more violence.

Nothing would comfort him; but sense took over. He must seem to be part of the team, part of their program, for that was the only way to survive. Bernard rose from the cot all smiles.

"You'd make a good clown," Rudolph continued to whisper in German.

Bernard shook the hands of fellow patients. There was no longer any discernible limp. A bottle of champagne opened, and then other bottles of vintage wine. The celebration had become a wild festival of bloodthirsty hyenas. However, Bernard could not tell them that.

Rudolph returned from the others to impart discouraging news. "I've been commissioned to march in the parade." Ben's quizzical expression prompted more. "We are told Reich Fuhrer Hitler will be in the capital to witness the celebration." There was a recognizable sense of pride.

"You will honour your country well," Bernard continued. Immediately he regretted his words. This was his Polish childhood friend wearing the Nazi uniform.

"Play the game," Rudolph cautioned.

"When?"

"This morning. Bye, my friend. I will never forget you." With that, Rudolph shook Bernard's hand, and then they quickly hugged. Rudolph smiled, "You will do well." Then he left.

Bernard watched his friend depart, talking with others before leaving through the far doors into the guard's quarters. Ben paused a moment and then joined others in the celebrations continuing to masquerade his vile contempt for each person in the Citadel.

Then Mephistopheles appeared.

Konrad Werner, having called for everyone's attention, proclaimed the conquest of Poland. The guards and patients yelled their approval as Werner described the defeat of the inferior race, declaring all Poles to be the scum of the earth and not just the Jews. "They have no right to exist!" he profaned God's humanity. But again, God was not present.

The initial tirade lasted a whole twenty-two minutes. Every German speech was about that same length. It was as if each member of the Nazi Party had attended the same college for elocution lessons. However this was no joke. Annihilation was his message. Inciting everyone to further action, he demanded, "to ensure the rights and security of the Fatherland."

"The Motherland," Bernard thought to himself. Poland was no more. This was now Germany.

Bernard remained behind others hoping not to be identified. Purposefully he chose to avoid Werner's gaze. Recognition could mean death.

Finally the ranting stopped, and more liquid was poured. These were festive times if you were a Nazi. Bernard thought for a moment about his friend Rudolph, how much he sacrificed, what he achieved, and how long his charade might last. Thoroughness was an essential for these invaders. Nothing could be left to chance.

Werner stood on the stage and continued speaking. He mentioned his brother. "They're like vultures. All the same," Bernard mused.

"My brother, your kin, has been invited by Herr Himmler himself to solve the infestation of vermin in Poznan. Ernst Werner is Commandant of Fort VII, a prison camp for these undesirables. Such means are necessary to ensure the rights and security of the Reich." So much of it was repetitious, yet it was necessary for all present to cheer every proposal knowing it had the approval of the Reich Fuhrer.

It was more than two hours after he first entered, that Konrad Werner chose to end his harangue. Ben returned to his cot. Perhaps the Nazi didn't expect him among the German wounded. How long would his luck hold out?

Mobility, Bernard was thankful for that. At least he would not be discarded among the invalids. He could thank Rudolph for that blessing. But the future was not bright. The hope that had long disappeared could not be conjured. Each day would have enough troubles of its own – that was an inescapable truth.

He shut his eyes again after talking with the young gentleman next to him. Too much said could give himself away. However he was able to learn that his tribulations were not isolated for him alone. So many were torn from their families, by forced conscription, to fight for a dream they considered a nightmare. No one used those terms, but in those first weeks of the war so much more could be read from what was not said.

Werner's orders compelled all to attention. He was no longer on any platform. His steps were direct, down the middle of the hall from one end to the other. The stares were warm from those appreciating the Reich, and cold from those fearing death. Death itself would on many occasions be kind, but Werner's reputation was one of torture, starvation, firing squads, or mutilation. "His brother's camp maybe better," some thought. However, they did not have to worry. They were German.

Bernard could not avoid Werner's glare. The commander turned immediately to his consort. Another approached Bernard. The questions were quick. The answers were concise as he had practiced: a Polish resident with German sympathies, assaulted in the initial attack as a result of a misunderstanding. They accepted the answers. Quivering finally stopped when they left.

Card games were part of the celebrations that night. Several guards played their instruments encouraging the festivities. Shepherd's pie and cake were followed by flowing wine. The Nazi troops were ready for more.

It was about 3 a.m. when Satan appeared, but this was no nightmare. Bernard was roughly hauled from his cot. Terrified he stood before Werner who gloated with his success. "Take him away!" The order was immediate.

Outside the hall, Bernard was repeatedly struck while being held by guards; and then after falling he was kicked several times. Gasping for breath was near impossible. He just wanted to die.

(I I I)

Poland was the land of diminishing options. Hades had frozen over with the terrorism of the Nazi occupiers. The vile annihilation in the first month was just a foreshadowing of the horror to befall the once proud nation.

Himmler had a mission and to assure his success he employed his Geheime Staatspolizei, the Gestapo, to thwart and destroy any potential resistance. The invaders had become the landowners and wanted to ensure their privilege for the stolen property. The Chief of German Police went even an unexpected step further by arranging four conferences with the Soviet occupiers to guarantee that all independent thought and action would have no place in Poland. The first of these conferences was September 28, 1939. The Gestapo was in charge.

From every flagpole in western Poland, the Swastika whipped about declaring the Police State. Aryan emblems disgraced once proud buildings. Polish pride had been replaced by German revenge. Convoys of Nazi troops continued to infest the countryside. The Wehrmacht filled the cities with brutish vigilantes. The S.S., Sturmabteilung, eradicated any suspicion of opposition.

The wartime curfew assured the Nazi regime that few would dare to contemplate any resistance. Shoot to kill. There would be no questions, and certainly no time for answers. Similarly, anyone suspected of looting would be shot. Suspicion was enough. In some communities the remains of homes were flattened to decrease any prospect of pilfering. In the cities, falling walls became flattened rubble. Food was scarce. Children starved. Schools were closed. The churches could offer little comfort. Bodies still lined the ditches. Decaying corpses still filled the laneways and driveways. Though bodies had been scraped from the ruins of city centres, the stench would never leave.

Leon Pawlowski played the game as best he could. It was a contest, a struggle to survive, to outbest the opponent, without concern for the dire reality that the cards were stacked in their favour. The Red Cross uniform bearing the insignia of the Aryan Eagle and the arm band of the Nazi Swastika – these were his ticket to survival. As to how long he could survive, he did as much as possible to control that factor.

Bernard lost fifteen pounds in that first month. A meal a day was a dream. Meals had become nothing more than uncooked leaves, corn stalk stubs, or the flesh of dead animals. It rained often after the fifteenth of the month. A tin can collected enough water to sustain him.

Leon's first concern after hiding those first three days was his family. In the blackness of night he was able to escape the city. Across fields he ran, but that took several hours for he constantly had to hide or conceal himself among the dead to avoid detection of roaming brigades. The Nazis had perfected the process of looting. Rape – that too had become their unrestricted joy. Jewellery was ripped from the dead. Wallets and purses were emptied. With each conquest of the vulnerable, the shrieks of Nazi-pleasure echoed through the valley.

Two days it took to get to his home. His heart was empty viewing the partially destroyed building. Was his family still inside? He took his time. While the invasion centred on Warsaw, more opportunities presented themselves for Poles in Poznan. The barn provided no prospect of any survival. The house – there could be some hope. He entered the basement using the same window that his son employed to escape. On the floor he discovered remnants of dried blood and immediately feared the worse. There he stayed until the morning. With the first sunlight he discovered the impossible situation. He couldn't stay, there was no benefit. The attempts to secure his documents, some clothes, food, anything from his home especially his family proved cruelly unsuccessful.

Behind the house he ventured into the field and realized nature was suddenly not his friend. The birds came, flew all around him, waiting for the grain, anything, for they too were hungry. Birds flying overhead could attract the attention of wandering Einsatzgruppen. He ran as quickly as he could to the closest woods, and there rested till dark.

The three closest farms made Leon shudder. Bodies and blood were everywhere. Jonas had a bullet hole in the right side of his head. Pavlov lay face down on his porch. Pavlov's wife was obviously forced to watch her husband being murdered. She was tied to a chair and shot through the heart. The broken windows and smashed doors were all symptoms of a crazed lunacy determined to fulfil Herr Hitler's insanity.

Days passed before he could make it to the farm he thought might offer remote hope. Leon knew the family. The woman was Jewish. Her husband was German. He had returned to Germany six years before the war started. Others told Leon that the German had secured papers wiping out all trace of Jewish heritage from their family. Reuben was the child's name. Bernard had called his friend Rudolph.

There was no one home. Where they were was a mystery. Leon conjectured that if anyone in the neighbourhood was to survive the Nazi onslaught it would be them. The woman had been a nurse. The man was Bernard's size. The home was remarkably intact although the two barns were destroyed. He left that night incredibly pleased with his disguise: the man's brown pants, his wife's medical smock, and the red armband in place. The cap with its metal badge was the right size. He grabbed a shovel, somehow inexplicably available. In the morning Leon walked away from the farm, as a medical employee of the Nazi regime with the aim to dutifully bury the dead.

(IV)

Bound with his arms behind his back and his chest shackled Wladyslaw Anders was thrown onto the frozen floor of his black cell. Like Christ before the Roman Procurator, he spoke not a word. He did not accept his fate, but there was no sense. The jeers of the celebrating Soviet Police shook the limestone block halls. Echoes of derision filled the offices. Beria looked up from his desk. He had accomplished his task.

Lubyanka Prison was the gate to hell, if not hell itself. No one to anyone's knowledge walked free. There were only so many cells and so many occasions to liquidate the cells. Torture was its specialty. Even the dumb spoke eventually. Standing all day for several days, sleepless nights, cuffs and leg irons, and systematic interrogation – these were the orchestrated steps of dehumanisation. Then there was the straight jacket, sensation of drowning, and being placed in deep pits. Ultimately firing squads or starvation would end the misery once family threats destroyed the will to live.

There was no light except the late afternoon rays from the barred window. With the autumn sun now lower in the sky, that glimpse of sunshine was no more than fifteen minutes each day. Limiting light would above all else send any man into a state of delirium.

Lubyanka Prison was a massive building, built forty-one years before as the head office of the All-Russia Insurance Company. After the Bolshevik Revolution, it became the headquarters of the Cheka, the Secret Police. In many respects Lubyanka Prison in 1939 could be compared to the Tower of London where the feudal king dwelled in lush quarters while his prisoners rotted in the basement cells. Lavrentiy Beria was its lord and master.

Beria knew he had seized the prize of the Polish elite, the intelligentsia some would call it. However Beria would never be caught suggesting anyone in Poland was intelligent. He had been resolute in his suggestion to Stalin that the General Secretary declare, "Poland no longer exists." Thus anyone that the Soviet Security Police seized would be Soviet property, a Soviet prisoner, and subject to Soviet justice – which didn't exist. Beria had carte blanche authority to seize anyone, anytime, and anywhere he wanted. His realm extended now from west of the Vistula River to the undisputed shores of the Pacific. Molotov's successful efforts had neutralized all tension in the far east making Siberia a feared venue for anyone who would disagree. Lavrentiy often laughed to himself, when he would let himself, at the suggestion that Siberia could be seen from the basement of the Lubyanka Prison.

Grigoriy Litvinov was a dutiful aide, with the incredible ability to express the correct opinion. The aide handed the document to Beria. Lavrentiy quickly glanced at it presuming everything was in order.

"This General Anders, we must safeguard him," Beria directed. "I know he's Polish, but he has value. Many I am told would make him their leader. As long as that is the case, he must be our slave. We must inconvenience him, but he must remain alive. The Poles don't need a martyr. We must not give them any reason to ever think they could rise against us."

Litvinov tried to endorse his commander's comments. "The Conference in Brzesc nad Bugiem was very specific on some issues …"

"We are aware," Beria advised. "Anders will remain alive. Is he still bound?"

"Yes, at least till morning."

"Release him now," Beria ordered.

Guards entered at Litvinov's call and left just as quickly to complete the instructions. Such diligence pleased Beria.

"What is your intent?" Litvinov enquired.

"Grigoriy, we are dealing with a General, a man who is still well respected. Twenty-five years ago Anders served our nation in the Czar's Lancers Regiment. Say what we may, that was then our country. True, he opposed us eighteen years ago as a commanding officer. Outnumbered, out positioned, yet he was hailed the victor by his nation. We could have used him then. And now, this month, he led his Nowogrodek Brigade against these Nazis at Lidzbark. Victor he again would have been, but he was wounded twice. And still suffering, he falls prey to our force, well planned to the end, until he could fight no more. Any sense of resistance must not have him as a leader or as a martyr. Be certain our doctors attend his wounds."

"And the sessions?" Litvinov asked about his role.

"Nothing now. Let him be. He has nothing more to add." Beria looked out the window at the troops marching down the street. Such precision made him proud. "We cannot feel secure. There will always be," he paused, "a sentiment opposed to our intentions. We will not tolerate it. I say to you, keep Anders alive, but perhaps not all."

"The camps are near full," Litvinov added regarding the number of captured Poles.

"Molotov said he spoke with Anders. Maybe this Pole is astute or just good at politics. Anders told our diplomat to never trust the Nazis. That is certain. We don't. But we must play the game. It is a game to them, someone wins and someone loses. For us though, there is no game. We will be the only winners. Molotov told me after that meeting that it would do well for us to release to Germany all of the Austrian and German dissidents we have captured. Why fill our prisons with those we cannot use? Do you agree?"

The aide concurred adding, "Let them deal with their own kind. We know what type of persons these are. They are the first to be rebels. We don't need Austria or any Austrian in our way. And for these German dissidents, let them be Hitler's problem."

"Well said. I often wonder about using the Poles. We have two choices: to use them as a wall between us and Hitler, or to wipe them off the face of the earth. If Poland is no more, then there is no need for Poles. Yet, can we trust the Nazis?"

"Iosif Stalin has been most direct on this," Litvinov noted.

"He has and those presently in prison are there as a result of the decree. The firing squads accomplished what we require. There is no opposition."

"There must be no opposition." Litvinov spoke boldly. "Our work must include all people who were once in Polish territory. They celebrate their independence from Polish occupation. They are with us. Let's not lose their support. Our Police are positioned firmly within borders.

All we need to do is nod, and the scourge will start. Let the Ukrainians and Belarusians do our job. Eradicate all trace of Polish influence, and then this Anders even if he is alive will have no people and no nation."

"This has been agreed upon," Beria informed his aide. He had a habit to conceal details before any discussion.

Litvinov stood awaiting further direction.

"These Poles. See what you can do."

There was a glint of delight on Grigoriy's face. Imposing terror made him sleep well at night.

Chapter Five
Christmas, 1939

The hymn Nawaiazuja zapowiadaja spiewaja aniolowie was a constant refrain in the emaciated prisoner's weary mind. Reaching for any joyous recollection was essential in these tormented times. Memories of Christmas, and Midnight Mass with his parents in the choir – these were images that Bernard could never allow himself to forget. They were festive times, never to come again. For three months now captivity was his destiny. His parents – he had no knowledge. His brother and sister – he could only pray. The refrain of Hark the Herald Angels Sing repeated itself once more, this time in English. This was the only carol he knew in that foreign language, something he learned for the school concert last year.

The wooden shovel could not in one sweep remove the inch of snow. Wood was all he had. All metal was reserved for their war effort. Plus, his captors would never trust any prisoner with a metal instrument. The path swung between the trees, and bushes lacking leaves.

In the autumn they were all in colour, a wonderful invitation. Then the discovery of the yard and stone wall beyond the path brought horror to the final remnants of any hope. Each day at the whim of the Schutzhaftlagerfuhrer prisoners walked this path to their destiny before the firing squad. Bernard took upon himself the task of cleaning the path as such chores had become his means of survival. But, who would be next?

Chica noc, swieta noc,

Pokoj niesie ludziom wszem

a u zlobka Matka Swieta

czuwa sama usmiechnieta,

nad Dzieciatka snem.

The carol 'Silent Night' remained so important to Prisoner 1237 for it was the hymn that his family sang together at the start of each Christmas Eve Celebration. The occasion was never just a meal, but rather a neighbourhood feast: first with the family, and then the doors were opened for any visitor. That meal prompted a multitude of memories from year to year as the children grew older. His brother for three years now was asked to light the centrepiece candle. Borsch was never Ben's favourite. The thought of carp never enticed him. He preferred his fish covered with thick batter. The best part was always the deserts. The taste and texture was amazing, even more than that, alluring. Always being able to have more than one made it all extra special. His parents liked the poppy seed cake, while his truly favourite was the piernik gingerbread cake with custard sauce. Prisoner 1237 would give anything to share another meal, any meal, with his parents, especially this evening.

Bernard knew it was Christmas Eve from the festivities in the hall, the music and the echoing laughter. One guard still occupied the tower. He was committed to keenly observing Bernard's every step. Last month Prisoner 1237 was caught piling two extra logs on the fire. Several prisoners had been suffering from typhus. Any warmth would be a comfort. Bernard was called to answer for his actions. The actual punishment was light. There seemed to be some understanding of his decision. A day without food was the only reprimand; but such a penalty did not have a great effect. Meals were restricted to once per day in any event. Starvation was the Nazi aim for all prisoners. In any event, three of those infected prisoners were dead within the week. Others, in the same cell, were compelled to walk the path. The echo of gunfire declared their destiny.

Each cell measured about five yards by twenty yards. At first more than fifty prisoners were crammed into each. There were twenty-five cells for men, and three for women. Two cells were empty. Ben reckoned that over two thousand Poles had entered the camp in those first three months. The Jews received the quickest attention. In October, approximately four hundred inmates arrived from the psychiatric hospital. These were not all deficient in any manner. After seizing the Citadel, many captured Polish officers were confined to that hospital. After that Fort VII Camp became their temporary home. There were many rumours regarding the gas chamber. All that Bernard knew was that two weeks after they arrived, no one from the hospital could be seen. Being gassed to death terrified Prisoner 1237.

Ernst Werner peered out the window. He had left the raucous laughter in the hall, for a quiet moment in his office. Inebriation was his daily affair, either with a bottle or with his pride. Many followed his weekly responsibilities, interested in methods, results and numbers. He was good at that – pleasing his superiors and keeping his subordinates equally attentive. Looking down onto the courtyard, he saw that prisoner for whom he once had a faint ounce of respect. His brother would have had him dead months ago; but Ernst was never one to concede to Konrad's will. Constant competition between brothers at times bordered on the ridiculous. Rumours persisted in this last month that Konrad would be sent to Warsaw, something about dissidents and rebels. He would be good for that, the Commandant conceded. For Ernst, there were no such prospects. He had his post and he was expected to exceed his Fuhrer's commands. This was his niche.

Ernst's eyes were fixed on the prisoner. He had a habit of talking out loud to himself in the confines of his office. "What makes that prisoner tick? Does he really think anyone listens? He knows we have rules? Why am I even letting him …?"

There was a knock at the door. Hans, his chauffeur, had noticed the Commandant's absence in the hall and came to enquire. Ernst dismissed his ride, begging him ten more minutes. He watched the prisoner again for another moment, then returned to his desk opening the side drawer. That rosary was still there. He took it from Prisoner 1237. No one with access to his office had any use for it. He could have had the prisoner shot instantly for just being in possession of such an idol. "And how did he get it in here?" The question was a legitimate one. "Never mind," his thoughts continued. "Look what he has done. But some day, I will have to say 'enough'."

Ernst Werner was well aware of the plans for the camp near Krakow and the ultimate intention to close this camp after liquidating all prisoners.

"Christmas," his mind continued forcing a grin. "Fraulein Adele is waiting." The young mistress was now his only family. His wife was left behind in Berlin.

She wouldn't come with him. They had gone through so much together, especially the depression. And now, when he was suddenly successful, she refused the career of the Commandant of Konzentrationslager Posen. Two months after his arrival, Ernst heard the rumours and concluded her suicide attempts had been successful. None of the past would dampen the expectation of his mistress in his arms. Christmas morning didn't matter that much. It was not a religious occasion, just a social event. One year, his father even called the Yule celebration a Communist conspiracy. That didn't make any sense at all to the teenage Ernst. He had heard enough about the Bolsheviks to know they did not even celebrate Christmas.

"Marry her? I must one day." Ernst Werner was well aware of the potential consequences for those who appeared to embrace an unmarried lifestyle.

The superintendent's eyes remained fixed on the prisoner. "Do any of them survive?" Werner knew of the habit of that prisoner taking the clothes from the dead, washing them and then handing them to those struggling to stay alive. "It's costing us nothing," he mused. "Anyway they will all meet the same fate, today, tomorrow, or the day after. Let them be. There is no harm, at least for now."

Ernst Werner took his coat from the stand. It was a heavy coat with enough thick lining to protect him in the dreaded cold. The celebrations in the hall reached a new level. "That's good." He smiled, satisfied with his accomplishments and then closed the door.

He no longer pondered who would not be alive tomorrow. Ernst Werner was not about to alter fate, just do his duty. His fraulein awaited him, and that was going to be a religious experience in itself.

Bernard continued cleaning the path to the edge of the yard. There were three logs for the fire place that demanded his efforts. It was a struggle to lift them, but using the wooden shovel he was able to shift them sufficiently for him to bend enough to lift and then drag them to the centre courtyard. There the logs were brushed clean of snow. From a shelf on the main building's wall he pulled the day's allotment of three pieces of paper and two matchsticks. In the cold, he prayed while trying to light the fire. Often he would pull the pieces of bark away using that for kindling wood. Fifteen minutes later, the logs were ablaze. The inmates in unison assembled around the central pit for warmth. They celebrated Prisoner 1237's efforts with expressions of gratitude. Gathered in the courtyard they could hear the Christmas carols from inside the hall. In unison they started their own. For more than that hour they continued. Bernard left to grab another log from the distant yard. The tower guard saw him and reported nothing.

Any possible Christmas joy resounded in their vocal harmony. The Christmas meal the next day would be the usual rations; but for some it would also be their last.

(I I)

The woman sat in the rear wooden pew, pensive, hugging her children, contemplating a bleak future, while praying for the best. Teresa could never express enough gratitude to the nuns of the Franciscan Convent. For three days after the initial bombing she had roamed the fields and laneways with her two children, no longer able to hide the carnage from the stare of their lost-innocence. The Abbess was decisive. There were no questions. There were others there too. Teresa and the children were given a basement room, one originally used by a noviciate. Access to the basement was by means of a stairway located under a counter cabinet in the sacristy. One room for each family, enough for shelter – the rule was strictly followed. Food was sufficient. The farmland provided necessary sustenance. Firewood had been stored in the barns since spring. The preparations were so complete causing one to wonder if the Sisters had been told by God about the war beforehand.

However, all who were sheltered knew a day would come when fears of the Nazi invaders would surpass the ability of the convent to provide shelter. Children could not be justified in a nunnery. The Wehrmacht had already entered the convent on two occasions. Each time their warning was severe. If the children were ever found, all of the Sisters could be brutalized. For Teresa in the fourth month of her pregnancy, any threat was very real.

The chapel was built in the centre of the convent, away from the outer walls, allowing it to be kept much warmer. Logs burned in the fireplace by the rear entrance. There was smoke, but no one complained. Smoke meant warmth. All was prepared for the Midnight Mass. The cave was made of twigs. Straw was real. Hand painted wooden figures completed the nativity scene.

Teresa remained seated, while others entering the chapel knelt in reverence. Her knees were sore especially on the rough wooden kneeler. Her back too was the victim of occasional arthritic pains. Weight loss made her even more susceptible in the winter season. No matter how warm a room could be, there was always the overbearing dampness that made her bones ache.

The children were less susceptible to the cold. However their spirits remained broken. There was no joy this Christmas. There were no presents. There was no hope. There was no understanding. Tears were a daily ritual. Words of reassurance would eventually subdue the inclination to cry, but kind phrases last only so long when the mind works overtime. Teresa hugged them, an arm around each, glad she was able through the kindness of the convent to provide them with warm coats. But her hugs did not take away the reality she had yet to tell them.

The Abbess made it very clear. In January they would have to leave. All of the religious orders in Warsaw, Poznan and Lodz had determined the Nazi occupation was exposing the seminaries and convents to potential horror if they were to continue to house families with children. Men could wear cassocks and collars. Women could wear habits. Sooner or later the children would be discovered. The Abbess of the Franciscan Convent disagreed with that directive; but the decision had been made for her.

Unlike those in other convents, she was able to offer choices. There were two: an apartment in Poznan with a job in the munitions factory, or transfer to the Siostry Seracanki in Czestochowa. In that location Teresa was told they would live in the farming complex next to the convent. The children could attend school. The sisters had already invited the Germans to review the curriculum. The Accord with the Vatican – Teresa was tired of hearing about it – had somehow guaranteed the security of that facility.

Teresa thought positively of that prospect. She had a warm affection for the Black Madonna, and being near the cathedral that would allow her to personally revere the portrait. It was enticing. Being on the Warta River too was further reason to consider the move. Getting away from Poznan would be good for the children. There was however one major issue: transit to Czestochowa. Being so close to the prior German border, safety could never be guaranteed.

That night, the public could attend the Midnight Mass. The nuns could not prevent that. Teresa prayed that no German officers would attend. She also begged God that her husband might suddenly appear.

(III)

Leon had buried thirty-seven bodies in that first week. On one occasion he was questioned by a German patrol. The captain confirmed his approval and asked if help was needed. Leon directed the captain to a fictitious cohort several miles away. Accepting the information, the patrol moved on.

The next inspection was not so congenial. Leon was ordered to stop. Appreciation was expressed for what he was doing, but at the same time he was told that others would complete the task. Leon knew the corpses would just be thrown onto a truck, and then burned at the garbage dump south of the city. That intrusion proved to be somewhat beneficial as he was ordered to report to the Citadel to assist in the production of daily needs for the occupying forces. Tin cups, canteens, metal plates, utensils – these suddenly became his saviour.

Fellow workers were many, all struggling to appease the occupiers. In the work places everything was positive. There were no complaints, for every worker knew the consequences of a misstated word.

That position lasted until mid November. At that time one of the guards, a German Pole, recognized Leon. Following that, he was back in his store with a staff of four workers preparing and mending garments for the occupying force. Leon had found his safety cushion. However, there was no family, no trust, and no hope. Christmas may well have not existed that year for there was no joy – just function and keep the captors who have no morals satisfied.

(I V)

O Come, let us Adore Him.

O Come, let us adore Him. Christ the Lord.

With the final refrain the choir immediately began the Sussex Carol. This hymn was the Prime Minister's favourite.

Neville Chamberlain with his wife Anne and their children sang with unrestrained enthusiasm. Although he professed the Unitarian faith, the Prime Minister, out of dutiful respect, shared the Christmas Eve celebration in St. Paul's Cathedral. The setting was grandeur in the supreme. Flowers, decorations and the nativity scene stole everyone's attention. Each member of the congregation was richly attired. Yet in spite of the splendour, Neville appeared timid. He was almost squeamish, unsure of himself. Prior to the service, he looked about as if fearing the worst. There should have been pride in his efforts, yet events within the last fifteen months had cautioned many to reconsider his capabilities. It no longer mattered that he enhanced National Health Care, that England survived the depression, or that he nationalized the coal industry preserving jobs and increasing wages. "Munich" would be the one word written on his tombstone.

Hymn followed carol with choral accompaniment. There's never a limit as how much any person can sing when ignoring events outside church walls. There was a homily, long and detailed, the type of sermon you know an English cleric would deliver. Further hymns preceded the final carol "Come, all ye faithful."

The Prime Minister returned home after greeting many in the congregation. Chamberlain was relieved, as much at peace with himself as he could be. He had been well received in spite of any fears.

In the morning, he rose from his bed. Warm in his thick dressing gown, he sat by the tree sipping his cider, very prepared to greet his family with an enthusiastic Merry Christmas.

Chapter Six
Europe, 1940

The PT31 locomotive pulled into Kalisz Station forty minutes late. Punctuality in Polish travel had disappeared one hundred and twenty-four days before.

The need to board was immediate, in spite of any apprehension. Quickly Teresa ascended the stairs, carrying Elzbieta. Ryszard became the young man not wholly dependent on maternal care. The passenger car with its wicker benches was more accommodating that the cracked boards and reek of the van that transported them out of Poznan.

In spite of the fears and inconvenience Teresa Pawlowski still felt she should be thankful. The Abbess's words tore her heart. To assure the family that she had their best interests in mind, the nun read from a letter delivered to the convent the day before. The Abbess had met the Governor only once before, but in that meeting Arthur Greiser was terse, direct, and unforgiving. The New Year's Day edict was very clear. Reichsfuhrer Himmler controlled the situation, and nothing would stand in his way. Any ambiguity would not favour any resident of Poznan.

Jews and Poles who have been ordered to move from some area of the Reich to the General Government, and who still remain in German Reich territory are to be summarily shot.

Teresa had to move hastily to a city within the borders of the General Government. Czestochowa, a prior option for her family, met that need.

The second part of her trek took her to Lodz. There the family had to board another train.

The direct trip would normally take three-and-a-half hours. With first the van, then two trains and waiting for the second train to arrive, the trip took nine hours.

During the last leg of the transfer an elderly woman, with obviously no friends nor family, nor income, chose the occasion to recall the tragic events of the first week of September. Teresa did not need to have such events repeated, but this woman would not be stopped. The smell of her rags became as vile as her story.

Guards on the train, those who accompanied the family and others from Poznan, chose not to curtail the narrative. There was no delight for them in her story, just no escaping the reality. Rudolph sat there with his comrades, realizing he knew the woman travelling with her children. However he would not let personal matters confound his way.

Czestochowa had been that derelict woman's home. Then on September 4, 1939, German troops stormed the city in a murderous rampage killing first Jews, and then any Pole they chose to suspect of being a Jewish sympathizer. Hostages were even forced onto the main square to die by the machine gun fire from novice soldiers.

Teresa hugged her children in the unheated passenger car finding no comfort in the story. With one arm around Elzbieta's shoulder, a hand covered the child's right ear. Ryszard cringed grabbing his mother's other arm. With the sun setting behind distant mountains, Teresa was thankful they could no longer see the rotting corpses in the countryside. Several times the woman repeated woefully that nearly two thousand perished that day. The guards hearing the story knew the figure was more. Teresa wanted none of this and searched her scrambled mind for the prospect of taking another train away from all this.

It was pitch black when they arrived at the Czestochowa train station. No one was there to meet them.

Rudolph and the four soldiers that accompanied the train departed the station with assigned groups to specific destinations. Families did as they were told, went where they were told, and never questioned instructions. Fear had no limits. It controlled everything.

Her entire being shook with fear realizing the plight of her family. Standing on the platform she never felt so totally helpless. Teresa did not have the formal identity papers. She did not have her work permit. She knew where she was supposed to go, but did not have the specific address. The Abbess had provided Baptismal Certificates to verify names, Christian lineage, birth dates, all something meaningful as long as the Wehrmacht did not suddenly turn on the Church. The Transit Papers, too, were her security. But her contact, where was he? Was it even a man?

Two Nazi Guards approached the family. Elzbieta immediately started to cry. Ryszard grabbed his mother's right arm staring firmly at the approaching occupiers. He would not cry. He had to be strong.

"Your names?" one guard demanded, speaking German.

Teresa did not answer. It was a double-edged sword. If she spoke German, they might conclude the family was Jewish possessing doctored papers. If she answered in Polish, she at least had the Baptismal Certificates and Transit Papers confirming her nationality and desire to move from the Reich District Land of Warta River to the General Government area. Such was sufficient to satisfy Herr Himmler's decree.

The question was repeated. Teresa understood even though it was in German, and she replied in Polish. Her papers were grabbed out of her hand. Slowly the guard read them feigning interest in the documents he clearly understood. It was troublesome standing there, wondering what irked him. He then thrust them back to the woman. Ryszard was relieved.

Other guards approached these two. The language was strange. Teresa prayed her husband could be there to understand. Slavic? Romanian? Certainly not German.

The original two guards returned to their post at the far end of the platform. Teresa could at least understand the German they spoke. Another train was expected before midnight.

Ryszard started to shiver.

Teresa asked if they could go inside to the waiting room. The answer was immediate and terse. The guard was obviously annoyed that a woman should even ask for anything.

"Slavic," Teresa concluded to herself. She continued imploring, pointing out that her children were cold and hungry. One of the guards laughed. Another left the group walking away, and then returned behind her. The moments were tense. He slid up against her. Teresa knew well enough not to protect herself. Instead she sheltered the children in front of her. The guard accosted her, and she said nothing. He continued with his exploring hands. The other guards smiled then laughed with derision.

"My children need warmth," Teresa said in a tone that suggested the lurid actions of the guard had no effect on her temperament.

He stepped away. They continued speaking in their foreign tongue. For another ten minutes they ignored her requests. She cuddled her children close to provide some warmth. Any warmth was a godsend in the cold January breeze.

The original two guards continued their patrol and eventually made their way back to the abandoned family. The other guards, the ones who spoke Slavic, left. Teresa watched them leave the platform on the far left. She was relieved.

Her request to these two guards received a similar reply. She knew there was now no prospect as the staff inside the waiting room were in the process of closing the premises. When hope dies, any aspiration for anything good is buried in the day's misfortunes. Teresa watched the waiting room staff knowing nothing would come of her wish for any food, warmth, shelter, rest, or any sense of humanity.

At that point when she was ready to collapse from the day's long journey and the insufficient food for herself, her children, and the child she was carrying; a gentleman entered onto the platform. His starched trench coat suggested he had a position of importance. The swastika armband affirmed his allegiance. His suitcase suggested he had the necessary documents.

"Teresa Pawlowski?" he enquired.

"Yes," she answered hopefully.

"Your two children?" He handed the papers from his brief case to the two guards.

They took their time to review them as they had done before. Returning the papers to the gentleman, they gave instructions that the family could leave with him. Relief was immediate.

The gentleman then directed the family to follow him.

Even in his car Teresa was uncertain of the exact destination. The information from the Abbess was at best ambiguous. Was it at the church itself, or on farmlands?

The journey from the train station took them past too many wandering refugees. The gentleman told them there had been "many incidents" and encouraged them not to offend anyone. "Keep yourself clean." The gentleman's Polish was very clear. Teresa had a sense of relief although short lived until they passed by another dead person lying by the side of the road.

An hour later they were in the rectory of the Pauline Church of Our Lady of Czestochowa. They never met that gentleman again.

(I I)

Ernst Werner held the letter firmly in two hands, re-reading Herr Himmler's every word. Then rising from the desk, he moved pensively to the window. Looking down onto the courtyard, the Commandant knew what he had to do. "It means their death," he concluded to himself.

Werner's mind shifted to the supply issue. He had difficulty focusing on any matter for too long. There was clearly not enough food. Only one meal each day, but even so there were problems arranging that. That had become an ever-present issue, expecting to feed so many.

Himmler's decree had to be followed. Prisoners had to be sent from his camp in Posen to the labour camp in Krakow. Werner understood the logic: that Krakow was in the General Government area. He felt sorry for some of these. Their conduct had saved their lives. Being sent to the new camp would make them the equal of everyone, with just as much chance to not see tomorrow's sunrise.

Bernard, not yet 15 having lied about his age, stood in front of the Commandant. One security guard was near at hand. It was the morning of the fourth day of January. The wind was biting cold. Prisoner 1237 was anxious, but pleased to be inside.

The commandant's advice was simple. "Your conduct has been exemplary. You have earned the opportunity to move to a new labour camp where conditions are better, where you will be properly fed, with adequate clothes and bedding. Thank you for helping us here."

Werner knew he said more than he had to. He was also careful not to say too much in front of the guard. Even the guards could be informants.

Prisoner 1237 was escorted from the complex back to his cell. There he picked up his shredded jacket, and then was taken to a waiting van.

On the train there were nine other prisoners. None of them were Jews. Three of these appeared so weak that even making it to the destination was questionable. Five guards accompanied the transferred inmates. The meal on the train was better than they had eaten in the last five months. Even going to the washroom was a relief.

The rail trip passed through Wroclaw then south-east to Katowice before the final leg to Krakow. By the time they could have viewed any mountainous scenery it was dark outside. The entire trip to the Krakow Train Station took seven hours. Time was important to anyone wearing a uniform, but to a prisoner it was just an undefined moment in any day that had no limit on uncontrolled events.

Prison 1237 never saw his Transit Papers. The guards kept those securely in their possession. Bernard had an immediate dislike for these. They were young, perhaps in their mid twenty's. They spoke Polish but fluency was not perfect. They didn't sound German. His mind questioned their nationality. Bernard said nothing because he knew silence was golden as silence was perceived to be agreement.

The van taking the ten prisoners to the labour camp was not heated. They shivered hoping the trip would be short. The driver gave the camp a name – Plaszow. They were told there were no Jews, and that the camp had just opened.

Being called scum was the most complimentary salutation. They were treated abruptly, with no attempt to provide any courtesy. Roughly they were thrown about. Their jackets were ripped from their shoulders while their arms were still tied behind their backs. A new Gray jacket was placed on Bernard's shoulders. He became number A08334. The first impression had been that this was not a large facility. However, the number suggested otherwise. He never questioned what happened to the eight thousand prisoners before his number.

The next morning Amon Goethe, the Commandant, introduced himself to the ten prisoners. The harangue was a forceful lecture about German virtues while reminding the inmates they belonged to an inferior race.

In daylight, Bernard realized the extremely dire situation. The cells were pathetically small, six persons to an eight foot by eight foot brick-walled room. The ground was the most disturbing. Beneath his cell there were two cemetery stones. "Jews," one of the inmates concluded.

Prisoner A08334 noted the double wall of barbed wire surrounding the camp. That was not unexpected. The guards' towers were too numerous to count. Machine guns were well placed. A fir tree and two oak trees obscured vision to the west. Only a few were occupied. Machine guns were placed. To the south side, there was a hill covered in budding daffodils.

The camp was situated on the right bank of the Wisla River near the train station. Near the barbed wire fence a prisoner could see the Kamieniolom Liban Limestone Quarry. To the other side, the Bonarka Brick Works was barely visible. Plaszow was an arbeitslager, a labour camp, and this would be the venue of their labour. Amon Goethe's second lecture was equally as forceful: anyone who could not work would be shot immediately.

Further observation allowed horror to become terror. Prisoner A08334 realized some of the guards were Ukraine Nationals. A couple of prisoners in that first week taunted them. These inmates were not seen again. Similarly, those frail prisoners on the train never made it to the second weekend.

Every morning, prisoners heard a gunshot and counted their numbers as being one less. The Commandant was an evil person, one to be truly feared; as he took delight in shooting one prisoner each morning before his breakfast. Herr Goethe had been a Commandant in Vienna. Bernard could not fathom why an Austrian would despise Poles so much. About ten o'clock each morning, Bernard was alive and thus pleased his number had not been called.

(I I I)

Reichsgau Posen did not celebrate the Feast of the Epiphany that year. Such festivities, religious or not, were banned by the governing Nazi Party. S.S. Obergruppenfhrer Arthur Greiser had absolute control of all events, all military actions, and all decisions concerning deportation, death, and extermination.

Archbishop August Hlond had no impact on the Gauleiter's decisions or conscience. The Prelate was alive solely at the whim of the Nazis to maintain an appearance of accord between the Catholic Church and the German State. Hlond's efforts in the first months were significant, and success was achieved safeguarding many with appropriate documents and security. However, safe houses became fewer, and trust became a vanishing virtue. There were always some who accomplished more than expected, but many of these were no longer alive.

Archbishop Hlond was never silent about the abuse, the pillaging, and the murders; but his congregation was becoming sparse. Fears ruled, and measures were taken just to survive. On that January 6th just being alive was a blessing.

Leon Pawlowski peered down the street looking for his employees. Several, who were always so dutiful, had not yet arrived for work. The main street too was oddly vacant, only a few elderly people sauntered about three blocks away. The operations manager returned inside to encourage the others to perform the necessary tasks. Leon was alive because he met the military quotas. His employees were alive too six months after the invasion alive because they too were part of the team that produced clothing, canteens, plates, and utensils. Poznan was the military centre for the Reich District. Production matched the demand. The salary did not compare to pre-war wages but it meant some income; and as long as the Nazis accepted the final product, the workers were alive. Some on the assembly line still had their farms and were able to sell some of their crops to the military for additional income.

Discussions were still an opportunity to express fears; however with time fears even involving discussions grew. Who had any connection or leanings toward the occupying troops? No one could be absolutely certain; for security was only as strong as the frailty of the tortured person. There was not an employee who had not experienced the loss of a family member.

Leon had difficulties sleeping. He had a cot in the back room. His wife? His children? The tormenting questions were many. It is impossible to count sheep when the mind is busy recalling the moments of terror.

The staff was afforded two meals per day. The workday was twelve hours. Those who might choose otherwise were still compelled to work sixty hours per week.

Affability with the German delivery and transport workers was essential. They would be the ones to report any difficulties. Boxes produced were always ready on time.

That day, however, the performance was not going to be met. Eight workers had not shown up for work. Leon, realizing it was more than a coincidence, noted that five of these lived in the same neighbourhood. He ventured outside again. While still on the sidewalk, he stopped suddenly. The sound of distant gunfire jarred his mind. He stepped back against the door. The barrage continued, echoing louder as if in the next block. Suddenly a woman ran from between buildings two blocks away. Her screams were silenced by machine gun fire. The young guards jeered in celebration, one even standing over the dead woman for a final volley.

Leon rushed inside and slammed the door, locking it instantly. He drew the curtains, and called his staff together in the back room. Machines were silent for those moments. The shock and expressions of woe could not control the horror each person felt. Hearts raced, minds wrenched. Several demanded to leave immediately. Leon did not stop them, but cautioned them to go to the right. Suddenly the roar and clamber of army vehicles shook the building. The women cried. Then with one thunderous blast a building in the next block was levelled. Leon tried to silence the wailing but could not succeed. Two men leapt past others toward the front door. They were followed by five others, all pursuing freedom from tyranny. Others bolted by the back door. The remaining staff, eleven in all, hid beneath the metalwork benches. Leon, the captain who would go down with his ship if necessary, stayed in the front room. The lights were out. The front door was locked.

Less than a minute after they fled through the front door, the barrage of gunfire defined their destiny. The screams and orders of the Wehrmacht echoed between buildings. There was another blast, and another building crumbled. Leon tried to look outside between the slats hoping to see the Nazis moving down the street away from his building. A patrol vehicle stopped obscuring his vision. He hid immediately.

There was a knock at the door with the demand for admission. Leon did not answer. The door was rattled. The dead bolt held. Faces were pressed closed to the glass peering inside. The darkened room suggested no one was present. The butt of a rifle broke the glass. Leon withheld his gasp. Voices and derisive laughter were heard. Another arrived. "Lieferanten!" His voice was loud intending to protect the firms supplying the military. The Germans moved on but not that far.

Next door they confronted Ivan, a tailor of fine suits and shirts. Minutes later Ivan lay in a pool of blood. Leon's prayer was silent for his friend. His mind returned once more to the terror outside and how much more, if anything, he could do to protect his workers. They were the only family he now had.

Lebensraum was intended to provide German lands for Germans, to remove all Poles from territory Germans called their own. On that January 6th the cleansing of Poznan began. Seventy thousand Poles living in the Reich District: Land of the Warta River were relocated to the newly established area of the Central Government. That policy alone hoarded Poles into one district making them: easier to govern, easier to torment, and easier to exterminate.

(I V)

Lavrentiy Beria's distrust for the Nazis was total. Herr Himmler was a falcon pursuing live game. Adolf Eichmann, sitting across from him, was no more than a disease-ridden rat determined to infect every Pole in creation. In that sense, Beria was really no different; but the Chief of the Secret Police had his clandestine methods. No one could ever accuse him of any mass murder, because candidly he would never allow any such evidence.

These Germans were all vipers, looking for every opportunity to strike and kill. The first impression of Herr Zimmermann, the Reich Fuhrer of the Radom District of the General Government, was exactly that. He had 'death' written across his cold stare – an inflexible man, determined to obliterate every Pole within his jurisdiction.

Zakopane in the Polish Tatra Mountains was the setting for the third of the Nazi-Soviet Conferences on dealing with the occupied nation. More specifically, the meetings were designed to establish preferred means to get rid of the Polish Jews, and then the intelligentsia, the Slavs, and ultimately all Poles in occupied territories. To the time of this third meeting, in the first six months of the war, approximately three hundred thousand Poles had been sent to their Creator. The barbarians were meeting at the Pan Tadeusz villa in the most picturesque mountainous setting in Poland. Snow-capped mountains with ski trails, sled paths, with streams and glistening lakes – no area in Poland could have provided such a contrast to the evil of their intentions.

Both sides clearly knew what the others had already achieved. Germany had declared all land it occupied prior to Versailles to now be Reich Territory. All Poles in these portions had to move to the General Government Territory, a large swath of land near Warsaw. The Soviet Delegation was well aware of Himmler's decree to the Polish citizens to move or be shot. Imprisonment, starvation, disease, firing squads, and mass murders – these were accomplishing the goal of obliteration.

Beria delegated the leadership of the conference to Grigoriy Litvinov. His Deputy had an incredible style of being able to present positive proposals to convince anyone the benefit of ending someone else's life. The primary fear of the Soviet Union was the leadership of the Polish forces. If ever these officers could escape or were set free, they could reasonably lead a massive assault on the Soviet Union. Such a force would include nearly all of Europe, the British Commonwealth, French Colonies, Far-East nations, and possibly the United States. Iosif Stalin had no reason or desire to believe the Nazi Empire would last one thousand years. The war would one day come to an end, and these prisoners would be set free. What then?

The Soviet distrust of Nazi Germany also stemmed from the Axis Alliance with Japan and Italy. Molotov invaded Poland the day after he reached an accord with Japan; and now Japan had joined Germany. Soviet troops were being sent east on the Siberian Railway, prepared to engage the Japanese forces. In the underbelly of Europe, Germany had made too many incursions. It wasn't just Italy. The Germans had shown more than an interest in Romania, Hungary, the Balkans and Greece. When would Hitler stop?

The Polish officers and intelligentsia also posed a significant problem, not just for what might happen after the war, but what could happen if Germany ever decided to set its sights east toward the Soviet Union. Would these captured Poles then fight with the Nazis to save their lives?

Unknown to the Nazi leadership, Beria had already established camps in Soviet territory as part of its program to annihilate Poles living in the Soviet Union. As early as August, 1937 Beria had been instrumental in such mass murder.

The representatives of both nations left the conference aware of the general interests of each other, while being committed to employing their own methods to achieve what definitely was a common goal.

The Soviet Union and the German Reich met once more in Krakow three weeks later. One of the topics was a prisoner exchange. This may have seemed to have been an odd issue bearing in mind they were already accomplishing genocide. However, Germany had become a venue for the extermination of too many European Jews. Other nations were actually paying Nazi Germany to exterminate their Jews in German camps. Hungary was paying five hundred Reich-Marks for each Jew it sent to Germany. Was it a moneymaking operation to finance the Wehrmacht? Yes, it was. Now what was the Reich to do with all of these foreign Jews? More camps would be built. More ghettos would be constructed. Methods would be improved. But, would the Soviets take some for their gulags? Issues were resolved; and after March 1940 the conspirators did not meet again.

(V)

Vyacheslav Molotov pulled the curtain back and looked out his window to the band playing the National Anthem. "Must be noon hour," the Soviet Prime Minister spoke to himself.

While Molotov was mouthing the final verse of the anthem, Sergei Ulanov excitedly knocked and simultaneously rushed into the room. "The Finns have surrendered!"

Molotov was elated. The victory gave unrestricted access to the Baltic, a chance for the Soviet Navy to display its might, to thwart any potential naval aggression.

111

"This is a brick wall to the Nazis in Norway," Ulanov stated the obvious.

Molotov smiled at his assistant's perception.

Returning to the desk, Molotov picked up the top page of a series of documents handing it to Ulanov. The script was legible. The assistant read it aloud.

We hold the spiritual forces of Christianity to be indispensable.

Ulanov was shocked.

Molotov instantly added, "It's Hitler. He's invoking their Christian God."

The assistant was puzzled.

Molotov raised his voice. "He expects his God to help him. Hitler thinks God is on their side. Do you know how dangerous that makes him?"

Ulanov did not have to answer.

"He will attack us. I know he will. He said this to encourage these Christian Poles to join him in his attack."

Ulanov's attention was drawn to Molotov's summation.

"An attack on us!" the Minister of Foreign Affairs screamed.

His Soviet war machine was already comprehensively organized, fully armed by factories and ammunition plants throughout the realm, for any conflict in the European corridor or on the Pacific Coast. The stability and increased range of the Soviet Navy just simply enhanced the nation's military capabilities in any confrontation. Long-range rockets were being developed. At any one moment, numerous fully armed divisions could be marshalled into action with coordinated communication. He would never allow for a debacle of the First World War when nations feared the size of the Russian force but quickly realized the incompetence of the Tsar in organisation and strategy.

Molotov was a genius at long-term plans, the movement of troops and counter-offensive operations. Today was always important, but tomorrow had to be equally so. He had taken upon himself the unilateral task of exceeding Stalin's military requests to ensure the Soviet Empire could never be subject to the fanatical enthusiasm of any German or Japanese maniac. Molotov was well suited to be Minister of War.

Molotov knew there was no choice, and that there really never was a choice. At the desk he picked up his copy of the Politburo's decree, handing the text to his assistant.

"Yesterday the decision was made …"

"It has to be," Ulanov quickly agreed. "Will you write?"

"This afternoon. Instructions must then be sent by Monday, in three days. That will give them three weeks. Hitler will use their God against us. That will not happen!"

"When?" Ulanov enquired.

"When the ground thaws. Trenches will become streams of Polish blood."

Ulanov was always committed to the Soviet cause, having a great ability to hide his inner feelings. Blood had to this time been spilled only in the combat of war; or, so he thought. However, now the discussion was involving imprisoned military, teachers, doctors, and even Polish clergy.

"How many more?" Ulanov silently questioned himself after leaving the room.

(V I)

The extent of human cruelty can never be truly measured. Throughout European's history there has been war, civil insurrection, bloodshed, oppression, torment, horrific acts, terror, mass killings, with a perpetual desire to be superior by forcing another group to be inferior. The capacity to be cruel is magnified by a self-righteous freedom of conscience allowing the perpetuator to be the judge, the jury and the executioner. In such cases, the executioner no longer has need for any judge and jury as he assumes all power and authority. Thus, Justice dies. Law vanishes. Cruelty reigns supreme.

Identifying a common enemy has prompted more factions and enemies to unite than we may ever want to admit. The Jews have been perpetually the victims of concerted efforts throughout Europe. On the road to Jerusalem for the First Crusade, Jews were assaulted and murdered in Germany. Two hundred years later a vessel with three hundred Jews on board was on route to the Low Countries when it became stuck on a sand bank at low tide. The vessel was set on fire, as planned, and all died. In Spain, Jews were exiled the day after Columbus sailed for the New World. All property was confiscated. In Czarist Russia, Jews were huddled together, impoverished, and then exiled. The recurring wars between France and Germany always involved the oppression and destruction of Jewish communities and property. In England following the First World War, the government would not hire a Jewish person, nor could a government employee be related to a Jewish parent or grand-parent. Prior to the Second World War, the United States, Canada and Cuba refused to accept Jewish refugees, returning them to their deaths. Therefore, should any prudent person not have expected the Nazi and Soviet commitment to oppression, terror and mass murder?

Lavrentiy Beria was committed even before Stalin's directive of March 5, 1940 to rid the world of Poland's elite officers. He would accomplish this by emptying the prisons and labour camps of all Polish military by mass execution. The murders were not restricted to the military but involved the mass murder of doctors, lawyers, professors, teachers, clergy and any Polish person or Jew that could be deemed to be saboteurs or enemies of the state.

Welcome to Katyn, a forest area near Gneizdovo Village about twelve kilometres west of Smolensk.

This was Ukrainian Territory. Unfortunately for more than one hundred years, Ukrainians had been oppressed by Germany and by Russia. The Ukrainian Nationalist movement developed as a result of foreign rule. Its difficulty became identifying the cause to which it should align itself. Following the Soviet invasion of Poland, the Ukraine was awarded land it felt was rightfully theirs. In many respects, many in the Ukraine became terrorized supporters of the Soviet Union.

Prior to Stalin's March decree, there was a faint hope that captured Polish soldiers and intelligentsia could be indoctrinated into the Soviet belief system. The realisation was quick that these attempts, being conducted in the prisons, were failing. From Kozelsk, Starobelsk and Ostashkov labour camps in the USSR, Polish officers were herded onto trains bound for Smolensk. There the rail line took the prisoners into a forest, where they were shot at close range. Their bodies were thrown into prepared pits. In the Kalinin and Khakiv prisons, inmates were placed in padded rooms and exterminated with a bullet to the back of the head. Bodies were then transported to the Katyn Forest and buried with the others.

The number of reported dead varies. Suggestions range between sixteen and twenty-five thousand, with most estimates in the area of twenty-two thousand.

These figures included these military officers: 24 Colonels, 79 Lieutenant-Colonels, 258 Majors, 654 Captains, 3,437 Other Officers and 7 Chaplains. The murdered intelligentsia included at least: 20 Professors, 300 Doctors, several hundred lawyers, 100 journalists, 200 pilots. Besides these the dead removed from prisons and labour camps involved more than fifteen thousand Polish citizens.

The massacre would be discovered by the invading Germans three years later. Stalin would deny any involvement, blaming the Germans for such a travesty. Britain on its part would choose to side with Stalin, as it wanted Soviet intervention to defeat Hitler.

(VII)

Mary Saunders sat at our desk attentively listening to the radio broadcast. The nun interrupted the scheduled

116

lesson allowing her class to hear the Prime Minister's speech. These were precious moments, living current events, in an era where everything seemed so tense, where everyone was so angry, where certainty knew only uncertainty.

Neville Chamberlain was very clear. He was retiring. The Prime Minister explained that for the benefit of the nation the decision was made. He repeated his view that England would have been better off if peace was possible. He explained he had no regrets about his policy of appeasement.

Miss Saunders regretted his decision as she would regret anyone not living up to expectations. Her parents had taught her well in basic virtues. Every evening since the prior September her family talked of events: those read in the daily newspapers, heard on the radio, or simply conjectured. In that respect, Mary was well aware of the Aryan doctrine and the horror inflicted upon the Jewish race even before the war. Miss Saunders often questioned why her beloved country was not adequately prepared to take preventative measures. "Why couldn't we stop the bombing of British vessels in the Channel? Why did the Germans bomb Kent killing innocent citizens? Couldn't we have stopped them? Why did England enter an agreement with Poland and not defend the country? Why didn't we stop Germany before it took over Norway? How could we let German troops invade Holland? Why are we so afraid?"

"It's good that he's resigning," Miss Saunders spoke up in class responding to her teacher's comment. Views were mixed, but the consensus was that the war end as soon as possible.

After the lunch hour break, the nun offered a prayer from Holy Cross School to the new Prime Minister, Sir Winston Churchill.

(V I I I)

Heinz Guderian stood atop his panzer tank in all of his self-glorifying superiority. The General was the epitome of Nazi perfection: destruction of every target, achievement of every goal, levelling of towns, murder of Poles, and extermination of Jews. Guderian had taken great delight watching many plead for his compassion before ordering their execution. All for the Fatherland! He had been decorated by Goering himself, and wore the Swastika proudly. Nothing would stand in his way. He made that promise before and vowed to keep it to his dying day.

Holland provided no defence. There was no need for the XIX Panzer Corps wasting any ammunition there. Belgium was opposed, but not for long. They both spoke German and rather quickly came to their senses to not oppose Aryan views.

As he positioned his tanks overlooking the valley, west of Ghent, he imagined he could see in the distance the assortment of French and English troops scurrying for survival. He waited there for the final order to motor his tanks west to the channel coast.

Norway was falling to Germany, and Britain would be next. The General had no difficulty imagining his XIX Panzer Corps in Trafalgar Square then on route to Westminster. The glory of certain victory drove Heinz Guderian to exceed even his Fuhrer's every expectation.

(IX)

The Polish Armed Forces did not completely disintegrate after the fall of Warsaw. Many fled south to Romania and reorganized there. The Polish Government in Exile was established in London. The remaining ground troops and air force reassembled in France.

A total of eighty-five thousand Polish ground troops were able to evacuate to France. These formed the 1st Grenadier Division: with four infantry divisions, a brigade of armoured cavalry and a motorized vehicle brigade. Together they fought vigorously in the Battle of France.

Polish pilots also played a significant role in the defence of France. One hundred and thirty-three Polish pilots joined the battle against the Luftwaffe. They already had significant experience against the German war machine even when they were clearly outnumbered. In France, the Polish pilots recorded the demise of fifty-five stukas and bombers. Unfortunately, eight Polish airmen were shot down.

Winston Churchill's worst nightmare proved true when the British Expeditionary Force and French were not able to thwart the advance of the Wehrmacht. Dunkirk suddenly became a temporary home to hundreds of thousands of Allied troops panicking to leave. Hitler, for reasons unknown, had stalled his assault. Allied forces on another front were able to temporarily halt the German advance. In one week starting May 27th, 388,000 soldiers escaped Europe in a flotilla of eight hundred boats.

Only twenty-five thousand Polish troops were able to leave. The Polish Air Force and pilots re-organized in England. There under the direction of General Sikorsky, leading the Polish Government in Exile, the Polish armed forces became the Jeden Korpus Polski, Polish I Corps. This included infantry divisions, and armoured unit, and the Polish Independent Parachute Brigade.

The Polish Air Force later played a very significant role in the Battle of Britain. Eighty-nine pilots flew in the four Polish Squadrons. Fifty more Polish pilots joined the RAF Although the Police Air Force provided only five percent of the pilots, it achieved twelve percent of the kills. Tadeusz Kosciuszko alone shot down one hundred and twenty-six German aircraft.

Though everything appeared so dismal with the fall of Warsaw, the spirit of Poland motivated its forces in France and England to thwart the Nazi advance that appeared inevitable.

(X)

Bernard stopped counting the dead. The hell-hole was going to be his death. It had to happen, some day, when he least expected it, in spite of what could do; but then there really wasn't anything he, nor any prisoner, could do to affect Amon Goethe's depraved mind.

The stench from the hill, Hujowa Gorka, penetrated even the frozen walls of the camp. Even the dead buried beneath the camp would roll in their graves. Plaszow, earlier that summer, had become Kozentrationslager Plaszow, a fully effective concentration camp to satisfy every vicious whim of the Geheime Staatspolizei. It was now more just a Labour Camp, and therefore it was fully expected that Goethe would engage every means to annihilate the humanity of every Pole.

Jews started to arrive to be confined in their separate section; but in three days they were not seen again. The Hungarian refugees too came in hoards by rail and truck. Some called these homeless persons 'Gypsies', others would name them 'Roma'. Their fate was the same, all dead within the week. For the Poles, the death was a slower process: disease, typhus, starvation, sometimes hastened by beatings or the firing squad.

Meals were limited to one per day, usually slop mixed with rice or discarded bread or vegetables. More often than not, this was restricted to only five meals per week, nothing on weekends. No explanation was required. However the reality was that nearly all of the farms were destroyed or farmers slain, and the livestock and foul that could still be found on these abandoned farms or from ongoing operations was being sent east to German lands.

The commandant's practice of delighting himself by murdering a prisoner every morning continued into the summer months. Occasionally more than one prisoner would be selected before the commandant's first meal. On April 20th to celebrate the Fuhrer's birthday, fifty prisoners stood like candles before the firing squad.

The prisoners, even after it became a concentration camp, still worked in the quarry or the brick works factory. The quarry produced stone blocks for the exterior walls. The camp had been enlarged to approximately two hundred acres. The factory produced bricks for several buildings in one portion of the camp. Prisoners realized that anyone who entered those did not walk out.

The gas chambers would all be fully operational early the next year; but now in the summer of 1940, they were already accomplishing the desired Nazi goal. The mobile gas trucks also made their daily visitation, taking away the weak and the disabled to another realm.

Some prisoners were given the grim task of digging the ditches and covering the bodies on the hillside. No one wanted the task but it preserved an inmate's life as long as he committed himself to the job. Other prisoners were wary of these inmates as more than likely they were carriers of typhus.

Young women received better treatment, at least the young girls chosen by the Commandant. These were fed well, and groomed to satisfy first the illicit behaviour of the senior guards. After being well used, they were set free to earn their keep. Many became permanently located in selected quarters away from the camp with the guardianship of the S.S. and Einsatzgruppen force. The Aryan philosophy had little use for the Sixth Commandment. But regardless, Amon Goethe was a happy man.

At Kozentrationslager Plaszow the Nazis knew exactly how to rile the anger and deflate the pride of every Polish prisoner. A majority of the guards were Ukrainian Nationalists. Vengeance for occupied land after Versailles, and seemingly inherent distaste were reason enough for these guards to extend the realm of terror. Beatings were a regular occurrence that left the victim incapable of work that in turn prompted the involvement of the firing squad. Such murders were taking place not only on Hujowa Gorka, but also in death marches beyond the mountain in neighbouring valleys. Residents cringed watching the victims being forced toward the open ditches; but fear silenced their consciences. These guards were easily exceeding Goethe's expectations.

In early summer, the Commandant provided an incredible favour to several prisoners. Two hundred of them were selected and forced, to join the Wehrmacht. The word spread throughout the camp that invasions and occupation of Hungary and Greece were planned. Goethe picked those who willingly voiced loud opinions averse to the Slavic peoples. Prisoner A08334 was not one of these.

Bernard's first task in the camp was in the brick works factory. This provided daily chores, eight hours per day, till early summer. After several days he had become numb to the idea he was making and delivering bricks for the construction of gas chamber buildings. There was no choice – do that or die. If Bernard chose the latter, there would always be someone else to do it.

By July 1st, the dead in the camp exceeded ten thousand. Thus when Bernard was told he would be assisting at the Krakow Zoo, he almost leaped at the opportunity. Prisoner A08334 was astute enough not to convey such over enthusiasm, but at long last his heart started beating again with the thought he might have a future beyond today.

Krakow's Zoological Gardens was a five hundred hectare lot in the Pustelnik Hill region about ten kilometres west of the city centre. The range of animals was immense including species from Africa, Australia, the Arctic and South America. The Aviary and Reptile Houses were favourites for those wishing to see rare breeds. The Przewalski Horses and a pigmy hippopotamus drew the most attraction. Bernard's job was to feed the wild cats. Fear was intense holding raw meat on a pole over the edge of the pit. His head was ready to explode each time he had to rush in to close the door to each outer cage so he could clean the inner den for each leopard, jaguar, and lion. The tigers were in absolute control of their quarters and terror of being ripped apart was very real. Sleep never came easy after a day at the zoo for his fears about tomorrow were very vivid. After the second day, Prisoner A08334 grabbed some raw meat at the zoo before leaving, consuming the same by the time he returned to the camp.

In spite of the benefit of having this task, Bernard started to fear that one day the truck would suddenly release toxic fumes.

Sleep never came easy at Konzentrationslager Krakow.

(XI)

For the celebration of 'Memorial Day for the Nazi Martyrs' on that Saturday morning, the ninth of November, 1940, the central market in Czestochowa was robust with the numerous vendors and their many customers. Enthusiasm had returned. Red swastika flags and banners with Hitler's portrait blew with the breeze, lining the avenues. Pots and planters of asters, poppies, chrysanthemums, and phlox decorated the entrance to each store and stall. Conversation was blissful. Even the guards seemed at ease.

Many attended, not just the financial and political elite. The display of fruits and vegetables was at its finest. The vegetables were not always fresh, but they were plentiful for a family feast. A few butchers placed their stands together. Their comparative prices reflected the vague appearance that this section of Poland still held onto some capitalist competitive leanings. Cloth, silks, and knitted goods too were in lavish supply.

Teresa Pawlowski entered the market from the sloping road on the far left. The opportunity to work near the cathedral and live on their farmland had been a blessing. She worked the farmland. Ryszard too was very active. The twelve year old cultivated the land, ensured the narrow rows for irrigation, picked the produce when ready, and drove the tractor for deliveries. Ryszard was very much self-reliant. He had filled the role of the independent son to the extent that he could – always mindful of the fears and anxieties of his mother, his sister, and baby brother.

Andrzej was five months old, smaller than normal, lighter than expected. Limitations on food never help an infant even if he is still suckling. His eyes told the incredible story of gratitude as if the infant understood the woe surrounding him.

Teresa was able to provide basic clothing and coats for the winter. However, the lining was often loose with no capacity to keep the feathery down in place. Baby clothes had been knitted by the women, for the many children in their care. Their own room was small with a half-size metal stove. One log per night, that's all they had, that's all it could take. Sleeping together was essential in the winter months just to keep warm. They had two beds pushed together. Washroom facilities meant waiting in line for the room in the basement of the rectory.

On the grounds of the cathedral they were safe. Inspections were regular to ensure the Church was not housing fugitive Jews and gypsies. However Christians with appropriate papers were secure.

Going to market, though, always created moments of apprehension. Surrendering sanctuary always made anyone vulnerable. The Einsatzgruppen mingled with the German military. There was no semblance of control and each group of guards was free to conduct themselves in the lurid manner they deemed justified. Ryszard played the appropriate game of being overly polite to the guards especially the young ones. They had come to know him, and he could sense those who might have only their own interests at heart. Elzbieta was always scared, nearly always on the verge of crying. She didn't have the poise or the courage of her older brother. She cared more for her mother and her younger brother.

Two guards approached the family as they entered the market. The demand for her papers was clear. Instantly her trembling started; and eventually she was able to produce them.

The younger guard started laughing immediately. He spoke to the two others again in that foreign language. Teresa knew it was Ukrainian. The older guard answered. He was definitely German.

That older guard became very direct telling the mother that the papers didn't mention the infant. Immediately her heart pounded. Questions concerning the child continued at a pace not allowing her time to answer. She fidgeted. Teresa had never been questioned about the child before. Ryszard was going to answer, but his mother held his shoulder encouraging silence.

When the German finally stopped his rant, Teresa explained that they were not able to obtain the papers having been in the process of being transferred from Poznan. Stumbling with her explanation she added information about the care and work at the cathedral. The older guard seemed satisfied. The younger one was not, and instantly started to inspect the pram. Blankets were pulled to the side. The infant wailed immediately. Ryszard reached for the handle of the pram. The young guard then reached in to grab the infant. Teresa instantly tried to stop him. She was pushed aside falling backward. Elzbieta cried. Andrzej screamed at the top of his lungs. In spite of his mother on the ground, Ryszard would not let go of the pram. Elzbieta too tried to stop the Ukrainian guard from touching her baby brother. Her hand was slapped. Ryszard turned his grasp from the pram to the left arm of the guard. He was brushed aside. They stared in disbelief as the young guard held the infant. The older guard, who would have let this all pass, now got involved inspecting the pram. The papers fell to the ground into a puddle. Ryszard pleaded for his brother.

"Resistance!" the older guard exclaimed.

"No!" Teresa snapped, grabbing for her child.

"Put him back," the older guard encouraged the younger one.

Andrzej was returned to the pram, but not in a gentle manner.

"Why?" Teresa asked.

"They do not mention your child. Jewish?"

"No! Mine!" the mother pleaded.

"My brother," Ryszard affirmed.

Teresa leaned over to pick up the soiled documents. While she tried to dry them against her tattered dress, the younger guard jeered at her. "They're all alike." His villainous sneer continued.

Ryszard's hands held the pram. Elzbieta worked quickly to wrap her brother in the blanket.

"Resistance!" the Ukrainian speaking guard screamed.

"No!" the mother cried searching for some compassion.

Then in one swift motion the pram was pushed forcefully away onto the road in front of a speeding van.

Teresa, unable to grab the pram, screamed in absolute terror; a wail that never stopped till her mind froze with fright. She never spoke again.

Chapter Seven
Europe, 1941

The second January following the Nazi invasion was bitterly cold. Sleeping, huddled together, was essential even in the wooden sheds where bunks were provided. Heating was a luxury; however a log lasted less than an hour. In the brick structures, still used for sleeping quarters, the conditions were no better. Prisoners in all sectors of the camp did whatever was necessary to stay warm. Even the prospect of death the next morning became inviting.

The sanitary conditions were degrading. There was no privacy. The early stages of the starvation process caused many to be incontinent. It was debasing to not even have control of basic bodily functions. Most inmates started whimpering, so often uncontrollably. Stuttering interrupted ideas. There were no ideals. Weakness permeated the limbs. Lifting even minute objects became a strain. Coordination was a struggle. Minds lost focus. Dreams were no more. Hope was ancient history.

Amon Goethe used the gender and sex issues to demean the inmates to the extreme. On more than one occasion he had a young woman stripped naked and violated in front of the starving male prisoners. One inmate tried out of sympathy to interrupt the debauchery, and was shot dead instantly. In each case the violated woman was left in a heap sobbing for the men to watch.

To celebrate the Fuhrer's Birthday, a grand feast had been prepared. The prisoners were again called to the courtyard, this time to watch the guards gorge on every morsel. In every attempt to destroy their spirit as a group and as individuals, the Commandant was succeeding.

Every day two more truckloads of prisoners arrived. Another truck also delivered prisoners, but these were already dead. The gas and vapours in the mobile unit were quick. The commandant remained consistent in his need every morning to personally annihilate at least one prisoner before his breakfast. Before noon hour, selected prisoners were dispatched to the hill to dig further ditches, then to watch fellow inmates be shot. Brutality was everywhere.

Then, the Jews arrived, more of them. Goethe was again consistent. They did not last long within the prison walls. Gas chambers quickly responded to Aryan needs.

Upon Ivan's arrival Ivan was assigned to the quarry pit, and after two months he was transferred to the brickyard. Transfers were common when the camp first opened, but lately a change in work venue; well, it just wasn't happening. Ivan had a strange dialect: a sort of twangy German as if he was from Switzerland or southern France. The first conversation did in fact confirm a Swiss connection – he had been in a short-term prison camp near Bern.

Ivan was filled with information from outside the prison walls. The stories terrified Bernard detailing how brutal the Germans could be.

Prisoner A08334 was cautious at first, friendly but careful. After hearing the reference to Switzerland, he started to think it was all very strange. Then when Ivan mentioned that some of the Poles had been in the camp near Bern Bernard's interest was aroused.

Their conversations were brief, as they had to be while being constantly watched. Ben was keen to learn more about the resistance movements and the safe houses. With the information, Ben became more at ease.

Ivan was very much against the perceived silence of the Church on the issue of labour camps and the exterminations. Bernard tried without any success to defend his Church but lacked the basic information to support his view. Similarly Ivan was deplored at France and Britain doing nothing to confront Germany at the time of the initial invasion. Bernard agreed with those comments. Ben's appreciation of historical events reminded him of the unfulfilled responsibilities assumed by those two countries.

Ivan had enough sense not to mention the massacre in Poznan. His own information was restricted to a couple of comments from fellow prisoners after his arrival in Bern. Bernard had never heard of the atrocity. The courtesy to never tell any prisoner about horrific events in his hometown was maintained

In one short discussion, Ivan mentioned that he heard "… things about Hungary and Romania." He had no further information and did not elaborate. A fellow prisoner having heard his comment hastily added that he would kill Himmler if he had the chance. Bernard had heard that name before, and sensed he was the German responsible for their fate.

At times ignorance could be bliss. Small ramblings on the other hand meant extraordinary fears and many more sleepless nights.

Bernard returned to his own bunk bed that night, choosing to be alone. The information he received that day was too much for him. He closed his eyes trying hard to picture his animals in the barn, their excited greetings, his favourite horses, and Sable who was probably still homeless. Most of all he thought of his family. Prayers, it seemed, were never enough.

(I I)

The nun sat at her desk at the front of the class. Her hands clenched the document as she read to the class.

This hour is in many respects a veritable

Hora Tenebrarum, in which the spirit of

violence and of discord is pouring a bloody

cup of nameless sorrow over humanity.

The nun paused finding it difficult to maintain her calm. She then continued reading from the Pope's Encyclical.

The people dragged into the tragic vortex of

war are perhaps still only at the beginning

of their sorrows. Already death, desolation,

lamentation and misery reign in thousands of

families. The blood of innumerable humans,

even non-combatants, evoke a poignant cry of

sorrow, especially for the well-beloved nation
of Poland, who by her service in the defence
of Christian civilisation, has the right to the
human and fraternal sympathy of the whole
world.

The teacher stopped when the tears began to flow.
With her family she had come to England from Poland
almost twenty years before. Her aunts, her uncles, her
cousins, her family: where were they?

Mary Saunders approached the desk to offer what
she could.

The nun looked up and offered while trying to hold
back the tears, "We should pray."

(III)

A few crocuses dotted the Hujowa Gorka. Temperatures
were rising. Bernard knew it must be spring, his second
in captivity.

Tyranny again assumed unfathomable limits. The
morning extermination of the chosen prisoner now took
place in the central courtyard. The atrocities were
becoming more visible. Bodies from the chambers were
loaded on wagons by prisoners. If family members were
prisoners, one sibling or child would have to witness the
torment of his relative.

It had been two days now since Bernard last saw
Ivan. That was his only friend in the camp. On that
occasion Ivan had mentioned a place called Oswiecim, a
town less than two hours away. He had his information

from a newly arrived starving Pole. The news was terrifying.

Ivan had been again called to dig the ditch on the hill. Normally he would return before the guards ate their supper. On that day, Ivan was not seen again.

Bernard's bunkhouse held thirty-two cots. It was filled a month ago. In the last two weeks, three inmates faced the breakfast brutality. Several died of typhus which spread faster in warmer weather. Others were told they're being transferred. Nothing more was heard. Now only five remained.

Who would be next? In spite of the anguish and misery, Bernard still feared death. Could he ever escape? Was there any possibility of anything good that could ever happen?

(I V)

The Sisters at Holy Cross School every Monday morning arranged their students into discussion groups. The junior grades received all of the good news. The senior grades talked about the reality.

The idea that Rudolph Hess, Hitler's Deputy Fuhrer, would have ever boarded a plane and parachuted into Scotland amazed the students. How stupid could he be? What was his mission? What did he expect to happen? Did Hitler even know?

Mary Saunders at that time did not appreciate the possible consequence of the Hess mission. She had heard her parents talk about Mauritius and the Seychelles the prior month thinking it was relative to a holiday.

Her home room teacher had received troubling news even before Hess jumped from his plane. Hitler wanted an accord with Britain that would ultimately involve dispatching the Jews in Britain to labour camps on the continent.

Mary would learn years later that the reference to Mauritius and the Seychelles was her father's view that they might have to leave England because Mary's grandfather was Jewish. That made the entire family vulnerable to any threat against the Jewish community in Britain.

Britain's victory over the Italians in Ethiopia, and the occupation of Bagdad received almost no comment. Her discussion group celebrated the sinking of the Bismarck and then held a moment of silence for crews of the HMS Hood and the Prince of Wales battleship. There was no group discussion of the British surrender in Greece as details were withheld. The remainder of their time was devoted to the bombing of London three weeks ago. The fears of the young women were very real; not just for themselves, but for their families, and country.

(V)

The five prisoners stood before the Commandant. In the centre courtyard they were at the mercy of the four guards carrying machine guns. Amon Goethe too had already drawn his luger.

They didn't move a muscle. Bernard squirmed inside. These were the last five in the bunkhouse. Empty it would be without them, perhaps fit for temporary residences of Jews and Roma, a place to stay for the moment awaiting the finality of the chamber.

Regardless, prisoner A08334 knew he would never look inside the building again.

Goethe's tone was fierce as expected. He really knew no other means of communication to those he thought were the scum of the earth. Yet, he was brief and strangely informative. There was no guessing of his intention or his direction. "Silesian Zoo." He told them. No one bothered to ask where or when. One of the prisoners knew it was in Katowice. The others would learn later. "The train will take you there," the Commandant advised. Turning to the senior guard he gave strict instructions concerning transit. Bernard was thankful for his knowledge of German.

One guard, Bernard knew; and he recognized Bernard. For reasons unknown, but perhaps because of this, there were no handcuffs. The van was cold. The turns were sharp. A fragile package would never have made the trip.

The five prisoners stood with the four guards on the train platform. The trip to Katowice would take just less than two hours. As a straight line it would be shorter, but with the many twists and turns, around hills and forests, the train would proceed slower than normal. The platform was the farthest away from the waiting room. This track would normally be used by rail traffic not stopping at Krakow. Thirty minutes later, the train arrived.

The locomotive was huge. Bernard knew little about different engine models, but conjectured from its size that it would have been used for cross continental travel. No one else was getting on the train. The stop was quick. The prisoners were forced into a boxcar. Two guards entered the diner near the front. Three others, including

136

the guard Bernard knew, entered the warm caboose. Guards also occupied a flatbed railcar equipped with a machine gun. The turret was an ominous sight.

The boxcar was a rebuilt flat bed with a wooden frame and slats. The wood appeared to be pine. The slats were rough spruce. Openings between the slats were narrow, but enough to determine the time of day. The converted railcar reeked of excrement, urine and blood. No one dare rest on the floor for the risk of terminal illness before the destination.

Tomasz knew every detail about the trip. He had only done it once in the opposite direction; however he valued his ability to recall events and times and use the information to his best advantage.

The train would go north-west to Zabierzow, and then turn sharp left to the west through Balic and Rudno. They should get to Rudno about forty minutes into the trip. The rail line then swung north. Tomasz was very specific. If they could jump the train it would be when they entered Krajobrazowy National Park. Excitedly he advised the others of the five natural reserves in which they would be able to hide.

Whistles were many in that first quarter hour. Tomasz suggested they were slower than expected. He then offered that if they wanted to try and jump they'd have to remove at least two panels. In their hearts they all considered the prospect, and the potential result. Bernard concluded it had to be worthwhile regardless of the consequence because even if they returned to Plaszow, they wouldn't have a cot.

Bartosz was the oldest prisoner. He was about thirty-five. Iwan couldn't be more than twenty. Jarek was so frail, his age didn't matter. He'd have severe difficulty just jumping. No one guessed Bernard had just turned sixteen.

It was Iwan who rummaged through the debris. Still covered in blood, he felt repulsed. Under the piece of clothing, he discovered the mallet. Skin, blood and tissue still stuck to the weapon. The prisoners were unaware this train was coming from Auschwitz. They were thankful suddenly that the Germans were not the cleanliest people. Together they could find nothing humane about their captors.

As the train squealed around the tight corner near Zabierzow they worked on the first board. It flew off in their attempts to grab hold of it. Fortunately the flying plank wasn't noticed as the train entered the shadows of the forest near Balic. Their inner gratitude for their little success caused them to work more diligently, this time with their hands pulling the plank away from the cross beams. Jarek conjectured that it could be easier to knock out the panel near the door and thus gain access to releasing the latch. Iwan directing the task continued slowly trying to make as little sound as possible.

Near Minkow the train slowed once more for a sharp turn, this time to the right. Two thuds forced the spruce panel loose. Tomasz clutched the panel bringing it inside. Daylight was ever so clear. The make-shift cattle car had its definite deficiencies. The cross beam was at a height of five feet for a nine foot high rail car. This allowed easy access under the cross beam when it came time to jump. Bernard started the process on the third panel which was easily detached during another screeching turn. They were ready.

Tomasz was becoming uncertain regarding the National Park. Was it best there, or before, or maybe when they entered the clearing? They passed the junction for Bolecin.

"Gotowy!" Tomasz advised his cohorts. "For God and Poland." Iwan saluted. They shook hands, hugged, and got themselves in line.

Ten seconds after they passed the sign designating the National Park, Iwan jumped. He landed on his feet, but the impact caused severe injuries, propelling him forward into brush. Before he even came to rest, Tomasz leapt from the slow moving train.

Tomasz arose from the ditch and hobbled as quickly as he could. A whistle blew. On board two prisoners froze. Iwan jumped. The whistle continued to shrill as the locomotive crossed the main road to the park.

Guards ahead of them atop the fourth car failed to observe the escapees. Those in the caboose too were not observant. Guards in the diner were drunk.

Bartosz waited until the train car cleared the intersection. He jumped as far away from the train as he could. Though having merit, his decision caused significant limitations. Impact with the stone ditch left him at the disposal of Aryan mercy.

Bernard was next. It was quick, but his previously injured hip gave way. He tumbled roughly, avoiding any scream of pain, and lay prone.

Suddenly the emergency siren blew. Guards atop the fourth car manned their machine gun. Looking to the east they could see nothing.

Then the last prisoner jumped. Jarek in his frailty screamed upon impact. Attention immediately turned to him. Brakes squealed. Jarek lay there for a second, and then tried to move. Machine gun fire ended his pain.

Two guards from the fourth car jumped down just before the train stopped. Fully armed, they were committed to being sure no one remained alive. Other guards rushed off the train from the caboose.

Bartosz could not crawl away from the inevitable.

Tomasz was into the forest quickly. Cuts to his face and arms meant nothing. He desired freedom more than he felt pain.

Iwan lay buried beneath the foliage of one bush and hidden by another. He breathed not a sound as guards approached looking into the clearing before the dense forest.

Bernard lay there at their mercy. Then the urge to survive took over. Guards from the caboose searched down the track, long into the distance. Others from on top viewed the clearings. He slid along the ground once more. Determination was all he had. There was no time for any hopeful expressions. He struggled, unable to rise. Then Bernard slid as fast as his painful hips would let him, between cars, over the coupling, then out the other side. Beyond the gravel he slid painfully knowing he had to get away from the train. There the bog partially covered him. It was the best he could do.

From atop the train orders were given to explore the forest. Tomasz had been spotted.

Machine gun fire blazed a barrage. Tomasz fell hit in the leg. There was no scream, just determination to get as far away as possible. Machine gun fire continued. Thickness of the tree trunks gave him some protection. As soon as it stopped, he continued running, seizing every moment to secure his freedom.

Then Bernard heard what he didn't want to hear. The Germans had found Iwan. He was ordered to his feet, and when he hesitated due to his injury, he was shot. Laughter defined the kill.

Tomasz was pursued by three Germans, more than five hundred feet into the forest. They chased as far as they wished then in unison stopped pointed their rifles into the woods and unloaded their ammunition. The older guard claimed they made their kill and joyfully they returned to the train.

Tomasz continued on, limping, not knowing where he was, and what or whom he could meet. After hours in the woods he became quite certain that he was not even in the national park.

Bernard lay motionless as the guards climbed aboard. "Rebels!" they would tell the commanding officer. Plaszow had many more to dispatch to the Silesian Zoo, many more that would not be missed, to delight the German children by hand feeding the lions.

(V I)

As Molotov expected, the Panzer divisions stormed across the eastern border of the General Government into the Ukraine and Belarus. On June 22, 1941, The Third Reich put into action the acquisition of its imperial dream. If the Reich was destined to live one thousand years then it would dominate all of Europe and Asia, from the Atlantic east to the Pacific. German lands for Germans!

Wehrmacht forces too from Romania and Hungary began their invasion. This both Molotov and Zhukov had expected. The size and swiftness of the attack was incomprehensible. All of the Soviet preparedness was not able to stall the thrash and control of the Nazi machine.

Italy and Romania simultaneously declared war on the Soviet Union. Germany's puppet states were on board to complete the rapid assault. However, Italy was becoming a non-factor. The month before Britain had seized Ethiopia from the Italians. Mussolini's force was unable to hold possessions in Africa. Romanian assistance too was suspect as a spirited alliance with Hitler was not possible following the murder of many Romanians.

"Home by Christmas" was the German promise, an inane repetition of that same vow made twenty-seven years before. In many respects it would become a glowing example of how history does repeat itself. It happens more often than not to nations whose vision is obscured by the blinders of racism. Himmler's intention to exterminate the Jews went hand in hand with every mile of Soviet soil the Wehrmacht conquered. That in itself would slow the process.

The Nazi atrocities knew no borders. The first six months of 1941 recorded butchery in Holland, Netherlands, France, several times in Paris, Romania, Bulgaria, Hungary, Yugoslavia, Czechoslovakia, Estonia, Lithuania, Latvia, Norway and Italy. Stories of exterminations on a small scale were heard from Switzerland, Spain, and Sweden – all neutral countries.

Molotov and Zhukov could not have imagined the Nazi tyranny on route to Moscow: especially in Lvov, Brest-Litovsk, Kaunas, Dubno in the previously occupied Soviet territory, Kovno, Vilna and Gordzhdy in Lithuania, and Kishinev in Romania. Throughout the conquered territories residents were compelled to exterminate the Jewish families or risk incurring the same fate. Extortion simplified the process of eradication.

Iosif Stalin was enraged, not only with the idea that Hitler with would even invade the Soviet Union, but equally so with the speed and thoroughness of the attack. Within two weeks Stalin was compelled to declare his Scorched Earth Policy.

Britain and the USSR entered the Mutual Assistance Pact, following the decision of the Soviet Union to renounce all prior decrees denouncing the right of Poland to exist. Meanwhile Himmler began his Final Solution.

(V I I)

An hour passed in silence. The east wind blew warmer in the afternoon sun inviting the destitute soul to rise. However caution ruled. Decisiveness returned to dispel impulsive whims.

The only noise was the wind blowing through the tops of trees in the distance. There were no moans. Trains had not passed. For the first time in two years, no one was yelling instructions.

Prisoner A08334 was no more. He was listed as dead by the guard responsible for his transfer. Bernard was alive; but terribly scared, cold, and hungry.

Motion was difficult. Swelling in his right leg prevented a full range of motion. Bending at the waist was difficult. Squatting became impossible. A cold breeze started blowing with a change in the wind direction. He had often heard how the breeze off the Tatra Mountains could change temperatures instantly. "Are they still alive?" he whispered to himself, realizing the probability was nil.

Bernard found Iwan first. The face was white. Blood stained his garment. He let himself fall to the ground beside the body. With mud on his thumb he made the sign of the cross upon the forehead. The corpse was now dead weight. Unable to move it, he unbuttoned the shirt, and pulled it up covering Iwan's face.

Jarek's body fell close to the tracks still on the gravel supporting the rails. The body was bullet ridden. "Death must have been instant," Bernard concluded. Not able to kneel on the rough stones, he did what he could to pull the corpse away from the tracks into foliage several metres away. Respect for his dead friend meant more than his pain or any risk of being spotted.

Ben was able to find Bartosz's body in the soft mud. Getting to his knees on the blood stained soil, he blessed the forehead of the corpse using the moisture from the cattail stem. Bernard looked dearly into his friend's open frozen eyes once more, and rolled the body to the side in order to remove the shirt. This Bernard wore immediately feeling very blessed by being able to don the attire of one he held in such esteem.

Standing up he looked around to search for Tomasz. The first to jump probably made it to the woods. "Perhaps he didn't." Bernard thought of the alternatives. "Is he near here?" He crept down in spite of the pain to continue his search. Moving south back down the line he spent another ten minutes in a final search. If fortune could shine in Nazi occupied Poland, it did. A German soldier's canteen lay on the ground. That was so quickly snatched up. "Water!" his heart jumped. Quickly it was gulped down not even thinking it may have been contaminated. It was such a relief, so little to generate so much energy. As if the pain had disappeared completely, Bernard set off again across the tracks, to the south, to where he felt he could survive. "Safe houses." He suddenly had a real goal.

The forest was to the north and east of the tracks. To the south the ground was flat, soft in many areas, without fencing. It was about two miles to the next growth of trees. That was his goal for the night.

Enough gratitude to his father could never have expressed in those first hours. In the woods near the family farm they had spent many hours exploring the undergrowth and identifying mushrooms and edible plants. Bernard found enough cattails to make a hearty meal, a feast compared to camp food. He knew the rootstalk was edible. Dandelion leaves were too a blessing. A small stream allowed him to wash himself and fill his canteen. Strength was returning to his injured leg. His enthusiasm for life was dispelling the pain.

Just before nightfall he came upon a farm at the edge of the woods. The pine trees provided sufficient shelter. From there he would not be able to witness the sunrise through the growth. Bernard felt he was still travelling west, and that was sufficient for now. The mattress was pine branches pushed together. These would be a deterrent to bugs and crawling insects. The extra shirt was his sheet. So accustomed was he to minimal bedding that a blanket was not needed.

The distant barking of German Shepherds aroused him. That he had not expected. Perhaps it was a sign of his naiveté. He hastily considered his position believing he was close to a town, or perhaps near a road, or maybe just a large farm. There was no activity around him, nothing at all. A few cows he could see in a distant pasture. The clothesline was bare. He crept closer shielding himself among the unpicked crops. The tractor, he concluded, had not been driven for many months based on the dirt on the chassis and the mud caking the wheels. He eyed another wooded area to the far left but that would take him to the south. The open flat land to his right would leave him vulnerable. Leaving his resting spot, Bernard eased away from the farm, and edged along the woods about two hundred meters a slight hill over an open area. Early stalks of wheat provided a golden glow to the entire field. This route could be a blessing. The ground looked solid. The early growth of wheat in the field yielded a surprise, a bundle of discarded clothes. The Gray attire he picked up, still leaving it in a ball. Beyond the wheat stalks, vines formed a makeshift border. Black berries were plentiful. He sat there obscured by the bushes, feasting on the abundance. Only when he again heard the yelping of distant dogs did he arise and bury himself in the safety of the woods.

At nightfall, Bernard slept on a grassy incline on the edge of the forest near the village of Pogorzyce. He had travelled a total of seven kilometres in that day and a half. The clothing he wore was warm. For his mattress he unfurled the discarded clothes, not noticing the yellow star design.

Fears became extreme the next morning upon awaking to the sound of angry voices of screaming Nazi soldiers. He rose instantly, grabbed the clothing and ran into the woods. There he discovered the yellow Star of David. Immediately he tossed the garment to the side and rushed deep into the woods. In the damp the mosquitoes were more than an annoyance. They were more voracious than he could have ever imagined. He tried swatting them, but viewed the alternative to be a better fate. Moving quickly provided some relief from the incessant biting. Into the opening he ran without thinking. There was no one there. Then a moment later the convoy of German trucks, with several vehicles loaded with machine guns, travelled north on a near-by road. Grouching down, he started to thank God for the mosquitoes that delayed his journey. He started to talk to God once more, mainly to ask about his family. Soon he figured he would get an answer. Perhaps in Czechoslovakia he would find them, working with the dissidents. Everything he had seen was better than the camp.

The convoy passed in three minutes. Bernard looked around, being very certain, and then moved stealthily through the wheat toward the road. He knew he'd have to cross it quickly. There was more vegetation on the other side for protection.

He had left the road about two hundred meters behind when the rain started to fall, lightly at first. Bernard could not avoid experiencing the propensity of the soil to absorb water. Dry furrows quickly became flowing rivulets. Bernard rushed up a slight incline in the field hoping he could avoid the increasing torrent. It was pitch black when the rain finally stopped. There were no dogs barking. They obviously had enough sense to stay inside. Convoys weren't moving. The quarter-moon appeared in the south-east to continue its nightly swing across the sky.

Bernard woke the next morning to the clatter and whistle of a train passing through the forested area he had left behind. He recalled the tracks were rather shiny on a line that looked abandoned. Rising, he tried continuing through the wheat field but the ground was too soggy and his tattered shoes got quickly caked in mud. He stayed the high ground until he neared the road.

Still uncertain he crouched until it was clearly safe to cross. Bernard followed along a stone filled embankment, then came upon another village.

The church steeple appeared beyond the trees. He presumed it was Catholic, then realized it might not be. Perhaps there was aid, a meal, direction, rest. Or maybe, it was abandoned. A broken road sign told him he was entering the town of Babice. Ben knew from his geography that there were several towns in Poland named Babice. Every administrative district it seemed had this name for the smallest and quaintest community. However there was nothing idyllic about Babice. The town was empty. A few of the seemingly prominent homes flew the Swastika Flag.

Bernard stole beyond the back yards. There were no fences. With no one home, he pilfered several clothes from a line. One garden gave him the opportunity to uproot beets and gather some beans. Another had a bountiful supply of cabbage and rhubarb. His feast in the woods was delightful. His clothes, someone else's, were dry. He then scurried along without saying thanks.

After leaving Babice, there were few wooded areas to give him shelter. The next road sign read "Olszyny 4". Bernard's hopes rose and with the next breath fell realizing this was his battle, and no one else's. The trust he lacked inside the camp had not reappeared.

He deviated to his right through open fields. Tall grass and shrubs provided a screen if ever necessary. Several armoured vehicles could be seen on the distant highway. The train whistles, he figured about ten kilometres away, could still be heard. There were no birds, just white clouds in the blue sky.

In the late afternoon, a foul odour whiffed through the region. It was repulsive, burning the nostrils. Then it would quickly go. An hour later, he found himself covering his face. Horrible thoughts ravaged his mind once more, just like those following the deaths in the gas chambers. Burning bodies, he thought then and now. Bernard looked around almost hoping to see a distant fire in some vast field, wishing it was the scent of burning crops and timber, but there was no smoke only the odour.

His freedom trip had taken him closer to Krakow, but he did not know this. At the very moment he was first repulsed by the smokeless odour, he was approaching Chelmek and Oswiecim. Any high-ranking Nazi would have told him their purpose.

If he had continued to the north-west, two hours later he would have walked into possibly his worst nightmare. The village of Zarki lay ahead through the fields on the outskirts of the Park Krajobrazowy. Zarki had been home to four thousand residents before the war. In two years, two thousand five hundred were gone, most to Oswiecim and some to Chelmek. The synagogue was in ashes. Many homes were looted. The remaining residents cowered behind Swastika emblems. They had no choice. It would have been everything Bernard would never wish to see.

Perhaps it was Divine Providence that told Bernard to turn to his left. Even though there was little shelter and fewer places to hide, Bernard felt he was making quicker progress over dryer terrain. He crouched occasionally when viewing distant traffic on the many dirt roads. The foul scent was a rare occurrence: an odorous wisp followed by fresh air. The streams provided a chance to fill his canteen, wash and then relieve himself. He was always certain of that order. As dusk turned to night, he used what appeared to be a seldom used road hoping to achieve more distance with less effort. A series of horns declared a convoy barrelling down the road. His dive to the ditch was instant. Three armoured trucks sped ahead of two vans equipped with machine guns, and four other vehicles similar to the mobile gas units he had seen in the camp. It was a cold reminder that the war was not over and that he had not reached his goal. Three hours later, Bernard lay in a field of alfalfa providing soft inviting bedding. But there were no pleasant dreams.

This time the young man was roused from his sleep by the barking and snarling of wild dogs. They stood feet from the lying boy, together as a team, yelping in an alarming pitch. As soon as Bernard moved slightly, the viciousness of their barks became even terrifying. "Stay still!" The order in German was given.

Bernard eyed the old man, his unshaven face, thick scarf, and plaid jacket. "Please," he begged.

The old man called off his dogs. "What are you doing here?"

Honesty instantly programmed his voice. "My family. I am alone."

The questioning continued about any friends, location, plans. The answers conveyed the youth's sincerity. In turn each question conveyed an appreciation for the youth's plight. Finally the old man asked, "Do you have a home?" After the answer, he bade the boy, "Come with me."

There was no choice. The dogs continued sniffing ready to do whatever at the stranger's command. The old man led the way. Bernard followed down the path, while the dogs checked his every step.

The farmhouse was compact, enough for two people to take care of an eight-acre farm equipped with a tractor and a barn. How much like home it looked.

Stanislaw and Aniela Wadja were in their sixties. Bernard became an ear for their tales of woe. So much was said about the first war, and how the recession destroyed their dreams. They regretted that cities recovered but that governments, both national and regional, did nothing to promote the agricultural communities. Then they started to talk about the war. Stanislaw was very irate and started to scream, even slamming a china cup onto the table. Their son was taken from them and forced into the Nazi army. They had not heard from him in these past twenty months and feared that he might be dead. Their questions of Bernard were many. He felt he could trust them and so he was not afraid to mention the camps. The old man took Bernard's arms searching for any identity code, but there was none. The young man repeated that he had been taken early and there may not have been the interest then of branding all prisoners. Aniela showed her concern by shaking her head, and in the same moment asked, "Do you have papers?" His answer gravely disappointed them.

Bernard was told he could bath, and then sleep in the barn. Stanislaw did not mention anything about any underground movement, or any resistance. There were still questions.

Late in the afternoon, Bernard completed several chores around the barn. The young man's impetus surprised the old lady. Though trust could have been an issue, the old man was willing to leave his wife alone with the boy. After supper, Stanislaw served each a glass of wine.

It was such an extraordinary taste. A good dizzy feeling made Bernard feel wonderful. The news made him even more so.

It again all started with a series of questions. The first answers confirmed they were all proud of their Polish heritage, and in spite of possible terrible consequences were willing to take chances to do what was necessary for the survival of their country. Stanislaw knew so much about so many issues. Contrary to the commandant's indoctrination, Poles were not stupid people. Bernard learned much about the Polish force in France, the exiled government in London, and the growing forces in the Levant. He was told about the underground network, and this more than anything enthused the youth even more.

"Tomorrow morning. Four o'clock."

Bernard would be awake.

He bid farewell in the early morning to Aniela with a long hug. It's hard to say goodbye when you're so thankful to people you will never see again. The two dogs were finally at ease with his departure. The trip in the pickup was only ten kilometres from Metkow to Podolsze through Janskowice. This was the route he had to take as the shores of the Wisla River on the outskirts of Metkow were heavily guarded.

Ninety minutes prior to the 6 a.m. whistle Bernard arrived at the factory. There was no prolonged good-bye. A man in a dark coat was already waiting at the door. Ben was quickly told what was expected of him. The duties included the manufacture of weapons. The rest of the conversation before the others arrived affirmed Bernard's innocence with respect to the real world. Ghettos had been established he was told. But he had no idea why or for whom. The commentary enlightened him affirming the Nazi desire to destroy every element of Judaism. The further comments regarding Auschwitz shocked him even more. Involving private citizens in a war sooner or later had to happen, but the full-scale annihilation of a race was beyond belief.

It wasn't until Maciej arrived that he was given any information as to what he could expect for his future. Nothing was assured and that was made very clear several times. Bernard was told that without his identity papers, he would have difficulty in Poland. Then he was again reminded of the activities of the holocaust within that area. He trembled, thinking of the Reich's desire to exterminate.

Ultimately a time frame was established, that the he would accompany the next shipment of completed armaments to Ostrawa, Czechoslovakia, with stops in Wadowice and Bielsko-Biala before crossing the border at Cieszyn.

Before parting, Stanislaw handed Bernard an envelope. Ben had his identity papers.

Words of gratitude were short before the truck drove away.

(V I I I)

Beria would have had him shot long ago had Stalin agreed. After being imprisoned for twenty-two months, the frail Polish former General stood before the Chief of the Secret Police.

Anders was bare foot, still clad in his lice-infected rags, squinting after years in solitude. The wreck of a man tried not to quiver. He was not scared for he could not endure any worse than what he had already experienced. The guards would say he was being treated well just to appease the Secretary Chairman's decision. His weight and appearance suggested otherwise.

"You are to be freed," Beria announced in Russian, a language in which Anders was fluent. "Not only that, this General Sikorski of yours, somewhere in Britain, has decided that you should be the one to lead a Polish Army. Not yours. Don't ever think it will be yours."

The news shocked Anders but he was more concerned with the origin of the information. "Who are you?" he replied to the KGB Chairman.

Beria announced his name.

"My medal?" Anders wavering voice enquired.

Religious medals had in every case been ripped from the interred. There was no possibility of any religious practice in Stalin's realm. Beria responded telling Anders he did not know. The frail Pole was quite accustomed to that advice.

"Meetings. And there will be more meetings," Beria continued in a superficial manner avoiding the specific details. Your General has made it clear that you are to form an army."

"Who?"

"Sikorski. Only with the approval of Comrade Stalin. You should also know that all decrees by our General Secretary concerning your beloved Poland are rescinded. Germany has invaded the Soviet Union. We can no longer keep you in prison because we are no longer warring with your nation."

"An army? Who?" Anders was ready to fall, but was held erect by Red Army guards.

"You will form your divisions from Polish prisoners in our camps."

"Still alive?" Anders challenged. He tried to convey his anger, but the weakness of his voice would not allow it.

"There are enough."

"How many?"

"Enough for four divisions," Beria announced.

"I am not understanding."

"That was expected." Beria knew it would get to this.

"It will be the Polish Army in the Soviet Union."

"For what purpose? To fight here? To return home?"

Anders's questions were many. The answers were confusing.

The discussion continued for more than an hour. Beria let it be known that the Wehrmacht was approaching Leningrad and had already captured Smolensk. The Chief of the Secret Police mentioned the Nazis were butchering civilians throughout Poland, and the Ukraine. The conversation ended when Anders was led to a private room with accompanying bathroom facilities. A tattered suit became his new attire. Then he was ushered away in Beria's private vehicle to a four-bedroom apartment where he stayed and rested.

Fifteen weeks later on December 4, 1941, The Polish Army in the Soviet Union was formed. Twenty-five thousand troops were organized into three infantry divisions. The troops were all Polish prisoners released from Soviet camps. Assemblies took place in the Soviet Union. Up to that time there were no definite instructions for the Polish Army's initial combat.

In early December, General Anders asked the General Secretary about the Polish officers that were taken prisoner in October 1939.

The answer was not immediate.

(IX)

The Polish Underground was not just one movement, but rather a series of organized groups determined to thwart and then destroy all foreign influence. In the five-year period there were at least twelve underground movements within the country. Together they were called the Home Army.

The anti-fascist factions were not limited to just fighting the Third Reich, but was also able to provide military information to the Polish Government in London. They became a communications network: decoding messages and sending information.

An additional aim of the resistance movement was to stop the Nazi atrocities against both the Jews and the Poles. The desire to save Jewish lives energized many communities to hide about one hundred thousand Jewish persons during the war.

The first resistance group established one month after the invasion was the National Military Organisation. One month later, in November 1939, the Secret Polish Army was organized. These were followed by the National Confederation.

In the Soviet occupied territory, two groups were established in 1941 to fight the communist influences. These were The Polish Socialist Party and the Battalion of Peasants.

In 1942, the Union for Armed Combat amalgamated several smaller groups. The same necessity to consolidate caused the National Military Organisation to become the National Armed Forces in 1943.

This National Military Organisation was achieving small but meaningful results that had a much greater impact on the German occupiers while Germany was committing many more troops and machinery to Operation Barbarossa.

With the turning of the tide in the battle of Stalingrad, the Polish People's Army was established by the Soviets.

By 1944, there were over 650,000 persons committed to Armia Krajowa, the Home Army. Together their influence was effective. Incidents of damage to locomotives and railway wagons exceeded twenty-six thousand. Thirty-eight bridges were destroyed. There were in excess of one hundred, sixty-five thousand incidents of intentional damage to factories and their production. Electrical grids were destroyed. Airplanes were damaged. Plans to assassinate the invaders exceeded five thousand incidents. And, Jewish lives were saved.

(X)

Ostrava, Czechoslovakia was home for now; but for how long? Bernard was allocated a small room with a bed on a top floor near the factory. The street was busy, and the noise endless. Still, it was better than he could have ever imagined. Bernard was routinely cautious in this foreign land. Even though the city was so close to the Polish border, Polish was rarely spoken. Czech and German were the common languages. In that respect his fluency was indeed a benefit. For the rest, he would have to assimilate.

Work was necessary to survive. Just having a job he considered to be his good fortune.

Bernard started as an apprentice to watch and learn. The factory made truck motors, and machinery for tanks. The completed parts were then delivered to Bratislava and Belgrade once every two weeks. The transit was in all aspects thoroughly scrutinized by the governing militia.

When not on the assembly line, Bernard had to shovel coal to keep the furnaces at full blast. Keeping the furnaces at full capacity was as important as finished product. In the new year, he was taken off the assembly line completely and did strictly coal shovelling.

Pavol Tesar was above all a gentleman. Enthusiasm for reality was his technique at work. At home or away from the factory his family was most important. His words always prompted more, encouraging both quality and quantity knowing by doing so he was protecting each and every worker in the factory.

Work was six days per week, nine to ten hours per day. His day off was always Thursday. Meals were twice per day. The cafeteria used to be a vacant brick garage. Wooden tables and kitchen facilities were added to accommodate the two hundred workers. Four shifts for each meal were the basic schedule. The food was obviously more nourishing than that offered in the confines of the zoo. As in the past, Bernard offered a silent prayer for those less fortunate.

Based on the violence he had witnessed, Ben had pre-conceived notions regarding German culture. In Ostrava, he used his one day per week discovering the university grounds, visiting the three music halls and the market square, viewing the canals, and observing the intricacies and mosaic windows in the Catholic and Pentecostal Cathedrals. Besides his factory, there were coal mines and several steel refineries. Ostrava had become known as the 'Steel Heart of the Republic'. Putting this all together, it was a culture and environs he did not expect.

Four rivers, the Ostravice, the Oder, the Lucina, and the Opava, flowed into and out of the city. Six major highways provided valuable access to move cargo and troops. It was the troop movement that astounded Bernard upon his arrival. There were so many moving east toward southern Poland and Hungary. Factory talk confirmed Germany was invading the Soviet Union. Bernard did not know exactly what to make of it, but he was happy he was not caught in the middle. Then, he wondered about his family.

The S.S. Sturmbannfuhrer visited the factory every month. On the first occasion Bernard had to present his papers. They were accepted. Even his heart smiled.

Emil Beier was the city's Nazi Governor. Upon receiving the appointment in 1940, he consolidated twelve suburbs into the one city, exercising greater control on the quality and quantum of productivity. Being able to supply many other German industrial towns with the necessary parts, supplies and equipment established Ostrava as an essential cog in the German military operation. As long as production exceeded expectations, there was no concern for the import and export of Polish labour.

Karina presented an option in life's daily opportunities. She was attractive, willing, and available even though she was his manager's daughter. Just being able to consider the potential consequence of a relationship, no matter how brief, complicated his mind. Karina was Slovak. Being Slovak, she was "one of them" in a land controlled by the Germans. Just thinking about her prompted Bernard to conclude how much he loathed everything Nazi. In the camps, sex and gender were taboos for prisoners. Men could not freely associate with women, and women could not be alone with men. Men slept with men only to keep warm in tattered clothes, but there could be no allurement. Hitler disposed of anyone who reacted during such companionship. He called them, "Gypsies." During his stay at Fort VII, a male prisoner, fearing others and homosexual tendencies, chose to sleep alone one night and froze to death. All sex, while he was still at the mercy of others, was avoidable. There would be opportunities later, moments made memorable by his ability to choose.

Bernard attended Christmas Services at the Pentecostal Cathedral because that was the most appropriate thing to do, to mix with German culture, to be seen as being one of them; so as one day he would have the chance to not be one of them.

Chapter Eight
Europe, 1942

Wladyslaw Anders despised everything about the Soviet Union. Everything about him, they controlled. Seemingly, he couldn't take a breath without their permission. But, he knew how to play their game. There had been discussions involving General Sikorski in December, 1941. Then in February of 1942, further discussions took place concerning the formation a Polish Army under the direction of the Soviet Union.

"Where are my officers?" Anders repeated, knowing he required experienced military officers to lead the brigades.

Molotov's patience was wearing thin. He had already answered the questions, although dishonestly. Anders was well aware that Soviet concerns did not include Polish interests.

"They were in your camps. Where are they now?"

"Comrade Beria has answered your question. They were deported to the east. Many escaped. Others? We do not know."

"You, Deputy Chairman, are not the type of person to not keep accurate records. You would demand it of anyone around you." Anders conveyed the common perception of Molotov's thoroughness.

Molotov however was reluctant to accept compliments believing they were a preamble to mistrust. "The Security Police have made it very clear. What you may hear in any rumour is not the truth. If your Polish officers were so cruelly murdered in the Ukraine, you have only Himmler's Gestapo or the Ukrainian Nationalists to blame. It was not the Soviet Union."

The Polish General was annoyed with the response. He paused looking out the window and then continued. "You call it a rumour …"

Molotov interrupted him wishing again to control the conversation. "Just look what they've done to your Poland! Does it exist anymore? Don't tell me it does, because it doesn't. Your country is overrun by these Nazi rats wanting to infest every aspect of your heritage. Each person is vulnerable, if not already dead. And the Jews …"

"They're in Poland because your Czar kicked them out of your country thirty years ago," Anders added the historical reference.

"But they were not slain. Only the Germans would do that, the same Fascists who murdered your people, and your officers."

Anders did not respond right away, so Molotov continued.

"Look at us. They are even swarming in the Soviet Union. Ukraine, you suggest. That is Fascist territory. You were hated on both sides by the Fascists and National sympathizers. They're the ones killing your people."

Anders was becoming even more irritated with the continuing lies.

"Just tell me, are they dead?"

"I believe they are. You tell me they are. You're an honest man."

Ulanov entered unannounced. "Major Zhukov will be here shortly."

"Defence issues," Molotov told Anders. The Polish General was already aware of Zhukov's role.

"The General Secretary appreciates your efforts to this time, that you have three infantry divisions with your twenty-five thousand soldiers. You've done well."

"And where shall we engage?"

"With Soviet armies, at Stalingrad. That was Beria's choice. Others say: assisting the divisions in Hungary and the Balkan states." Molotov was obviously saying too much not in accord with usual Soviet practice where the opinions of others are never divulged.

Anders, on his part, clearly understood from the tone of the advice that the Polish Infantry would be on the front line. "And yours?" he enquired.

"I would move your divisions south to Tashkent. There we can have more of your prisoners released, enough for still another infantry division. Would that be your choice?"

The game continued. Anders knew that Molotov was trying to tie him down so that he could use the Polish General's reply at a later time. The three existing infantry divisions all wished to fight as a unit to restore Poland's independence. Putting the army in Tashkent would basically shunt them aside where they could have no influence on Poland's future. Serving at Stalingrad, they would suffer the same starvation and death as the millions of Fascist and Bolshevik forces. To enter Hungary and the Yugoslavian region would, too, be certain death trapped between opposing forces.

Anders offered a smile. "We will fight for Poland, for an independent Poland between you and your mortal enemy."

"Unfortunately that is not possible." Molotov was aware of Zhukov's plan to sweep across Europe. "You will serve in the front lines."

Anders was aghast.

"The General Secretary is very firm on this. You are the Polish Army in the Soviet Union."

"Your Stalin's agreement with the Polish Government in London was clear. We will fight as an independent ..."

"That was never said," Molotov sternly directed.

Ulanov entered once more. Zhukov had arrived and would not be kept waiting. Molotov looked over at the Polish General advising him that he can wait, and they would meet later. Anders, although frustrated, respectfully acknowledged the advice.

Molotov's meeting with the Defence Minister took forever. Anders was not seen again until the next day.

Beria was present for that second meeting. The exchange was less than colloquial. Beria was no one's friend.

The Soviet advice to the Polish Army was simple, "Fight in the front lines or rations will be cut to your troops and to all Poles in the Soviet Union." Mass starvation for over 300,000 persons and soldiers – that was Beria's ultimatum.

Molotov then pulled rank with Beria advising Anders that if his army chose not to fight on the front lines, then it could leave the Soviet Union. "You have one month to leave." Molotov was very direct. The Soviet General knew something had to be done to ease the demand on military rations.

"To where?" Anders anxiously enquired.

"Iran," Molotov stated definitely, being aware of the Soviet influence in the Middle East. "You will still be the Polish Army in the Soviet Union. You will not be independent. You will never be a Polish Army in Poland."

"Transportation?" Anders enquired.

"You have two feet!" Beria flatly decreed.

In March, 1942 three divisions of the Polish Army started their journey out of the Soviet Union. In total, more than 110,000 Polish persons escaped the poverty, disease and starvation of the gulags, by boat across the Caspian Sea. Others fled on foot, around the sea, through valleys, over hills, to a desert land of hostile factions. Many grumbled. Others were elated. A rare few were willing to risk life remaining in the Soviet Union. Others couldn't leave. To Anders, undergoing a prolonged death experience in Siberia was not an option.

(II)

Rumours were becoming just as terrifying as the reality. The stories of so many atrocities everywhere were mind wrenching. It was inconceivable that this could ever be happening. Where are the English, the French, and the Americans? Bernard had gone through enough: captivity, two camps, on his way to a third, the escape, friends being shot, running the countryside, being transported out of the country; and then in Ostrava it was almost as if he was a forgotten commodity. The growing number of refugees was becoming a real hazard. Factories were overcrowded. Workers were falling over each other. Boarding houses forced three persons per room. Food was becoming scarce. Three meals per day were no longer possible. In this milieu, personal importance had to be closely protected. Thus when he was moved from coal shovelling back to the assembly line, Bernard was most thankful. However he never conveyed anything more than a subtle hand-shake of gratitude. Over enthusiasm was still considered a display of fragility.

Working with metal and machinery gave him a valuable trade. Within the week he was assembling the transmissions and gears for Panzer IV tanks. When he had to fill in for other workers it was usually working with electrical and lighting circuits. Multi tasking provided a real advantage. If or when the war ended, he knew he would have definite employment skills.

Although he was not yet seventeen, he looked much older. The factory manager, Pavol Tesar, treated him as he would any employee. Being able to run and exercise on his one day off each week triggered significant muscle development and endurance. Unlike others,

Bernard was having no difficulty with eight to ten hour shifts.

The young man eventually allowed himself liberties with Karina. In early January, she insisted and he replied. Their moments were nothing more than an exchange of friendship. Both realized the day would come when he would leave and she would remain. Perhaps it was Karina that got him the job on the assembly line. She may have had some influence with her father, but it was never said.

Bernard was on the assembly line about six weeks when he was called to the cut-away office upstairs. The walled cubicle was situated above heavy machinery, preventing anything said in the office from being heard outside its walls. A heavy set, rough-faced individual stood in the corner. "Radomil," he introduced himself extending his hand. Ben was pensively scared, even though he should have been pleased upon hearing a Polish name. His manager and this gentleman continued their conversation in Slovak first. Minutes later, Radomil spoke in Polish to the youth. His smile could not be hidden. Bernard would be leaving in two days. "Budapest," he was told. "Trust me," Radomil offered. Bernard extended his faith in a series of questions confirming his interest.

They met again that evening in the beer hall, frequented by German guards and Nazi sympathizers. This venue seemed so extraordinary to be discussing the transport of weapons and Bernard's departure from Czechoslovakia. Three steins were Ben's limit. Radomil drank the same without being affected. Young guards at the next table however had trouble with their consumption. For whatever reason, Bernard offered the boisterous guards another round of drinks. Their gratitude was instant. Radomil didn't smile; he just told Bernard quietly that he was rather shrewd.

The convoy of six trucks left the factory the next morning fully loaded with machinery. Two of the guards, who were the recipients of Ben's generosity, arrived at the factory just before departure. In little time they approved the entire shipment.

They travelled south-east to Hranice, a factory town with minimal military production. At that point, instead of taking the main road towards Prostejev, the convoy turned south on a secondary road heading toward Kromeriz and then Breclav. At that point the trucks returned to the main highway travelling the eighty-five kilometres south to Bratislava.

Nazi flags were everywhere within the city. German was the predominant language, actually the only language allowed, at their depot. The temperament was clearly one of cautious frustration. Answers were never direct. The boisterous enthusiasm in pre-war Bratislava had disappeared. Bernard was informed Vienna was only two hours away. He had been sternly warned to watch his words, to be agreeable, and to respond quickly. Having already heard so many terrifying things about Austria, especially Germans in Austria, Bernard felt most ill at ease.

The inspection at the Bratislava military base took almost three hours. The inspectors were away for lunch when the convoy arrived and returned two hours late. They were young, terse, Austrian S.S. Guards, and had no patience for any explanation. This was obvious from the tone of their questions and the short answers they accepted. This convoy was at least the eightieth from the

169

Ostrava machinery factory. Still, everything had to be checked including the transit papers of each person on board. Bernard had his papers ready.

Eight hours after leaving Ostrava, they were on their way to Budapest. The Hungarian border waited for them less than thirty minutes away. The documents approved by the S.S. in Bratislava provided prompt approval at the border. Bernard was suddenly so grateful. A tremendous weight had been lifted off his mind and from within his heart.

The trucks continued on the main road for the last leg of their journey. Normally the winding roads of the last two hundred kilometres could have been completed in three hours. The drivers purposefully went slower not wishing to arouse the interest of any security police surveying the roads. Convoys of trucks, many in derelict condition, were speeding in a seemingly continuous line north to Bratislava or Vienna. Throughout this portion of the trip, transport trains frequently disturbed the distant horizon with their clatter and incessant whistles.

It was pitch black when they arrived at the loading docks. A train with a series of flatbed cars waited on the other side of the parking lot. Bernard prepared himself for another prolonged inspection process. Each piece of machinery, every motor and transmission, all of the tractor wheels, and locomotive parts, even the nuts and bolts had to been counted, and signed for. Thereafter they had to watch while another crew transported these from the loading dock to the train cars.

Seventeen hours after leaving Ostrava, they left their empty trucks on the lot and retired to rooms provided for them.

In bed that night Bernard thought about Karina, the factory, these truck drivers, and the Wadja family in Poland who gave him hope and assistance. Ben almost regretted sleeping on a mattress thinking that perhaps his own family, if they were still alive, never had such luxury.

A middle-aged stranger entered his room in the early hours the next morning. Bernard was startled by the suddenness of the intrusion, and stretched for anything he could use as a weapon. The man's voice was calm. "I'm here for you," he whispered in Polish. That was immediately reassuring.

The man was not clean shaven, and the stubble was almost Gray. Scars marked his face, one across his forehead. There had been no attempt to comb his hair. Clothes bore the odour of cheap cigarettes, and spilt booze. He held a flashlight fixing it against the palm of his hand, providing only a dim light. The explanation was detailed, and then repeated focusing on what Bernard had to do. Ben realized this was the Polish Underground in action. No one asked a name, but the man obviously knew who Bernard was.

Before the sun rose above the mountains, Bernard was at the dock assisting others load the Gray panelled truck. "Monfalcone Shipping" was the script on both sides of the vehicle. The fork-lifts were already busy filling the vehicle in the prescribed manner.

S.S. Guards were closely observing the entire process. The Monfalcone vehicle had to be loaded, the gate secured, and the approval sticker applied. Six trucks had to return to Ostrava with empty compartments, and the same number of drivers and personnel.

Bernard entered the same truck, perched next to the driver, two others squeezed in next to him, all ready to return to Ostrava. The convoy of six trucks, after Nazi approval, left in single file. The S.S. Patrol vehicle followed the last unit out of the parking lot and onto the highway. Meanwhile, the Monfalcone Shipping truck remained at the dock waiting for its drivers.

The German Patrol followed the convoy out of Belgrade. In less than thirty minutes they would reach the Czech border. As was usual practice, the Nazi Patrol discontinued its pursuit within five kilometres of the border guards. At that point, the last two trucks left the highway at the last ramp. The other trucks simultaneously pulled alongside each other obscuring the guards' vision.

Within five minutes after leaving the highway, the trucks stopped at an abandoned service area. The overgrowth had almost obscured the venue. Five riders including Bernard immediately on queue jumped out of the vehicles. The two trucks then hastily drove away returning to the highway and their position in line at the border crossing.

The Monfalcone Shipping truck arrived just as planned. The five refugees boarded the truck through the passenger door, entered a concealed passage behind the front seat into the rear, and hid among the boxes and equipment. The seal on the rear door of the truck remained intact.

The man, whom Bernard first met at three o'clock that morning, was already in the rear compartment. His advice was simple, "Nothing is assured." The refugees were informed in great detail about events in Hungary, Slovenia, Trieste and Monfalcone. The Italian-made vehicle was lacking a durable suspension, so that every bump became an arcade ride.

Bernard learned enough to re-ignite his fears. There was nowhere to run. That would be a major issue if they were ever stopped. No one disagreed. No one knew each other's names.

The refugees then heard about the dismal reality of Hungary, that the Germans were in control of the west including the capital, that the Soviets were infiltrating the east, and that many Nationalists were fighting for self-preservation. "They can't trust anyone, especially the Fascists," the man advised.

The prolonged darkness generated headaches, making it impossible after a while to even concentrate. Closing one's eyes became preferable rather than trying to distinguish objects in the black. Seeing nothing outside the vehicle also meant not knowing what to expect which only caused fears to escalate.

If the refugees could see outside their truck, they would have identified the course of their trip through Szekesfehervar, south-west to Nagykanizsa, then onto the Slovenian border. There were innumerable bridges across the many rivers flowing from the mountains.

The vehicle slowed approaching the border with Slovenia. Germany considered Slovenia as part of its empire so there were no questions to be asked at this border. The vehicle had to stop however for the seal on the back gate to be inspected. The refugees trembled in silence, then breathed signs of relief when the truck moved forward once more.

The trip through Slovenia was hidden from them. The mountains and the scenery would entice any tourist;

however they just wanted out of the country. Winding roads caused the vehicle to bounce profusely. The sad condition of the screeching breaks was evident during the descent from the mountains. The cold was becoming too much for some. Kidney pains compelled several to relieve themselves. Fumes were not an issue in the sealed compartment. By the time they had reached the mountain pass through Celja four of them were fast asleep. The trip from Budapest had to that point taken almost nine hours for the five hundred kilometres. There was still one hundred kilometres before reaching Trieste.

Unknown to the passengers the driver had no interest in entering Trieste. About forty kilometres from the port, the vehicle turned to the north-west away from the Nazi occupied territory. The Fascists, relying on the pact with Italy, had seized the port of Trieste and the territory of Dalmatia following the acquisition of Croatia and Slovenia. In essence the Germans controlled the Adriatic.

Italy was perceived by both the Axis and Allies as being a weak link. If the truck from Italy could return to Italy, not much would ever be questioned.

Thirty-five minutes after turning away from Trieste, the loaded truck pulled into a parking lot and backed up to the dock. It was just after seven o'clock in the evening. The moon was obscured by clouds in the darkness.

Italian Guards were not there. The driver and dockworkers didn't bother to wait. They wouldn't have waited in any event. The refugees raced off the vehicle, not bothering to gasp at fresh air, ran through the facility and into the basement. There they waited the inspection.

The wait for these five was absolutely bewildering. Shouldn't they be running?

The Italians eventually arrived. Immediately, loud voices echoed from the dock with complaints that the truck doors were already open. The explanation was repeated several times before it was accepted: they had to load the equipment for the return trip very early in the morning. Fortunately no one asked: "Where are the goods you just delivered?" The co-driver pointed to a distant transport vehicle and that sufficed.

In the basement, two Italian Officers entered. Their austere appearance matched the black uniforms. As soon as they started, the pretext of formality vanished. A cursory view of the papers – that was all. Bernard figured they couldn't read Polish, Czech or Hungarian; and he was thankful for that.

The man, whose name no one knew, stood at the side. He spoke Italian to the guards asking if there was a place to stay and when they would start to work. The answer conveyed the normal routine. The five refugees were then asked to follow him.

It was not the best of accommodation, on the ground floor, adjacent to a busy street, three rooms with two beds per room, and one bathroom for all. A meal was brought to each person from an elderly gentleman who appeared to operate the facility.

They slept well that night. Poland, Czechoslovakia, Hungary, and Slovenia were all in the past. Before they awoke, the man of many languages who had done so much, was gone. At six o'clock sharp an even more decrepit vehicle arrived to take them to Monfalcone Shipyards.

(III)

General Anders was Moses to the impoverished tribe of imprisoned Poles, with the promise of freedom in a distant land.

One million, seven-hundred thousand Poles had been taken captive by the Soviets since September 1939. Approximately five hundred thousand were government officials, lawyers, and the intelligentsia. In February 1940 about one quarter million were taken from the rural communities and exported to Siberia in cattle trains. Two months later, three hundred thousand women and children were transported to Kazakhstan and Altai Krai. In the summer of 1940 another four hundred thousand were seized and transported to the gulags in the eastern Soviet Union. The last seizure of Polish citizens took place in June 1941 when two hundred, eighty thousand persons were deported to various regions of the Soviet Union. In those labour camps known for their horrendous brutality nearly fifty percent died of disease, the cold, starvation, beatings, or mass murder.

If Polish prisoners would fight for the Polish Army of the Soviet Union, they would be released. Starting in March, 1942 more than one hundred thousand men, women and children commenced their journey leaving Soviet servitude behind. Many of these included families. The number with previous military experience was approximately twenty-five thousand. To put the total number into perspective: less than seven percent of the Poles who were seized by the Red Army or the Soviet Secret Police were in a position to follow Anders out of the Soviet Union.

After leaving their gulags, many who were inspired by the ambition of fighting for their country did not complete the trek. Typhus, freezing temperatures and malnutrition ended their dreams.

The exodus took place in two phases: in March, and then in August. There were two routes: by sea and by land. The masses boarded vessels in Krasnovodsk in Turkmenistan and sailed across the Caspian Sea to Pahlavi, Iran. The land route left Ashgabat, Turkmenistan requiring the refugees to walk the three hundred kilometres to Mashhad, Iran.

In March, 1942 the Krasnovodsk port recorded the departure of 33,039 military personnel, and 10,789 civilians.

In August, the departures from that port were 44,832 troops, and 25,437 civilians.

The number of Poles who died on route or shortly after arriving in Iran confirmed their general weakness. Health did not necessarily return once they left the gulags. Typhus, thirst, hunger, scarlet fever, dysentery, and the permanent scars from hard labour all claimed their victims. Cemeteries at Dulab, Tehran, Pahlavi, and Ahvaz still bear tribute to the many who didn't live to experience freedom.

In Iran, the Shah Reza Pahlavi, and the Minister of War, Aminollah Jahanbani, welcomed the refugees. Five transit camps were established: one for the military and four for civilians. Two thousand tents answered the immediate need for the first flood of refugees. Villages sprung up with care facilities, schools and orphanages. Religious orders in Isfahan and Mashhad provided shelter and education for the eighteen thousand children.

Every person entering Iran was required to shed their clothes and be disinfected. The rags from the gulags were burned to destroy any disease. Malaria was becoming a major issue, an ailment not seen in frozen Siberia. When typhus again appeared as a devastating malady, those who were infected were segregated from the others. Ultimately a hospital just for the Polish citizens was built to address the spreading ailments.

The refugees leaving the USSR included many persons of the Jewish faith. After weeks in Tehran, many of the Jewish soldiers and citizens abandoned the Polish camps and journeyed west to Palestine. Anders chose not to pursue these for abandoning the force, although he had every right to do so. Anders clearly understood the importance of fulfilling national dreams.

General Anders was proud of these initial results, in spite of the fact that so many leaving the Soviet Union were nothing more than walking skeletons. They bonded, and celebrated their freedom.

(I V)

Ryszard hung the vestments in the sacristy closet. "Still have to clean the pews," he whispered to himself. It was all part of his daily routine. Sweeping the aisles would follow.

In the maze of greenhouses Elzbieta helped her mother. On the Saturday before Palm Sunday there was still so much to do. They had already separated and organized the palm branches. Red and white tulips were prepared to adorn the sanctuary during the parish mission. Then there were the herbs that the nuns needed for seasoning their meals. In addition, other herbal plants

178

required clipping. Daffodils were also gathered into bunches. Military personnel would arrive soon to pick these up and deliver them to various institutions and offices. The spring tomatoes and kale would later be picked for the Saturday market, where Elzbieta and a young nun would sell the produce for charity.

They would be kept busy all week with the preparations for Easter Sunday on April 5 of 1942. Busy was good.

The shrine was a godsend. Czestochowa was still a haven of misery, where Fascist violence could erupt at any second. Most of the Jews were gone. The Sisters heard they were transported to the General Government. The church had helped some of the Jewish families: hiding them on premises, getting jobs in factories, altering identification papers, driving them into the hills or leading them into the protection of the Polish Underground.

Teresa was silent and remained deaf. Her children were everything to her. They had developed an intricate sign language that started and ended with smiles and hugs. The Sisters and clergy were accommodating in every respect. The mother and infant Andrzej were given one room. Elzbieta shared one with a young Novice. Ryszard was housed with the seminarians.

Each night in bed she said a silent prayer invoking visions of hope as she closed her eyes. Dreams were becoming the wrapping paper of her bundle of fears.

(V)

The Monfalcone Shipyards had been in operation since 1908, equipping the Italian navy for the First World War. The capacity of being able to work on four hulls at the same time made it extremely valuable to the regional economy, and made it a substantial prize for any invading nation. Germany used the territory well – from Venice to Trieste and down the coast onto Croatia. Basically, the Axis Powers controlled the Adriatic.

The German Schutzstaffel (the S.S.) was not willing to let its partner control the governments, settlement, or the factories along the coast. Trieste was the centre of the Nazi operations. The murders and brutality there were no less than elsewhere in Europe. In fact, to assure himself that there would never be pro-Allied sympathizers, Himmler moved Franz Stangl from the Treblinka Death Camp in 1943 to govern Trieste. Fully being aware of the dangers within the region, the shipping truck from Budapest purposefully avoided Trieste. Dealing with the Italians was so much easier.

The van picked up the five refugees at 6 a.m. sharp. First impressions count. The courtesy exceeded expectations. There were no terse orders, still everything happened with such precision. The jobs were fully described. A co-worker was present to meet each new employee. Salary as expected was minimal. The size of the shipyards was mind-boggling. Farthest away, a transport vessel was near completion. Two empty hulls were secured and afloat with workers being dropped by rope and crane to complete the structural welds. The fourth vessel on the far left was still on land. Ropes secured the welders to the outside of the ship where they welded and filled the joints.

Bernard should have been apprehensive because he never worked on anything so complex. The workers, even those fellow refugees, appeared all in their thirties. Would anything be said about his age? In the locker room Ben was given his gloves, knee pads, and helmet, being firmly told not to lose them.

Guglio was his co-worker, a delightful fellow. Everything he said seemed so positive considering the surroundings. Bernard was sure there were contrary feelings inside, but Guglio was not one to ever say anything that might compromise his well-being. The Italian lad loved his family and returned home every night. They had to move to Monfalcone from Rimini at the direction of the Italian government. Ben was certain the Germans had more to do with that decision.

Bernard was lowered into the hull with other workers. He watched for a moment and then started without further prompting to complete his welds. Any pain or discomfort in his hips and legs was negligible compared to the enthusiasm from just being that productive. Compliments meant so much after that first hour. He knew he was being closely watched.

Supper with the fellow refugees was nothing less than a feast: cold cuts, pasta, and a glass of wine. All present retold stories of the day's events. Bernard wished his father was there. He could do this job.

Everything remained positive for that first month. Then rumblings of discontent surfaced with expressions of distrust. First of all, three of the refugees wanted to get away feeling they were never meant to be there for the duration of the war. Others, whom Bernard figured were also refugees, were fearful of Allied bombing feeling the shipyard would be a main target. Bernard that also was a major worry, but he never spoke of it. Their identity papers were locked away in the shipyard office.

A week later, Easter was mentioned, only to remind everyone that work would continue on Good Friday. The manager continued advising there would be two hours for worship on the Sunday. Guglio brought a portion of a palm branch for Ben. The symbolism was most appreciated: not that just Guglio practiced his faith, but that he was willing to risk assisting others to do so. Bernard learned significant Italian in that month, suitable for the factory environment and late evening conversations. Events at work were transpiring to his benefit.

In mid April, both Guglio and Bernard were transferred to the vessel almost ready for its inaugural voyage. They formed part of a crew of thirty workers to complete the fabrication, finishing welds, primer coats, and final painting. Bari would be the ship's first destination. That news spawned wild imaginings. Were there Poles in Bari? Perhaps there were ships to take him to the Polish troops in Syria? But first, he knew he had to get to Bari.

Guglio had this incredible ability to read minds. He was always one step ahead of his manager and co-workers, always able to say that the task has been done or at least started. This earned him the appreciation and respect of many, giving him greater access. It was on the Thursday night, before the Italian Ship Isadora set sail, that Guglio handed his Polish friend an envelope. Bernard hastily opened it. There were his identity papers, and a transit document allowing him to be on board in a maintenance capacity. "I will be with you," Guglio told his friend, speaking Italian. Bernard understood the generosity and expressed his gratitude in Italian. Ben always felt that the first words a person should ever learn in any language were 'Thank you'. It was very handy on that occasion.

Bernard was told the trip would take more than a day. "About seven hundred kilometres," he was told. Ben really didn't care how long it would take, this was an adventure, first time on board a ship. His broom he held firmly, knowing that it was in a strange way his ticket to freedom. Whenever he thought someone might be watching, he became appropriately active.

The voyage rocked the boat consistently with the north winds driving south the full length of the sea. Waves became an issue after leaving the harbour area. As the ship neared Ancona, they topped four meters. The air remained cold, and the strong breeze accentuated the freezing temperatures. As many as possible found shelter inside. However there was no room for the deck hands. Ben stayed close to the left side bridge taking advantage of any shelter it could provide.

Bari was the most beautiful seaport he could have ever imagined. "Heaven," he thought. The castle dominated the horizon, perched above the city as it looked east across the Adriatic towards Montenegro. The history of the Middle Ages was alive with all of the tales of Roman and Norman fleets, and the invading Saracen and Byzantium forces. The commercial inlet was immense spreading for what seemed miles with endless piers, and fishing vessels. Guglio and Bernard sauntered along the Luongo Mare, the sea wall walkway; then returned through the gardens amid the government buildings. The Cathedral of San Nicola was the final stop before returning to the park near their vessel.

There they joined several other seamen. Two were from Croatia. Three had arrived from Tunisia. Another group was Maltese. Bernard smiled at Guglio and shrugged his shoulders. His Italian friend clearly understood as a gesture of surprise: no Italian, no German.

They purchased a basket of seafood for their supper. On board the ship they received a minimum wage: usually enough for two meals, a pack of cigarettes or a weekly hooker. Bernard had no interest in the latter two, so he ate well. They finished the meal sharing a bottle of Vecchio. Bernard had no idea what it was, but it looked like dark wine and tasted like a weak sherry.

The Isadora was to be in dock for three days before sailing onto Egypt. As was the usually practice during war, advice changed every day with the latest announcement that it would sailing to the French coast. Guglio laughed mentioning Monte Carlo, then seriously suggested that this was more than a cargo ship. He reasoned that more than likely the voyage to France had something to do with Rommel enlisting the Fascists from southern France to assist his troops in Africa.

"How much does he know?" Bernard felt wary. "How could he know so much?" he asked himself. An itinerant seaman having so much knowledge just didn't seem right. Ben never offered another word about such issues but realized that he had to get away from there.

The next morning, Bernard left early to walk the Luongo Mare by himself, sat on a bench in the gardens and stopped at the church, ultimately to go anywhere where he might hear a word of Polish.

184

Guglio wondered about his friend when he wasn't there that morning. He knew what would happen and he wished him well.

Prayers do work. Finally Bernard found the courage to speak to the priest. The cleric immediately called for the assistant pastor. An elderly clergyman arrived, looked at Bernard, and started talking Polish. Bernard was in heaven. He let his enthusiasm instantly show by hugging the priest. They went to the office behind the altar.

"Do you believe in Father Christmas?" Reverend Pawel asked. "Swiety Mikolaj?" he repeated.

Bernard continued to smile. The answer was obvious in this church. "Tak."

The elderly cleric encouraged Bernard to talk about the events of the last three years. The tears were many and the napkins several. The priest conveyed his need to give Bernard the opportunity to let everything out of his system. Thereafter he heard Bernard's confession.

Lunch was served in the garden behind the church. It was a quiet, incredibly peaceful area. The flowers were all in bloom and the vines were covered in buds. Pussy willow trees were a mass of soft fur, making Bernard realize the world could still be a beautiful place. The cleric's concerns returned to the horrific events in Poland, the concentration camps and the invasion of the Soviet Union. The priest then talked about his own experience, being Chaplain to Polish forces in Romania and then fleeing there when it became the battleground between Fascist and Bolshevik forces.

Ultimately, the conversation turned to plans for Ben's future. There were many Poles in and around but mainly north of Bari. "A ship will be leaving on the thirtieth of the month from Trani."

When the priest invited Bernard to come with him, the youth followed. Bernard then appeared in the sanctuary minutes later wearing a clerical cassock and collar. The next morning Reverend Bernardo was the front seat passenger in the parish vehicle on its way to Katedra de San Nicola Pielgrzym, twenty-five miles north of Bari.

Bernard thought of Guglio often after that. His prayers were for his friend as much as for his own family. Gratitude knows no limits, and the expressions of appreciation should never be silent.

In December 1943, nineteen months later, the port of Bari was heavily damaged by massive bombing. Over one thousand people died the first day aboard the twenty-eight vessels. Many more died later suffering excessive skin burns caused by a cargo of mustard gas. Bernard even then prayed for his friend Guglio that he was not one of the victims.

(V I)

Sooner or later the day had to arrive when even the Nazis would realize that the production of trinkets was no longer a viable industry. Leon had prepared himself for that eventuality. On his infrequent days off, he ventured around the farmlands realizing there was still potential for life outside the city.

Poznan was strained in every direction, its heart torn by devastation. The city was never meant to be German, yet German it was forced to become. Every Polish family, Leon knew, had experienced sadistic violence. No family had escaped. Of those still alive, many had been transported to the area of the General Government, or worse still directly to urban ghettoes. There were now only one in twenty left. Leon was one of that five percent. He never understood why, but then he never desired the alternative.

He drove his rusting vehicle past what would have been the family home. The entire area was absent of any life. Nothing had changed in three years. Nothing was growing. He cursed the Germans once more for such destruction. They claimed they had to cleanse the land for their own people, yet in many areas the Germans never came.

Leon could play the game as well as anyone. Every Friday evening he visited the local beer hall to drink with the security police. There was nothing to hide and he was as open and jovial as could be, except he never told them to rot in hell.

Ultimately then when these same guards entered his factory with advice it had to close, there was no harsh language, no orders and no ill feeling. It was going to happen and it did. In the confines of the beer hall he had already impressed upon the senior officials the potential benefit of having his staff return to farming to feed the many of Germans who were bound to settle in the area. They thought then it was a wonderful idea, and upon attending Leon's factory claimed the strategy to be their own.

Leon invited them into the back office. He had no idea how far he could go. However, he took the risk. Leon stressed the churches, and the need to use the grounds of religious institutions to maximize crop production. He had a list prepared that included the convents, one closed seminary, several abandoned churches and the archdiocesan grounds. Leon realized Archbishop Hlond would be very favourable to this idea.

The German officials were easily sold. Throughout the Aryan Empire they were stretched too thin for both manpower and supplies. Any solution was workable.

Everyone in his factory would have a job. Leon felt so relieved he could do this for these who responded favourably to his ideas that got them this far.

The next week found Leon scurrying through the area inspecting potential farmland. He didn't have the courage to ever recommend to the authorities the street on which he lived, the vacant school ground, or even his old farm. "Count your blessings," he told himself.

Fate required him to visit the Franciscan Convent. Leon suspected his family may have at one time sought shelter in such a place, but convents like other institutions were forbidden to maintain records of visitors or even of their own postulants. Same was true for the abandoned school and seminary. There were no surviving records. Leon again cursed the Germans for such attempts to hide their crimes.

Farmland to the north of the city was the venue of his new enterprise. Frequent discussions with authorities affirmed the acreage and that work was available and the entire area was suitable for settlement by the German population. But, in many suburbs they did not come. However, their trains continued east, not stopping to eat his produce.

The concept of greenhouses the city officials considered innovative even though they were commonplace in other communities. At times it was difficult to understand how the German nation could have ever organized itself to invade any country when it seemed to know so little about the basics of food and life.

Kale, lettuce, beans, tomatoes, potatoes, pumpkins, squashes, beets and peas were the first year's crops. Leon got the authorities to pay for the orchard of apple trees. He completed an inspection of other farming operations and provided detailed reports. The Germans had bought every aspect of the project and were pleased they didn't have to complete their inspections.

Jewish refugees were able to find shelter on the farms and again in the religious communities. Sufficient documents were arranged to suggest their Christian heritage in order to preserve their Jewish lives. The terrifying news of events in southern and eastern Poland ripped the hearts of so many people. Suicide in Poznan was still an inescapable reality. The future was brighter but still very much opaque.

(VII)

The fortnight at the Cathedral of Saint Nicholas the Pilgrim were days of impatience, and nights plastered with images of Plaszow's horrifying terror. There was no calm, only nightmares.

With the assigned garb, Bernard spent most of each day in the church, in one of the front pews on the right. It had to appear that he was a cleric and not a refugee. Any questioning mind must be satisfied that the priests were not involved in the exportation of Allied supporters or sympathizers. Other 'clerics' arrived in the week before

189

departure. The bells would peel every hour from six in the morning till nine at night. The appearance of a conference, or novena prayers was able to conceal their ultimate intent. This would be their ninth such delivery to Tripoli, Lebanon. Everything reflected the precision the clergy demanded.

The vessel was nothing more than a very large fishing boat. The two massive engines had been moved to the rear section of the hull. The front section of the hull could accommodate twenty persons. The other ten would be on top hiding among the four lifeboats and netting. There were no life jackets. Falling into the cold water in the mid Mediterranean with three to five meter waves created conditions that made any life preserver obsolete. They boarded the vessel just before 2 a.m. Three hours later to the second, the vessel departed.

All of the passengers had been told during supper the night before to not ask questions, and to be patient as the voyage might take longer than expected. If they were approached by a German cruiser, they were all to claim to be refugees fleeing North Africa, and to profess their allegiance to the country that would accept them. If there was a torpedo, there would be no time to pray.

The food was dried flakes, nothing more than porridge three times per day. Fishing poles were in use to create the proper impression; plus, having a fresh catch never hurt anyone's supper plate. If any vessel was seen on the horizon a crew of eight had to immediately disguise their mission by working on the nets. Washroom facilities were overboard.

Some of the passengers eventually had to ask about their destination, who they would meet, and to where they would be taken. There were no direct answers. Only one term was ever used to answer such concerns, "Refugee Friends".

The voyage took them south from the Adriatic Sea to the Ionian Sea. To the north and west Turkey and Greece were far beyond the horizon. Once into the Mediterranean, the vessel sailed south of Crete, and then as it neared Cyprus the vessel turned north-east to approach the Levant.

All were on the main level viewing the approaching port and the town beyond. The excited exclamations were many. No one was quiet. All had been warned not to be too over enthusiastic in the event something or someone on shore may not be as planned. However, their fervour could not be constrained.

There was trouble at first docking against the deteriorating wooden planks. Realizing they have achieved the best possible docking, the engines went silent.

They all disembarked in a hurry. No sooner was the last person off than the boat restarted the engines and moved out to sea. It dropped the anchor about a hundred meters off shore and watched the events.

The first blue panel truck arrived followed by a second one minutes later. Polish was the only language the drivers spoke.

The two vehicles drove the prescribed route carefully: no speeding, no dangerous turns, nothing to attract attention. They journeyed north along the coast reaching the Lebanon-Syrian border after thirty minutes. Bernard could hear the border guards. Everything was in French.

The mountains lacked any set design. There was not one range, no consistent geological feature. Some were high, rounded and stretched for miles. Others had jagged peaks. Suddenly one would just appear out of the desert after miles of wind driven sand. To the distant north a range appeared on the horizon. That stretched for the entire last leg of the trip. The final portion of their journey took them into the valleys among those hills, then up one slope and treacherously descending another.

The vegetation and crop production were left behind on the coast. There were several oases on the route with villas surrounding each of them, relishing in the benefit of unlimited spring water. There were camels, and even more camels. Sure every Polish boy had seen a camel at the zoo; but these were trained animals, forming a caravan. Children played with one camel outside a small village. In another town, several of the animals were roped together outside a series of tents. This was a different land.

The passengers on the two vehicles could not silence their enthusiasm. Amid the many exclamations, there was the recurring theme of hatred for the Fascists and Bolsheviks, and the inherent desire for retribution. "Revenge. That's the reason they're joining the army," Bernard concluded.

There were actually some already in camp who were not there to even fight at all. They left the camps in the Soviet Union under the guise of wanting to join the military but really had only the intention of abandoning the troops once they arrived in Palestine.

The trucks reached their destination just before midnight. In the first week of June, it was still incredibly hot that late in the day. That first impression was quickly buried in the appearance of more than one thousand tents. They went on for at least a mile. The Polish flags had already been lowered with the evening ceremony.

The refugees formed two lines for the initial inspection. There were very few questions, just name and place of birth. A distinguished gentleman entered from the side. His uniform gave the impression he was a Lieutenant or General. Others saluted him. He was obviously one who was much respected.

The General directed his cohorts to bring the new-arrivals to the available tents. From the hand direction given, it appeared they'd be sheltered at the far end. After the new recruits were dismissed, the General unexpectedly turned in their direction. "Ever carry a rifle, better still shoot a rifle?" It was an immense feeling to hear Polish spoken especially by a person who seemed interested in their well-being. Polish was no longer a language for concealed conversations.

"Third Carpathian Division," the General instructed those who had nodded. "Six o'clock. We will meet then."

In this manner Bernard became a member of the 3rd Carpathian Rifle Division of the Polish II Corps. He was on top of the world.

(V I I I)

"Does the end justify the means?" The substitute teacher posed the question to her class expecting a lengthy discussion.

Mary greatly enjoyed these sessions, at the end of the school year, when the regular curriculum texts were closed, exams completed, and students were expected to think without being graded for their opinions. Even during the school year, the Principal would allow such occasions into the class schedule just to encourage the girls to consider alternatives and to develop the ability to stand up and convince classmates of the validity of her opinion. Public speaking and assertiveness were the planned result. The school had already achieved significant success in many public speaking debates.

Many of the girls in her group were equally inclined and similarly gifted with respect to the expression of thought. In her seventeenth year, there was so much still to learn, and Holy Cross School was providing that opportunity. The A-Level exams would be completed next year. Mary felt assured of her success. Giving others the chance to express their views was an enticing prospect because even though they may have had the wits, they did not always agree. So when the question was posed concerning the end justifying the means, the expressions were many, and the discourse insightful.

"Let me expand on that. Was the assassination of Reinhard Heydrich justified?"

Faces lit up with enthusiasm to express keen thoughts. The discussions continued into the next day expanding the conversation to include the war in Russia and the ultimate consequences to Europe. Treblinka, Auschwitz and Wannasee were names that would never be erased from history nor ever again dismissed in such discussions.

(I X)

Two weeks after arriving in Homs, Bernard was on a
wobbly bus heading west into the hills at Hadida. The
wooden plank seats were incredibly uncomfortable.
Windows that couldn't shut completely allowed the hot
dust to blow through the vehicle. The journey of thirty
kilometres took about an hour with several sharp turns
through the valleys and up the inclines. The time
allowed the comrades to recall the tribulations that
brought them together.

Conversations always started rather low-key and
ended with angry, loud expressions. So much of the
resentment was indeed justified. Bernard spoke little of
what he experienced in Plaszow. Of the ten on that bus,
he was the only one who had been held inside a German
camp. Four of those had experienced Beria's brutality.
Three had escaped early into Romania and encountered
incredible barriers trying to leave. The other two came to
Syria via the Balkans. They all had hope for a Poland,
independent of the Germans and the Soviets.

Though it had not been specifically said, the
impression was that they would train in Syria and then
be transferred to Palestine. Many of the troops had
already left for Quastina. Becoming proficient was the
step before such a transfer.

Each person on the bus was equipped with a
backpack weighing fifteen kilograms, a short-handed
shovel, and a semi-automatic rifle. Ropes were flung
over the left shoulder. Belts held the ammunition. The
boots were heavy, and the hard helmet secure.

The bus stopped on a levelled lot among high rolling
hills, part of a chain that appeared to go on forever. They

195

started by discarding their apparatus and then were instructed to commence a twenty minute run: up the incline, along the edge, and back toward the bus. Only after that could they enjoy beverage from their canteens.

Then fully loaded with their gear, they headed up the slope having to manoeuvre off paths among scrub brush, and loose rocks. Within one hour they had to arrive at a designated spot. All of the training was timed to develop endurance. After drinking again, they headed higher up the slope, and then split into pairs. Overlooking the valley they had to prepare dug outs in the rocky terrain among the boulders. Fingers bled. Lips were parched. An inspection of each rabbit hole was completed before each pair could proceed with the trek. Up higher they climbed, using ropes along the jagged edge. Then the path dropped sharply demanding incredible agility on the loose rock. Near the bottom they were required to cross a small stream, the only flowing water they had seen since arriving in Homs two weeks before.

The next trip to the mountains repeated much of this training, but also introduced methods used in mine detecting. Firing weapons became a staple of training exercises on the fourth visit to the hills. The fifth visit was overnight surviving alone and in the cold.

Rest in the camp, no matter how loud, always came easy after these adventures. No one had regrets about any portion of the training. It was all necessary to assure victory.

Five weeks after arriving in Homs, Bernard was on a troop transport, no more than a modified flat bed, to Quastina. The trip was about four hundred kilometres starting on a dirt road going south between Beirut and Damascus. The hills were a perpetual annoyance diverting the vehicle several kilometres to the east or west constantly. After five hours, the transport passed Haifa and continued further south hugging the coast.

Quastina was a village thirty-eight kilometres north of Gaza. The area was flat, elevated above the coast. Population may have been as high as seven hundred, Bernard figured. There were clearly less than two hundred homes, most makeshift shacks. On the outskirts there was an adobe style edifice that some had said was the local school. The community, before the British arrived, had been strictly Moslem. The British military camp called Beer Tuvia was established just three kilometres south-west of the school building.

The 3rd Carpathian Division with its cadet school was situated on the outskirts of Quastina. Nearby hills provided the venue to enhance the training program. Being away from the Russians in Iran, and the French in Syria gave this division its own Polish identity which was essential for morale.

Produce was more than just a basic staple. Wheat and barley provided bread. Goats and chickens provided meat, eggs and milk. Lemons, bananas, and grapes were the regular crops. Honey was plentiful from the many hives used for pollination.

Strength and endurance remained the objective of all training exercises. Being able to outlast your opponent was essential as nearly every conflict to that point, outside of the initial Blitzkrieg, had basically become a prolonged stalemate with the victor being the one capable of enduring longer. Manoeuvres included actual re-enactments of conflicts that compelled each cadet to fully employ all mental capabilities on the battlefield.

Rest came easy in spite of the work. Enthusiasm for the first action made everyone eager.

(X)

He was almost certain there were no devices; but still, necessity demanded further inspection. Anders had to be very cautious as he walked on water between the sinking Soviet skiff and the British ocean liner. How best to describe his peril? The General was a master at demonstrative comparisons. His troops loved it. The message was always clear.

Anders struggled with the probability that his Poland would be no more. Even his presence in this Cairo hotel suggested his priorities were not theirs. Everything that had happened since the First of September almost three years ago attacked Polish pride.

Leopold Okulicki was an astute assistant, always able to add the appropriate incite at the opportune moment, especially in those hours waiting for the British Prime Minister.

Okulicki's formal role was Chief of Staff. He had been a trained officer in the first war, and was one of the few Polish officers still alive after Stalin's purge. It was at times a godsend that Okulicki's patience exceeded Anders's fervour. If it didn't, Anders would not have been there in Cairo then, or at any time.

The Chief of Staff's inspection confirmed there were no listening devices. His experience with decoding and deciphering transmissions had indeed been beneficial, giving Anders instant first-hand knowledge.

But knowledge is not always a good thing. The General regretted that at times he knew too much. It scared him.

"Why did Churchill meet with Stalin?" Anders's concern was very real. "How could the Prime Minister have any respect for that dictator?"

Anders knowledge of military affairs would never let the past sleep. In that mid afternoon in August of 1942, his mind continued to search for the rationale of recent events. He knew Churchill and Britain sided with the White Russians against Stalin and Soviet Russia. "How could he be so friendly with a person he considered such an enemy?" This question was even more apropos when Anders reflected on the audacity of Stalin ten months ago when the dictator asked Churchill for military aid. "Only friends do that," Anders contemplated. Whether Churchill and Stalin had become friends really didn't matter that much as long Churchill still had positive plans for Poland.

"Over Fifty Thousand," Leopold replied to Anders's query. The support for Communism in Britain was increasing. "Exponentially" was Anders's term. That had to scare any person wishing to stop the spread of Communism in Europe. Okulicki was not a psychologist but knew enough about the subject to realize that the existence of a common enemy had greater ability to unite factions than having any common interest among participants. In this case, Hitler was the entity everyone hated. "When hatred unites nations, more than one nation will suffer," the Chief of Staff concluded.

Bored with sitting in their room, the General and his Chief of Staff moved to the tearoom. Chandeliers, mosaic windows, refined table clothes, and the finest china reminded guests of the elegance of Cairo's French and British heritage.

"Sikorsky strains to maintain their interest," Okulicki continued after sipping his tea.

"I am too aware," the General added. "Stalin refuses to acknowledge our government in exile. Even Roosevelt was indifferent to the Fascist-Bolshevik division of our country. We cannot count on him. I am not going to be his ostrich and bury my head in the sand."

"The Prime Minister has been firmly opposed to any attempt by any nation to control Poland's destiny."

"My friend, Churchill was never elected by his people, he was only appointed, selected to save Britain, not Poland. No one can assure you or me or any Pole that tomorrow he will hold to any opinion that Poland must be preserved. He has to deal with Stalin and the US I tell you neither one favours our future. The events of this year have been most evident in this regard. Only two months ago, the United States and Britain committed themselves to invade Africa, not Europe. In Eastern Europe we seem to be not much more than an after-thought. Millions die and still there is no help. I admit they made a weak gesture, an attempt at Dieppe that was doomed to fail, sending thousands of Canadian troops to die below the cliffs. Tell me about Communism.

"I'll tell you what I know. World Domination! That's been their one goal this past quarter century. That will not change this week, next year or any time thereafter.

"But let us be specific. The Nazis started to empty the ghettoes exactly four weeks ago today. Is anyone stopping them? We are forbidden to try.

"American troops have been in Britain for seven months now. What are they waiting for?

"And now, this month's events. We are called to Moscow to meet with Churchill. Instead of meeting with us, Churchill spends more time with his friend Stalin telling this dictator that they are continuing with the invasion of Africa, and will not now invade Europe, but may do so someday, and that the Allies will be willing to share military information, especially that which we Poles decode. So what happens, Churchill doesn't meet with us. Instead he spends hours feasting with the General Secretary. We return to Iran and then three days later we are ushered here to Cairo and are still waiting."

The Chief of Staff had nothing to add. They paid the bill leaving more than enough for the tip, and returned to their suite.

Although General Anders had very real concerns about the past and how it might affect the future, he acknowledged that he was still a general with the duty to lead and motivate his army. He already had more than twenty thousand troops in various camps, in several divisions. At the very time he was in Cairo, another forty thousand were leaving the Soviet Union to join his army. How best to lead them? That issue compelled his meeting with Churchill.

General Anders was called to the foyer at about four o'clock in the afternoon. He had only Leopold Okulicki by his side. Churchill arrived with his entourage. The meeting room was altered at the request of the British, a tactic designed to make sure the room was not bugged.

The Prime Minister was very cordial, low key, with his usual embracing style. Churchill was a good listener, or at least in the meetings with General Anders. Now as to whether appropriate action would result, that was the unknown factor. War never really allowed for a fixed position. Both Churchill and Anders appreciated this reality. Being able to quickly adapt with full use of your resources, this Churchill told Anders was, "Always essential."

Churchill, however talked in generalities after telling Anders that he declined the Soviet request for aid. The decision to not invade Europe in 1942 was also repeated to Stalin. Anders didn't raise the issue of Dieppe. Churchill then apologized that they did not meet in Moscow.

General Anders was direct. He anticipated his Polish Army would exceed seventy thousand by month's end. Anders reminded the Prime Minister that his force was still very much a Soviet controlled military unit, and that every day they feared orders compelling them to fight in the front line against the Nazis. This would happen in any event, whether fighting for the British or the Soviets; but fighting with the British held more hope for Poland than the Soviet dream of European domination.

Churchill did not disagree. After supper, they continued the meeting.

Anders's request was direct, simple, and beneficial to both. "It is in the interest of both of our countries, and for the benefit of our Allies, that the Polish Army in the East be no longer aligned with the Soviet military.

Therefore we request your approval that Polish army, devoted to the Allied cause, with the support of our government in London, become one with the British, under British control. Thus we would become wholly submissive to the government of Poland in Exile, servants of His Majesty the King, and fight together with the British High Command."

The request was well received bearing in mind Churchill's own views that the forces in the Levant should have already been either part of the French Expeditionary Force or of the British High Command.

General Anders returned to Iran with the agreement that his troops, his camp, and all of the Polish civilians would move to Iraq and eventually enter combat under the direction of the British High Command.

On September 12, 1942, the second exodus began, this time from Iran and Iraq. Forty-one thousand troops made the trek. The 5TH Kresowa Infantry Division, an Armoured Brigade, and an Artillery Group were formed from the assembled troops. Factories and ammunition plants were established to ensure Allied forces were well equipped.

General Sikorski in London re-named the entire force the Polish Army in the West. Its Commander in Chief was General Anders. Although camps were situated throughout the Middle East, headquarters was established at Quizilh, Iraq. General Karaszewicz-Tokarszewski directed affairs affecting the battles in North Africa from his base in Quassasin, Egypt. Bernard also moved, with the 3rd Carpathians to Quastina, Palestine.

(XI)

The train to Marylebone Station arrived as scheduled, which was a good thing as the snow had just started to fall. That December was unusually cold, and even more bitter with restrictions on coal consumption. Still, her thick coat kept her warm. Just having a coat was a luxury.

The morning train was packed as expected. She found a seat next to a business gentleman. He was courteous enough to move his brolly to the side. The office worker was lost in the morning edition of the Daily Mirror. Mary had heard so much of such "rags" her father called them. "One's the same as the other." Then looking out the window as they passed the local cricket pitch, Mary smiled thinking of her father and how he would offer disgruntled comments about everything in the paper until he got to the sports page with the racing results.

There was only two other women in the car. She thought about it for just a moment and then turned to the purpose of her journey. The School Debate was scheduled for twelve noon. Being there two hours early would give her time to once more rehearse her opening presentation. She had written enough, rehearsed daily, and explored every possible rebuttal. 'Does the End Justify the Means?' The topic seemed to be a ritual in nearly every academic discussion.

Then her topic took on greater significance came to light once more with an article in the gentleman's newspaper.

The British Foreign Secretary Anthony Eden

told the House of Commons yesterday about

the Mass executions. Jews from every nation

are being transported in cattle cars to

extermination camps in Poland.

She shook her head being repulsed by such reality and sickened that obviously nothing was being done to stop it. The bombing of German cities caused so much destruction and many deaths. "Was all that justified? Should there be more? Should they be more focused? Are there alternatives?" Her mind raced.

Mary's stern expression reflected on the glass as they neared Wimbledon. She was astute enough to realize not enough was being done.

"Could they once again bomb us?" She knew the answer to her question. With war, there is always fear of destruction and death. The Book of Ecclesiastics did not offer comfort for it did indeed remind the Christian world that 'There is a time for peace, and a time for war.' The latter obviously had to precede the former – that was the history of Europe.

The train emptied quickly after arriving at Marylebone, everyone rushing to their offices. Mary was the last to leave, picking up the discarded newspaper. She planned to read it while on the Bakerloo Line to Regent's Park.

That afternoon at Queens College, Mary exceeded her own expectations.

Bombing the enemy's cities, even if it meant hurting innocent people, was justified if no other means was possible to stop its extermination of humanity.

Her opinion was enthusiastically received. The entire debate was actually more of a political statement encouraging action by the British in the war against the Hun. The opposing side had a challenge it could, during war time, never win.

Thirty-three days later on January 20, 1943 the Luftwaffe in a day time raid dropped a series of bombs striking Sandhurst Road School near London. Forty-one children between the ages of six and fourteen died along with six of their teachers. Death was more than just a probability. Fears and tears were inescapable.

Chapter Nine
Europe, 1943

Twenty-six years after the fall of the Tsar, the Soviet Union would resolve its differences with its minorities. Two years earlier, the Lithuanians, Latvians, Romanians, Volga Germans, Tatars, Caucasus Greeks, Crimeans, Balkars, Karachays, and Finns experienced the misery and death of forced relocation.

Following the invasion in 1939 the Red Army inflicted Sovietisation on eastern Poland. The government was Soviet. The systems were Bolshevik. The ideals were Communist. Anyone suspected of processing any thought contrary to Soviet practice found himself or herself on a cattle car heading to Siberia. That deportation number totalled 1,700,000. Stalin let Anders and more than 100,000 Poles leave the Soviet Union; but he still had several hundred thousand Poles living in his empire. The Poles were a minority in the USSR, and were destined to be treated like other minorities whom Stalin and Beria already sought to exterminate.

By the dawn of 1943, the assimilation of the Poles into Soviet society had progressed reasonably well. There were schools, hospitals and community centres. Polish people in the Soviet Union were not living the best of lives, but they were not being annihilated by Germans. The majority wanted to be good Soviet citizens realizing the alternatives were Germany, gulags, or death.

Therefore it came as a complete shock on January 6, 1943, when the staff of the Polish Embassy in Moscow was served with a notice to close its welfare & social agencies including the hospitals and orphanages.

Ten days later, the USSR advised the Polish Government in London that all Polish people living in the Soviet Union, and who previously lived in Poland or any country occupied by the USSR would be considered Soviet subjects.

In March, 1943 all Poles in the Soviet Union were compelled to accept Soviet citizenship.

Weeks later, Stalin and Beria reinstated the program of forced deportation for many minorities. 1,900,000 persons became refugees on wooden railcars bound for Siberia. Approximately forty percent did not survive the transit to the frozen gulags.

Stalin was losing grip on the reins of the Soviet Bear, and had to eliminate every possible enticement for discontent. Silencing the potentially dissatisfied was one remedy.

(I I)

The German war machine was tragically short of bodies. Hitler had two goals: expand the German Empire and murder the Jews. The first objectives did not have enough humans. The second objective illuminated humans. To any pragmatist the entire mission was doomed to fail.

In the course of planning the campaigns in North Africa and against the Soviet Union there had been opposing sentiments. However the words of dead people are seldom recorded by their assassins. In North Africa, the German dead and captured approached five hundred thousand. The Soviet invasion cost Germany at least two million lives. More soldiers were needed.

The Inferior Races were not the solution. Children in the military were considered. Getting women more involved was a prospect.

On January 13, 1943 Hitler issued his decree "on the full employment of men and women in the defence of the Reich." The aim was to get 500,000 more men into the armed forces. The Fuhrer added that all women between the ages of seventeen and forty-five were required to register for work in the Reich's factories.

Two weeks later the Reich's radio broadcast announced compulsory military registration of all men from age sixteen to sixty-five, and for all women between ages seventeen and forty-five for factory work.

Leon Pawlowski was weary of the German game. The contest was survival. The clothing factory, the munitions plant, farming production – all these kept him alive, even in most unfortunate circumstances. His friends he had seen shot. The stories of cattle cars and gassing sickened him. Why were Poland's friends doing nothing to stop the murders?

Then the Gauleiter, Arthur Greiser, arrived. The questions were many concerning production, alternative means, improvements, shipping, and staffing. Leon was beyond trembling at such inquisitions. The answers were candid. There was no rebuttal and twenty minutes later the Governor was gone.

The issue however had not passed without further comment. The Gauleiter's three associates continued. It was easy to discern right away that together they knew nothing about everything.

The eldest, the one with three stars on his uniform, informed Leon that he would have to return to the factory and supervise a unit of twenty women. The second associate reminded the others that food production was an essential service. The third German wondered if a woman could best supervise women, and then quickly countered his statement with the suggestion that his idea would never work.

In the course of the discussion, Leon was again informed of the Fuhrer's decree and reminded that Poznan was the Reichsgau Wartheland (Reich District Land of the Warta River). The assertion received equal emphasis. "Poznan is German territory, German land for Germans only."

Leon obliged immediately offering to obey their request. That left two of the Gauleiter's associates indecisive. Then the senior officer asked for the identity papers. He always had them secured in his buttoned front pocket. The review was quick. "Polish. He speaks German, but he is not German."

Leon received the papers, and placed them back in his jacket. Just as quickly, the senior guard saluted him. Leon acknowledged he was being challenged. "Heil Hitler." His mind choked on the words but his voice was brisk. Then they left.

Leon remained on the farm continuing to serve the Reich in the production of crops. For every German national holiday, a sumptuous meal with the finest produce was made available for the festivities. Records were produced, although not always accurate, assured the appreciation of the Reich. Leon avoided the use of Polish except on the very rare occasion. He did everything possible to ensure his job serving his overlords.

Factories, that had been abandoned less than a year before, were reopened. Uniforms were a priority setting many of the women to tears as they prepared the garments for their own children to wear in defence of the Fascist Empire.

(III)

General Anders stood before the multitude of Polish troops, absolutely elated with the news he was about to impart. Recognition meant everything in the world. No longer would his band of refugees be called the Polish Army in the West. That day they became 'Polish Second Corps'.

In June, 1943 at Anders's headquarters in Gaza, the cheers echoed across the desert. The celebration would not stop. Forget the reality that these troops were supposed to remain at attention. Everything has its place, and every explosion of joy causes a tidal wave of elation.

The enthusiasm was unlimited. The Polish General dispersed the troops but spent hours well into the night talking, laughing, and relating his dreams. Such events were wonderful opportunities to allow the weight on every soul to be eased, with the realisation there is international recognition for their cause, and with that, the hope for the assurance of post war Polish independence.

In Quastina, Palestine General Sikorski, on a visit from his London headquarters, delivered the same news receiving a similar celebratory response. Discussions with a select few, following his address, imparted his views concerning the officers found murdered in Katyn and the role of the Soviet Union. He concluded by mentioning how proud he was in the achievements of the Polish troops listing the battles in France, the Romania Bridgehead, the flight from the USSR, the conflict in North Africa and the continuing role in the Royal Air Force. They all shared his pride.

There were very few soldiers in Gaza and in Quastina who did not ask the question,

"When?" Unfortunately, both in Gaza and in Quastina, the answer could not be given.

General Sikorsky left the Middle East with a stopover planned for Gibraltar. Back in England he would use his influence to define the role of the Polish II Corps and thus be able to answer the question of his countrymen.

With the re-designation of the force as Polish II Corps, international military recognition prompted respectful interest. On July 22, 1943, US General Clark asked General Anders to have the Polish II Corps ready for the invasion of Italy. One month later, Prime Minister Churchill, in conjunction with the Quebec Conference, decided to have the Polish II Corps sent at the appropriate time to Italy.

(I V)

On July 4, 1943 at 11:07pm, a Consolidated B-24 Liberator aircraft ascended from Gibraltar Airport with eleven passengers and seven crewmen on board. Sixteen seconds later, the plane crashed. Polish General Wladyslaw Sikorski was dead. Only the pilot survived.

General Sikorski was returning to England with his daughter and his Chief of Staff on board. As President of the Polish Government in Exile, he had been visiting Polish troops in the Middle East to provide current news and assurance, doing what he considered necessary to secure and maintain morale.

Three months before the crash, two significant events occurred involving his relationship with the Soviet Union.

The Nazis invading the Ukraine had discovered more than twenty thousand corpses in the Katyn. General Anders, personally acquainted with Soviet treachery, blamed the Soviets. Stalin blamed the Gestapo. Because both the Americans and British required Stalin's military alliance, they accepted Stalin's explanation and attributed blame to the Nazis.

General Sikorsky felt that the Soviets were involved in the massacre as the USSR had seized these officers, held them captive and had exclusive opportunity to inflict the butchery. However, his government was housed in Britain where there was seemingly a growing love affair with Stalin's military influence.

With Stalin's program of nationalizing Poles living in his empire, Stalin withdrew his recognition of the Polish Government in Exile in London. It was Stalin's intention to govern Poland as a puppet state of the Soviet

Union. Accordingly he did not want Sikorsky telling him otherwise. Stalin didn't even acknowledge Sikorski as the leader of any government.

While on the tarmac, the Sikorski plane was parked near a Soviet aircraft used for its ambassador, Ivan Maisky. Maisky had met Sikorski two years earlier and had at that time finalized the arrangement for the Poles to be freed from the gulags to form the Polish Army in the Soviet Union. The consequences of that arrangement were an embarrassment to Ambassador Maisky: the Polish troops joined the British, never fought on the front line for USSR, and had just become Polish II Corps. Therefore Maisky may have felt he had the reason and the opportunity for retribution and may have had his staff sabotage the Sikorski aircraft.

Some of the dead were never recovered, which led to the wild assertion that Soviet personnel may have either shot or stolen the bodies.

The Soviets blamed the Germans for damaging the controls suggesting that Sikorski was blaming the Gestapo for the Katyn Massacre. This was never proven.

The Polish Navy brought the plane to England for the analysis. Opinions followed immediately that the mechanism was purposefully compromised.

The official report said the cause of the crash was the jamming of elevation apparatus on take-off. As to how the equipment became jammed, the report did not attribute negligence.

Subsequent inspections suggested other causes: a half empty mailbag may have jammed the stabilizer, or that the aircraft was overloaded, or that the take-off altitude was too low for the weight, or that the auto-pilot was already applied at take-off. None of these versions discussed liability.

Regardless of the cause, General Sikorski was no longer alive to lead the Polish Government or to provide influential support for the Polish troops. Poland lost its leader, and the one government official whom the British and American diplomats respected.

(V)

Lieutenant General Bernard Montgomery led 220,000 troops of the British 8th Army to a very significant victory at the Second Battle of El Alamein on November 25, 1942. In doing so, he repelled the counter offensive of Field General Kesselring.

The success of the British army occurred just fourteen months after its inception in September 1941. The British 8th Army in that time had become an organisation of seven international divisions and brigades, all sharing the same goals: to stop and defeat Germany. These included seven regiments from the British Commonwealth: British 70th Infantry Division, 1st Army Tank Brigade, British 7th Armoured Division, 2nd New Zealand Division, 4th Indian Infantry Division, South African 1st Infantry Division, and South African Infantry Division.

Following the initial designation of the army in 1941, several military formations joined the British 8th Army. These included: 1 Canadian Corps, British V Corps, British X Corps, British XIII Corps, British XXX Corps, Anders's Polish II Corps, and the Polish Carpathian Brigade.

The military prowess and reliability of the Eighth Army was perhaps questioned, though not vocally, in light of the number of commanders – five in total - who led the army in just twenty-six months.

Lieutenant General Allan Cunningham was the first Commander. Ten weeks later on November 26, 1941 he was replaced by Lieutenant General Neil Ritchie. Eight months later General Claude Auchinleck took over leadership. Then two months after that on August 13, 1942, Lieutenant General Bernard Montgomery assumed leadership of the British 8th Army.

It was Montgomery's leadership that led the offensive against the Germans in North Africa with the eventual result being the withdrawal of the Italians and Germans.

Sir Bernard Montgomery led the British Army in Operation Husky – the invasion of Sicily. Once the island was captured, The British 8th Army succeeded in Operation Baytown – landing in Calabria, and in Operation Slapstick – landing at Taranto in the 'heel' of the Italian peninsula.

From Taranto and Calabria, Montgomery pushed north, east of the Apennines along the Adriatic Coast toward Ancona. When the American 5th Army became embroiled in a prolonged campaign north of Naples, the British 8th Army moved several divisions west (leaving just one on the Adriatic) to assist the American cause in the capture of Rome.

Sir Bernard Montgomery was overly eager to engage Kesselring in conflict one more time. Victory at El Alamein was sweet. Taking Monte Cassino would be syrup. However, even the Lieutenant General's best laid

216

plans could not guarantee his participation in that venture. On December 23, 1943, Lieutenant General Sir Bernard Montgomery was transferred to England for Operation Overlord in which he was assigned the role of Field Marshall.

(VI)

Twenty-two months after the attack at Pearl Harbour, the United States 5th Army successfully completed Operation Avalanche in September, 1943. The one German army defending Salerno, Italy was unable to prevent the landing of the American 6th Corps with the support of Allied naval and air force battalions. Lieutenant General Mark Clark was at the apex of his career. The 47 year old Allied Commander had the confidence of Five-Star General Dwight Eisenhower, and did not let him down.

World War One experience as a commander had already displayed Clark's ability to lead an army: encouraging the force, directing the strategy, and accomplishing the goal.

The United States had committed itself to fighting the current war on two fronts. An invasion of Europe was definitely necessary. An attack, while the German armies were pinned down in the Soviet Union, was advantageous. Discussions with Churchill deferred that plan making the invasion of North Africa the priority.

Operation Torch was the American strategic plan to land its troops on African soil. Germany was already occupying these nations with the assistance of Italian forces and those of Vichy France. The French troops in particular were a question mark. France was an ally of the United States. On which side would the French troops from occupied southern France fight?

Lieutenant General Mark Clark was commissioned in October 1942 to secure the allegiance of the Commander in Chief of Vichy France. The covert operation was a success. The French General still in France was whisked out of the country for his safety. The French nations in North Africa would not oppose the Allies. The United States was ready to attack.

On November 8, 1942 operation Torch – the invasion of North Africa – began with landings at Casablanca, Medhia and Safi in French Morocco, and at Oran and Algiers in Algeria. The forces were secure, although the advance was slowed by the military strength of Rommel's Afrika Korps.

Lieutenant General Mark Clark was then assigned the task of establishing, organizing and directing the United States 5th Army. The army, with approximately a quarter million troops, was formally activated in January, 1943 with the initial task to secure Morocco and Algeria. However, the ultimate assignment was Italy. However, Italy would have to wait. The American force still had to deal with Field Marshall Rommel and the German military units. Decisive battles at Tobruk and El Alamein followed in the summer of 1942. On May 13, 1943, Germany and Italy conceded defeat in Africa.

The focus turned to Sicily. On July 9, 1943, the Allied troops stormed the island. Thirty-eight days later, Sicily belonged to the Allies.

In September 1943, Lieutenant General Clark invaded Salerno, Italy. His US 5th Army included the troops of American 6th Corps and British 10th Corps, with support from the American 82nd Airborne. The assault also included more than six hundred warships and landing craft. The immense task was completed with precision and sacrifice.

The Allies were once more in continental Europe.

(VII)

The glory of Rome had long since died. Attempts at reviving that esteem under the guise of the Holy Roman Empire had also become ashes in history's blaze. War upon war ravaged civility and destiny. For several centuries animosities confronted alliances – friends today and enemies tomorrow. The political whims of the Italian peninsula had changed like the winds off the Adriatic, from the Alps, east from Gibraltar, west from Crete, or flowing north from the Africa continent. Italy has in the last millennium toyed with communism and democracy. In the twentieth century monarchy established the rules for the political game allowing a brand of tyrannical fascism.

Prior to the First World War, Italy was a partner in the Triple Alliance with the Kaiser's Germany and the Austrian Empire. When that war started in August 1914, Italy did not immediately support Germany. In fact, it declared war on Austria. Then after it realized the strength of the French forces and their potential threat, Italy chose to support the Kaiser's Germany. However that did not last till the end of the war. When the French and English offered Italy the Austrian territories of Tyro and Trieste, Italy changed sides and joined the Allies.

The Treaty of Versailles did not grant Italy the further territorial possessions it sought in Africa. The dismay quickly became frustration with the Allied Nations. The Italian Army, reflecting this disgruntled opinion, invaded Ethiopia in 1935 with Fascist Mussolini leading the onslaught.

Following the German invasion of Poland in 1939, even though Mussolini and Hitler professed to be close friends, Italy again did not immediately support Fascist Germany. In fact Italy waited nine months before declaring war in June 1940.

Hitler counted on Italy, his Axis partner, to conquer North Africa and Malta, seize Crete and Corsica, invade Greece, and participate in attacks on the Balkans and Slavic countries as well as the Levant. The Italian forces did not meet Hitler's expectations, compelling the Wehrmacht to direct the battles, supply the troops, and support the provisional governments in these territories. German troops, that would otherwise have been involved in Operation Barbarossa, had to assist Italian forces.

Italy had become to Germany a weak sister, or as Field Marshal Rommel described, "A German colony."

The Allied countries too viewed Italy as villainous being the Nazi's partner, and as ineffectual in terms of its military strength and reliance.

Before the summer of 1943, all participants in the war were uncertain of Italy's impact and permanency of its allegiance. Would it again alter course? Would it continue to be the weak link?

The humiliation in North Africa resulting in surrender and then the captivity of a quarter million Italian and German troops on May 13, 1943, opened the door to the Allied invasion of Sicily, Mediterranean islands, and the Italian peninsula.

American bombers with almost no threat bombed Naples on May 31st. In the two weeks following, the Allies captured the islands of Pantelleria and Lampedusa, making another eleven thousand Italian troops prisoners.

On July 9, 1943, the Allies commenced Operation Husky – the invasion of Sicily. Palermo was captured two weeks later. Then following the bombing of Rome on July 19th, major political upheaval followed in the Italian capital.

Benito Mussolini was arrested on July 25, 1943. Fascism was dead in Rome. It had become obvious the Italian armies were not able to secure North Africa, lost Sicily, and could not prevent the bombing of Naples and Rome. Friendship with Hitler ended for many Italian politicians and citizens. Following Mussolini's arrest, King Victor Emmanuel III appointed Pietro Badoglio to form a democratic government.

Events in August confirmed the perilous state of Italian defences. On August 11th, Italy began to evacuate its troops from Sicily. Two days later, the Americans repeated the bombing of Rome, while the Royal Air Force bombed the German strongholds of Milan and Turin. Following the bombing of Rome, the Italian Prime Minister Badoglio declared Rome to be, "An open city", meaning the city had no active defence force.

On the last day in August, the Allies considered Italy to be a defeated foe. It had not denounced its relationship with Germany. Bombers were able to destroy urban infrastructures, communication systems, and affirm the threat of ongoing hostilities to which the Italian forces could not defend. Realizing the no-win situation, Italy entered into secret negotiations with the Allies. On September 2, 1943, in those discussions Italy pledged that the ports of Brindisi and Taranto would not be defended. The Italian government basically said: "Benvenuto. Rimanere unpo. Welcome. Stay a while."

The next day, the British 8th Army invaded Calabria, the area of the Italian peninsula closest to Sicily.

Five days later, on September 8, 1943, Italy surrendered to the Allies. The Italian Navy did not thereafter defend its ports; and in accord with the amnesty, the twenty-two ships yielded to Allied authorities at Malta. Meanwhile the King, Queen and Prime Minister prepared to leave Rome for security at Brindisi.

The next day, Allied forces were quick to react. The British 8th Army landed at Taranto, while the US 5th Army came ashore at Salerno.

On September 10, 1943, the Germans also reacted by occupying Rome. Once the capital was secured, General Kesselring declared all of Italy to be in German hands.

Adolf Hitler decreed that German controlled Italy was divided into three sectors: territory south of Rome, the central Apennine mountain region, and the Adriatic coast.

German participation aided Mussolini's escape from prison. The dictator was then established as the head of the Italian Socialist Republic with its capital in Venice.

A prompt Allied victory was not going to be achieved in Italy. The entire peninsula had within days become a stalemate. Although the Italians had surrendered, the Allies were confronted by the more superior German forces. This was not going to be trench warfare, but rather mountain warfare. The American 5th Army suffered forty thousand casualties while advancing only seventy miles. On September 18, 1943, preparing for a long confrontation, Kesselring established lines of defences across Italy. In conjunction with this strategy, he ordered the destruction of bridges and dams.

The island of Sardinia fell to the Allies on September 19th. This battle confirmed difficulty experienced by the Italian troops. Were they to fight with the Allies or for the Germans?

In Rome, the Germans acted as if they owned the country. Gold was absconded from the central bank. Jews were deported to concentration camps.

In the south, the Italian citizens favoured the liberating Allies. Troops from New Zealand, Canada, India and Poland were landing in territory secured by the British 8th Army. In Taranto, Brindisi, Bari, and north to Ancona, the sentiment of the Italian residents and troops was clearly with the British Armies.

In Naples, the citizens revolted against the occupying Germans. They had already been bombed by the Allies. Their country had surrendered. They did not need nor want another invading force to control every aspect of their lives. Three days after the citizens' revolt, Americans marched into Naples to secure the freedom of the city.

At that point, every principal port in southern Italy supported the Allies.

The Nazi hierarchy was infuriated with the manner in which the Italian troops changed sides. Germany vowed to treat Italy as if it had always been the enemy. On Cephalonia, an island off the coast of Greece, that Italy had seized and controlled on behalf of the Germans, the German forces seized, briefly detained, and then slaughtered five thousand Italian soldiers. Vengeance was theirs!

Kesselring after capturing more than three hundred Italian soldiers had them slaughtered in a prisoner of war camp.

Germany generally offered the Italians the option to fight for the Fatherland. Approximately ninety-four thousand soldiers accepted the offer. Those who refused to fight for Germany exceeded seven-hundred thousand. These were designated as being Military Internees and were sent to slave labour in Germany.

It was a tumultuous time for any Italian sergeant or corporal leading his band of soldiers anywhere in the country. Who could be trusted? In many cases, even the Allies continued to doubt the allegiance of their Italian hosts. Definitely, meeting a German brigade meant death. Like the Poles, the Italians had little impact on the outcome of the war in their own country. The major players were now involved – face-to-face – leaving every Italian citizen and soldier vulnerable.

(V I I I)

With the failure of Germany to seize Stalingrad, the Great Patriotic War began. Stalin vowed to never stop until Hitler and his gang were wiped off the face of the

224

earth. In the process, the Soviet Union pursued its expansion into Eastern Europe.

By the middle of 1943, about 3,700,000 German troops were trying to stall the tsunami of the Red Army. Every additional kilometre into Nazi occupied territory created an unstoppable wave of more than 6,000,000 Soviet troops. Every foot was a goal, every mile a dream, every village an object, and every dead German a celebration.

By August, 1943, the Germans could no longer control the Soviet counter offensive and retreated back to the Dnieper River approaching Minsk in Belarus. The citizens, those who were still alive, viewed the Red Army as liberators from the treachery that had been Nazi occupation. The German decision to retreat was a costly alternative as the Nazis surrendered the resources and crops they had valued so much. Hitler, angered by events, instructed his generals to hold the ground at the Dnieper and commence a counter offensive utilizing its 4th Panzer Army against the First Ukrainian Front.

By the end of the year, the Red Army was approaching the Soviet-Polish border. The Soviet troops who had so proudly defended the prolonged engagement at Stalingrad were sweeping south, taking control of the Baltic States. Gdansk, East Prussia and the Polish coast were next.

More than four hundred thousand German troops were killed in action on the Eastern front in 1943. There was no one left with military prowess to stop the Soviet onslaught. Children donned Wehrmacht uniforms to defend the dying Nazi realm. The destruction of Berlin itself was no longer a vague Soviet dream.

The death of a free Polish state was also fast becoming a cruel reality.

(IX)

The five-foot eight-inch baptized-Catholic stood at the rostrum exhilarated by the adulation and the results of the thirty-five divisions of his Waffen Schutzstaffel. His Armed Gestapo now rivalled the German army for size and influence. The forty-three year old Himmler had been appointed the Minister of the Interior, a far reaching position with no boundaries. If Germans believed in the Reich's creed of imperial and racial domination, Himmler was their prophet.

He had been raised Catholic, but those truths were anathema since his discovery of Hitler. It was said of him that he brought the Book of Job to life for more than six million Jews.

In earlier speeches Himmler used the term 'evacuation' referring to his plans for the inferior races. However, he really meant 'extermination'; and those listening to his enthusiastic diatribes consciously understood what Himmler meant by 'evacuation.'

I am talking about the evacuation of the

Jews, the extermination of the Jewish

people. It is one of those things that

is easily said. "The Jewish people is

being exterminated," every Party Member

will tell you, perfectly clear, it's

part of our plans, we're eliminating the

Jews, exterminating them.

There were no limits to his evil as he considered the annihilation of women and children.

We came to the question: what to do with

the women and children? I decided to

find a clear solution here as well. I

did not consider myself justified to

exterminate the men – that is, to kill

them or have them killed – and allow the

avengers of our sons and grandsons in

the form of their children to grow up.

The difficult decision had to be taken

to make this people disappear from the

earth.

The raucous celebration and applause was expected. The site was well chosen – Poznan in the heart of the Reich District Land of Warta River. The entire district since the German invasion had become home to approximately four hundred thousand Germans. Himmler was at home in Poznan.

His speech on October 4, 1943 roused the emotions of the many determined to eradicate the Jewish race. Himmler justified his decisions, their actions, and the end result. He then provided additional firm instructions: not on the techniques of murder, but on the necessity to hide the atrocities.

Whether the other races live in comfort

or perish of hunger interests me only
in so far as we need them as slaves for
our culture. We shall never be rough
or heartless where it is not necessary;
that is clear. We Germans, who are the
only people in the world who have a
decent attitude to animals, will also
adopt a decent attitude to these human
animals. I speak to you here with all
frankness of a very serious subject. We
shall now discuss it absolutely openly
among ourselves, nevertheless we shall
never speak of it in public: I mean the
evacuation of Jews, the extermination
of the Jewish race.

Thirteen days later, the process of closing Treblinka II Extermination Camp began. It was destroyed, buried, and replaced with a farmhouse. However even Himmler, who thought himself to be a god, could not hide his crimes.

(X)

Albert Kesselring was a proficient military officer, committed in every respect to defending the territorial gains of the German Nation. In the First World War Kesselring was a cadet with an artillery regiment, and later became a balloon observer. Even though he was significantly wounded during that first war he continued to serve the Kaiser in the front line.

With the start of the re-armament of Germany in 1933, Herr Kesselring was appointed to be the Head of Administration of the Luftwaffe, a position that directed the manufacture of the aircraft, and supervised the training of able pilots. Three years later, he was designated Luftwaffe's Chief of Staff.

A disagreement caused his demotion, even though he was still well respected for rebuilding the air force. When the Second World War started, Albert Kesselring was Commander of Luftwaffe Air Fleet 1, directing the aerial blitzkrieg of Poland.

Six months later he was the Commander of Air Fleet 2 during the invasion of France. He was reluctant to provide the Allied Forces any opportunity to leave Dunkirk. However his decision was counter reprimanded and the Allies were able to flee.

The war in North Africa introduced Kesselring to action in Tunisia where he directed the transfer of Axis troops, and in Libya where he was appointed Commander of the Axis Forces. Unfortunately, he was not initially able to hold Libya, and was forced to withdraw to French Tunisia. There he suffered another defeat in May 1943 before his major counter offensive.

On November 21, 1943 Albert Kesselring was appointed by Hermann Goering as Commander In-Chief South to defend the Italian peninsula.

Kesselring had for some time recognized there were critical issues concerning Italy. The Italians forces were considered to be unfit for prolonged campaigns, and were lacking in weapons, aircraft and tanks. It was well known and not appreciated that Italy, although an Axis partner, had no interest in the war in 1939 wishing instead that the battles be delayed for three years. The incidents of June 10, 1940 infuriated Herr Kesselring. On that day Norway surrendered to Germany alone, Nazi forces were approaching Paris, and realizing he had little to lose and perhaps much to gain Mussolini decided it was time to declare war on France and England. Ultimately expecting to gain from his declaration of war, Mussolini anticipated receiving territorial concessions from France. That self-righteous expectation from a partner was inexcusable.

To make matters even worse, Kesselring had no certainty as to which side the Italian troops or citizens favoured. Mussolini had been arrested on July 25, 1943, and was freed from prison by a rebel mob seven weeks later. Whose side was Mussolini on? Were the Italian troops dependable? The fears for Albert Kesselring and his German 10th Army were very real.

In the course of the conflict, Kesselring even ordered the murder of Italian prisoners who were caught supporting the Allies. There was no mercy for anyone who was not willing to declare his allegiance to the Axis Pact.

The 10th Army itself was not as strong in manpower as he would have preferred. The Wehrmacht had lost countless troops in the invasion of the Soviet Union, and now troops, some even young teenagers, had to be employed to stop the attacking Soviet armies. Failures in North Africa and the commitment to the occupation of the Balkans and Slavic nations also cost Germany much needed manpower. Regardless, Kesselring was most adept at maximizing skills to defend the Reich.

Bridges crossing the many Italian rivers were destroyed to thwart the American 5th Army and British 8th Army.

The Gustav Line was established in the Liri Valley. Kesselring added the Winter Line, and then the Barbara Line that followed the Trigno River. The Adolph Hitler Line and Caesar Line were formed to stop access towards Rome. He also added the Gothic Line across Italy from Pisa to Rimini. Taking into consideration all factors, Albert Kesselring was well prepared to defend the eventual invasion of Italy.

(XI)

For twenty-four days from October 18 to November 11, 1943 the foreign ministers of the United States, Soviet Union, Great Britain and China met at the Kremlin. This was the third of a series of meetings in Moscow to discuss plans for post-war Europe. Iosif Stalin and M. Litvinov, Deputy of the Peoples Commissars for Foreign Affairs, also attended the conference.

The mutual agreements included the establishment of the European Advisory Committee. Two communiqués were issued in accord with the EAC assuring the independence of Austria, and democracy in Italy. These were small concessions compared to Stalin's ultimate interest in Europe. Plus, assuring the independence of Austria assured the Soviet Union that Germany would lose its pawn. Disputes with Austria in 1914 forced Russia into the first war, and Austria acquiescence with Germany compelled the Soviets to react in September

1939. Italy, was a country prone to kings and dictators. There was nothing said at the conference that could ensure its decision to opt for democracy.

In the second week of the conference, a declaration was signed regarding the Nazi wartime atrocities with the desire to have the villains held accountable.

... evidence of atrocities, massacres and

cold-blooded mass executions which are

being perpetrated by Hitlerite forces in

many of the countries they have overrun

and from which they are now being steadily

expelled ... those who committed these crimes

be judged on the spot by the peoples whom

they have outraged.

The concept for the Nuremberg Trials was thus approved. The document added that criminal offenses involving Germans in various jurisdictions would be punished by a court established by the Allies. Steps were actually being taken to hold the mass executioners responsible and to punish them for these outrageous crimes against humanity.

However, the declaration only mentioned the Nazis as being responsible for the mass murders, and never acknowledged the approximately two million that died in Soviet gulags or who were murdered in the forests, deserted areas or public squares of those countries the Red Army occupied.

That declaration affirmed that the atrocities were taking place not just in Poland but in all nations occupied by the Wehrmacht. Thus when the Red Army declared its surprise upon discovering Auschwitz, it was a lie!

The further tragedy is this: the signatures of Franklin Roosevelt and Winston Churchill appear on the document.

(XII)

The woman screamed in pain. Repeatedly she was violated while her husband, with his hands bound behind his back was forced to watch. The guards had their way with her, as they had done with other women. Always the same, the brutality, and if the husband ever chose to say a word he was shot. The Commandant did not deter the guards; in fact he even encouraged the debauchery.

Prisoners too were compelled to watch the depravity, pitying the woman in their hearts, while begging inside for the violation to stop. When one guard finished himself inside the devastated woman the next jumped aboard. Repeatedly they raped her, while their cohorts cheered and derided the devastation. Finally they ended that punishment. The crime was being a Polish woman. As she lay on the stone courtyard, one guard cut her hair. She did not have the strength to object. The tears were incessant. Another grabbing a bucket of water threw it on her, exclaiming that it was her baptism. The delirious laughter accosted the hearts of those forced to watch. They could not close their eyes, unless they risked being shot.

The husband repeatedly whimpered straining within the rope around his chest. His whispered pleas meant nothing to the oppressors. If they heard them, the abuse would only be worse, not for him, because he no longer cared for himself, but for his wife.

She lay there in the winter cold: naked, defiled, frozen, almost lifeless. Her whimpers meant nothing. The guards walked away, leaving just the two who were restraining the devastated husband.

Amon Goethe had watched from a distance with his right hand on his luger. As the satisfied guards left, he approached the woman. His jeer was Satan's. He dared not touch the tragic victim's torn dress. Goethe just kicked it towards her. She would have clutched it, but her broken wrist would not allow such motion.

Following the Commandant's grin toward the two guards, the husband was pushed to the ground. They stood over him doing the Commandant's will. Then the two guards simultaneously pressed the points of their revolvers to the husband's head. Within a second he was dead. The woman raped of her identity screamed in shock until bullets silenced her torment.

The prisoners did not react. If they did, the same fate would be theirs. However the prisoners all realized how sadistic the Nazi killing machine had become. Only one of the revolvers was loaded, so that each guard pulling the trigger could always think the other one was responsible for the deaths.

Those memories would not leave Bernard's mind. Forgetting Plaszow Concentration had been easy at first. Just being free was a blessing. However, as he waited at El Khassa camp, fully trained, for his first combat duty, moments became, hours, then days, and weeks, and never ending. He did not have to recall any details to know why he hated the Nazis so much. But not being

234

able to erase such deplorable memories affirmed the brutality to the mind. Forgetting was a joy, but Bernard could not forget. Time only made some recollections worse. How would he react when confronting his first German soldier? Bernard just wanted the opportunity to make that choice.

In spite of any desire for any retribution, he prayed daily for that woman, her husband, and every man, woman and child slaughtered by the invading Hun. Some called them 'Gerries'. Any such name clearly gave them too much respect. Why would anyone ever give them such deference?

Those who helped him – these too he prayed for, not just to say thank you but also for their safety during the continuing Nazi blitz of oppression.

Then there was his family. Those prayers never stopped, mingled always with questions that were never answered.

The moments before five o'clock every morning were his time. The quiet minutes with the morning sunrise were a silent embrace of the Moslem friends in El Khassa that befriended the thousands of Polish troops. Reputation meant so much to these people, stories of valour and defence. The Carpathian Brigade stopping Rommel's offensive was now more than folk lore. As much as the people were thankful, Bernard and many others were equally so for their care and hospitality.

Accommodation was mixed: some in three storey buildings, others in rows of barracks, and there were those still preferring tents. Food, like that in Quastina, was not overly plentiful, but nourishing. Respect meant security and that was a dimension whose importance could never be measured.

The oases with the tall palm trees, the lone hills jumping out of desert sands, and the one pyramid were all cultural icons of an era blessed with centuries of dreams and success. Viewing that pyramid, the first time he saw it, drew his recollection to the Jews being forced into Plaszow Concentration Camp, and how the Star of David was fixed within a triangle was patched on their clothes. Triangles were a strange symbol; meaning death to Jews, glory to Egypt, and the Trinity to Christians.

The move to El Khassa, just six kilometres south of Cairo, from Quastina seemed at the time so providential. It spawned so much hope that immediately the force would be engaged in battle. Delays had not been good, causing many to become frustrated, anxious, and unusually loud.

Among the forty-five thousand troops, Bernard had only four close friends. Others would confide at times, but in times of war it is best to, "Watch yourself."

Franciszek was three years older than Bernard. His family fled their home in Krakow on the second day of the war, escaping into the mountains. From there they made it to Romania. Franciszek knew his father died. He didn't know by whom. "Russians, Germans, they're all from hell!" Like Bernard he had no hope or even dwelt on ever seeing his family again.

Hendryk was abrasive. Perhaps he had the right to be as he knew more than the rest. He was older than the others, maybe ten years more than Bernard. His experience meant so much too many. He had been in business, worked at a law firm although he himself was not a lawyer. Having escaped the purge on the intelligentsia, Hendryk felt very fortunate to be alive, yet vengeful against the Germans for the livelihood he lost.

Piotr was on the verge of entering the seminary when the war started. That never happened, as the religious congregation fled once the seminary grounds were bombed. He was a kind and compassionate person, the kind of person you could always trust.

Eduard was the cold and factual one. There were only two sides to every issue: the very right and the very wrong. "Every German can go to hell!"

The Polish II Corps totalled 45,000 troops, and the 3rd Carpathian Rifle Division comprised 13,200 of these. Pride was becoming the most essential quality to survive and both army affiliations gave soldiers like Bernard the opportunity to be proud. He once explained to Eduard that they were the only army without a home to go to, and so they really didn't have a choice but to fight. This was their home, and pride surrounded the welcome mat.

There were times for being pensive and times for serious thought. Being pensive gave Bernard the time to justify any deep thought. As he walked amid the buildings toward the wooden barracks he allowed himself to ponder life's blessings. He struggled with the process, but that didn't take long, ending with the light-hearted thought that perhaps it was good to be slightly schizophrenic as it justified recalling the ugly so vividly while being able to conjecture the best. Bernard was at last satisfied after the morning walk. Tomorrow would be the big event – November 14, 1943 – when General Anders would review the troops – all forty-five thousand

– and the Polish flag would for the last time be lowered at Camp El Khassa.

Al Quassasin, one hundred kilometres north-east of Cairo, awaited them.

(XIII)

Tehran was the site for the first Conference involving the leaders of the three major Allied Powers. For the four days from November 28 to December 1, 1943, Iosif Stalin had every reason to feel at home as his forces were already stationed in Iran and controlled most of Eastern Europe.

Prime Minister Winston Church had met with General Secretary Stalin on several occasions before this conference. They were acquainted with the interests and styles of each other.

President Roosevelt was the new element in the triumvirate. The United States did not enter the war to stop the Nazi menace controlling Europe or in response to the invasion of the Soviet Union. Was it wise to moor all of your major battleships and naval force in one island harbour? Though Stalin was silent on the issue it is appreciated that the Soviet Union's naval strategy was to spread the arsenal wide removing the possibility of one fell swoop destroying the nation's naval might. United States entered the North Africa conflict and had difficulties with decisive victories. Ultimately, troops landed in Italy only to be stonewalled by the German forces before even reaching Rome.

The Soviet Union in contrast stalled the full force of the German war machine, and was rebuffing them in a display of power throughout all of northern, eastern and south-eastern Europe. The German Wehrmacht was no match for Soviet Union's might, strategy, and desire. Eradicating Germany completely would be a pleasant delight.

Thus when they met at Tehran, Stalin had his clear agenda. He knew the negotiating weaknesses of Britain and America. They were not in any position to make any demands as they had yet to set one foot in the core of Europe.

Stalin was well aware that the USSR bore the brunt of the German Armies since June 1941, actually since May 1940 when the British left the continent at Dunkirk. Stalin did not want to go it alone against Germany. But at the same time, the Americans and British did not want to allow the Soviet Union to be the only Allied troops on European soil. There was no suggestion Germany could quickly be brought to its knees in the Italian peninsula. They had to invade Europe. Stalin wanted them to invade Europe. Stalin demanded that Churchill and Roosevelt affirm that commitment. They responded accordingly assuring Stalin of their joint efforts in Operation Overlord.

Stalin then went one step further in his demands. He knew the Americans and British would not allow Germany to become destitute and impoverished prompting yet another war.

Stalin was also keenly aware of the industrial complex within Germany. Therefore he seized the opportunity to propose splitting Germany into Allied zones of occupation following the war. There was no major objection.

Iosif Stalin then made his only promise. It wasn't much of a promise as he was going to do it anyway. As soon as the Allies defeated Germany, the USSR would declare war on Japan. It is difficult to comprehend how naive the other participants were on this issue. The USSR had been at war with Japan before 1939. Then on September 16, 1939, the day before it invaded Poland, the Soviet Union achieved a peace pact with Japan solely to allow Soviet forces to concentrate on Eastern Europe. There was no real cultural appreciation between Japan and Soviet Union before the Tehran Conference. Obviously after the Soviets swept Europe it would turn its attention to the warring nation in the Far East.

Stalin then added that if the Soviet Union declared war on Japan, then it was to receive a portion of the Sakhalin Peninsula and two ports on the Liaodong Peninsula. It is questionable as to whether Britain and the United States ever understood the request. Forces of the United States and Britain had entered Russia in the 1920's via the Far East to confront the Bolsheviks. Perhaps there was a feeling that this area was not worth the argument.

With respect to Poland, Stalin was forceful in his demand that the Soviet Union's western border with Poland be established at the Curzon Line, first suggested by the British Foreign Secretary in 1920. In return the USSR would allow, if the Politburo consented, Poland to move its border with Germany west to the Oder River.

Stalin wasn't finished with just Germany and Poland. He expected Lithuania, Estonia and Latvia to be incorporated into the Soviet Union pledging that this would only be accomplished following a plebiscite in each Soviet occupied nation.

President Roosevelt was satisfied that both Stalin and Churchill agreed to the concept of the United Nations, as an international organisation to ensure peace. This was the first item on his wish list.

Stalin made the greater requests and achieved the most concessions. He returned to the Kremlin very satisfied with the assurance that the Soviet Union would control Eastern Europe.

(X I V)

The parade of trucks was like no other he had ever seen before. Sure they had transferred from Homs, to Quastina, to Al Khassa; but though there were many trips in the past, there were always only a few trucks at a time. Now more than thirteen-thousand were being mobilized to Egypt's Port Said. Would this be the last time they would ever see Egypt, or taste Egyptian sand in their biscuits, or relish the unique tastes and spices? Actually, very few even thought of that. The excitement was intense. Finally, they would see action!

The journey from Al Quassasin to Port Said took the eager troops into Ismailia where more troops climbed on board for the last stage to the Mediterranean port.

No one thought about Christmas, four days before the event. December 21, 1943 was a memorable day for Polish II Corps, and even more so for the 3rd Carpathian Rifle Division and the Independent Infantry Commando Group. These two forces would be the first of the Polish troops to land in Italy. Participating in the war, holding your weapon, coming face to face with the enemy, resurrecting the pride of Poland – all this is why they were there.

The more than seventeen thousand troops boarded the six vessels as quickly as possible. With changing tides and the winter winds from the north-west, leaving port before noon was essential. The artillery was already loaded when the troops arrived. The commanders and senior staff accepted no preferential treatment on board. They were a team, one force for one country.

The ships docked at Taranto in southern Italy the next day. Camp was established near the Adriatic north of Brindisi. The site was a series of tents, many tents going on for what seemed like miles.

It didn't take long before shock hit. Two days after their arrival, the news spread quickly: The General of the British 8th Army, Bernard Montgomery, was being transferred. His re-assignment was disappointing to many Polish troops because the Polish II Corps was fighting as part of the British 8th Army, and it was also well appreciated that Montgomery and Anders were almost like brothers. Now, Montgomery was headed to England, and Anders was still in Egypt. The Poles had basically lost a close relative before even the first volley.

Other news spread consternation in the camp. That the Polish force was being considered as less than proficient was an opinion hard to quell. Bernard too heard the scenarios wondering if there was truth in the suggestions. Montgomery's British 8th Army had been fully engaged in combat in Italy since the first week of September. When he called upon his forces to assist the Allied cause, the 8th Indian Division, the 78th British Infantry, the 38th Irish Brigade, the Canadian 1st Infantry, and 2nd New Zealand Division, and the British 5th Division had all been called to action. The reality that the Polish II Corps was nowhere near first choice tempted some minds to question their purpose, the strategy, and the possible results. Still others considered the delay in seeing their first action to be a blessing. Too many grey vans were returning south to the ports carrying the bodies of dead troops.

On December 29th the Independent Commando Company participated in the first Polish action as a diversionary raid in the vicinity where the Garigliano River ran into the Adriatic Sea. Immediately following that, troops of the 3rd Carpathian Rifle Division were engaged to back up other Allied forces belonging to the British 8th Army.

Action was a blessing.

Chapter Ten
Capturing the Hill, 1944

The determined soldier of the 3 Dywizja Strzelcow Karpackich trudged through the camp with mud thoroughly caked to his boots. His uniform, too, was no stranger to the inclement sediment. The mess hall, though appearing so near, seemed perpetually far away. Fatigue was not his issue, or at least he would never let anyone know. The rains started three days before, and did not stop. There was no thunder, just ominous dark clouds that refused to move.

Drops fell from the brim of his helmet onto his shoulders, around his neck and down inside his shirt. Not needing glasses was perhaps the only blessing. His soaked gear no longer kept him warm, but he was no worse off than anyone else. His pants were heavy, drenched with the inescapable mire, held up by a course leather belt tightened to the extreme. His backpack he left in his tent with his sleeping bag. Like everything they were completely soaked. Rivulets from the hill and mounds became gullies first and then streams. Latrines were swimming pools. Supplies remained on the carts stuck in the winter rains.

The first week in Italy for the Polish Corps seemed to last forever: waiting to be actively involved, to fulfil their commitment, and to avenge their plight. Vengeance was a cherished invitation. Being in Puglia brought them nearer to the front, but they were still south of the Sangro River. The British Eighth Army had already crossed the river more than five weeks before heading north through the eastern flank of the Gustav Line toward Ancona. That holding pattern continued for the Poles on the streaming hillside and muddy farmland. The existing order was simple, "Be Prepared." They knew who the enemy was. "Just tell us: when and where."

Bernard eventually made it to the mess hall, having taken the upper expanse farthest away from the riverbank. Even so that route had its own issues. The path, made clear on the first day, had become a series of potholes and tire tracks, providing the inevitable slippery, mushy, sinking feeling.

The hall was an abandoned old wooden barn. The slats, once bluish-Gray, were colourless and rotten with age. The building's one saving grace was that the walls appeared to have been reinforced about twenty years before. The barn typified Puglia. Bernard conjectured, "Too many empty farms. Was it the first war? Or were they forced to join the Fascists?"

The barn floor had already been swept clean, a necessity six times each day. Mud coated the floorboards the instant troops arrived for their rations. Even without the muck, the dirt would have been extensive. So often the broom was replaced by whisks made of straw, or by carved slats scraping across the porous planks. Hay still filled the attic space along the north and south sides providing a temporary solution to leaking rain. Regarding the roof itself, there were many prayers hoping it would survive. Electricity was provided by two generators, one in a very makeshift condition. The

Germans had completed their scorched-earth policy on a number of villages, especially those within ten kilometres of the Gustav Line. Four rows of tables ran the length of the barn being able to accommodate about five hundred at a time. There were at least six other barns available to Allied troops from appreciative Italian residents.

Bernard was at the far end of the hall stirring the pot, when their commander entered. All stood immediately.

Commander Bronislaw Duch had their earnest respect. His 3rd Carpathian Rifle Division was the first of the Polish forces to leave Egypt. Anders trusted him that much. The commander always had words of reassurance and hope, never an impossible promise, but lots of encouragement, all centred on the basic aspirations of the many Poles as individuals and as a group. Often he had imparted the logic of being prepared, noting that it could be only a matter of days before the division received orders to engage the enemy. Commander Duch admitted he was not certain who would provide such orders with Anders still in Egypt. Perhaps it could be General Oliver Leece, Commander of the British Eighth Army; but he had met General Leece only once. That meeting had been courteous with many accolades offered to the Polish force. Success at Tobruk still echoed the initial comments of the Australian troops following that battle. But, that was years ago. The enemy, although the same with even the same commander, was different. This time the Polish II Corps was fighting in Europe against a German force that stood between them and their homeland. Leece clearly understood the Polish need for retribution.

General Duch was a master at mobilizing the aspirations of the thirteen thousand troops in that massive encampment. He was well aware that regardless of how much each person may have been committed to the cause of Poland, he was equally concerned about his family. The General could not avoid the reality that there were many under his command who had personally witnessed the butchering or starvation of their dear ones; and that these were wholly committed to the cause of German annihilation. The commander remained always cognizant that his division was composed of the prior Polish Brigade from North Africa, many who were released from Soviet gulags, others who came from the Romanian Bridgehead, and those who later escaped occupied Poland. Regardless of any other factor, there was one common denominator: they all despised the Germans and vowed revenge. Bronislaw Duch was able to marshal this sentiment to maximize the commitment of the 3rd Carpathian Rifle Division.

The division was composed of two infantry brigades, the 12th Uhlan Podolski Lancers a reconnaissance regiment, three field artillery regiments, an anti-tank force, and one anti-aircraft regiment. Each had its own sector within the sprawling camp, spreading themselves over the terrain of at least twenty farm sites.

Most of the force was stationed to the south side of the hills avoiding any German aerial surveillance. Anti-aircraft artillery was prepared for any such incursions. Abandoned homes and villages provided residence for some. Hospital units were available and prepared in the southern extremity beyond the camp. The women too had their own base camp. They were prepared and equipped to complete repairs and maintenance. Tents were covered with designs resembling cultivated land patterns. In spite of all the precautions, the Germans were not going to engage the Polish force south of the Sangro River. The Wehrmacht was farther north thwarting the advance of the British Army.

Concerned expressions ended at every mealtime. There was always light banter, much off colour humour, and laughter to relieve any tension. Faces usually remained caked in mud even during the meal. So thick was the mire that the rains could not wash it away. Wine was a luxury, but vino was limited to only once every third day.

Lunch was the prime opportunity to discuss whatever wounded minds could conjecture. Bernard's group of Hendryk, Eduard, Piotr and Franciszek had grown to include the pensive Franck, Jerzy who vowed to personally kill every German, Wiktor a wild youth, and Dawid a stoic individual. Such groups never included soldiers all thinking and believing the same. This was war.

Sex was perpetually the number one topic. Several girls in the villages had apparently become the latest conquests for several soldiers. The men proclaimed their exploits as if they were the culmination of their sole desires. Such rationale was inevitable under the circumstances. Bernard, though, remained politely quiet. The images of the couple being violated and then murdered at Plaszow still violated his senses. Others may have also witnessed such horror, but such recollections they never openly discussed. Perhaps adventures in the villages were their way of disposing of the past.

Franck was the most serious of their group, so often others wondered, "How does he know?" Regardless, there was a flow of information into the camp. There were the informed sources through the commander's office. Then there were the stories from the villages. Word from the front was always passed to the support troops waiting in the rear. Many of the stories, so many wished were untrue. Differentiating between truth and rumours had become a game of skill. The progress of the Red Army horrified the Polish troops. There was no one in camp who did not express dismay. Equally so, suggestions about the Tehran Conference, first heard while they were still in Egypt, continued to be worrisome, invoking anger in many, and in the others betrayal. There was no love for Roosevelt. That was a definite. Any appreciation for Churchill, particularly his inability to stand up to Stalin, waned. By January 2, 1944 many even questioned the relationship of the Polish force to the Allies. But to have any impact, the 3rd Carpathian Rifle Division still had to fight under the auspices and direction of the British Eighth Army.

(II)

Albert Kesselring stood outside the southern wall of the Benedictine Abbey from where he could look down to the south-east upon the town. His mid morning walk provided the usual undisturbed moments when he could feel self-assured. Everything was quiet in the valley. His troops had absolute control of the town.

The terraced gardens, outside the abbey wall, were still void of growth in late January. He had expected more. If the plants were not yet sprouting in late January, could a second crop ever be certain? Remembering his university days at Padua, he was intrigued by the climate of the Italian peninsula. Being so, he expected warmer temperatures and some sign of vegetation to produce the crops for his troops. He would speak to the monks. They would have the answers.

The fir trees were varied in their height, their breadth, and hues of green. To the General they were the ultimate plant: standing so tall and so in control of their destiny. Looking to his left, he knew that somewhere in the distance beyond that hill his troops were anxious for battle. Yet, at the same time he was certain there were many among them who had no interest in further conflict.

Turning back to his right, he expected the courier to arrive any moment with the report. "Where were the Allies?" It was the most obvious question for the Commander In-Chief for the conflict in Italy. He was well aware that the US Army had landed in Salerno more than three months before. Kesselring was equally cognizant of the fierce and prolonged defence established by his valiant army.

War in Italy was so different from the battles in North Africa. In place of sand storms, he encountered persistent rain. The desert plains were replaced by mountain ranges and broad valleys. The residents of the towns and villages in North Africa clearly identified their allegiance. Here, the Italians could not be trusted.

The Fuhrer supported his every decision on defence lines and required troops. Kesselring would never admit his surprise, but he was somewhat stunned when two divisions were moved from Operation Barbarossa to defend Europe's under-belly. More than one hundred and twenty thousand troops were at his disposal to secure the Gustav Line: defined by the Gariliano, Liri, Rapido, and Sangro Rivers and their valleys. His Tenth

Army included: the 71st Infantry Division, the 94th Infantry Division, the 98th Infantry Division, the 162nd Infantry Division, 278th Infantry Division, the 5th Mountain Division, the 51st Mountain Corps, the 26th Panzer Division, the 29th Panzer Division, the XIV Panzer Corps, the 66th Panzer Corps, the 15th Panzer Grenadier Division, the 90th Panzer Grenadier Division, and the 2nd Parachute Regiment and the 1st Parachute Division. This last group would later be the Polish nemesis.

Kesselring had no time to be patient, and no patience for anyone who didn't value his time. Just because there was no active gunfire, that didn't mean there were no tasks to be accomplished.

"Where are the Americans?" The General was becoming more concerned. He had expected their attack in early December, thinking that would have been their appropriate time being the second anniversary of Japan's invitation to the Americans.

Kesselring contemplated the prospect that perhaps the Americans were waiting for the Tenth Army to make the first move and surrender their advantage. "That will never happen!" Kesselring vowed.

Heinrich von Vietinghoff arrived, late as expected. Kesselring didn't want to hear the word "Overcast"; but that was the clear message. The conversation continued without any apology for the lack of specifics, clearly frustrating Kesselring. Von Vietinghoff knew enough to excuse himself as quickly as possible.

Information from yesterday's meeting regarding the conflict on the Adriatic was still bothersome. "Could we entice the British into a trap?" Kesselring's best plans followed discussions with himself. "Why can't we hold them?"

"Australians?" Someone had proposed. The General had had enough of them in Africa. Then someone else suggested; "They're Kiwis." Kesselring quickly translated the term identifying the New Zealand force. He then ventured that if the British Army was engaging the assistance of one Commonwealth nation, then there would also be others. He had already been told of the Canadian and Indian Corps.

The General had no choice regarding the conflict on the Adriatic Coast. If the German Army did not remain actively engaged there, the Allies might send their reserves west to join the Americans. That, he didn't want.

General von Vietinghoff reappeared moments later carrying another document. His summary told Kesselring what he expected to hear, that the troops on all of the surrounding hills and in the valleys and in the town itself were all ready and prepared to confront the enemy. The messenger had no answer to Kesselring's repeated question regarding the Americans. It had become a series of conjectures exploring possibilities and probabilities. "Send a battalion from the town. Explore Venafro and Marzanello." The instructions were radioed immediately.

General Kesselring continued his walk westward till he got to a point where he could view the Liri Valley. To the far end the river flowed. Beyond the valley the Aurunci Mountains rose forcing any American interested in Rome into the open firing range in the valley. Those mountains he had been repeatedly told were impassable. Kesselring had no reason to believe otherwise.

Once inside the Abbey the General ascended the stairway to his favourite vantage point: looking north to Monte Cairo. The limestone God-created structure rose more than a mile (1,669 meters) above the Liri Valley to its west. That was more than 3,500 feet (1,100 meters) higher than Abbey. Superlatives were the immediate reaction every time he viewed the massive hill. He imagined God handing the German nation His Aryan Commandments on that very hill top. The General would not himself ascend the precipice as he was never one to tangle with ice and snow. Yet, it was the melting snow, God's gift as it were, from that mountain that gave life to the valleys. On that very issue, Albert Kesselring was very proud of his ability to have situated the various camps and barracks in such key positions to take advantage of the terrain, the climate, and the soil. Although he felt the need for crops in his immediate area, there was sufficient for the German forces already stationed.

In the five kilometres between the Abbey and Monte Cairo there were numbered hills all fortified with troops, artillery, anti-tank, and anti-aircraft weapons. Hill 593, only two kilometres from the Abbey, was guarded by the Third Battalion of the German 2nd Parachute Regiment. The Snakeshead with Phantom Ridge, steep hills beyond the Abbey, were also key defence positions. Attacks on those hills were the most probable if the Allies wished to ultimately seize the Abbey. But that was never going to happen as long as the King of the Hill ruled the valley.

The monks and abbots, the priors and friars: they all looked worried in spite of many reassurances. Kesselring could have stayed within the confines of the Abbey itself but chose not to do so. Appearances counted. He wanted to be seen as one of the many, to be one in unison with the troops, not to be privileged, nor to be seen as one thinking himself as overly important.

He already had the respect of his many divisions, corps, and battalions. He didn't have to lord it over them. There were some troops staying inside the Abbey. Basically they were there to provide reassurance, support, and affirm the perception that the German Tenth Army was in Italy to protect the interests of the Italian population. When Lieutenant Colonel Schlegel and Captain Becker removed the sacred scrolls, writings, paintings, and artefacts from the Abbey in October 1943, expressions of gratitude were extended not only from the Benedictine Monks but from the Vatican as well.

Vowing to protect the interests of the inhabitants had become just verbiage. Kesselring had been fully involved in pledging one thing and doing another. Villagers had been moved prior to the destruction of dams. Farms became flooded. Men were forced into battalions supporting his army. Women were left alone, victims of assault and rape. In any age when women were rarely employed outside the home, opportunities and alternatives became drastically limited to war-widowed women. Young boys, too, as young as fourteen, were being forced into Fascist battalions. Then there was the produce, the poultry, and the cattle. So much was seized to feed the occupying army.

There were no doubts about the last insult to the civilian population. Kesselring knew it had to happen and took no time to complete the task. Bridges were destroyed. Then dredging equipment widened and deepened the rivers. Where the task of such machinery was prevented, bombs completed the job. Roads were destroyed by the weight of heavy machinery and the movement of so many troops. By the time the Germans were in place, the roads had become trenches and potholes of disintegrating, flaking clay. Ditches became deeper than vehicles. Rains perpetuated the destruction eroding the remaining dirt into the flooded fields. Seeing no benefit to any repairs, the roads were abandoned in that pathetic state. For the citizens, there was no life outside the home. Produce could not be taken to market. In any event there was no produce. There was no market. If anyone grew food, or had poultry, perhaps a lamb or a goat; these were hidden from the invaders. Children could not go to school as most schoolteachers were forced to wear German uniforms. Even if there were teachers, the schools themselves lacked utilities. Life in Italy ground to a dismal halt.

Inside the chapel, Kesselring dutifully received communion.

(III)

On Thursday, the Sixth January, the rain finally stopped. Cheers throughout the camp would have revealed their location if the Germans at that point even cared. The conflict on the Adriatic Coast had moved farther north into an all out engagement.

The 1st Polish Brigade was out in force immediately hanging clotheslines and drying personal gear. Dislodging the carts became prime importance. It took days in some cases even with the help of mules. Others in the 3rd Carpathian Rifle Division busied themselves scraping the muck, and cleaning the campsites. Latrines were moved to ground away from the flooding river. The mess hall was mopped repeatedly. The mechanics guarding the trucks and fuel tanks finally got a break too. The all night sentry protection of the vital armaments had been hell in the pouring rain. Naked souls ran into the river to wash off the mud. There was no shampoo. The cold flowing water accomplished the task.

Smiles returned and frowns disappeared. "Enjoy it," Commander Duch implored, for they all knew the rains would return.

The need to feed so many troops would eventually require more supplies. The responsibility was not just to provide for today, or next week, but to consider and acquire for the future. The request was extended to each battalion and division to again explore the villages, farms, and all surroundings for any available produce, poultry products, or meat. Bernard and Franck volunteered.

For miles on the rough county roads, there was nothing – no crops and no sign of life. After driving fifteen kilometres south, they took an even more forsaken laneway west into a valley between rolling hills. The comments of the five backseat drivers reflected fears of being stuck in a remote stretch away from any civilisation. There was also one other issue they had all contemplated – language. The inhabitants had never talked much and did not always have answers to the important questions. Information, as helpful as it may have seemed, was not always reliable. There was also the issue of the Pugliese dialect. Almost none of the Poles could understand it. Bernard too encountered difficulty comprehending the vocabulary in spite of what his former friend, Guglio, had tried to teach him.

It was at least thirty kilometres before they passed the first farmhouse with any sign of life. There had been two other farms before this where the autumn crops had not been picked. Outside this particular farmhouse, a woman's garments hung on the clothesline. There were no men's clothes and no children's attire, a whiff of dark smoke blew from the chimney. That was promising.

Knocks at the door triggered no reply. They got louder but the silence remained. Bernard tried a few words in Italian stressing "Alleati." Assurances that they were not "Nazista" encouraged a frail woman minutes later to peek through the blinds. Bernard signalled to his badge 'Poland'. That was sufficient for the woman.

Words of greeting blessed with smiles encouraged her need to hug each man. They remained on the porch while using broken sentences and hand signals to convey their interest and queries. The Germans had taken her husband and raped her daughters. The woman's tears would not stop. One soldier handed her a military napkin. She dried her eyes and looked at the khaki linen. Another soldier handed her bars of soap, a gift graciously received for she appeared to have not washed in weeks. A bowl he found and pumped the handle to prompt enough water from her well. They all knew what the word "Grazie" meant. Appreciation was the brilliant smile on her tragically worn face.

A kettle was placed on the pot belly stove. One of the soldiers went to the barn and there found some firewood still reasonably dry. Two others joined him, and twenty minutes later they returned with a chord of wood.

Much of the continuing dialogue included some hand drawings. She seemed so delighted that anyone would even care for her opinion.

There were cattle available, on a large estate among the hills about thirty minutes away. That farm belonged to her "Tio". However she made no promise regarding her uncle's intention saying in verse, Bernard understood, that she did not even know if he was still alive. Such was life and death in southern Italy.

Before leaving, Bernard handed the woman his medal of Our Lady of Czestochowa, one that his mother gave him and that he still revered. She in turn handed the Polish soldier her medal of St. Francis. It hung with his dog tags for the duration of the war.

In the truck, Franck lamented on how the Wehrmacht had absconded with crops and poultry and slaughtered the livestock it could not transport. There was to be nothing left, not even for the Italian widows.

"Tio" was dead, or at least the young woman believed so. She was his niece, the only survivor of the German raid to seize and butcher. The time was well spent. She had cattle. They had food and supplies with them. Perhaps exceeding their authority they offered her protection. Common sense was the accepted standard for prudence. The variables were many in wartime situations. Two animals were slaughtered that day and hung in the shed. The soldiers left and returned the next day with two trucks: one for the meat, and the other for vegetables that had still been in the ground.

Teodor, a twenty-two year old from Warsaw, re-attended with the other troops on that second day. With permission, the young man stayed behind to provide the security that they promised. Two flags hung from the edge of the barn roof: the tri-colour Italian and the bi-colour Polish. Teodor became Auriel's spouse, custodians of a Polish outpost in the foothills of the

Apennines. Commander Duch approved the process noting Teodor held the post of an informant in occupied territory.

As for the 3rd Carpathian Rifle Division, everyone ate reasonably well. The support among the Italians for the Polish force became reliable. The stories were all true.

(I V)

One quarter million troops awaited the commander's order to attack. The United States 5th Army was camped, waiting south of the Gustav Line near the Tyrrhenian Coast. Operation Avalanche had been a success. The troops dreamed of another quick result. However, dreams are not always reality.

Lieutenant General Mark Clark was an astute leader. However, some of his decisions have allowed history to consider him vulnerable. Nevertheless, he was firm and always ready to consider alternatives. Every campaign had a plan-B. The Lieutenant General was very proud. So few, in the military, had advanced so quickly. At age forty-seven he was about to lead the largest American force assembled in Europe.

When he landed at Salerno, the British X Corps and the American VI Corps were under his command. As they prepared themselves for an assault on Kesselring's Mountain, the VI Corps was replaced by the French Expeditionary Corps. The French General Alphonse Juin had the military mind of a genius. He always prepared his troops to do the unexpected. Surprise was his means of exceeding the expected.

Even before the Allied attack of Sicily, Lieutenant General Clark was burdened by too many preconceived notions about Italy and its dictator. Those opinions were easy to grasp when everything Italian was the enemy. However, in America for years Italy was not the enemy. Mussolini had done so much so effectively to resurrect the Italian economy after the first war. El Duce had defeated communism in Italy, and was celebrated for his socialist programs to improve the daily lives of every Italian. Even the Italian newspaper in America, Il Progresso, available just around the corner from Clark's home, told Americans how wonderful the Italian peninsula had managed its recovery.

Then American preconceived notions became alternatives, question marks, and hurdles to immediate goals. Even after Mussolini's arrest some still loved him. Other Italians hated him. Italy was Germany's ally. Italy turned its back on Germany. Italy had also done that in the first war. Some Italians welcomed the Americans. Other Italians despised the 5th Army. Who was to trust whom? Mark Clark could deal with Kesselring because he knew the enemy. But could the US 5th Army trust the Italians for support?

On January 17th, Lieutenant General Clark ordered the British X Corps to attempt a crossing of the Garaliano River as a start to the ultimate goal of establishing a bridgehead across the river. This British Corps, consisting of the 5th and 56th Infantry Divisions, even before entering the valley was confronted by the German XIV Panzer Corps, and the 94th Infantry Division.

With some success in that initial raid, the British 46th Infantry Division then launched its attack at the fork of the Garaliano and Liri Rivers.

The next day, Clark sent his US 36th Division, composed of the 141st and 143rd Regiments, across the Rapido River. It was his plan to expand the front over a twenty-mile front. The US Regiments were quickly rebuffed by Kesselring's 15th Panzer Grenadier Division. Ultimately, the Allies were pushed back across the river. Casualties were extremely heavy. Of the 2,100 in the 143rd Regiment, only forty survived.

Clark attempted another river crossing on the twenty-first of the month. Would he have done so, if he didn't have so many troops at his disposal? By sunset, the Americans who were still alive had again be forced back across the river.

Kesselring was preparing himself for a long drawn out conflict. Having made the order, the 29th and 90th Panzer Grenadier Divisions arrived from Rome.

Clark and the US 5th Army rested for two days to explore possible alternatives. The eventual decision was firm. Clark designated the French Expeditionary, particularly the French Moroccan and Algerian troops, to participate in an attack across the Rapido River to the east of Cassino. The assault would be supported by the US 34th Infantry Division. Hopes were high when the battle started. Then everything went awry.

The American Division became engaged in fierce combat for a week against the German 44th Infantry Division. There was considerable success in their campaign as they were able to establish a bridgehead on the other side of the Rapido River.

The US 135th and 168th Infantry Divisions then joined the battle focussing their two-pronged attack on the Abbey and Cassino town. The latter was essential as German forces in the town could attack the Allies from the side or rear once the Americans crossed the Rapido. The attack toward the Abbey followed the success of the 34th Division's bridgehead across the river. Ascending the hill, the American 135th Infantry was able to get within a kilometre of the Abbey. In spite of heavy mortar fire, machine guns, grenades and close combat, they held their position and even captured several Germans. These prisoners advised that there were Paratroopers stationed within the Abbey itself.

At the same time, the 34th Division circled Cassino Mountain capturing Hill 455, a round top hill slightly below the Abbey. The ultimate goal though was Hill 593, about two kilometres north of the Abbey. Hill 593 would have provided a panoramic view of the Liri Valley and was definitely in artillery range of the Abbey. However, the 3rd Battalion of the German 2nd Parachute Regiment held firm. The capture of Hill 593 was not achieved. On Hill 455, the Americans were surrounded and became rifle range targets for German artillery from the Abbey and the many dugouts on the mountain.

After one week of intense fighting the American 135th and 168th Infantry Divisions suffered almost an 80% casualty rate. Out of three 3,200 troops, 2,360 bodies littered the hillside.

On February the twelfth, the Indian 4th Division relieved the US Infantry Divisions. The battle continued, but the Indian Division could not repel the German onslaught.

The number of German casualties as a result of this offensive was also considerable. But, Germany was still in the position of dominance and control.

(V)

The Algerian and Moroccan forces, acting on the order of Lieutenant General Clark, were involved in the first attack on Monte Cassino. The United States General clearly understood the importance of the French Expeditionary Corps, a unique army with incredible skills. Mountain warfare was its specialty.

General Juin commanded the 112,000 troops in the French Expeditionary Corps. His army included: 1st Free French Division with three brigades and two regiments; 2nd Moroccan Infantry Division with five regiments; 3rd Algerian Infantry with five regiments; 4th Moroccan Mountain Division with five regiments; and General Reserves consisting of the Moroccan Goumiers in three regiments. About sixty percent of this army was North African. Hatred of the Germans, after the conflict in North Africa, had become instinctive.

The role and success of the French Corps in the first assault on Monte Cassino was significant.

When the US 34th Division crossed the Rapido River on January 24, 1944, the Algerian Infantry, the Moroccan Infantry and Moroccan Mountain Divisions fought alongside, securing the bridgehead across the river. From that position, the Moroccans and Algerians were able through the mountain passes and over the hills to gain access to positions north of the Abbey.

The Moroccans captured Mount Cifalco, to the north-west of Monte Cairo. From this position, ten kilometres from the Abbey, any Allied offensive would pose significant risk to the Germans.

At the same time, the 3rd Algerian Division captured Colle Abate, just west of Mount Cifalco and about nine kilometres north of the Abbey. It was a decisive victory but it cost almost two thousand lives.

To hold these two positions, Reserves were required. The request was declined. With that decision to not support soldiers actively engaged in fierce conflict, the first battle for Monte Cassino came to an end.

(V I)

Lieutenant General Clark had promises to keep and a major conquest to achieve. "Rome by October" had been General Eisenhower's expectation. Unfortunately landing at Salerno in September 1943 did not mean marching into Rome one month later.

General Eisenhower had been clear about this war in Italy, considering it as a "divergence." With his presence required in Britain, the attack on France was clearly seen to be more important than any conflict in Italy. The final battle was to be the Allied victory in Berlin. To get to Berlin the Allies would have to land in France. Italy was not that 'landing'. Eisenhower's public or private views on the Italian war were not imparted to the troops for the sake of morale. However, to the more than half million allied troops, this war in the Italian peninsula remained essential for liberty in Europe.

The hours after February 9 1944 were exceeding long. Clark had lost his first battle. He had made the decisions on where to attack, who to send and the fateful decision to avoid sending reserves to the hills already captured in the north. However even before the final result of the failed campaign, Clark had already determined the necessity to open a second front.

An amphibious raid at Anzio, a town on the Tyrrhenian Coast beyond the Winter Line, would certainly divert Kesselring's divisions away from Cassino. Under the command of Major General John Lucas, and with the support of General Sir Harold Alexander, Commander in Chief of the Allied Armies in Italy, thirty-six thousand Allied troops landed at Anzio. This force included: the United States troops of the 3rd Infantry Division, a Ranger force, and the 509th Parachute Infantry Battalion. The British 1st Infantry Division also took part in the raid. The Polish Navy, too, participated in the landing operation. The German troops already in the town were not able to repel the initial Allied attack. Swiftly the Allies seized control of the area.

Communication in the course of military campaigns is essential. Accuracy and full disclosure are equally important. Clark, in January 1944, appeared to encounter difficulties meeting expectations. The under-manned attack for Cassino on January 12th was followed by his non-disclosure of vital information to Major General Lucas before the landing on January 22nd.

Anzio was a beach surrounded by marshlands and farms. Beyond these were mountains. Clark knew the terrain and the military consequences of not acting immediately to get away from the beach and flat land. Unfortunately, Major General Lucas did not.

Major General Lucas was ready to celebrate after the successful landing and decided that his 36,000 troops of the US VI Corps should camp at Anzio while awaiting word from General Clark or General Alexander to proceed north towards Rome or south behind Kesselring at Cassino. What Clark did not tell Lucas was this: if Lucas just stayed in the area of the beach, his men would become a shooting gallery for German artillery.

Lucas waited for advice. Germany responded.

The German counter-offensive began immediately with twenty thousand soldiers. This was followed by the German 14th Army and the reserves of the German 10th Army. Then the Hermann Goering Panzer Division arrived. The Allies were able to muster 186,000 troops. The German force numbered 155,000 plus two Fascist-Italian battalions.

The attacks and counter offensives continued for weeks. Lodged in the hills, the Germans were able to employ mortar guns with a range of a half-mile, machine guns with more than fifteen-hundred rounds per minute, and the massive K5 Railway Gun with its five hundred pound shells and a range of fifty miles.

One month after the landing, and with the Allies forced back to the beach, General Clark relieved General Lucas of his post. The new commander at Anzio, General Lucien Truscott, was ordered to commence a counter-offensive immediately; but that was not possible. Clark also removed two British infantry divisions, replacing them with the US 34th and 36th Infantry Divisions. Operation Shingle had become an

American battle with American leadership and American troops. Proudly they fought, and eventually, but after too many casualties, they achieved victory.

Those casualties exceeded twenty-three percent and included 7,000 dead and 36,000 wounded or missing. Anzio proved to Kesselring that he could repel the Americans but that his defence of Rome might be vulnerable.

(V I I)

On February 6, 1944, General Anders said farewell to the African continent. Leaving Egypt, he sailed across the Mediterranean Sea into the Adriatic and on shore at Bari. The General was well versed in the exploits of the Polish Independent Commando Company on the coast, who with the British 8th Army were proceeding north. Anders was also aware of murmurs of discontent in the 3rd Carpathian Rifle Division concerning the absence of action. On the Italian west coast the Armoured Division was set to come assure. Naples was the scheduled port.

General Anders also had sparse information on the first raid at Cassino and the landing at Anzio. He sincerely wondered about any role that the Polish II Corps would play in the conquest of Italy. No one would give him answers. Information from General Leece, too, was a rare commodity. Just getting to talk to him was a monumental task. There had been significant camaraderie between Anders and General Montgomery. That had always been encouraging, for Sir Bernard Montgomery was there at Tobruk to witness the effectiveness of Polish troops. What would Leece have the Polish force do? Anders did not know.

However, fighting on the Adriatic Coast had a definite advantage for the Polish troops. So much had been heard about the Soviet advance against the retreating German army. Eastern European cities, counties and countries were now occupied by the Red Army. Poland was ominously vulnerable. Victory on the Italian west coast could allow the Polish forces and equally importantly the Allies to advance north through Austria, or west into Hungary and then north with the ultimate goal of fighting for Poland's independence.

With headquarters established in Italy, the Polish II Corps would have greater exposure, being seen as ready, and would become active participants in the campaign. Meetings with Generals Leece and Duch were a priority. Anders knew he still had much to learn and much more to give.

(V I I I)

The decision had been made. German troops were in the Abbey. Captured Nazi soldiers had told the Allies. How else could the Germans so dominate the terrain unless the troops had security within the walls of the Abbey? Obviously, the Allies could not win if the Abbey remained a German fort.

Those views echoed the military assessments of Brigadier Harry Dimoline and General Bernard Freyberg. Freyberg was the commander of three divisions: the 2nd New Zealand, the 4th Indian, and the 78th British. Dimoline's role was leadership of the Indian 4th Division. Both generals on February 11th had recommended to General Clark that it was necessary to bomb the Abbey as they deemed it evident that the

Germans were using the Abbey as a fort to attack Allied forces.

The leaflet was candid. The warning, in Italian to Italian residents, was definite.

Italian friends,

Until this day we have done everything to

avoid bombing the abbey. But the Germans

have taken advantage. Now that the battle

has come close to your sacred walls, we

shall – despite our wish – have to direct our

arms against the monastery. Abandon it at

once. Put yourselves in a safe place. Our

warning is urgent.

The note was signed by the US 5th Army.

Doomsday was February 15 1944. Two hundred and twenty-nine American B-17 bombers from the US 96th Bomb Squadron dropped 1,150 tons of high explosives on the Abbey, completely destroying the monastery. The sacred shrine was reduced to rubble.

The following morning, over-kill was completed when 59 bombers returned to complete the pulverisation of rubble.

As soon as that attack was completed, General Clark ordered the Indian 4th Division to attack Hill 593, two kilometres from the ruined Abbey. Clark believed that with the Abbey destroyed, Hill 593 provided visual and artillery access to the valley. However, the American bombs never touched Hill 593. Again Clark appeared deficient in his command. The Germans still on top of Hill 593 had not been weakened by any bombing and had no difficulty repelling the Indian 4th Division. Casualties were again heavy.

On February 17th, Kesselring seized his opportunity. His German 1st Paratroop Division occupied the ruins. The debris provided artillery positions for his machine guns, cannons, and even tanks. With all of the dugouts, and shallow caves created by the bombing, Clark's decision to destroy the Abbey had benefited Kesselring's defence of the Gustav Line.

After failing to take Hill 593 the day before, the Indian 4th Division were again ordered into action to attack the Cassino hill. At the same time the 28th Maori Battalion of the New Zealand Division was successful in crossing the Rapido River and establishing a bridgehead.

Unfortunately neither the Indian nor the New Zealand forces were able to maintain their positions. On February 18, 1944, the second attack on Cassino was abandoned.

(I X)

The 5th Kresowa Infantry Division was ecstatic about the decision in late February to move its base to the Italian peninsula. General Anders had moved his headquarters just weeks before. Once established the general called for the remaining Polish troops to leave Egypt. It was in many respects a sad ceremony to watch the Polish flag lowered for the last time at Al Quassasin.

Commander Nikodem Sulik directed the transit of his 12,900 troops across the Mediterranean to Bari and then north to Barletta. From there they travelled west along the southern perimeter of the Garaliano valley.

His Division included troops from Wilno, Wolyn and Lvov in eastern Poland – territory invaded by the Red Army in 1939, occupied by the Nazis in 1941, and re-taken by the Red Army in 1944. The 5th Kresowa Division actually existed prior to the second war, but with the invasions of 1939, the division disbanded. With the reassembling of troops in Iran and Palestine, the 5th Kresowa Division breathed a second life. Being able to unite troops that were previously together was a military advantage. Being already acquainted meant so much for morale, enthusiasm and professionalism. The Division was composed of two infantry brigades – the 5th Wilesnka and the 6th Lvovska, a reconnaissance regiment being the 15th Poznanski Lancers, three artillery regiments, an armoured brigade, anti-tank and anti-aircraft regiments. Engineers were also part of the division with duties relating to signals, decoding, construction and repairs.

The insignia of the brown bison on an amber background was embellished on its uniforms, trucks, tanks, and equipment. Unlike the 3rd Carpathian Division whose focus was the occupying Germans, the 5th Kresowa's attention was directed to dealing with the Red Army once the Germans were out of the way. Together the divisions fought for an independent Poland, a concept that was never abandoned.

By the thirteenth of March, the 5th Kresowa Division was stationed at Castel San Vincenzo to relieve the 2nd Moroccan Division. Castel San Vincenzo was a village east of Cassino, along the Garaliano Valley about half-way across Italy. The village was situated in a

271

valley surrounded by snow-capped peaks, in many respects a dream home location, but they were in the middle of a war. With the 5th Kresowa in this position, and with the 3rd Carpathian Division to their east in the same valley, the British 8th Army had restricted the German capacity to head east from Cassino to join the Adriatic campaign.

(X)

The Ides of March for the Allies was planned to be just as ominous for Kesselring as it had been for Caesar. The third assault on Monte Cassino commenced that day, not with an infantry attack on the Abbey ruins, but with an assault on the town.

"No more lives will be lost. Bomb the shit out of them!" The instruction was adamantly clear. Allied forces moved away from the front like the retreating tide before a tsunami.

Cassino town had been your picturesque romantic hideaway, nestled at the foot of the mountain below the Benedictine Abbey. Beyond the Monastery, Monte Cairo towered over the valleys and rivers. In the centre of the town there was the usual fountain, foliage and market square. The market was busy three mornings every week. Buildings were predominantly three to four storey apartments with at least one business on the ground floor. Large estates bordered the southern perimeter.

In the spring of 1944, the town was home to three hundred soldiers of the German 1st Parachute Division and the 2nd Battalion. From that position the Germans were able to face the Allies head-on, or attack them from the rear or to the side. The town too had a fully functional railway and depot that the Germans had used to transport their supplies, tanks and artillery.

At 8:30am on March 15, 1944 the Allied bombing of the town of Cassino began. During a barrage ending at noon, 775 US bombers dropped 2,500 half-ton bombs on the town.

There was a rest for thirty minutes, and then 748 guns started a bombardment of more than 195,000 shells that lasted until 8:00pm.

In the dark the New Zealand Division entered the rubble and engaged the remaining Germans. By the morning of March 16th Cassino town belonged to the Allies.

(XI)

The third battle for Monte Cassino had two distinct aims: first to eliminate the German threat in the town, and second to attack the Abbey.

Although the town had been captured, the accesses on the incline to the Abbey remained fodder for German artillery. From the south-east, the road between the town and the mount was an uphill winding snake making any invading force extremely vulnerable. Troops and tanks would have to proceed north through a series of six twists and turns for 1.6 kilometres, then go slightly downhill for 750 meters, then north uphill for 600 meters, then south-west for 1.5 kilometres with a twist in the road to the west, then east sideways up the hill for 400 meters, then on a steeper incline about 400 meters to the north-east, then back down the incline for 300 meters to the south-west, then back up the incline in the north-west direction for 600 meters, an about turn east for 600 meters, then 650 meters in the north east direction to a position behind the Abbey, then 500 meters rounding the Abbey to the point of entrance.

In the west, German troops remained in control of the Liri Valley.

The New Zealand Division, having already captured the town and without fear of counter-attack, secured the bridges across the Rapido River inside the town and downstream. Tanks followed immediately expanding the bridgehead well into German held territory. The Allied attack achieved its initial goal with the capture of Hills 165 & 236 to the north-east of Monte Cassino.

The Indian 4th Division Gurkhas coordinated their attack at the same time capturing Hangman's Hill, the hill below the Abbey's southern wall. That hill, also known as Point 435, was only two hundred, fifty meters from the Abbey ruins, and as such was considered vital to the Allied cause. The exchange of artillery was intense. The Indian Division had relied upon its tanks to destroy German positions on the way up the incline. The tide was in their favour; then the German counter-offensive began. Within hours, nineteen of the Indian Division's tanks were destroyed, blocking the road. In spite of their lack of mobility they were able to maintain their stronghold as long as possible.

At Anzio, the German guns were not silent. The Americans of the Sixth Corps were tied to their defensive position near the shore, unable to advance.

With the New Zealand and Indian Divisions well away from the town, the Germans encircled the ruins of the town. By midnight on the seventeenth the Germans once again occupied the remnants of Cassino. Among the debris they established their machine guns. Key positions enhanced the use of grenades. Trip wires and mines endangered any soldier approaching the city. By mid morning the Germans surveyed the destroyed rail lines and with their engineers planned the repairs and reconstruction.

Upon realizing they had lost the town, the Allies started bombing supply lines to destroy any prospect of the German army re-arming their artillery positions.

Death and fatigue were everywhere for the Allies. Under the veil of night, the New Zealand Division withdrew from the two hills below of the Abbey ruins. Also in the black of an overcast night, the Gurkhas were able to descend the hill.

Two days later on March 19th, on Cavendish Road, north of the mountain, thirty-seven tanks of the New Zealand Armoured Division were proceeding south toward the Abbey. The New Zealand and Indian engineers had been influential in securing and maintaining this road and others between Monte Cassino and Monte Cairo. The Kiwi force knew the road well.

The plan of the New Zealand Armoured Division was to commence a tank bombardment from Hangman's Hill. To accomplish this, the tanks passed west of Colle Maiola at the northern expanse of Snakeshead Ridge, to the north of the Abbey ruins. From there, the tanks moved west along a narrow road to a position overlooking the Liri Valley. It was on route from there to Hangman's Hill that the German 4th Parachute Regiment attacked. The first twelve tanks were destroyed preventing any mobility. Almost one thousand, seven hundred New Zealanders died in their attempt to capture the ruins.

On Thursday March 23rd, General Harold Alexander, Commander-in-Chief, ordered the withdrawal of the Allied forces from the hills around Monte Cassino. They could not maintain their positions. Trying to do so would be suicide.

(XII)

General Anders knew there was an inevitably to Stalin's retribution. The Soviet Dictator was never one to be trusted by anyone at any time. "Stupid fools!" the Polish General often called Stalin's cohorts, especially Beria. The Dictator always called them comrades as if to elevate their status. Did Stalin really believe that no one could see through his deception? Yet the sick reality remained that anyone who said anything against him was no longer alive to say another word.

Considering the treachery that purveyed the Soviet Union, and his own imprisonment, Anders questioned in his heart how he ever got so far.

Anders asked Stalin to release Polish prisoners from Soviet gulags. The dictator did that.

Anders accused Stalin's inner circle of murdering the Polish officers in the Ukraine. Anders lived to see another day.

When Stalin announced Anders's army would be a Soviet Army of Polish soldiers, Anders fought the issue and won.

When Stalin told Anders his army would fight for the Soviet Union in the front line against Germany, Anders said, "No!"

When Stalin suggested Anders could leave the Soviet Union, Anders took more than seventy thousand Poles with him.

When Stalin arranged the supervision of Anders's Army in Soviet-dominated Iran, Anders fled with his troops.

Instead of being a Soviet army, the Polish II Corps became part of the British force.

General Anders sat in the rickety wooden chair in the tent of Lieutenant General Oliver Leece holding the letter in his two hands. Anders had a marvellous ability of controlling his temper. He was clearly in that frame of mind. A wry smile was his initial response. That bothered Leece.

Leece told Anders it was very damning. The Polish General let his British superior continue. The diatribe lasted the whole of five minutes.

"None of this is true," Anders told the Lieutenant General. Leece paused, and Anders continued explaining all of the factors that would prompt Stalin to orchestrate such lies.

"How do you know Stalin was involved?"

Anders's reply started with an historical reference to Trotsky and how he met his fate because he voiced an opinion that differed from Stalin's idealism.

"You're shrewd," Anders was told. To this comment, Anders repeated his earlier advice on how Stalin might have felt being challenged by Anders's snub.

Leece took the letter from the table and read it once more.

"This comes from our war department."

"No," Anders corrected, "it appears to be based on an article in the press by someone we do not know."

Leece acknowledged that, but added that the British War Department was involved.

"Does the author even know the Polish Government in Exile exists?"

"General Sikorsky is dead." Leece was direct.

That issue was close to Anders's heart, because it was part and parcel of what appeared to be a scheme among several nations, including Britain, to appease the Soviet Bear by wavering Poland's right to independence.

"Our General was killed by the Soviets."

Leece was ready to argue that at length based on British information. "I could tell you the reports do not confirm Soviet involvement. In any event it is the British who raise the issue of your participation with this army."

"This person that penned your letter, do you know him? Does he even work for the war department?" Anders paused for a moment waiting for an answer. "Do you agree, my Lieutenant General, that the English would never have written such a letter to you or to anyone if Stalin was not involved?"

Leece had only one answer, and delayed speaking it. Anders continued.

"I know your advice. You do not have to say. The letter says we are an inept fighting force. It suggested Poles just ran from Poland. It says that we are not dependable, that we will again run, and that we will not fight when the request is made. Rest assured we will fight, we fought in Tobruk, and will fight again with our hearts committed to you and to ourselves. You have but one enemy. We have two: Hitler and Stalin. Don't believe a word either dictator ever says to you. They dance the tango with the devil."

The discussion continued for more than half an hour. The Lieutenant General was impressed with Anders's calm, in spite of the accusations. Even when the term 'mutiny' was mentioned, Anders did not blink. His voice was passionate but even keel, sincere but not loud.

General Anders was also aware that there were factions in the United Kingdom that were challenging British support for the Poles. His thoughts were based on what he had heard from more than two persons about Clement Atlee, the Deputy Prime Minister and Leader of the Labour Party. Atlee, being oriented to workers' rights, had the support of the communists in Britain. There was no doubt that he would need their votes to defeat Winston Churchill in a general election. A British government with the support of a communist faction would be willing to dismiss the Polish Government in Exile and favour the imposition of Soviet rule over Polish territory. As long as that prospect existed, the operation of the Polish II Corps under the auspices of the British 8th Army could be in peril. But then, Anders also knew that if it wasn't with the British, it could be with the Americans or perhaps the Poles could even leave Italy and fight for freedom in the Balkans, Hungary, Austria or Czechoslovakia.

The events on that April afternoon affirmed that nothing in war was certain, not even your support.

It was General Anders, his style, his thoroughness, and his professionalism, that convinced Lieutenant General Leece to disregard the foul accusations against the Polish troops. Realizing that there had to be growing discontent by just waiting for so long, Leece advised Anders his force would see action not on the Adriatic but in the campaign on the other side of the Apennines to free Rome.

Anders was delighted with the prospect that at long last his army could prove its worth.

(X I I I)

The first reaction confirmed the consensus of the Polish troops. "West to Cassino" was the cheer. Then the enthusiasm had dimmed almost completely for so many with news of the article printed by the British press. England, that at one time welcomed the government in exile, now seemed to be in bed with the Soviet Union. Perceptions count.

General Anders had few words for his troops about the Soviet scam. He was more concerned that the British press even considered any truth to the Soviet allegation before stabbing the Poles in the back. In spite of anything Anders may have said to his men, there remained the historical reality that after the Nazi invasion of Poland, Britain did nothing in spite of its defence agreement with Poland.

Some of the Polish troops just wanted to quit, but they didn't have a home. To where could they return?

Bernard sat on a ground sheet in the tent with Piotr and Jerzy. Hendryk had left almost an hour before for the latrine. He was so easily side tracked. These moments at the end of each day were opportunities to relieve the troubles in each person's mind. War was painfully long and forever sheltered the memories that would never fade. Conversation was the one remedy they had.

Jerzy said the news about the British article didn't bother him. Later he added that perhaps it was a good thing as it brought him closer to killing Germans.

Piotr was far more philosophical about the future. "After we win, where do we go?" On a couple of occasions he was close to tears when thinking about the family he would never see again.

Bernard too shared that melancholy concern. "Justice" he called it, not revenge but justice, for what happened to his family, his farm, his friends, and his country.

Comparisons to the first war meant a lot in such conversations. Piotr conjectured that this second war was progressing better than the stalemate in the first. Jerzy referred to the dynamics of this conflict involving Africa, Japan, and the Pacific.

Food supplies were again a topic for conversation. Only two meals per day, it couldn't get any worse. Yet how were they ever going to be fed when crossing the peninsula?

"When?" was the question repeated often by all within the camp. It was already one week after Easter.

"Is it raining there too?" was another common query.

About preparedness, an oft-mentioned issue was the tanks. Eventually an informed source advised that the Polish Armoured Division would be landing at Naples. "To help us and not the Americans?" Bernard asked. Such questions never received answers from superiors.

Piotr returned to his pet peeve "The Italians?" He had trouble with the trust issue.

The 3rd Carpathian Rifle Division commenced the trek west in the third week of April. With vans transporting as many as possible they moved quickly for the first two days. After that the progression was slow through the valleys and over the hills, staying away from the rivers that formed the border for the Gustav Line. Most movement in open plains was done at night. Although the territory had been yielded to the Allies, there was still the prospect of informants. The rains had made the fields impassable, so nearly all of the trip was completed on the roads and developed laneways. Support from the inhabitants throughout the journey was rare, but definitely a blessing.

The 5th Kresowa Division, already half way across Italy, left later joining the other division at the final camp.

The final camp was situated south-west of Cassino town in the valley between Monte Lungo and Sesto Campano. As more troops arrived, a sector was established closer to Bivio Mortola. In all cases they were protected by anti-aircraft and anti-tank weaponry. From the hills, bordering their camp, they could look north toward the Abbey ruins. However on most mornings, fog obscured the Cassino summit. The slope of the terrain blocked their view of the river. Constructing bridges they knew was necessary.

Fog, too, became a defence mechanism, creating smoke to obscure the camp. There were no lights so as to not give away their position. There were no walkie-talkies or radios. Everything was camouflaged: the tents, the portable mess halls. Tree limbs covered all equipment. The forest had not come to Macbeth, it had arrived at Cassino.

The first night there, Bernard and several others went on patrol. They had to adjust themselves to the terrain, to the shadows among the hills, to the echoes, to the night crickets, soaring owls, and the silence of the corpses littering every vantage point.

Bernard could not avoid the necessity of prayer. He had seen much, done much, survived much. "The Final Camp", he hated the expression but could not avoid the possibility of that reality.

(X I V)

His headquarters several miles north of the Abbey ruins was safe. Self-preservation was an essential trait even for military commanders. The knock at the door preceded the usual instructions, salutes and greetings. It was really getting laboriously repetitious but then this was war and discipline and standards were required.

The news was not what he wanted to hear, but everything he expected. General Kesselring looked dismayed, and dismissed the messenger. The aerial report was exactly not that. Again, nothing could be seen regarding any troop movement south of the Rapido and Garaliano Rivers. He knew they were there, all of them, destined to do whatever they could. But where were they?

Kesselring ventured they would head south then go across Italy through the southern valleys. His army conceded that portion of Italy to the Allies. He fought Hitler's design as much as he could, the edict to concede the south to the Allies and then defend the central portion. Giving away the south allowed for just this: troop movements without detection. Kesselring would have fought the invasion to death, and many of his loyal soldiers did just that. But as he prepared himself for what he conceded would be the inevitable battle, he was paying the price for the military decisions made in Berlin.

"How many?" That too he questioned. Available surveillance confirmed much of the British force was no longer on the Adriatic.

"Should I start a major offensive there, so they wouldn't move west?" The prospect was inviting. "If we could drive them south to the heel, then we could circle back and trap them here on this coast. Damn Americans!" Kesselring was becoming very prone to talking out loud to himself. Perhaps he conjectured no one could give him the answer he didn't want.

At his desk he checked his papers. "They have lost more. When will they give up?" However Kesselring knew the Allies were not going to fold. "There aren't enough ships to take them all away," he regretfully mused, realizing the inevitability of Armageddon.

"Deplete the defence of Rome?" Kesselring had already removed two divisions to fight at Cassino and Anzio. He could not afford to remove more troops. Rome was still the military goal of this entire Allied campaign, he realized. As long as Mussolini was alive somewhere in the north, and as long as Mussolini was Hitler's friend, Rome had to be defended.

There was his own military pride, too, that was taking a beating. North Africa, Sicily, Salerno, Calabrese, Taranto, Bari, the beachhead at Anzio, and the bombing of Turin and Pisa: all showed weaknesses in an empire that could never last one thousand years.

Kesselring took the advantage of such quiet moments to reflect on all of the mistakes Berlin had made. He would never tell the Fuhrer this; but those who tried to tell Hitler about the facts-of-war were no longer alive. "Silence may be golden, but it is also the highway to the end," Kesselring often surmised.

"Why did we ever invade Russia?" He had often asked the question realizing how much he could have accomplished if he had those divisions at his command, and if the dead were not dead.

"The Jews?" Kesselring opposed the exterminations. He was proud of his German heritage, but he was not a disciple of the Thule. He had read Mein Kampf, but he was not an Aryan terrorist committed to disposing of every other race. He was German, and Germans lived with the French and the Slavs in the best of times. Kesselring was a commander knowing his role was to mould men into fighting machines, taking all of the ingredients of every part of their lives and nationalities and sentiments. Mobilizing men into one unified source did not involve the annihilation of men who could fight for the Fuhrer.

Kesselring also wondered why Hitler ever befriended Japan, and why Toto suddenly became an acceptable word in the German vocabulary. Without Japan, we would not have had the Americans on Italian soil!

The German Commander, regardless of how pensive and rational he could be, was also prone to obsessive bursts of violence. He would again do it. Trusting the Italians – that was something he didn't have time for. There were groups of militant inhabitants ready to attack his army. No matter how uneventful the attack may have been or how harmless the result, punishment was a necessity. More than three hundred belonging to an Italian resistance movement met their fate at the Ardeatine caves. He would do it all again.

How many would there be? Man for man, Kesselring realized he would soon be outnumbered. As much as he loathed any outcome that was not victory, the commander conceded that there were decisions that could lead to his demise.

"Motivation." His voice rose from the silence of the room. "Who is more motivated? Who has the most to lose? The Americans in Italy or Germany defending its ally?"

That discussion with himself did not continue, for he feared the answer. After looking once more at the notes on the deficient surveillance, he tossed the page in the garbage.

"Where are they?" His mind would not let go of the question, for he feared the Poles most. "They have nothing to lose."

(X V)

Ten Downing Street had never been the victim of so much smoke. The Prime Minister's office had survived the Nazi bombing, but this attack of the senses was indeed too much. The Maharaja, the representative of Colonial India, excused himself for a breath of fresh air, as clean as air in London could ever be.

Standing by the front door, pictured so often by the British Press, Hari Singh, the Maharaja of Jammu and Kashmir observed the surroundings. The response of the press was quick. A security guard stepped between them advising Mr. Churchill would give a speech. That was it, it was all about Churchill. To the Maharaja there were more pressing issues, for India, an end to colonisation.

He stood there in those moments expecting a High Commissioner or one of the Prime Ministers to join him, but that did not happen. There were businessmen walking by: perhaps politicians or others dressed to impress. Hari Singh returned to the meeting about ten minutes later having inhaled as much British air as he could take.

Winston Churchill had not moved from his high-back chair by the curtained window. A side table separated the British Prime Minister from his Australian colleague. John Curtin from Canberra diplomatically listened hoping to discern more than the agenda. The meeting was into its seventh day, an incredibly long time to do nothing. Sure they met one another, but such

287

impressions were not startling discoveries. They all cherished the British Commonwealth, all participated in the war, and had similar problems at home.

To the far end of the room the Canadian Prime Minister, William MacKenzie King was speaking at length with New Zealand's Prime Minister Peter Fraser. Jan Smuts from South Africa joined the group. The High Commissioners spoke among themselves, while those in attendance from Churchill's Cabinet too were primarily interested in their own agenda. In that respect the meeting was no different than any other business session at that time or in the future.

The sixteen-day period from May 1 to May 16 in 1944 provided the various Prime Ministers at the First Commonwealth Prime Minister's Conference the opportunity to meet one another and to appreciate the concerns of each nation realizing the issues in one were very much common to others.

Winston Churchill reported on the Moscow Declaration and his agreement with Stalin and Roosevelt. Italy would be free to pursue democracy after the war. The representative of Malta was keenly interested in the future of Italy. The Prime Ministers were told that Austria could no long align itself with Germany in any military pact. That information was nice but it really didn't impact them. There was reference to the agreements on Turkey and the Balkans, but again the impact on the Prime Ministers was nil. India had concerns about Iran being granted independence under the Shah Mohammad Rez Pahlavi. India questioned how Churchill could agree to independence for Iran, but couldn't ensure India the same independence. "Does

Churchill understand that Iran is not just one people?" the Maharaja asked himself.

Information flowed on a more pressing issue: the course of the war. Churchill responded referring again to the Moscow Declaration and the promise of the British and Americans to open a front that is to invade Europe within the year. As to when and where, the questions were not answered.

The atrocities afflicted upon so many innocent people were discussed for more than one day. The troops of all of these nations had reported upon the rumours and stories, the tales of refugees, and destroyed villages. The atrocities, too, of the Japanese in Manchuria, in Malaysia, on the continent, in the Philippines, and on Pacific islands were frequently mentioned. Few of the Prime Ministers or High Commissioners were acquainted with details of the Soviet deportations. When Churchill mentioned that the Nazis were being held responsible for the atrocities in Europe, they were satisfied.

Questions arose regarding the Tehran Conference. Churchill paraphrased the meeting by referring to the agreements with Stalin. He repeated the information on Turkey, realizing that he had already mentioned that. The need to centralize the Balkans was understood. But again, those issues had no impact on countries more than nine time zones away.

The issues of the Red Army, and Soviet expansion were troublesome. Who could stop them? Nations in the Pacific were rightfully worried. If Japan was defeated, who would fill the void? Reports that Bolshevik influences were already present beyond the Pacific borders of the Soviet Union had the Prime Ministers in a quandary. Churchill turned once again to criticize the former policy of appeasement. At the same time, as he usually did, he implored the others to focus on the future.

It came quickly to the Prime Ministers that Eastern Europe would be lost to the Soviets, that the United Kingdom and its allies could not conceivably remove the Red Army from Poland, or the Baltic States. The Soviet Union's control of Poland was bound to happen.

On the morning of the seventeenth of May the Prime Ministers were preparing to return home. Their forces would continue to fight: some under the direction of the British, and others with the Americans. They had all been informed, realizing there was little they could do to alter reality.

(X V I)

Security was extremely tight at the four ends of the camp, especially at the northern extremity near the Rapido Valley. To the east of the Polish camp the Indian Divisions were stationed. The New Zealand force with its tanks and artillery were positioned between the Polish and British 10th Corps. The US 5th Army remained near the west coast, positioned for its assault north toward Anzio. South of the Americans, the French Expeditionary Corps was camped with some of these troops being about fifty kilometres from the Gustav Line. Utilizing its position near the Tyrrhenian coast, the US continued with simulated amphibious raids attracting German attention on more than one occasion.

In the Polish II Corps camp, the 5th Kresowa Division was separate from the 3rd Carpathian Rifle

Division. Brigades, too, tended to be apart. Each belonged to the entire Corps, but being a part of a smaller group tended to enhance morale. Bernard found himself and his fellow troops to be seemingly too close to the Rapido for their comfort. That required them to keep watch at night for any activity approaching the river.

The next day, the Second Brigade was in action, not fighting, but assisting the engineers positioning trucks and equipment to hastily establish bridges. There had been five bridges leading into the town of Cassino and to the east of the town that had to be restored. In the black of night, with the moon concealed by clouds, two bridges were established. These would be a morning surprise for the waking Germans. It was astounding, Bernard thought, that none of them woke during the operation. "Try doing it when they're firing on you," a New Zealander told him.

Others in the Second Brigade were ordered to complete the task of mine detecting within a tenth of a mile of the south bank. War being war, the Germans would have left these buried after retaking the town. "Doesn't make sense," Bernard said to Piotr. "How would they get themselves home?" The Polish invention of the mine detector was very handy in those first two days discovering more than ten German mines.

Getting rest was an easier feat without the constant rain. With so many divisions for so long in place prior to the arrival of the Polish II Corps, the provision of food was already a refined process. But in spite of the well-planned organisation, the Allies still had to deal with the German capacity to flood the plains destroying the crops and severely hampering transit routes.

Besides the provision of sustenance, the general support from the residents was very much a necessity. Some of these had already joined the Italian Royalist Army supporting the Allies. "Know your enemy," was one of Anders's most common reminders. The corollary to that of course was, "Know who to trust." The Poles, in that respect, were more tolerated than the Americans who were first considered invaders, or the Germans who were considered the tyrants. The Italians were sick of the war. The countryside ridden with potholes, the roads destroyed by shrapnel, and fields void of produce and cattle justified their feelings.

General Clark's vehicle entered the Polish sector with the usual fanfare: one security vehicle in front, and American flags on his vehicle. General Anders greeted him with a flamboyant display of camaraderie. There was much seriousness about the meeting once inside Anders's tent.

General Clark was there to encourage the Polish to accept his plan. Clark would normally have met with General Leece of the British 8th Army, but Leece had not yet arrived from the Adriatic coast.

The American General started his discourse by stating the obvious. "We have to get them out of there. I know there is not much left, rubble, but enough of it to give them caves and shelters from which they cut down our troops as if they were just tin cans in target practice. My friend, we have another reason. There will be no invasion of France until we take Rome."

Anders was surprised by that comment even though he had heard it once before, being the reason for Eisenhower and Montgomery being dispatched to Britain.

"I should add," Clark continued, "it is not just that. Perhaps I said it too simply. Reality is they expected us to march into Rome last October. They say much but like yourself we get only pieces. Communiqués do not mean troops. All of the words ever spoken will not put more men in our ranks."

They paused while coffee was delivered to their table. It was very dark as expected, like a full cup of cappuccino.

"Have to teach them to grind their coffee beans," General Clark quipped.

"From Morocco, I believe," Anders added.

A sip was all the American General tasted before continuing. "We have suffered dearly, no, may I say severely. We lost more than 15,000 troops from the moment we landed at Salerno until we arrived at Cassino. On the coast, that hell-hole Anzio, the General tells me the killed and missing exceed 30,000. In the first battle here, we lost more than 4,000 troops. In two other battles the French, the Indians, and the Kiwis lost more than 7,000. The second battle here was worst of all. Casualties exceeded fifty percent. You can understand our position. We have suffered greatly. Our men are weary, weak and famished. Surely we can take them away from the front, but not for long."

"So much has been sacrificed by so many. But unlike your troops, mine have nowhere to go. I tell you this not to lessen our commitment, for our steadfast loyalty is whole. No one will ever say we were ever less than one hundred percent. Remember us, please? We will do whatever you request and fight wherever you battle."

General Clark was appreciative of the commitment, and took the opportunity to recount his request. "I asked for you in March. I know the process takes time, but I, no, we are glad you are here."

Anders continued, "We have a common enemy. That unites us here more than any other factor. 'No more Germany' my troops vow. 'Stop Stalin' my troops declare. We are friends because we share our goals, our lives, and our enemy." The Polish General then reflected on the role of the Polish Navy in the Mediterranean referring to the landings at Calabria and Salerno. Using those examples, Anders repeated the pledge of the Polish troops to the Allied cause.

A second sip of the coffee convinced Clark he was better off talking than listening. The American General continued with his personal plans to actively engage the Polish divisions in capturing the Abbey ruins.

"They have weapons that can hit targets fifty miles away. If they ever brought such a weapon to the top of that hill, then nothing would penetrate their defence. They have such a weapon against us at Anzio. The Germans must not be given the chance to have that weapon here." Clark's urgency was more evident.

General Anders too had his agenda, principally the American plans for Poland after Cassino. Clark, although appreciative of Anders's concerns, would not commit himself. In spite of Clark's decision to hesitate on the future of Poland, Anders repeated the commitment of his troops to the Allied cause. Obviously if Clark saw the need to meet Anders in Anders's tent, then General Clark must have shared Anders's views regarding the effectiveness of the Polish force.

(XVII)

Sir Harold Alexander, Commander-in-Chief on Friday
May 5, 1944 met with General Clark of the US 5th
Army and General Leece of the British 8th Army. The
sun was setting quickly, just moments before it hid itself
behind the mountains. To the north the Liri-Garaliano
valleys seemed barren, void of activity. Trip wires, and
buried mines do not move until greeting the soldier
about to surrender his life. Germans buried in pits and
trenches, behind boulders, and from caves – these too
were stationary. The mist would consume the plains in
the morning as it had for these many months. Tanks and
trucks, mortars and cannons these too were lost in the
stalemate. The crickets were long gone. The roosters had
become supper. The sheep and cattle too were basic
meals. Silence, silence, and more silence.

General Alexander had already reviewed his plans
for the fourth attack on the hill. It was his style to
communicate, encourage discussion, and then affirm the
consensus.

Using the incredible abilities of the Algerian and
Moroccan Divisions, these were to cross the Garaliano
River into the basically undefended area of the Aurunci
Mountains. These mountains were to be scaled where
necessary, with the intent to enter the Austente Valley,
and cross that into the northern portion of the Liri Valley
and then turn south to attack the Abbey ruins from the
north. Ultimately the quest was to establish control of
the route north to Rome.

General Leece's British Army, particularly the
British 4th Division and the Indian 8th Infantry would

repeat the attempts to cross the Rapido and establish a bridgehead on the northern side of the river. Once this was accomplished the Canadian 5th Armoured Division and the British 78th Division would move north toward the Abbey ruins across the terrain littered with boulders, destroyed tanks, and rotting corpses. The British 6th Armoured Division would follow in reserve to support the Canadian tanks and destroy any German defence trying to flank the Canadian and British divisions.

General Clark's US 5th Army was to relieve the US 6th Corps at Anzio. The might of the 5th Army would force Kesselring to move more of his artillery and troops away from the Abbey ruins. The 6th Corps, once relieved of its task at Anzio, would drive to the north-east to take control of the city of Valmontone. This city was on the main route between Cassino and Rome, the very route the Allies had hoped to secure with the first landing in Italy eight months before. Valmontone was forty-five kilometres from Rome, and ninety kilometres from Cassino. Taking Valmontone would be a gem! Considering the military prowess, the Americans in Valmontone with the French controlling the west, and the British attacking from the south and east, meant the Germans at Cassino would be basically surrounded.

The last section of General Leece's plan involved the Polish II Corps. Their divisions were to be the ones to climb the hill and capture the Abbey ruins.

Just bombing the ruins was always an alternative. However, there were significant hurdles. The Germans were not all in one location. The fuel and planes were limited. With the departure of Eisenhower and Montgomery five months before, and with all of the promises being made, the invasion of France was far more important, meaning the supplies for the Italian campaign were restricted. Further, with the German anti-aircraft capacity, too many lives and planes would be lost with such an attack. With all of the devastation already, the enemy would still find ways to fill the manholes and caves with their artillery.

In the camouflaged tent, with two flash lights covered by Leece's jacket, the generals agreed on the campaign for Operation Diadem. They had less than one week before their men would perhaps fight their final battle.

(X V I I I)

In the early afternoon of May 10, 1944 General Anders stood before the thirteen thousand troops of the 3rd Carpathian Rifle Division. He would in due course speak with the Kresowa and Armoured Divisions, but this was his time with the Carpathians. Anders never played favourites, but many in the Carpathian Division were raised in Poznan, the city of his birth. He felt an affinity to their cause and commitment.

Following a series of meetings in the prior five days Anders's task had become straightforward motivation. The plan of attack had already been described, and the instructions given in detail. Brigades were to act independently performing their special assignments, yet at the same time they would work together as a unit, everyone protecting everyone. A meeting two evenings before ended with such raucous, enthusiastic cheering that it almost brought Anders to tears. At a time when every Pole in camp had reason to despair and candidly just turn his back on the whole war effort, the Polish troops celebrated their opportunity to have an impact.

On May 10th, there was no written speech. Anders rarely prepared one. Speaking from the heart, he started by appreciating their sentiments and every issue that gave rise to their determination: Hitler, the blitzkrieg, extermination camps, Stalin, the gulags, and the occupation of Poland.

> Let the spirit of a lion direct your
>
> actions. Keep the love of God ever in
>
> your heart. Honour our land – Poland!
>
> Go! Take revenge for all of the
>
> suffering in our land, for the many
>
> years you suffered in Russia, and for
>
> all the years of separation from your
>
> families.

There was no need to say more.

(X I X)

Zarowas Maria, laskis plena pan z toba

> blogoslawionas ty miedzy niewiastami i
>
> blogoslawion owoc zywota twojego Jesus

Piotr continued Bernard's Hail Mary prayer.

> Swietas Maria, Matco Boza, modl sie za
>
> nami grzesznymi teraz i godzinie smierci

naszej. Amen

Prayer had become an evening ritual, in Bernard's tent, with the flash light buried under his wool sweater.

There was the realisation in spite of any morale boosting speech that this evening of May 10, 1944 may be the last together, and possibly the last for any one of them on earth. The cold reality was inescapable following General Anders's mention of how many had already died. The prayers continued.

The tent that was just enough room for four sleeping bags was the men's den for eight persons that evening. Two were already in bedding: Jerzy and Wiktor. Neither had any use for prayer.

Jerzy struggled to sleep amid the praying comrades. "Put an end to it. God had nothing to do with this war or He would have stopped the Germans long ago." He was exasperated with how naive these six seemed to be.

No one paid attention, and continued with the Rosary.

Wiktor, the youngest in the tent, two months younger than Bernard's eighteen years, turned in his bag to watch the others. He was wild, but not that against God. It was always good to have God on your side. Following the final prayer he asked the ultimate question, "Will we see each other again?"

There was no immediate answer. Hendryk eventually whispered, "Yes, of course we will. Not tomorrow for we fight, and perhaps not the next for we will be together on the hill. But on our way to Rome, yes we will."

Franciszek clutched his hand in confident agreement.

Piotr lightened the moment posing the comment with a tone of envy, "Wonder how Teodor is doing?"

Hendryk quipped, "At least two children by now. Lucky bugger." They tried to keep their laughter quiet.

"They're home," Bernard concluded.

About Teodor, no one really knew much. He was a quite person, but helpful and always involved. Though he claimed to be born in Warsaw, Teodor first came on the scene in Egypt. There was thought even then he might not stay. He would not be compelled, just as long he did not join the enemy. General Anders had previously allowed Jewish members of the force to leave their company in Palestine. There was however a corollary to such actions: any troop member who left would never be allowed inside an independent Poland or in a Poland ruled by the Communists.

After the Poles had left the Adriatic coast, Teodor and Auriel continued to supply produce, eggs, and meat to the reserves and to those returning from the front on the Adriatic.

"Their decision," Piotr added.

"Do you ever wonder about the others?" Bernard pondered.

"Who?" Hendryk interrupted.

"The friends we left behind. Our families obviously we think of them, but the friends for whom no one prays."

"How did you ever escape?" Wiktor whispered still lying in his sleeping bag.

Bernard's story was detailed attracting their attention. However he didn't need their interest for it to be real.

Dawid concluded that Bernard was very lucky. "And, what of that other one who escaped?"

Bernard had no information on Tomasz.

Franciszek wondered why the Allies suffered so many deaths. The question had been asked as many as five times each day. "After they bombed the Cassino, why didn't they just finish off the Nazis?"

No one had an immediate answer.

Hendryk repeated the information he had received. "Many of those Jerries were not on the hill until after the bombing. They just moved into the rubble, filling the holes with their tanks and mortar guns."

"So why do we even care about the hill?"

"Because at one mile high with guns that could shoot more than thirty miles, there is no access to Rome," Hendryk concluded.

"What will happen to us?" Piotr returned to being serious.

"We will win!" Franck stated unequivocally.

There was a pause regarding Piotr's comment that had more to do with the aftermath than about any battle at this mountain. Hendryk added the obvious, though an unwanted answer, "We don't know."

Franciszek conveyed his dejection. "Do we have a choice? Look at us. Poles fighting for some other country. So what if we win? What then? I'm not going back to Poland. I saw what Stalin did and what he will do. And, the stories we hear. No one cares."

Bernard offered, "They have problems caring."

Franck was offended. "Bull shit! They don't care. The British don't care. Churchill kisses Stalin's ass. This Roosevelt doesn't give a damn. The Americans here, they tell us to fight their battles. Will they tell Stalin to set Poland free? Will anyone say 'no' to the Bolsheviks? While we are here, who's defending Poland?" Will we ever see Poland again?" The comments reflected the consensus of many in camp.

Bernard offered this perception. "We can do nothing, and let the Germans win. Are we better with Hitler or Stalin? There aren't enough camps to satisfy Hitler. Yet, there aren't enough gulags to keep Stalin happy. With Hitler, there is no life. With Stalin, some life. If we fight and win, what do we have? No one knows."

Franciszek couldn't avoid his irritation, "You're dreaming again."

Witkor's voice was heard from his sleeping bag. "Just sleep."

Bernard responded to Franciszek's quip, "It's better to dream and think big, then bury your frustrations in your death."

"The poet!" Franciszek interjected. Others laughed.

"What would you have us do? Run? You won't get far. You have the British on one coast, and the Americans on the other. Or do you run north into a machine gun while you trip on a land mine?"

"Tomorrow night, we will be out there," Dawid deliberated.

"It will be hell." Franciszek stated the obvious.

Bernard pondered a response thinking in terms that everything was in God's hands; but he said nothing.

"What's it like to shoot someone?" Piotr asked. Franciszek, Dawid, and Hendryk said they had never done so.

Wiktor, still turned away from the others, spouted, "Give me your biggest mortar. I won't care." They chuckled.

Franck advised that he had shot at a German soldier who died; but he did not know if it was his bullet. "He stood there and we shot him at the same time. No one claimed credit. Killing makes Poles into Germans. We lose our dignity."

Bernard retorted, "You're the one who wants to kill every German you see."

"And did you ever meet one you liked? You've never shot a man, have you?"

Bernard shook his head.

"What's it like to see 'em die?" Piotr questioned.

"Don't think about it. It's either him or you."

"So true," Hendryk replied to Dawid's comment.

"Should be more to it than that," Bernard added.

Franck turned the conversation to the subject of fears. It was a regular topic for evening discussions. However, on this occasion, it had more significance.

Piotr followed with the comment, "My worst fear is a land mine." There was no disagreement.

"Still being alive with only half your body. Never. Shoot me right away," Dawid expressed his fear of suffering.

"They never tell us how many are in their hospitals," Franciszek commented. "And the number that never leave, except in body bags."

Jerzy rolled over, awake in his sleeping bag. "Don't be so stupid. There are no body bags. Where would they send them? The Bolsheviks won't take them. Float them out to sea, or just bury them in Italian soil."

Franck added his jest, "Maybe that's why the soil is so good."

"What will become of us?" Piotr continued.

"We will win."

"You never stopped dreaming," Franciszek retorted.

"What's wrong with dreams? It is better than sitting here at the base of this mountain. Look out there. There's only rubble on the hill. What's wrong with dreaming beyond this hill?"

Franciszek did not reply to Bernard's comment.

Hendryk returned to the issue of the battle. "They say there will be tanks following us."

"Hopefully they will miss us," Jerzy jested.

"Canadians as well as Poles," Hendryk added.

"As long as they both drive on the right side of the road," Jerzy continued, trying to make light of the issue.

Piotr enquired, "Has anyone ever met them?"

They all agreed they hadn't.

"We're more than fifty thousand here, just Poles. And the others, it's said together we are more than half a million," Hendryk quoted from his discussion with General Anders.

"Do we get to march into Rome?" Dawid ventured.

"Probably just the Americans. It's the only reason they're here. Claim all the credit," Franck asserted.

"We should all be part of the celebration. It's not just their war," Piotr added.

The realist Franciszek had to include his comment. "Do the others even care? Easy to celebrate when you can leave the war behind."

"But do we really expect the war to end the moment we greet the Pope?" Franck continued. There was consensus that the war would continue and that the fall of Rome alone would not compel Kesselring to surrender. "Only when we take over Berlin." Franck concluded,

Dawid's concern for his homeland continued to be the focus of his thoughts. "What if the Soviets arrive there first?"

"There'll be no kicking them out of Poland."

"Then what are we to do?" Piotr's comment drew silence from the others. They talked about the risks, and repeated concerns about the future. Talk about the war, the plan of attack, and the prospect of death were thus avoided. Thought about events after the fall of Berlin dominated their further discussion.

It was well after the final role call when sergeants could at long last close their eyes, that the chaplain visited the tent to bestow his blessing. There was a strange solemnity, a ritual not always done because there will always be a tomorrow, but perhaps there may not be a tomorrow.

"Good night," Bernard whispered after the last guest closed the tent flap.

(X X)

The mock attack exercises continued into the early afternoon. Then a late lunch was followed by three hours of rest. After a brief supper, the troops prepared themselves. Engineers guarded the camouflaged bridges. Allied trucks were fully gassed ready to bring troops to the front. Tanks were assembled in formation. Generals reviewed maps pinpointing the hills, the laneways, and positioning of the German forces. The diagrams however did not include the bunkers, the caves, the trip wires and the land mines. Rather than a dread fear of death, desire for victory perked their enthusiasm. All were ready to prove they were better than the Krauts that started this war.

The Americans of the 5th Army were on the move first, skirting to the south-west and then circling north along the coast south of the Gustav Line. They waited for the simultaneous attack on the German front.

Bernard stood with his comrades, at ease, ready for the final order. Before that day, there had been uncertainty. Now there wasn't. The medium brown uniform, he wore with dignity. The curved 'Poland' badge, applied to each sleeve, conveyed his pride. The

306

3rd Carpathian badge clearly displayed his allegiance. The Division was everything to him.

The barrage started at 11 p.m. on May 11 1944. One thousand, six hundred artillery guns let loose over a twenty mile stretch of the Gariliano-Rapido Line. Of these guns, one thousand and sixty belonged to the British 8th Army. The American 'Long Tom' gun with its 155mm calibre could propel nine-two pound shells a range of five miles. For forty minutes these Allied guns blasted German positions.

The Allies had the equivalent of 108 battalions that included these guns, about 2,000 tanks, and more than 3,000 aircraft. These planes included the American B25 Mitchell Bomber, the B26 Marauder, and the B17 Flying Fortress. The Germans at Cassino could muster only the equivalent of 57 battalions. Kesselring had devoted other divisions to the Adriatic, to the combat at Ancona, and to the defence of Rome. These diversions were a significant component in the Allied campaign to defeat the Germans at Cassino. The reality was: Kesselring under-estimated the Allied force. Allies had the equivalent of thirteen divisions while Kesselring had only six.

At 11:40 p.m. the Royal Fusiliers and the 21st Lancers crossed the river as Allied mortar shells flew overhead aimed at locations on the upper hill. The goal of the Fusiliers and Lancers was to secure a bridge allowing Allied tanks to cross. As soon as they crossed, the German 10th Army with heavy mortar and artillery rebuffed the Allies.

To the west, the 1st Free French Division and the Moroccan Mountain Division of the French Expeditionary Corps crossed the Gustav Line moving north into the Aurunci Mountains. This mountain range was positioned between the Tyrrhenian Sea and the Liri Valley. Though German troops occupied the southern portion of the Liri Valley, not much attention had been spent defending the mountains. They were considered impassable.

Prior to the attack, the French force was required to trek the fifty kilometres from its camp to the front. They were firmly committed to the destruction of Germany after what Kesselring had done to Morocco, Algeria and Libya. It was not difficult to motivate these troops.

If the French troops were able to scale the mountains, transport artillery equipment along dangerous paths, keep their feet on wet rocky terrain, and transgress flooded basins; then they expected to meet the Germans in the valley. Monte Petrella was 1,533 meters high, just less than the height of Monte Cassino. Monte Sant'Angelo was about one hundred fifty meters lower than the Abbey ruins. The task was monumental but getting around and over the mountains was just the start. The United States II Corps assisted the French in this campaign.

At the same time, the US Fifth Army moved up the coast to relieve the US Sixth Corps, allowing the latter to move north-east to Valmontone. Opposition was at times intense, but the Germans weakened under the relentless attack by land and sea.

The British 13th Corps, part of the British 8th Army, crossed the Rapido River and encroached upon the lower outskirts of the town where they confronted the Germans firing from concealed positions and partially destroyed walls. From there the British moved east to establish a bridgehead across the river.

The fighting on all fronts continued into the night.

At 7 a.m. on May 12th, the Allied air attack began. After several hours, the armoured and infantry divisions took over.

The American 350th Regiment, fighting with the Fifth Army, encountered brutal artillery and mortar fire in trying to capture Monte Santa Maria Infante. The hill, near the mouth of the Gariliano River, was strategic for supplies, reserves, and movement in all directions. Capturing it would prevent the Germans from any counter offensive from the rear. After several hours, the American offensive failed to secure the objective, resulting in significant casualties.

In the Aurunci Mountains the Moroccan 8th Rifle Division was successful in capturing Monte Feuci and Monte Maio. On the same day the Moroccan 4th Mountain Division with the assistance of the US II Corps captured Monte Faito. However these were still more than thirty kilometres from the Cassino summit. If Kesselring shifted more troops into the Liri Valley to protect that advance he would make himself vulnerable elsewhere. The success of the surprise through the mountains elated the Allied commanders.

East of Cassino town, the Indian 8th Division and the British 4th Division joined forces with the British 13th Corps enlarging the bridgehead across the river. With the bridges secure, the Canadian 1st Armoured Brigade joined the battle.

The Gustav Line had been breached in several locations. Allies moved forward in some areas as much as 1,500 meters. Journalists described the launch as 'a massive offensive' claiming that 'the first objectives had been attained'.

(XXI)

They waited impatiently, no longer at attention, but fully equipped and ready for battle. Rifles weighed upon their left shoulders. Ammunition, grenades and wire cutting shears were in place for rapid use. They could barely see the summit covered in rubble before them. Enthusiasm had passed. Good-byes had been said. It was time for performance. Stern, determined expressions pierced the midnight black.

Across the river, between the mountains other troops of the Polish II Corps waited, having relieved the British 78th Division three weeks earlier. These soldiers too were ready for the final assault. Superlatives for total victory rang loud in both camps.

At 1am on May 13th the Polish troops marched into action. Crossing the Rapido River to the west of Cassino town the Polish officers led the 3rd Carpathian Rifle Division and the 5th Kresowa Division into battle. The Carpathian Division was assigned the task of securing Hill 593, Hill 444 and the final ascent to the Abbey. The goal of the Kresowan Division was to take Phantom Ridge and remove the Germans from Colle Sant'Angelo. The 5th Kresowa moved to the right of the Carpathian Division for sweeping access to the Ridge.

The rubble and debris took on a fourth dimension with the extraordinary time necessary to climb, descend and avoid the hazards. It was difficult enough just getting across some of the bridges still littered with rocks and boulders. The Allied bombing and mortar fire created more difficulties than anticipated. The Germans were still in place. Having to climb over boulders forced the Allied troops to become openly vulnerable to machine gun fire. Injuries, strains and fractures became immeasurable. Barbed wire also took its toll on many soldiers. It was just not the cuts or the ominous impediment. Doing anything to cut the wires or gain access repeatedly exposed the soldiers. To the eastern extreme, the flooding caused by the ruptured dam, still slowed any battalion wishing to quickly cross the plain. German tanks, even in broad daylight, were concealed by boulders and debris. Caves, created by the Allied bombing, provided the Germans with security. Only the blaze of machine gun fire revealed their location. The Germans, from their pillboxes, were able to surprise many unwary as well as prepared soldiers. Anti-tank guns were positioned to thwart the Allied ascent. Kesselring had positioned more than three hundred artillery pieces to maximize the deaths caused by inescapable cross-fire. All of these presented incredible perils to even the most attentive soldier. In the black of night, the time when most raids took place, these risks were intensified.

Commander Duch arranged for the troops to be in groups of about thirty to magnify the number of orchestrated clusters attacking in sequence. Within hours, the Carpathian Division was directly attacking Hill 593, its prime initial objective. The Hill 593 had another ominous name, Mount Calvary. It would be the death of many soldiers. Battalions of the Carpathian Division simultaneously fought their way into the gorge adjacent to Phantom Ridge. From that position and from Hill 593, the troops began an assault on Hill 569. That region exposed an immediate problem: there was no communication access.

Meanwhile, the 13th and 15th Battalions of the Kresowa Division reached Hill 517. Unfortunately, the cost was extreme, suffering approximately a twenty-percent casualty rate.

The Armoured Divisions provided support throughout the assault on the various hills. However, the roads and laneways were still littered with destroyed and damaged units. The Germans had positioned their tanks and anti-tank artillery to maximize the kill factor.

The 13th Battalion of the Kresowa Division continued forward under heavy fire, reaching its goal of Phantom Ridge. The Ridge was essential because from that position there was artillery access to the Liri Valley and ultimate road access to the abbey itself. At dawn the Germans began their counter offensive. The Polish troops on Colle Sant'Angelo, Hill 505, Hill 575, and Phantom Ridge became extremely vulnerable. Another battalion joined the Polish ranks, but even that proved to be ineffective against the German onslaught.

On Hill 569, the Germans began a massive assault, driving the Carpathian Division back to Mount Calvary. There the Polish force withstood several counter attacks involving bombing, snipers and paratroopers. In the lull following a German offensive, several Polish troops were able to scramble up mounds of concrete rubble and along potholed narrow footpaths into abandoned German foxholes. This was becoming trench warfare. While they fought to maintain their position on Hill 593, Polish casualties on Hill 569 had become disastrous. Only one officer and seven soldiers survived. The German artillery then focused its attack on the gorge between Phantom

Ridge and Snakeshead. There, machine gun and mortar fire destroyed numerous tanks and shortened the lives of countless soldiers. Before sunrise, the Carpathian Division had lost about one thousand men.

At dawn, to the north of the abbey the Carpathian Division with the 2nd Armoured Brigade began an assault on German forces at Massa Albaneta. The German anti-tank machinery had already been positioned for such an offensive. The casualties were again heavy.

At 7:15 a.m., Allied bombers began a bombardment of German positions. Unfortunately the Polish troops were in close proximity to the enemy on many fronts. The casualties on both sides were severe. The benefit to the Allies of this air raid was the destruction of the headquarters of the German 10th Army and of a post belonging to the XIV Panzer Corps.

On Mount Calvary, one officer and twenty-nine soldiers remained alive to confront the German 14th Corps. There was no time for fear or trembling. Death was all around them. Comrades were dead. Friends were no more. The stench in some places was so pungent that soldiers searched for their gas masks. There were lulls. But each time the volley that broke the silence was that much more intense.

Bernard huddled behind boulders, obscured from machine gun fire. His rifle he held securely in his left hand. A German machine gun rested against right arm. The brim of his hat he had pressed down to his eyebrows, as if protecting more of his head might save his life. Among the thirty left in the Carpathian Division on that hill, not a word was spoken. They covered a large area, one or two soldiers to each protected strongpoint. Minutes became hours. There was no time for any meal.

No one was hungry. Eyes pierced every shadow. Ears perked to the sound of every breeze. In momentary silence, the screams of dying comrades still echoed in their minds. It was a perverse world of self-preservation.

The German offensive against the two battalions of the Kresowa Division continued from dawn until late afternoon. Casualties mounted quickly, and would have been greater if the Polish troops had just fled. Mowing down running troops was more of an adventure. The exhausted Poles continued to engage the Germans in heavy combat but lacked further reserves. In the dark, they seized the opportunity granted to them to withdraw.

At night on Mount Calvary, the remaining Carpathian troops were joined by others, making their force comparative in size to the Germans. Night patrols were completed to survey enemy positions. While doing so, it was difficult to avoid stumbling on the corpses. Trip wires were still a deadly hazard. Throwing a rock to disturb the silence and then seeing if there was any reaction – this was the best method. Ducking was mandatory. Not much was accomplished that first night nor the next morning. The paratroopers then commenced an offensive on the afternoon of the fourteenth. The exchange of mortar fire was intense. Boulders and debris could no longer sustain the impacts, and could no longer hide the enemy. Volleys of gunfire filled the air. More lay dead. Others were critically wounded. Some, painfully gasping for life, preferred death. The Germans would not be moved from their bunkers. Grenades were a possible means to compel such flight, but both sides had already hurled their grenades leaving so few in reserve. For the Germans, it was near impossible to bring fresh supplies to their bunkers. For the Poles, access from the secured land on the slope was possible.

Just before suppertime, Bernard clutched his grenade. He was angry. Something had to happen. He hadn't eaten for almost two days. That perhaps above all made him so determined. He looked at it once more. "This is it," he thought. The soldier knew he would have to stand to properly propel the weapon, and that appearing above the height of the large boulder could mean his death. Looking up he noticed the movement of the clouds. The breeze had been strong all day. One benefit to afternoon warfare from their position was that the Germans were staring toward the setting sun. As soon as the clouds moved, the sun would shine and that must be his opportunity. He thought again of his alternatives. All of the training in Syria, Palestine and Egypt taught them to be prepared. Part of being prepared was making the best choice. Bernard put down his rifle, and in his left hand he held the machine gun. It may have taken as much as five minutes, but brightly the sun did shine. With his left hand on the trigger, Bernard released a short volley of machine gun fire to the far left into the area of the last mortar fire. Then rising and in the same second with the clip released, the grenade was thrown. It flew heel-over-head toward its destination. In that very same moment, Bernard dropped to the ground covering his head. The blast blew debris. Men screamed. German machine gunners were ripped apart.

Voices echoed among the rocks. Another Polish grenade found its mark. However, the rest of the Germans, as if glued to their bunkers, did not move. The quiet that followed was frightening. "What next?" Bernard thought. There were no instructions from any superior. German tanks and artillery remained in their position to maximize the death caused by cross fire.

Late in the evening of the fifteenth, the Carpathian troops engaged the Germans once more. The German reprisal was less than expected, but still significant. The Polish troops held out. Another lull followed; but this time it was the Poles that broke the silence. The exchange last more than a half hour. Then in the black of night, with prisoners bound and muffled, some of the Carpathian troops withdrew to their camp.

Before dawn on May 16th, the rest of the Carpathian Division, after successfully destroying several artillery stations, withdrew.

For three days, eight hundred well-positioned German troops were able to withstand the attacks of two divisions. The Polish II Corps lost 3,503 soldiers and 281 officers.

Bernard returned to camp, more psychologically damaged, than he had ever been in two concentration camps. The saving grace was the death of enemy soldiers. He was amazed he had no difficulty pulling the trigger.

(XXII)

To the west of Cassino, into the Liri Valley and through the Aurunci Mountains the Allied forces penetrated the Gustaf Line. The American and British Armies employed the full force and reserves of all of the divisions and battalions at their command. Whereas the Poles were directed to attack the Ridge and three Hills close to the abbey ruins, the others did the necessary to win access to the route north to Rome.

The British 4th Division, the British 78th Division, the British 13th Corps, the British 6th Armoured Division, the Indian 8th Division, twenty regiments and three brigades of the French Expeditionary Corps, the Moroccan Goumiers, the Canadian 1st Infantry, the Canadian 5th Armoured Division, the American 10th Brigade and the New Zealand force – all prepared with specific assignments to complete the defeat of the German 10th Army and all of its aligned panzer units, divisions, and paratroopers. This was to be Armageddon if that was required.

The two specific objectives were to rid Cassino town of all German artillery, soldiers and influence, and to defeat the German forces guarding the Liri Valley and access to Rome.

On May 11, 1944, the French Expeditionary Force crossed the Gariliano River and engaged the German forces before the foothills of the Aurunci Mountains. By the next day, the French had defeated the German infantry and were entering the mountain region with the Algerian, Moroccan regiments at their command. On May 13th the French had captured Monte Maio. This mountain range provided a view of southern part of Liri Valley with the capacity to maximize artillery usage.

The British 13th Corps had also entered the Liri Valley after subduing a less than determined German Corps. The Axis defence though committed was progressively weakened by fatigue. It was becoming more difficult to protect a sprawling front of over twenty miles for such a long period of time. The weather was no longer on their side. Supplies were stretched to the limit including food. The general malaise of troops in a foreign country, with all of the problems at home, diminished the will of the German soldiers to keep fighting. However, the fear of the firing squad compelled many to stay focused. If the Italians weren't fighting to preserve the Axis pact, why should the Germans waste their lives fighting this multi-national force. As the British 13th Corps drove north, the success at Monte Maio became even more important as it allowed the Allies to fire on the retreating Germans.

On that same day, the British and Indian Divisions with the Gurkhas captured Sant' Angelo Village north of the abbey ruins. The repairs and security of the bridge on Pignatarro Road provided direct access to the abbey for the Canadian 1st Infantry Division and the British 78th Division and the Indian 8th Division.

As much as Kesselring may have feared the revenge-factor of the Poles, he similarly had military respect for the retribution the French felt toward anything German. For the past one hundred years, there had been five major conflicts or wars with the French. Each time the determination on both sides to wipe out the enemy was intense. Therefore with the French overcoming the German defence in quick fashion, Kesselring committed his cause to stopping their advance. However he was considerably less than successful in this objective. In fact, he was losing. The French in the Aurunci Mountains overcame the German counter attack and captured Mount Faito and Castleforte. The 1st Free French Division and the Moroccan Division captured Mount Girofano. With the Goumiers attacking at night, they advanced to S. Apollinaire and S. Ambrogio.

With the French in the mountains on the west, with British and Indian Divisions overlooking from the east, the entire Liri Valley was not a secure home to any fleeing army.

Farther to the west, at Anzio, the US 5th Army under the direction of the Lt. General Clark relieved the US 6th Corps. The American Corps then commenced its march to the north-east toward Valmontane on the route to Rome. The speed of its progress was thwarted by a series of German counter offensives that lasted almost two weeks.

With the access to the Liri Valley secured, brigades from the British 13th Corps circled back and then moved east toward Cassino town. There they confronted the remaining Germans from fixed positions among the craters and rubble. By the end of the day on May 15th, the British 13th Corps over ran the remains of the town.

On that same day the French Expeditionary Corps seized control of Cresasola, San Giorgio, Ausonia, Esperia at the base of Monte D'Oro, and Monte D'Oro itself. It had control of the Aurunci Mountains and several vantage points looking down onto the valley. It was those mountains that Kesselring had been told were impenetrable.

On May 16th General Oliver Leece ordered the British 78th Division to drive further into the valley to open the route north to Rome. At that point the Axis defence held firm. Counter attacks followed and the British Division succeeded in quelling the stiff defence.

By evening on the May 16, 1944, the highway through the Liri Valley was mostly in control of the Allied forces. Still, the Germans held the summit at Monte Cassino and from that vantage point no Allied soldier was safe.

(XXIII)

Bernard sat in his tent, trembling, terrified by the absence of those who did not return. Throughout the camp exclamations of distress and the wails of loss broke the night. There was not a gentle word, just repetitive damnation. Piotr was there, too, in the tent, silent and shocked. His bloodied tunic he had discarded; but the absence of clothing could not make him feel any colder. Piotr was stunned. He was never much for religion, and he certainly had no need for it now. The flaps of the tent rustled in the cool breeze from the mountains. Fires were lit to warm the wandering souls. They were so contrary to camp regulations. Concealing your camp was paramount. But on this night, rules were not meant for the dead. The chaplain roamed among the groups of distraught soldiers offering as many conciliatory words as possible. The sparks and flying embers ascended to the heavens dividing the ebony-spirit that pervaded the camp.

Bernard's battalion returned across the river after that three-day face-to-face combat with the enemy. Other members of the 3rd Carpathian Rifle Division returned to their temporary camp north of the Monte Cassino. "Perhaps they went there." Bernard repeatedly thought of Franciszek and Hendryk. Piotr didn't think. His silence and dread were all he had.

General Anders, too, was shocked by the more than 3,500 fatalities. He feared there may be others also unaccounted for, victims of machine gun or mortar fire just lying there, injured and not able make it to safety. There were prayers too for those as they lay dying. There was no longer a desire to conceal his tent. The lamp was

320

lit, the maps unfurled. The problems he knew were almost insurmountable. Any enthusiasm had basically died. They knew the routes to ascend the hills. That was an obvious benefit. Hopefully they, too, recalled those areas where they might be most vulnerable. That was essential. Leadership was now a key issue. He lost over 250 officers. The number was still counting. Because of this a complete roll-call had not been done. How many soldiers he had on this side of the river could only be an approximate. Who would now lead them? Like others in the camp, he prayed that many ventured north instead of south across the river.

Perhaps it was good news that he had not heard from the French. General Juin would have certainly reported any misfortune. Good news for the French would definitely mean Kesselring would have to divert more troops away from the abbey ruins. But then, even if most of his Tenth Army with all of the divisions and paratroopers left, a handful of soldiers could man the bunkers, tanks, and pillboxes to wreak havoc once again. It bothered him that some were equipped with up to five machine guns at each location. The Germans were that well prepared and seemingly had committed their entire defence to that hill. "But if the French broke through?" Anders conveyed a hopeful smile to his two sergeants.

An officer wandered from tent to tent announcing the plans for the seventeenth. It was about 10 p.m. when he ventured into the sector of the camp where Bernard was stationed. "Pięć godzin," he announced. At 3am they would be back in action.

Bernard lay back and pulled the sleeping bag over his head.

(XXIV)

Before dawn on the morning of May 17th, a stern, angry commitment veiled the emotions of the Carpathian camp. There was no robust enthusiasm. There was a job to do, and come hell or death this was going to be the day. No one could say that for sure. In war nothing is certain. However, when desire becomes buried in anger, everything, including the remote probability of victory, becomes more than a possibility. Vengeance had peaked. One soldier even declared the mountain before them to be, "Zamontować Zemsty." 'Mount Revenge' became more than a name; it was their military objective.

The Carpathian and Kresowa Divisions maintained their prior goals. This allowed for the obvious knowledge of the terrain, the German defence positions, all such hazards, and the best areas for concealment and mortar deployment.

At 6 a.m., the Kresowa 5th Division headed for Phantom Ridge. Success came quickly, and within the hour a foothold was established on the ridge. The Germans refused to fold and from their pillboxes inflicted an ominous defence. In spite of the volley of artillery from hidden craters, the Kresowan Division was successful in destroying the German defence on the ridge. From there the division drove toward Sant' Angelo. Again Axis firepower from the obscured craters thwarted the Polish advance. In spite of the deluge of mortar fire, the division held its ground.

At the same time, from a position two miles west of Cassino town, the Carpathian Division crossed the Rapido River. Defence was almost non-existent. Earlier bombardment had eliminated German positions in the lower valley. Those Axis that expended any artillery were destroyed. The armoured units would not let them survive. The initial objective was to secure the gorge below Phantom Ridge, attack Mass Albaneta, and then focus the assault on Mount Calvary.

Fatigue was ever present. Each soldier felt it. It was inescapable. Sticking to the main road for the first mile eased the grumbling aches. Then when they had to abandon the path for the rubble and boulders, every discomfort was magnified. The ability to overcome such pains was the mark of a true soldier. The fears were many to discourage the many, but an able soldier would not allow any sentiment interfere with his ability to defend his division, his battalion, the officers, and his fellow troops. To Bernard, climbing the debris truly meant nothing to himself in those moments.

After crossing the river, Bernard did not see Piotr again. Commander Duch split the troops into seven per unit. "Powódź (tsunami)," he called it. There was a land mine device with the trained technician in Bernard's group. That was indeed something for which to be grateful.

The pain in his legs was at times almost unbearable. Thirty minutes climbing the boulders left him vulnerable with each movement. The Germans were still out there. In the distance he could hear the exchange of gunfire. Then there was the blast of mortar artillery. Each time those in his company would duck. Then rising, they would carry on, climbing further. When they achieved a position where they were partially sheltered on one side by a row of pine trees, they rested. From there, they viewed the valley below, and the Polish troops streaming into the gorge below Phantom Ridge. Members of the

Kresowan Division could not be seen. Bernard guessed they may have already achieved control of the ridge.

A swig from his canteen, that's all he would afford himself. Ben closed his eyes for those moments as did five others. One always stayed alert to keep watch. Hands signals conveyed their plan. They did not speak, being that high on the hill, and not knowing where the Germans were.

Then suddenly all hell broke loose in the gorge. The Germans, still the division of paratroopers, were firing upon the Poles from both sides. The blaze of crossfire ended the advance. Carpathian soldiers in the valley fled for cover, but there was none from the crossfire. Meanwhile the Germans were commencing their counter offensives against the Kresowan Division at Cole Sant' Angelo. Those Poles were occupied defending their own position, unable to assist the troops in the gorge.

The signal was simple. The hand dropped. Immediately Bernard's company rushed from its security, descending slightly and then hiding behind strewn boulders. From there their gunfire was directed toward the Germans who were firing on the Poles in the gorge.

To assist the Allies in the gorge, the Carpathian troops, who had camped north of the abbey ruins, fired upon the German positions on both hills. At the same time, battalions were climbing Mount Calvary. There they met the onslaught of the German 14th Corps still protecting the Hill 593.

As this battle was ensuing, on that same morning, the American 2nd Corps was capturing Formia, and the British 78th Division was pushing farther north securing more territory in the Liri Valley. However, regardless of any conflict elsewhere, the Germans defending Monte Cassino were there to the end.

From their position above the German snipers, Bernard's company fired upon the enemy. Four of the locations were silenced. Bernard himself ended the lives of two enemy gunners.

The gear carried into this battle was so much more than five days before. They vowed to not return and therefore took everything with them. Climbing the hills thus became a more arduous chore with all of the extra equipment. Three grenades were standard. Bernard took four. Piotr grabbed five. The canteen and a dried sandwich were all the nourishment allowed. Bullets for rifles and machine guns were plentiful. Unlike the Germans whose supplies were restricted, the Poles had artillery fresh from the navy at Naples. Such ships, especially in the Mediterranean had become more than troop carriers.

Once the four pillboxes were silenced, Bernard's company moved still further below, hiding to avoid detection. The conflict in the gorge had become a full-scale exchange of artillery. Toward Colle Sant' Angelo, the Kresowan Division was overcoming the German paratroopers.

Armoured Divisions were active, too, in the various valleys, along the many paths, and decidedly against enemy tanks. As difficult as it had become for Allied tanks to advance on the roads, and in the fields; the German Panzers were in a similar position with almost nowhere to go without first removing the tanks they had already destroyed. Wreckage was not beneficial to either side.

Mount Calvary was still occupied by the Axis forces as the sun was setting on May 17th. Phantom Ridge and Colle Sant' Angelo were captured by the Polish forces. Cassino town flew the British flag. The British and French Divisions were pushing north in the Liri Valley. The American 5th Army was still engaged by the Germans at Anzio. The lull in the gorge below Phantom Ridge lasted more than normal, more than an eerie few hours.

As dark fell upon the valley, volleys from German snipers broke the silence. Polish forces shot back to positions on the hill not knowing whom, where or if. The rest also ended for Bernard and his company. Firing into the darkened gorge was not an option. They turned around and headed once more up the incline. The climb was even more difficult in the night. Germans had to be there somewhere. But where? They came to rest just before midnight in a setting concealed by boulders on three sides.

Back in camp the news was exhilarating. A message was decoded revealing, the Tenth Army was, "on the verge of retreating." However that communiqué could not explain the Axis firepower in the gorge, or on the hills or from the summit. To coincide with the message, at about thirty minutes before midnight on May 17 1944, enemy flares were ignited, being an order to retreat.

The flares were not hidden from the Carpathian troops. They knew what it meant, that victory could well be theirs. However, it could also be a trick encouraging the Poles to expose themselves to German fire. Regardless of any order to retreat, there were no Germans jumping out of the craters or from behind rocks retreating, running away, or waving white flags. They cautioned themselves. This was still war.

Bernard's group of seven were surprised to meet others from the 4th Battalion on the hill. They spoke at length about what they had seen. One soldier was actually able to pinpoint the German defence positions. He had lost three friends four days before.

The hill became that much more difficult: steeper with loose rock. Pain was no longer an issue. Realizing they could come into the view of a German sniper at any time, each step forward meant hugging the ground.

Members of the 12th Podolian Cavalry Regiment had already ascended the incline and were concealed by the limited brush and leafless bushes that withstood months of prior bombing and gunfire. As a reconnaissance unit they had mastered mobility at night.

Below them the gunfire was being replaced by cheers. The Carpathian and Kresowan forces in the gorge and on the ridge were moving toward their final objective.

Mount Calvary was the now the objective of the Carpathians from the gorge. They moved swiftly but again met the fierce resistance of the German 14th Corps. Bernard threw his last two grenades. There were at least twenty hurled in the direction of four German placements. However the ability to stand and brace oneself on sloping ground and then hurl the weapon with full might was considerably restricted. At least four Polish soldiers, Bernard saw die, in those hours. Each German pillbox or crater was the home to at least three machine guns. Mortar weapons were aimed at key locations. The German 14th Corps was so well protected not just by boulders around each position but also by the rocks and bombed-debris preventing close access. The need to take out the final German defenders was essential.

Bernard slithered between the rocks. Crawling on his stomach over the sharp rocky rubble was painful, but so was death. His tunic was ripped, his pants torn, his knees bloodied. He continued to his right unseen by the enemy firing overhead. He was about fifty feet away when the German Paratrooper was clearly in his sights. A volley of five shots ended that German soldier's life. His scream told the story. Rolling away he found the security of a massive boulder. In the distance Ben saw one paratrooper rise. The Polish guns were instantly pointed at him.

"Kapit ..." The enemy could barely speak.

At 10 a.m. on May 18 1944 the Polish force repelled the final German volley on Monte Cassino. The last meters to the top of the ruins were quickly climbed. The exhilaration was imaginable. Lieutenant Gurbiel of the 12th Uhlan Regiment hoisted the flag above the abbey ruins. Bernard and other members of the 3rd Carpathian Rifle Division were there with him to celebrate. A bugler from the 3rd Battalion played the Hejnal Mariacki, the Krakow Anthem, in celebration of the victory.

They looked down upon the ruins, to the troops celebrating in the gorge and on the hillside, to the town of shattered concrete, on the hill strewn with rotting corpses, over the lane ways and fields with destroyed tanks, and on the red poppies struggling to grow between the rocks.

(X X V)

After celebrating the victory at Monte Cassino, General Anders wrote describing the summit and battlegrounds.

There were enormous dumps of unused ammunition, and here and there heaps of land mines. Corpses of Polish and German soldiers, sometimes entangled in a deathly embrace, lay everywhere, and the air was full of rotting bodies.

Crater after crater pitted the sides of the hills, and scattered over them were the fragments of uniforms and tin helmets, tommy guns, Spandaus, Schmeissers, and grenades. Of the monastery itself, there remained only an enormous heap of ruins and rubble with here and there some broken columns. Only the western wall, over which two flags flew, was still standing. A cracked church bell lay on the ground next to an unexploded shell of the heaviest calibre and on shattered walls and ceilings fragments of paintings and frescoes could be seen. Priceless works of art, sculptures, pictures and books lay in the dust and broken plaster.

More than 55,000 Allied soldiers died in the four battles for Monte Cassino. This figure is about five percent of all of the available troops.

Troop numbers were unfortunately not always accurate based on many factors. The divisions and battalions on both sides were regularly in motion: towards Anzio, defending Rome, to and from the Adriatic, Axis divisions from the north, Allied divisions from the south and the coasts, rapidly moving panzer divisions, Italian soldiers fighting on both sides, and all of the additional divisions, brigades and corps that formed the Allied troops. This latter contingent included troops from at least twelve nations or colonies. In addition, this conflict caused the deaths of many officers, those who would account for the number of their troops. Following the fourth battle, some troops were transferred to the Pacific Front, while other divisions and brigades were disbanded. Also, there were the troops Missing In Action who were too innumerable to count. The stench on the mountain was beyond measurement.

Historians vary on the actual number of Allied troops. Some suggest a half million, others about one million. Taking into account Montgomery's more than 200,000, Clark's 250,000, the Polish 50,000, and then adding to these the Canadian, French, Moroccan, Algerian, Indian, South African, New Zealanders, Australians, Irish and members of the Commonwealth. The number easily exceeds 1,000,000.

Considering this was such a prolonged bloody conflict, the fatalities would reasonably have been expected to be far worse. However, at any one time as much as forty percent of the entire force was not actively engaged at the same time. Taking that into account the Killed In Action and the Missing In Action net figure is approximately eight percent of those actively engaged in battle.

The Germans reported only 20,000 casualties. This figure historians accept, but it may not be totally reliable as the Nazi figures for other battles were easily refuted.

The Polish Divisions had 56,000 troops at Monte Cassino. Of these, approximately 4,000 were killed or missing in action. The casualty rate for the Carpathian and Kresowan Divisions was just higher than seven percent, comparative to the entire Allied force.

The injured was an equally devastating figure. More than 5,700 Polish soldiers were so severely injured they either could not walk, had lost a limb, were blinded, suffered chest or head injuries, or were impaired so that they could no longer join the Polish Divisions in further conflict. Their fate was doubly cruel as there was no longer a sympathetic independent Poland to offer them care.

With almost ten thousand troops either dead or disabled, the Polish force was severely lacking manpower to ably continue. Its divisions had paid a heavy cost to achieve victory on a mountain covered by rubble. But, such was their fate and their accepted duty.

However, the ten thousand dead or injured was not the cruellest blow to the Polish II Corps. Reports surfaced that the Germans offered no defence in the final attack. An internet report more than sixty years after the battle still promulgates that view, "the summit was undefended." To quote the name of that source may in fact be slander so the identity will remain confined to the inaccuracies of history. Initial reports suggested limited protection of the summit. Others identified specific numbers for the Germans protecting Monte Cassino. Some said thirty. Others espoused only thirteen. Another reporter accused Kesselring of abandoning "sixteen injured soldiers" to fight off the advancing Allied troops. A few suggested the Germans left with their artillery. A report citing the number of Germans as being less than twenty came from a journalist who at the time was reporting on the conflict at Anzio. Another war correspondent stationed in Britain reported on the minimal number of Germans defending the mountain. Still, another, so called expert, asserted that the entire summit was defended by only one officer and two soldiers of the 1st company of 1st battalion of German 3rd Parachute Regiment.

Perhaps these reports were concocted to dispel the heroic influence of the Polish troops. Perhaps they were an attempt to support the interests of the Soviet Union, its Ally to whom they had already conceded Poland. Stalin did not want any accolades bestowed on Anders's Army. Stalin would not tolerate any prospect of opposition in Communist Poland. Perhaps they were attempts to claim that all of the Allied troops were responsible for the victory. The reality was that there was not one Allied Flag representing all of the united forces. Therefore the flag or banner that would be waved atop the summit would be the one carried by the first troops there. There was never any intention by the Polish II Corps to dismiss the efforts, the lives, and the results of all of the Allies.

The reality was some of the German troops and regiments had already left the ruins of Monte Cassino. These had indeed left to defend the Hitler Line to confront the French Expeditionary Corps and the British 78th Division in the Liri Valley, and to confront the Americans at Anzio. German Divisions necessary to defend Valmontane would move the shorter distance from Rome where they were stationed. But to suggest Kesselring abandoned the summit leaving behind only thirteen, or less than thirty, or just three is more than a gross exaggeration.

Kesselring had at his command the German 10th Army and the XIV Panzer Corps as well as Paratroopers, with more than forty regiments belonging to several divisions. The total number of troops, including the two divisions that came south from Rome in January, exceeded a quarter million. If approximately twenty thousand had died, there would have been more that 200,000 German troops to move out of the way between 11:30pm on May 17th and 10am on May 18th. That was not possible.

The Allies prior to May 17, 1944 had basically encircled the summit. In the east along the Rapido River the British 8th Army and the Polish II Corps were stationed. To the south, on the other side of the Gariliano, the New Zealanders, Indians, and armoured divisions waited. To the west beyond the Aurunci Mountains, the US 5th Army controlled the venue. In the Liri Valley the French and British were pushing north. The other route away from the summit was north toward Mount Cairo. But in that area, there were the battalions of the Carpathian Division, and the infantry regiments of the New Zealanders, Indians and Canadians. None of these reported such a mass exodus.

Kesselring had established barracks about ten miles east of Cassino town on the same side of the river. What happened to these? There is no historical report that they had previously abandoned their locale or had been killed. There is no report of their mass exodus toward the Adriatic or to the north-west beyond Cassino.

What happened to the German tanks, machinery, large guns, and artillery? If the Allies were controlling the southern portion of the Liri Valley, how did the German divisions just pass them unseen? There are no such reports. However, the Germans were able to gather at the Hitler Line, eight miles (12.5 kilometres) north of Monte Cassino. From that reality, the conclusions can be drawn that the French and English did not have full control of the Liri Valley, and that the German troops had a route in the same valley to vacate the summit.

Prior to the Polish assault on the summit of May 17-18, some of the Germans had left, but there were still several battalions and or divisions there to defend the mountain. It would have been impossible to move 200,000 troops in less than eleven hours.

One explanation, recorded in Italian right after the war, provides this information: the German 1st Airborne Division left the region of the summit for the Hitler Line on May 16 and May 17; and two German Battalions went north starting on May 17 to Massa Albaneta and then to the village of San Lucia, eventually occupying Pizzo Corno and the slope of Mount Cairo.

It's unreasonable to suggest that the Germans did not leave sufficient troops to adequately defend the summit on May 17-18. If the German troops were not still defending Monte Cassino who confronted the Poles for ten hours in the gorge below Phantom Ridge? Who fought the Poles on the Ridge and on Colle Sant'Angelo? Who fought the Allies at Massa Albaneta? Who was firing on the Carpathian Division in the valley? Which Axis force was occupying Mount Calvary? How did approximately five hundred Polish troops die on that last day of fighting?

Untruths can hurt more than German bullets.

Chapter Eleven
Beyond the Summit

As long as there were victories to be won, the Polish II Corps would never rest.

As long as the Germans were in flight, the Poles would be chasing them.

After losing the summit at Monte Cassino, the German force fled to the Hitler Line, the 1st Airborne being the first to leave. Two battalions went north to Massa Albaneta and then established camp at the village of San Lucia, five kilometres from Cassino. The next day, the same day that the Polish Carpathians celebrated atop the ruins, a portion of these German forces established key positions on the slopes of Pizzo Corno and Monte Cairo. The majority of the German troops headed north, to the northern section of the Liri Valley to defend the Hitler Line.

If the German figures on its casualties at Monte Cassino are to be believed, then Kesselring would have had at least 200,000 troops at his command.

The Hitler Line was a seventy mile fortified line from the slope of Monte Cairo west to the Tyrrhenian Sea. The eastern extremity also included the incline of Pizzo Corno, the village of San Lucia, the town of Piedimonte San Germano. From there the Hitler Line stretched into the Liri Valley through the towns of

Aquino and Pontecorvo. After that it rose into the Aurunci Mountains, where it was not well protected, to end in the sloping terrain at the Tyrrhenian Sea. Throughout the valley, the defended line was five hundred to one thousand meters thick.

The British 8th Army had committed the British 78th Division and British 13th Corp to the Liri Valley. The task of the Polish II Corps was to defeat the Germans in the eastern extremity of the Hitler Line. This meant capturing the village of San Lucia, neutralizing the influence on Monte Cairo and Pizzo Corno, and seizing the village of Piedimonte San Germano.

The 50,000 soldiers in the Polish II Corps following the victory at Monte Cassino included: 13th Battalion Kresowa, 15th Battalion Kresowa, 18th Fusilier Kresowan Battalion, 5th Battalion Carpathian Fusiliers, 12th Uhlun Lancers, 9th Regiment Field Artillery, 10th Heavy Artillery, 11th Heavy Artillery, 7th Antitank Artillery, 6th Armoured Regiment, various battalions of Carpathian troops, and the General Staff of the 2nd Corps. With these troops the Indian 8th Division proved to be a valuable asset.

On May 18, 1944, the Polish troops busied themselves removing their dead from the hillside of Monte Cassino. In doing so, they encountered the continuing machine gun and rifle fire of German troops still in the valleys.

Just before midnight on that same day, the Indian Division had advanced five kilometres and seized the railroad line and train station outside of Piedimonte San Germano. Troops of the Polish Corps seized the village of San Lucia that was basically undefended.

The orders of General Oliver Leece to General Anders on May 19th were very direct:

> Make contact with the Hitler Line. Poles are to be in constant contact with the Germans as if there was to be a massive assault. Capture Piedimonte and protect the right flank of the British 13th Corps.

The attack on Piedimonte San Germano was not only to seize and control the eastern extremity of the Hitler Line, but also to compel Kesselring to move troops away from the valley to facilitate a breakthrough there. Actually, with the Poles tying Kesselring to the slopes and to defending Piedimonte San Germano, the British 13 Corps was able to make rapid progress.

The Lancers of the 3rd Carpathian Rifle Division were initially stopped the German troops firing down from the Pizzo Corno slope. Thereafter, the Poles began their daily assault and bombardment on Piedimonte San Germano. By May 23rd, the tanks were within 200 meters of the town. Still, the progress was halted by the enemy using grenades and anti-tank artillery from close range. The Polish force lost nineteen tanks in those first five days.

Good news was received by means of a decoded message on Wednesday, May 24th. In spite of the failure of an assault by ten Polish tanks and an infantry battalion that morning, the Germans were allegedly planning a retreat. The Polish II Corps immediately activated the 13th and 15th Kresowan Battalions. Any plan for any retreat was not immediate. A fierce exchange took place resulting in significant casualties. These two battalions continued their assault and ultimately the next day took control of the slopes of Pizzo Corno and Monte Cairo preventing further artillery attacks from above.

The German troops, that were not killed or captured, fled to try and reorganize themselves and their units. Those fleeing the eastern extremity of the Hitler Line included components of the German 10th Army and the 1st Airborne. They were fleeing the Poles whom they hated more than the British. Actually, they were heading from one hell to another.

On May 25th the Polish Carpathian reconnaissance force entered Piedimonte San Germano to the cheers and celebration of the surviving residents who had hid without food, water and rest for more than a week. The success of this campaign cost the Polish II Corps 189 lives.

Bernard continued his efforts with the Polish Corps bravely carrying his weapons into battle when required, and helping those they saved when needed.

(II)

While the British pushed north in the Liri Valley, the American force was approaching the Hitler Line along the coast. It was the ultimate intention of General Clark to march his troops into Rome.

In the Liri Valley, four kilometres west of Piedimonte San Germano, the town of Aquino was situated. Five kilometres to the south-west, Pontecorvo lay in the plain. Between these towns Kesselring established his zig-zag fortifications. Having rained so much in March, the rivers were still at flood levels. Bridges had been destroyed preventing the Allies from

338

any rapid or even any progress. Water filled the craters made by German bombs. Most fields were impassable. Rolled barbed wire covered miles of open terrain. Pillboxes, gun placement pits, panzer tank enclosures and anti-tank land mines complimented the German defence system. So detailed was the resistance that it truly required superlative military skill to even contemplate any assault.

However, in spite of all the best laid plans and thorough analysis of alternatives, defending Hitler Line over this seventy mile stretch required troops. Kesselring was well aware he did not have the soldiers he required. In his 10th Army the German Field Marshal maximized the accomplished military skills of the 90th Panzer Grenadier Division between Aquino and Pontecorvo, the 26th Panzer Division between Pontecorvo and Pico, and the XIV Panzer Mountain Corps between Pico and Itri. Kesselring himself was stationed at Army Group C Headquarters sixteen kilometres south of Rome at Frascati in the Alban Hills.

The US 5th Army included these divisions and the regiments aligned with each: US 2nd Corps, US 85th Division, US 88th Division, 337th Infantry Division, 338th Infantry Division, 349th Infantry Division, 351st Infantry Division, 601st Artillery Battalion, 697th Artillery Battalion, and the French Expeditionary Corps. General Clark commenced the American attack on the Hitler Line on May 15, 1944, three days before the capture of Monte Cassino. The United States 5th Army followed the coast along the western slope of the Aurunci Mountains. At the same time, the French Expeditionary Corps was working its way around and over these mountains. The initial objective was to seize control of Monte Grande and from that position cut the line of communications between Itri and Pico solidifying and facilitating the Allied position on the coast.

On May 16th, the 351st Infantry reached Monte San Angelo and progressed north toward Route 82, between Pico and Itri. The XIV Panzer Division was not able to stop the American Infantry in the mountains. Within the day, Kesselring was shifting his forces from the Liri Valley to the under-defended mountains. Before the German reinforcements even arrived, the American 85th Division was advancing north along the coast, and the French, after transgressing the northern slopes of the mountains were approaching Pico.

On May 18th following bombardment of the town of Itri and its bridges, the 351st Infantry approached the ruins. Monte Grande was taken, while the French were nearing Pico. Kesselring had to face the reality that his XIV Panzer Mountain Corps were defeated, that his 71st Division had only 100 soldiers left, and that the 29th Panzer Grenadier and 26th Panzer Divisions from the valley were delayed because of all of the impediments he had established to prevent mobility by the Allies. In Kesselring's favour, the Germans defending Aquino were able to thwart the attack of the British 78th Division.

With the victories that were within their grasp, General Alexander ordered General Clark that same day to entrap the German 10th Army between the US 6th Corps in Anzio and the British 8th Army in the Liri Valley. This would be achieved by the American II Corps and the French Expeditionary Corps both moving toward the junction of Route 82 (west-east) and Route 6 (south-north) in the valley. This would completely interrupt the German line of communications, its

340

mobility, and ability to defend the Hitler Line. The German 10th Army would be completely defeated.

General Clark did not follow that order.

On May 19th, the British 78th Division resumed the attack in the morning fog that covered the terrain and obscured their assault. However, the midday sun burned off the fog leaving them tragically exposed in the fields south of Aquino. They were easy prey for the German artillery.

On the coast, the American Infantry Divisions were continuing the ongoing battle for Monte Grande. The 349th Infantry Division occupied the ruins of Itri. The French could not take Pico.

To make sure that did not happen, Kesselring moved the 15th Panzer and 90th Panzer Divisions from the Liri Valley. With the German Panzer units defending the central and eastern portions of the Aurunci Mountains, General Clark directed his 5th Army along the coast toward Anzio.

During the next two days, the US 338th Infantry reached Terracina, the port on the Tyrrhenian Sea that was the western extremity of the Hitler Line. At the same time, Clark ordered the French Expeditionary Force to move east from the mountains into the valley encircling the Germans and preventing them from moving further troops west to the coast. In doing so, the French captured Pico.

On May 23rd, the breakout from Anzio began when the General Lucian Truscott led his US 6th Corps and five divisions against the German 14th Army. Kesselring did not have any available reserves.

But in the Liri Valley, especially along the main access of Route 6 to Rome, the campaign had been stalling. To end the stalemate, General Leece gave these orders: The Canadian 1st Infantry Corps with the aid of the British 13th Corps will attack Aquino, the French Expeditionary Corps would descend from the mountains to continue the assault to Aquino, the Canadian 1st Infantry Corps will breach the Hitler Line at Pontecorvo.

On the morning of May 23, 1944, the Canadian bombardment of Pontecorvo commenced with 810 guns blazing. Germans attempted a defence of the seven kilometre stretch from Pontecorvo to Aquino employing the 90th Panzer Grenadier Division with the 51st Corps, 361st Regiment 576th Regiment, the 1st Paratroop Division, and regiments of the Mountain Division.

At Aquino, the Canadian 1st Infantry and the British 13th Corps were delayed by the mire following days of continuous rain. In spite of the rigid German defence, the 2nd Brigade of the Canadian 1st Infantry Division was victorious and entered Pontecorvo on the morning of May 24th. Those Germans that were not slain in the final assault or captured, had fled. The Canadian 5th Armoured Division followed the infantry and overtook them pursuing the Germans eight kilometres beyond Pontecorvo. From that position, they could trail the Germans even further or turn to the east to assist the Allies in capturing Aquino.

The Germans continued to taste success against the British 13th Corps (part of the British 78th Division). Whilst the Canadians were to focus their attention on Pontecorvo, Aquino was going to be the British acquisition. Unfortunately that was not happening. Regardless of all other victorious battles, Aquino was the key as it controlled the flow of traffic north to Rome. With revised orders, the Canadian 5th Armoured Division from the north-west, and the Canadian 1st Infantry Division from the west directed their focus to Aquino. Kesselring was in a bind. He was lacking troops, pathetically low on supplies and manpower. With the onslaught of the Canadian forces, the German 10th Army fled Aquino to fight another day.

Rather than encircling the fleeing German 10th Army, General Clark ordered General Lucian Truscott and the US 6th Corps to head north toward Rome. General Truscott later conjectured that Clark was afraid the British 8th Army would be the first to celebrate in Rome. General Mark Clark said that he chose to avoid having the US 6th Corps battle the Germans because of the Corps' need for a rest. History will continue to judge.

(III)

While the Polish II Corps was completing its second assault on Piedimonte San Germano on May 21, 1944, a plane took off from Naples destined for Poland. General Leopold Okulicki, the Chief of Staff and assistant to General Anders, was returning home. His commitment was total, not only as a combatant in Italy, but as a freedom warrior to save his own country.

Leopold Okulicki was born on November 12 1898. At the age of sixteen, he joined the Polish forces in the First World War as a soldier with the 3rd Legions Infantry Regiment. After 1918, he remained with the Polish Army to fight against the USSR in the Polish – Bolshevik War. After that victory he completed his studies at the Warsaw Military Academy, and then taught the Infantry Program for the Polish Military. Ultimately he became the Commanding Officer of the Polish 13th Infantry Regiment.

Then came the second war. Infantry could not stop the Blitzkrieg. After the capitulation, General Okulicki joined the Polish Victory Service, an underground resistance movement. In 1941, in Lodz within Soviet occupied Poland, he was taken prisoner. With so many other Polish officers, he was imprisoned in the Soviet Union. Concerning that confinement, Okulicki's comment was very direct even to the extent of being prophetic.

In comparison with the NKVD, the Gestapo methods are child's play.

With the creation of the Polish Army in the Soviet Union, he was released from prison, and became the commanding officer of the Polish 7th Infantry Division. Leopold completed training in London with the Cichociemni, the Polish resistance – spy group where he obtained knowledge of the decoding process. He already had acquired engineering skills in his military training. In the Middle East, he was then assigned Chief of Staff to assist General Anders.

The Polish Resistance Movement never left his heart. With all of the tales of exterminations and vanquished uprisings, General Okulicki felt compelled to do more than just fight the battle in Italy.

The parachute worked.

In Poland, he joined the Polish Home Army, the Armia Krajowa of over 400,000 Poles committed to the reality of an independent Poland free tyranny. Although the Home Army was originally an anti-Nazi force, with the terror of the occupation shifted its focus to all occupying forces. From its inception in September 1939 to May 1944, over 240,000 deliberate acts had disrupted the invading forces. Commitment was total to the cause. Death in Poland was better than imprisonment in the Soviet Union.

(I V)

After the fall of the Hitler Line, Kesselring withdrew his 10th Army, 14th Army, and the panzer and infantry divisions north to the Caesar Line. This sector was aptly named as it would be Germany's last line defending Rome from the south. The Caesar Line crossed Italy from Ostia on the Tyrrhenian Coast to Pescara on the Adriatic Coast. In doing so, it crossed the Alban Mountains. It was in these hills that Kesselring had established his headquarters.

In September 1943 with the surrender of Italy, Rome had been declared an 'open city'. This meant there would be no defence offered to any invading force, and that accordingly there were no troops within the city, and the city would never be bombed. When General Kesselring assumed control of Italy, Rome at once became a bastion to troops defending the city. It was there to be bombed, and to be taken if they dared.

Following the breakout from Anzio, American General Truscott with his US 6th Corps advanced north along the coast. By the end of May, they were in control of Valmontane, situated south of Rome on the major route north to the city. The Caesar Line was breached.

General Clark assumed total leadership of the advancing force as it approached Rome. The British 8th

Army were to remain in the rear acting as reserves in the event of battle. However, the divisions within the British Army were advancing faster than Clark anticipated.

On the last day of May, the German 14th Army retreated from the Caesar Line to take its position at the Trasimene Line north of Rome. The City of Rome was then declared to be an 'open city'.

On June 3, 1944 when the occupation of Rome was inevitable, General Harold Alexander sent a message to General Clark requesting the Americans to allow the Polish II Corps to participate in the entry into Rome because of its victory at Monte Cassino. Clark did not reply.

The next morning at about 3 a.m. the Canadian Infantry Division entered Rome. There was no celebration. The Canadians continued straight through the city, remaining focused on the pursuit of the German 10th Army to the north of the Capital. Later that day General Clark entered Rome with his troops claiming credit for liberating the city.

On June 5, 1944, they celebrated in Rome with the parade and the appreciation of the citizens. The Poles were not there. The Canadians were not there. Meanwhile, the German 10th Army that could have been surrounded two weeks before continued its retreat north to the Gothic Line, there to commit itself to a stern defence costing the Allies many more lives.

Hours later, Operation Overlord commenced.

(V)

After the Poles had been shunned at Rome, General Alexander encouraged their participation in an assault on Ancona, north of the Trasimene Line on the Adriatic Coast. The campaign on the Adriatic had very much become second fiddle to the assault on Rome. The last major battle on the Adriatic took place at Ortona in December 1943 when the Canadian 1st Infantry was victorious against the German Parachute Division. That conflict required the Canadian force to cross rivers, transgress rough terrain, thwart concealed anti-tank and machine gun placements, and engage in house to house combat throughout the city. British and Indian forces also participated in the Allied force which after nine days of fighting celebrated while remembering the lives and commitment of more than 1,500 soldiers.

The job of the Polish II Corps was to continue that assault north. General Anders moved his headquarters east to Ortona. His force included British, Indian and Polish troops: 3rd Carpathian Rifle Division, Royal Artillery, British 7th Queens Own Hussars, 17th Heavy Artillery Regiment, 26th Heavy Artillery Regiment, and the Indian 4th Division. The 5th Kresowa Division and the Armoured Division arrived later within the week.

The British 5th Corps had already been in the area controlling any thought the Germans might have concerning any counter offensive. The territory from Ancona to the Trasimene Line was covered by many rivers, and several pockets of German resistance north of Ortona. One hundred ninety kilometres separated the Allied troops in Ortona from its objective in Ancona.

From June 21 to June 30, the Polish force confronted the Germans at the Chienti River, about fifty kilometres

347

from Ancona. The Chienti River starts in the Apennine Mountains, twisting and turning, and then joining other rivers before flowing into the Adriatic Sea.

One week later the Allies captured Orsini, ten kilometres from Ancona. The casualties were again heavy. Thereafter the armoured division progressed north encountering insignificant defence and began its assault on the city. The Germans were there to defend Ancona and the Trasimene Line to the end. Hitler demanded it.

On July 17th the Polish II Corps captured Monte della Crescia and Casenueva outflanking the Germans. The British troops seized Montecchio and Croce di San Vincenzo. This allowed the Polish troops to continue the assault encircling the enemy force at Agugliano.

On the morning of July 18th, the Polish II Corps advanced from Augliano to capture Offagna and Chiaravalle. The Armoured Division drove forward reaching the sea north of the city. On land, the Germans were trapped. Vessels were quickly loaded and hastily departed under Allied fire. Other German troops fled north through the Allied troops only to die in the attempt. In mid afternoon on July 18th, the Allies entered the city of Ancona encountering little resistance from the German troops who were unable to flee.

Ancona was another success for the Polish II Corps. The Poles, dead or wounded, numbered 1,423. The British experienced 167 casualties. The Germans Killed In Action exceeded 3,000. Also, more than 3,000 German troops were taken prisoner.

Following the military achievement at Ancona, the British received public recognition and commendation for the victory.

(VI)

After the loss at Ancona, the German troops headed further north to the Gothic Line. These troops included the German 10th Army, German 14th Army with the infantry and panzer divisions. They were ordered to cover a line of defence from LaSpezia on the Tyrrhenian Coast to a point between Pesaro and Ravenna on the Adriatic Coast. To accomplish this, the Germans had installed 2,376 machine gun positions, 479 guns, barbed wire, anti-tank mines, ditches, and concrete bunkers. The terrain itself supported all defence efforts.

The Allied force was the British 8th Army that included: British 5th Corps, British 10th Crops, British 13th Corps, Canadian 1st Infantry that included the Greek 3rd Mountain Brigade, Indian 4th Division, and the Polish II Corps. This force would normally have totalled more than 150,000 troops. However the campaign in France diverted at least 50,000 of these. With 100,000 soldiers, the Allies were confronting Kesselring's two main armies.

For the Polish troops, this battle offered the remote prospect that a victory on the Adriatic Coast could encourage the Allies to direct their assault toward Austria and Hungary thereby becoming a significant threat to the Soviet Union's dominance in Eastern Europe. That hope was quickly dashed when former Prime Minister Churchill met with General Anders. The Polish General was told that this would be the last battle for the Polish II Corps. The Polish force was insulted by Stalin referring to Anders as being a wicked man. Anders had been the saviour to so many Poles in Europe because it was Wladyslaw Anders's impetus that got them out of the gulags and out of the Soviet Union. Churchill then confirmed his information concerning the Polish Home Army, the Warsaw Uprising, and the deaths caused by Soviet tyranny. Churchill wanted Anders' commitment that the Polish II Corps was still committed to defeat Germany even though the thoughts of so many troops would dwell on issues in Poland. Anders gave Churchill that assurance.

On August 22, 1944, the same day of the meeting with Churchill, the Polish II Corps fighting alongside the Canadian 1st Division, crossed the Metauro River, about forty kilometres north of Ancona. The river flowed rapidly more than one hundred kilometres from the Apennine Mountains presenting a significantly wide obstacle. The Allied force surprised the insignificant defence, capturing a hill overlooking Pesaro.

Kesselring did not know how to react. Was this the major offensive? Was he to move reserves away from Bologna? Would the Americans attack there as soon as he deployed the reserves? Whether or not the document was a military ploy remains uncertain, but Kesselring was provided with a note dated August 28th indicating that in fact this Allied attack on the Adriatic Coast was a major offensive. He immediately deployed three reserve divisions to that coast.

At the same time, the portions of the German 10th and 14th Armies on the west coast were joining their forces to confront the Americans, who were anxious to end the war in Italy as soon as possible.

While Kesselring was waiting for his reserves, the Allied troops were moving north through defended positions toward Rimini.

In the first two weeks of September, the British Corps and the Indian Division were engaged in a series of prolonged battles with the German 98th Division. After twelve attacks, the British and Indians were able to capture the town of Gemmano. After three days battling the German 278th Infantry Division, San Marino was captured by the Indian Division on the seventeenth of September.

Four days later, the Canadian 1st Division, the Greek 3rd Mountain Brigade, and the New Zealand 20th Armoured Regiment occupied Rimini. The autumn rain season began as if to quell the celebrations. Rivers swelled and roads flooded almost stopping advances on undefended terrain. General Kesselring, realizing the situation, re-established his headquarters at Bologna.

For the Polish II Corps, even though it had been informed that was their last battle, that scenario did not occur. In fact, they had more troops now than at Cassino, with the addition of Poles being released from the German prisoner of war camps.

(VII)

In July, 1944 the Polish Armia Krajowa, the Home Army, accidently got into bed with the Red Army. The organized Polish resistance movement was determined to rid Poland of all German influence. The Soviets had the same intention. By the middle July the Red Army had already captured Vilnius, had seized Minsk, occupied Western Ukraine, and had swiftly crossed the

Polish border. The determination of the Soviet force matched the commitment of the Home Army in their goal to defeat Germany.

The Home Army, under the direction of General Okulicki, planned to orchestrate a series of rebellions in the Poland's major cities, starting with Warsaw. There was no doubt that the entire Home Army of more than 400,000 men were committed to the cause. They called their plan, 'Operation Tempest'.

Iosif Stalin, prior to 1944, had established the Polish I Corps within the Soviet Union. This was not the Polish I Corps organized by General Sikorski and the Polish Government in Exile. Then in 1944, General Zhukov reorganized his 200,000 soldiers into Stalin's Polish People's Army. The Polish People's Army was then split into the Polish First Army and the Polish Second Army. The Red Army totally commanded their campaigns. When the Red Army entered Polish territory the headquarters of the Polish People's Army became based in Poland, and was the military wing of the communist ruled People's Republic of Poland. Because of the tyranny inflicted by the Nazi occupation, many Poles were receptive to the presence of the Polish People's Army. They were assured that that army totally represented the interests of the Polish nation. Once the Red Army crossed the Polish border, there was limited defence offered by the Germans. The Wehrmacht had spread itself too thin defending Ukraine, Belarus, the Baltic States, Hungary, Romania, and the Slavic region. Kesselring's demand for troops in Italy had also limited the defence Hitler could offer. The entire German force of 3,300,000 throughout Europe could not control the invasion of 6,400,000 Red Army soldiers. The Polish Resistance, believing it had Soviet support, felt that the urban rebellion in Warsaw would end quickly and ultimately force the Nazis back to the pre-war eastern border. The Warsaw Uprising commenced on August 1, 1944. Success came quickly for the Poles when they seized control of the central city. A prolonged street-to-street, house-to-house battle took place. Six weeks later, extreme fatigue and dwindling ammunition grossly affected the Home Army's ability to battle the larger German force. The Wehrmacht was no stranger to the boulevards and side streets providing the capability of encircling factions of the Home Army. "Where is the Red Army?" The question was first asked by many with the full expectation they would soon arrive. The Soviet Air Force was only five minutes away. The Soviet troops were camped on the bank of the Vistula River. The same question was repeated again but with the outraged acknowledgement that the Poles had been duped. Even Winston Churchill urged Stalin to help "Britain's Ally". The Soviet dictator refused. The Royal Air Force then risked their safety flying over occupied Poland to drop two hundred loads of supplies to aid the destitute Polish force. The Polish Airmen, as part of the RAF, were able to do as much as they could to help their countrymen. However that was insufficient. The United States then became involved asking the Soviet Union for clearance to use their airfields. The reply from Stalin was a complete refusal. Stalin, Molotov, Beria, Zhukov, and every devoted commander in the Red Army were pleased to see the Germans eradicate the Polish resistance.

Although there may have been the urge to aid their fellow Poles, the soldiers in the Polish People's Army were held at bay by the Red Army. From the bank of the Vistula River they watched their capital city become rubble. On October 2, 1944, the Polish force in Warsaw surrendered. Almost instantly, many fled for Krakow. The Home Army was organized away from the Capital. Casualties were extreme. At least sixteen thousand Polish men and women died. About six thousand others were severely maimed or wounded. These were left to die or died awaiting non-existent medical care. The Gestapo and German soldiers had a field day going from house to house annihilating the residents. Those Jews, that the Polish Underground had kept safe, were forced from their hiding places to be subject to mass executions throughout the city. The number of Warsaw civilian victims exceeded 150,000. The German casualties, dead and wounded, were only seventeen thousand.

A quarter of the city of Warsaw was destroyed in the battle. After the surrender, the German Armoured Division destroyed another third of the city. By the time the Red Army occupied Warsaw three months later, 85% of the city was destroyed. The news ripped every sinew and blood vessel in every heart in the Polish II Corps camp. Men cried, trembling, knowing that any chance of ever seeing any family member ever again had finally expired. The Polish Chaplain had no words to comfort the grieving.

(VIII)

The Guard loosely boot stepped his path across the cold concrete factory floor. It wasn't the formal military step that the workers had so often seen during parades or disciplinary processes. The guard appeared moderately uncomfortable to the watchful eye, quicker than expected, yet seemingly just as determined. Workers, after hastily observing his presence, returned to their jobs. Churning inside they were all hoping he would just continue on. The young German did eventually stop. Leon Pawlowski turned cautiously away from his machinery.

Not a word was spoken. The Guard handed the Polish factory worker an envelope.

"Danke," Leon expressed, very much surprised. The Swastika was ink-stamped on the centre of the five by eight inch envelop.

"Be surprised," the officer assured Leon speaking in an almost inaudible tone. Leon was suddenly at ease with the messenger's smile.

"I know you," Leon whispered in German.

"Our families," Rudolph offered. Then he stood back. Everything was to appear to be as customary.

Leon looked again at the envelop noting the hand written word 'Czestochowa' on the reverse. He looked at the young guard once more trying to glean from his expression the contents of the document.

"You will be pleased." Those words seemed so foreign from a German official. Then the guard clicked his heels, saluted, "Heil Hitler," and left. The co-workers continued to stare with many questions to be answered.

The envelope, Leon folded and placed in his apron pocket. It couldn't be that important if his answer was not immediately required.

History will never be kind to Iosif Stalin, and he should never be the beneficiary of any kind thought. His malicious attitude and actions toward the millions he considered to be his inferiors demanded that he, like the fascist leader he detested, annihilate anyone and everyone for whatever reason.

Knowledge of the atrocities in occupied territories could not be concealed. The debates in London, accusations over Katyn, news reports on the prison camps, statements in Parliament, the knowledge of dignitaries, the Moscow Declaration, and the reek of burning flesh – all affirmed that the Europeans, the Allies, in fact all of the world, knew of the mass murders and deportation of millions by the Nazis and the Soviets. It's still impossible to count the number of blind eyes.

After defending Stalingrad, the Red Army forced the Wehrmacht to retreat, spiralling backwards toward Berlin. The Soviets maintained their hot pursuit with three million more troops, with more than twice the tanks and artillery, and with the valuable supply of fuel. Reports suggest the Soviet thrust toward Berlin averaged more than thirty kilometres per day. It is accepted that in two weeks, the Red Army had crossed from the eastern border of Poland to the Vistula River outside Warsaw.

The Red Army purposefully allowed the mass murders to continue even though the Soviets were in a position to stop the annihilation. The Red Army entered Hungary on August 31, 1944 and waited 165 days until February 13, 1945 to seize control. They marched inside Slovakia on September 8, 1944 and took control 207 days later on April 4, 1945. The Soviets swarmed into Danzig and East Prussia on January 13, 1945 and declared control 75 days later on March 30, 1945. The Red Army entered Poland in August 1944, crossed to the Vistula River overlooking the Capital, and then 155 days later occupied Warsaw. Much could have been done to stop the ongoing slaughter of Polish citizens before then.

The Red Army claimed the Soviets discovered the Auschwitz camp in early January, 1945. However, Stalin was well aware of its existence in November 1943 at the time of the Moscow Declaration. And, after the Soviets first discovered Auschwitz, what did they do? The Red Army extracted many prisoners and led them away on a death march. Then three weeks later, after many more had died, the Soviets closed the camp.

In each case the Red Army could have seized full control of each country or of each situation. They could have saved lives. Why did the Red Army not act appropriately?

History cannot hide the reality of the Soviet desire to remove any prospect or possibility of any resistance. Stalin let Hitler eradicate the inferior races before leaving, or let the population with nationalist sentiments remove the weaker links of society. The Warsaw Uprising openly conveyed this policy: get rid of the Poles that might cause the Soviets a problem in the future, and let the Nazis do it.

The Red Army occupied Warsaw on January 17, 1945. The task was rather simple: cross the river and enter the devastated ruins that the Germans had abandoned three days before.

Two days after the occupation of Warsaw, the Home Army was disbanded. There were enough deaths.

In June, 1945 Polish Resistance Leaders were tried by Soviet authorities in the infamous mock Trial of Sixteen. The sentence was predestined as well as the harshness of captivity. He was never able to serve his ten year sentence. On Christmas Eve of 1946, General Okulicki was murdered in Butyrka Prison. His body was then burned and the ashes buried.

Dante's Inferno has a closet for Stalin and his band of thugs – in the vilest place in Hell.

(X)

The Polish II Corps didn't realize there was a word in the Polish language for 'pinata'. It was 'Anders'.

First, General Leece demeaned General Anders and the Polish force with the article from the British Press; then there was Prime Minister Churchill telling the Poles they're finished; and then in March 1945, General Richard McCreery, Commander of the British 8th Army, provided Anders with the specific details and consequences of the Yalta Conference. Wasn't it enough that Anders had to deal with Kesselring, the two German Armies and a multitude of panzer divisions? Why wasn't anyone seemingly on his side – on the side of the Poles?

General McCreery's advice was candid. He tried to keep his calm realizing the inevitable reaction of the Polish General. Anders had lost his ability to be calm, when being called into meetings with his superiors from the network of British Generals. The news was never good.

In accord with the Yalta Conference, Poland was to become a communist state. Actually this was already known to Anders. The communist state, the Soviet People's Republic of Poland was already in power.

McCreery then advised that the 5th Kresowa Division, because it had been based in eastern Poland prior to the war, was to become a sector in the Soviet Polish People's Army. There was loud debate on this issue with Anders sternly telling his commanding officer that he would never surrender the lives of his troops to Bolshevik labour camps and tyranny. McCreery tried to tell the Polish General that the matter was already decided, but there was no hearing that advice.

General Anders had already realized the dire straits of the Polish nation. The invasions, the exterminations, the Red Army, the failure of the Home Army, the occupation of Warsaw, and most of all the entire tone of appeasement toward Stalin – these he could no longer suffer. Wasn't it enough that the world condemned Chamberlain for his pleasantries with Hitler, and now they shared a bedroom with the Soviet Dictator. "Why?"

The Polish General would give no quarter in the conversation that had become a debate. Whether General McCreery had on that occasion known of the views of the British Foreign Secretary was uncertain.

The two generals met later that month. The news was rather pleasing and certainly reflected the conscientious and caring nature of the British nation. The soldiers in Anders's Army, who chose not to return to Poland, could after the war establish residence in the nations of the British Commonwealth. Time Magazine reported on the advice that month.

British High Command promised Anders that those of his soldiers who did not want to return to the new Poland could find asylum in the British Empire.

Argentina and Brazil were also reported ready to offer them homes. But Britain thought the best solution would be for them to return to Poland, and Britain was circulating an appeal through the Polish Army containing the Polish Government's pledge to treat the soldier exiles fairly. Anders argued that he could not advise the soldiers to return to Poland unless the Polish Government promised elections this spring.

Bevin, too, wanted immediate Polish elections, but both men knew that the chances were becoming slimmer.

At least there was hope.

(XI)

Bologna was Kesselring's headquarters. He vowed it would be his last. This was going to be an all out battle. The Reich had to be defended.

The American 5th Army was already camped south of the Senio River. "When?" was the question often asked in the German camp. Reconnaissance had revealed the British 8th Army was also moving into position. Following the battles at Ancona and Rimini, divisions in the British Army were no longer tied to the Adriatic Coast. Bologna was only 110 kilometres away. There were no obstacles to the British 8th Army joining the siege on Bologna.

British High Command once more swung the piñata stick at the Polish troops. Churchill's message was repeated: the Poles were no longer needed. General Alexander, General McCreery, and General Clark dismissed those instructions, and encouraged the Polish II Corps to continue to fight with the Allies. On his part, General Anders relieved himself of some of his duties and awarded the role of Commander of the Polish II Corps to General Zygmunt Bohusz-Szyszko. The Polish troops immediately mobilized their remaining enthusiasm and crossed the Senio River allowing them to move to the north-west toward Bologna. The river itself and its tributaries flowed from the Apennines. They could have followed that route to Bologna.

Then three days later, on April 12, 1945, the Allied campaign was shocked with news of the President's death. A period of respect occurred. By the time that news reached the Polish divisions, they were about to capture the town of Imola, only forty kilometres from Bologna. The German 1st Parachute Division reacted swiftly with its own offensive causing intense fighting for the entire week. Ultimately, the 3rd Carpathian Rifle Division captured Bologna. Doubly sweet was the reality that the German 10th Army was at long last defeated. Bernard with the many comrades celebrated for days with the festive inhabitants. The curse of German autocracy in Bologna was gone.

Of the 55,780 Polish troops available for battle; 234 were killed in action, and just over 1,200 were injured in the thirteen days of war.

Within the month, the Polish II Corps had grown to more than 228,000 soldiers when more Poles were released from German camps and with the end of forced conscription in the German army.

With that massive force, what was next?

(XII)

In spite of having more than 200,000 troops, on April 22, 1945, the day after its victory over the German 10th Army at Bologna, the sad news was affirmed. The Polish II Corps was removed from the front line. It had fought its last battle.

One week later, Allied troops crossed the Po River in northern Italy. Four days later on May 2, 1945, Kesselring and his German divisions surrendered in Italy.

The Italian Campaign was costly in terms of casualties for both the Allies and the Germans. Figures vary, but clearly each side suffered more than 300,000 casualties. These included the killed in action, the missing in action, and those too numerous to count who lay dying on the hills and in the valleys.

The numbers for American casualties range between 114, 000 and 120,000.

The British casualties were approximately 89,000. This figure did not include the Commonwealth or Colonial armies.

The casualties for the Polish II Corps were approximately 11,000, more than 20% of the entire force. A dear price was paid for valiant victories for an uncertain future.

(XIII)

On the very day that the Polish II Corps was celebrating the victory at Battle of Bologna, Stalin had his hammer in his hand ready to bang the final nails into the coffin of an independent Poland. It wasn't enough that the Soviet-controlled Polish People's Army was the military wing of the Bolshevik People's Republic of Poland. There would be no opposition to USSR's brand of communism. To solidify that control Stalin arranged for a formal pact between the Soviet Union and his Poland. On April 21, 1945, representatives of the Provisional Government of the Republic of Poland (same as People's Republic of Poland) signed the Treaty of Friendship, Mutual Help and Cooperation between Moscow and Warsaw.

Stalin had the entire European continent wrapped around his fists as he tightened the noose in Eastern Europe. Poland, the Baltic States, Hungary, Bulgaria, Romania, Czechoslovakia were all controlled by the Red Army that entered, occupied, and never left. Beria's KGB was so ingrained in these societies that fear was the daily breakfast. Refugees fled. To counter any misperception Stalin repeatedly asserted that Soviet control of Eastern Europe was necessary to prevent any future German invasion. No matter what reason he could provide, there should have been no recognition of Stalin's good will, for benevolence was void in his realm.

To please the Western Allies on June 28, 1945, Stalin renamed his Polish government and established the Provisional Government of National Unity. This was done by order of the State National Council in Warsaw. With this act, Stalin also promised that there would be an election in Poland within the year. Britain, France and the United States were pleased; even if this was the third time Stalin renamed the Polish nation in one year, and even if Stalin in the past had never kept a promise of any benefit to anyone other than himself.

The Polish Government in Exile in London, England immediately declared it did not recognize the Provisional Government of National Unity.

As if enough had not been enough, the United States on July 5, 1945 declared its recognition for this Provisional Government of National Unity, and withdrew its recognition of the Polish Government in Exile. On the next day, Britain likewise recognized the Provisional Government of National Unity as being the only government of Poland. Similarly, the British Parliament withdrew its support for the Polish Government in Exile.

Less than two weeks later, former Prime Minister Winston Churchill met with President Truman and Iosif Stalin at Potsdam. The agreement affirmed that Poland was a communist state. The pact also included conditions relative to the Polish soldiers who fought in the war. Though not specifically stated, these applied to the Polish II Corps – that is Anders's Army. Stalin was not finished with his need for retribution. In March 1945 the Soviet Dictator had promised that Polish troops could return to his Polish nation without fear of any retaliation. That changed. As a result of the Potsdam Conference, there was no pledge of safety or security to returning Polish soldiers. Members of the Polish II Corps could return to Poland with no guarantees.

The fate of those soldiers was bleak. The number of soldiers in the Polish Armed Forces under British High Command totalled 194,000 in May 1945. Added to this were 46,000 Polish civilians and dependents. From the 240,000 persons who identified themselves as belonging to the Polish II Corps, 105,000 of these returned to Poland. Perhaps it was the feeling that they were betrayed by both Britain and the United States that caused them to take such seemingly inordinate action. Perhaps too it was a case of the devil they knew compared to the devil they didn't know. Perhaps, they felt they had nowhere else to go.

On October 16 1945 Communist Poland joined the United Nations as the only true nation of the Polish people. Hopes and alternatives had disappeared. They were a homeless tribe.

(X I V)

The austerity of the Gestapo was in complete contrast to the flaking concrete platform. A corrosive chemical had obviously been spilt at the far end. Leon walked around the stained concrete. The guards closely observed him, one even turned completely to face the visitor as he ambled toward the waiting room. Generally it would be just a turn of the head. There was an obvious tension as there had been on the train from Poznan. No one seemingly wanted to be there, yet they all offered opinions suggesting they no longer had any interest in staying in Poznan. Five days, that was all Leon was afforded. Things would have to happen fast. It didn't help that the train seemed to take forever.

His family did not even know he was arriving. Rudolph had handed Leon the letter with the advice concerning his family. At the factory he also left Leon's director with a formal letter demanding his presence elsewhere. Leon was so ever grateful for this good fortune. At the same time, he couldn't get his mind off Rudolph and the boy's family: all which prompted so many queries. War had changed the colloquial greetings in Poland. It was no longer appropriate to ask, "How are they doing?" It was better to keep quiet and wonder, "Are they still alive?"

The waiting room was empty. The few, who had still been on the train at its terminus, had left quickly. That pace was usual to Poland. Leon regretted that. There was no more room or time for peaceful coexistence. "Peace" was such a foreign word. "First the Nazis, and now the Communists," Leon regretted. Having worked in the armaments factory, the war was never far away. Leon no longer pondered about the political future, just "Being alive" was his goal. The transients in his rail car were a harsh group. They didn't have much to say that was polite about anyone or anything. "Best they're not here. We'd be arrested," Leon mused as he left the waiting room.

There were no taxis. It was not yet dark, but overcast. The cold-grey, eerie surroundings were not a pleasant greeting to Czestochowa. There was no guarantee of any warm temperature on an August evening this close to the mountains. Yet, knowing his family was there, somewhere in the city, probably near the cathedral, as the note had said: he found himself still warm inside.

Leon started walking toward the distant spires. Military vehicles constantly passed him. No one stopped. There was no help to be had. Commercial vehicles were almost non-existent. Automobiles were few. None of the drivers were women.

It was well after ten o'clock when he knocked at the door to the cathedral rectory. There was no response to his repeated knocking in those first five minutes. He was ready to walk away and return the next morning, but that light was still visible inside. Eventually a voice responded on the other side of the door with a series of quick questions. It was Polish. That was gratifying. There had been too much German in Poznan.

After slipping the Reich's letter inside the door, Leon waited. He could hear someone unfolding the letter, and then a question was asked, this time in German. Leon understood the query and his heart leaped. Teresa was there, but they didn't know the exact room. Leon was asked to come inside. His expression was a broad smile. He knew he should conceal it because smiles were almost not allowed in Nazi occupied territory.

A woman who had the necessary information was roused from her bed. She was a heavy set individual. "Panzer tank," Leon thought to himself. He shouldn't have even contemplated such thoughts because the woman was so helpful. But in Poznan, she would have been the size of two hungry women.

He knocked at the door. Again there was no answer. A second knock produced no response. It was the fourth rap that aroused the person inside. Seconds later Leon's arms were wrapped around his wife. The tears of joy were immediate. Two hearts raced. Exclamations of joy shook the hallway. Lips covered her face in so much appreciation. Words were replaced with endless gratitude.

Elzbieta stood there, too, crying, unable to comprehend their good fortune. She joined the family hug, then split for a second to bring her younger brother. Leon stared at Andrzej, so overjoyed. He immediately reminded himself that Teresa had told him that she was pregnant less than two weeks before the Germans invaded. Had it been that long?

Leon joined them on bed that night, all cuddled together.

As for Ryszard, they planned to surprise him in the morning. The family would attend Mass together and he would appear from the sacristy as an altar boy. His tears of joy were immediate.

The next day was spent together tending the gardens. One of the guards made his customary visit to ensure the produce would be ready for the market. Leon was brave enough to introduce himself. Although the guard would not offer a word, he was inside quietly delighted by the reality of such a family reunion.

Leon returned to Poznan as was required. However before leaving the plans were finalized for Teresa and their family to return. He would stay in contact.

(X V)

After the Provisional Government of National Unity came into being in June 1945, the Communists in Poland worked diligently to control every aspect of the government, the military and the electoral process. At Yalta, Stalin had promised the Allies that there would be elections within the year. He had one goal for those elections and only one result in mind. In the June 1946 election, the Communists claim they received 86% of the vote. Many declared the election to have been rigged as the Communists controlled the entire electoral process. This did not involve just counting the votes, but also included many threats. The Volunteer Reserve Militia had dispersed approximately 100,000 activists with weapons to achieve the result. Stalin had the decision he wanted. Another vote in January, 1947 proved Stalin could control elections.

The Communists remained in absolute control of Poland for thirty-one years and nine months, until a Polish cleric stood on the balcony of St. Peter's Basilica.

(XVI)

The nightmares did not stop with the end of the war. There was no calm to be had. The cruel winds blew cold across Europe even in July 1945.

The Polish Corps was snubbed, not allowed to even march in the celebratory parade in London. Troops in other forces could and did return home. But for the Poles, there was no home they could recognize as home.

What would happen without Churchill? There were enough reasons to doubt the Prime Minister and his allegiance. However they knew or at least they seemed to know where he stood. Then there was Clement Atlee. There would be really no need for any Pole to have any interest in English politics, except for the fact that Mr. Atlee was receiving the support of the faction that favoured appeasement with the Soviets. There were so many rumours and so much second hand news. What was to be believed?

Bernard's belief was founded on his present situation. There was no need to entertain dreams of a future that could never be. In the absence of aspiring thoughts at night, nightmares ruled the mind. The images of the concentration camps, the gunfire, the blood and corpses all rattled his being. There were so few in camp who could thank anyone for anything. Many in the Polish force had moved to the ports: Genoa, Pisa, Rome, and Naples. A few brigades dispersed to the east: Bari, Venice, and Rimini. Some even remained in the area of Bologna. Their tents were all they had for housing. Wooden barracks were being dismantled. Food, that was scarce during the war, had become at times almost non-existent. With the Soviet takeover of Poland, the national government would never support this Polish Corps in Italy. Britain, too, was short of funds. English financial support was not assured.

Soldiers in the Polish II Corps were allowed after the war to disperse with permission and knowledge of their whereabouts. Keeping that many restless souls in camps was impossible. Some soldiers left to finally spend time with their families who left the Soviet gulags with those committed to the army. Others out right left the force to take permanent employment in Italy. More than 450,000 Italians had died mostly male soldiers; leaving many vacancies in required jobs. Then there were those who returned to Poland. Many of those belonged to the 5th Kresowa Division. At the same time, the British Government was encouraging Polish soldiers to "Volunteer for Repatriation."

Bernard was still proud of his uniform, the eagle on his cap and the Carpathian crest on his tunic. The belt was lighter now, void of grenades, weapons and ammunition. The pants were perpetually dirty, knees still slightly torn, and the cuffs shredded. The end of the war had relieved many of the continuing aches and pains. However the headaches still persisted. They filled the void of lost causes. Bernard remembered everyone whom he had met since his capture: some with fond memories, while others he vehemently deplored. The prayers for those he thought of fondly were becoming too repetitious. Nothing was being gained. He felt assured they were doing well if they were alive. And about his family, he really had no hope. Western Poland was flattened by the Nazis, and every living thing was destroyed. There were too many horrific tales to avoid that conclusion. Heading north was a prospect. Bernard with others considered it. Then several businessmen from the local towns approached the camp. They had jobs, in the fields, lasting until the harvest in October. Maybe good fortune would shine again.

Bernard jumped at the opportunity; and that afternoon in early July, he was operating farm machinery digging irrigation rows. Being in an open field and not fearing stray bullets, land mines or machine gun fire: it just seemed so strange, yet so wonderful. In the quite moments he couldn't avoid reflecting on the many stories and figures. No one had exact details, but the proposed figures were astronomical. Poland's war casualties included 240,000 soldiers and 5,500,000 civilians. He would have been absolutely shocked if he had ever known the true extent of the extermination programs. In the field, he had the opportunity to bury the past in glowing sunshine. In many respects he was successful. The wages from the farming job provided enough funds to purchase personal hygiene and clothing items. Ben had just enough ready for an emergency as long as it did not include costly medical or dental care.

When he returned to the camp in October, Bernard found many had already left. He dreaded to think that a considerable number had returned to Poland. "Perhaps the stories weren't true," was his hope concerning those searching for any better life. As for his friends in the

371

army, Ben couldn't find them. So many died at Cassino. Piotr, he never saw again after the battle at Piedimonte. Two in the camp were planning to head north through Europe with no final destination in mind. Bernard decided to accompany them.

From Milan they headed north, hitch-hiking through the Alps until they got to Zurich. It was too German for their liking. With that in mind Bernard couldn't understand why the others chose Salzburg, Austria for their next destination. Austria was even more German than Switzerland, and still objected to Allied interference. Wearing the Polish tunic and cap was not recommended. At that point, the others proposed Hungary or Slovakia. With that also not being to Bernard's liking, he let them go on. Ben would never hear of them again.

In Salzburg, after visiting the castle, he spent the last of his Italian Lire on food. That night he slept on a park bench. Racing police cars startled him before dawn. At that point he was on his feet walking to wherever. Being lost and poor in a German speaking city was not smart especially when he was still wearing his Polish uniform.

He made his way to the chapel at Nonnberg Convent just before nine o'clock one morning. After Mass, he didn't move, not because he was reverend, but because he had nowhere to go. On the church grounds he saw workers in the course of renovations. He asked them if they needed help. Minutes later he was working. The tasks at the convent though many came to an end by mid December. Bernard celebrated Christmas on route while returning to Italy.

The port at Pisa was his destination. While there he met several and then hundreds of stranded Poles. The majority of these were soldiers, the rest civilians. Rumours consumed their discussions, too many and too wild to be readily believed. In a camp, he found rest. In the morning the mess hall provided nourishment.

Discussions could not avoid the same rumours. Then Ben heard that General Anders had been in the camp the prior week with his words of enthusiasm.

Contrary to initial perceptions, the existence of the Atlee Government in Britain was not the worst case scenario for the Poles. In January 1946 Ernest Bevin, the British Foreign Secretary, received confirming advice regarding the conditions in Poland. The violence in Warsaw and throughout Poland had been orchestrated by the communist policy of the Polish Provisional Government. Any Polish soldier returning to Poland from elsewhere in Europe could be the victim of violence or death. The Soviet military considered any person affiliated with Anders's Army to be a terrorist. In February, 1946 the Foreign Secretary declared in the House of Commons, "Terror has become an instrument of national policy in the new Poland." On May 21, 1946, Ernest Bevin advised General Anders, while the Polish General was in London, about his program to transport troops of the Polish II Corps to Britain. "A Polish Resettlement Corps will be established." Anders received Bevin's good news. Many would have dismissed the prospect. The reality of so many words with no meaningful action in the past had created a doubting crowd. Yet the reality was Italy was not going to keep them forever. Anyone who may have doubted Bevin did not have to doubt for long.

The next day in the House of Commons, the Government announced the establishment of the Polish

Resettlement Corps. This would be the family of Polish soldiers and civilians, who fought under the direction of the British High Command as Polish II Corps. The program would involve mostly the Carpathian Division as many in the 5th Kresowa Division had chosen to return to Poland.

In spite of this inspiring program from the British Government, the Allies barred the Polish II Corps from participating in the Victory Parade in London on June 8, 1946. Having already acknowledged the Communist Government in Warsaw to be the actual government of Poland, the invitation to participate in the parade was sent to Warsaw and not to General Anders. When Communist Poland delayed its reply and did not send troops, the British Government asked the Polish pilots who belonged to the Royal Air Force to participate in the celebrations. The airman refused saying they would not attend if the soldiers and navy were not invited. Ernest Bevin then invited Polish soldiers at the last second. They refused. Poland was represented in the parade by only one dignitary of the Communist Government.

Before the end of June 1946, nineteen thousand Polish soldiers and civilians boarded ships leaving Italy behind for their new home in England. Those first vessels did not file full passenger lists. Bernard could see, hear and feel the exhilaration of those boarding the vessels. He imagined sailing the Atlantic, envisioned landing on the south coast, and pictured himself at home in a Polish camp in Britain. This meant a future. This was the best that any Pole in Italy could ever imagine. The Polish II Corps was disbanded in 1946, and the Polish Armed Forces under British High Command ceased to exist in 1947. The Polish Resettlement Corps had become home to more than 120,000 Polish soldiers plus thousands of civilians. The future shone upon them. While waiting his turn, Bernard smiled in his heart with an expression that never dimmed.

(XVII)

Bernard ambled along the wooden docks under the full moon sky, trying earnestly to slow himself down. The ship, R.M.S. Andes, was already moored, ready to take up to the Polish soldiers to their new home. So many had left before, and now it was their turn, Bernard's turn. Naples had been his home for the past two weeks. He was provided with transit papers in the camp near Pisa, and given specific orders to board the ship on a certain date. The emigration was so meticulously organized that efficiency alone created images of a very organized and caring nation. Everything that may have been expressed or conjectured about the English while the Poles fought in Italy was now becoming so untrue. These were compassionate people. Bernard was not going to miss out on this opportunity. Being in Naples early was a necessity.

The Neapolitans were still very receptive to the former Allied soldiers. This was indeed a benefit in getting a room and incredible meals for no cost. The family was ever so basic in so many aspects of their life: breakfast and supper together, prayers and Mass, walks and bicycle rides, daily ventures to the fishing docks, and visiting elderly friends and relations. "This is why we fought." Bernard concluded on more than one occasion. The boarding plank for the R.M.S. Andes slid onto the dock at sunrise that morning. The troops were all ready, each with a small knapsack and their identity card. Bernard's tunic and clothes had been washed the day before. He felt so very properly attired. This was a formal occasion. Many of the soldiers he had already met in the camps. The vessel, once the 856 Polish soldiers, supplies and crew were on board, rapidly departed. Bernard waved good-bye to Italy. It wasn't the smoothest ride: west through the Mediterranean, past Gibraltar, north along Iberia and French coasts. The Atlantic was its usual rough in September. The night air was very cold compared to the warmth of the midday sun. There were three floors below deck and two above. Ben was in the second lowest floor. Throughout the trip his transit document remained secure in his vest pocket. The document, prepared before his departure, listed his age of nineteen in 1944. Instead of his first name, it recorded his middle name: 'Pawel Pawlowski 19'.

The ship docked at Southampton on September 30, 1946. Each soldier bounced down the plank onto the dock, enthused with unrestrained prospects. British citizens were there to greet them, among them many women whose husbands died in the war. Regional council members ushered the troops to the appropriate processing facilities. There were more than enough translators. Bernard had lined up like once before, behind other Poles; but that was at Fort VII in Poznan. This was so incredibly different. It was amazing how joy had so instantly become loud, cheerful and unbounded.

The train trip took them north toward London, and then veered to the north-west to a station north of the Thames. Those, for whom there were no trains, road in military vehicles. One of the conductors entered the car all full of dutiful emotion for the Polish soldiers. He used a term that prompted some concern, "Polish Displaced Persons Camp." Bernard and the others had never heard that before. Even with adequate translation there were still questions about the term "wysiedlonych." He wasn't 'displaced'. All of this, this new life in England, had been promised. The translator continued reminding them that the Polish II Corps was disbanded, and that the Polish soldiers were only in England because of the generosity of the British Government. After telling the Polish soldiers why they had to be grateful to the British people, the translator continued with essential details.

There were many such camps, and the ones already established had been medical clinics. Some had been constructed for possible use as prisoner of war centres. They had wooden barracks, and long house structures. There was a chapel, a community hall, a school, and facilities for family life. Employment was possible in the neighbouring towns and cities. The more he spoke, the more enthused Bernard became. At the train station there were more army vehicles waiting. That portion of the trip was about another fifteen minutes. It was late afternoon when they arrived at the camp.

Hodgemoor Woods presented an encouraging vista, surrounded with acres of pine, fir, birch and oak trees. There were rows of wooden barracks. The first of the pre-fab long-house structures was near the entrance. Others could be seen in the distance. The newcomers were all assembled together, a mass of soldiers all belonging to the 3rd Carpathian Rifle Division. The camp was already home to many soldiers and their families who had previously arrived. They provided an aura of enthusiastic commotion as they headed to the mess hall. There was an air of happiness that was quickly recognizable. The information given to the soldiers on the train was repeated again to those who did not hear it. They would have a bed with proper bedding. They were responsible for daily chores and maintenance of the camps. Information regarding prospects of employment was repeated. Bernard paid strict attention to that aspect. The smiles were many when they were promised classes in the English language. At the conclusion of the speech, one of the group commanders and the chaplain were introduced. Then the Polish flag ascended the pole as they all jubilantly sang their national anthem. Bernard and all of the soldiers had to hand over their transit cards, and in turn received a British Identification Card. This bore his proper name and current age.

The next morning, he was awake as normal, ready for the raising of the flags. Both the Polish Ensign and the Union Jack were raised on separate poles to the music and singing of the national anthems. Then as if led by some angel, Bernard was kneeling in the chapel. Attending Mass on a Tuesday morning had never been a priority. Regardless of how much he had experienced, he was in those moments alone with God praying for his family if they were still alive, for those still in Poland, and for himself. There was so much to say; yet at the end of his litany Bernard wondered if God even heard a word. Bernard maintained the practice of his faith. It was expected that if you were Polish in a Polish camp; then you would go to Mass on Sunday. Reverend Jozef Madeja led the congregation in Mass three times each Sunday. After that, he toured the camp identifying the location of community hall, the post office, and the school. The community hall also provided a pub, entertainment, dancing, meals, and a billboard for employment and language opportunities. There was a second mess hall. The Polish immigrants provided their own kitchen and laundry facilities. Gardens were plentiful, near each barrack. There was also a choir and musical groups. In the far distance there were the garages for the military vehicles. Bernard was interested. Within the hour he had a wrench in his hand and was busy working on a truck's suspension. That task proved his worth and ability. Before the end of the year Bernard had employment, albeit only on a temporary basis, in High Wycombe. Learning English was essential. Some troops took that responsibility seriously. Others seemed to think the camp would last forever. Bernard was too young and enthusiastic to ever draw that conclusion. He was given a ticket to get to England and he needed a ticket to get out of the camp. The many, among the six hundred families, who wanted to learn English could not all be taught in the community hall or school. Most of these teachers came from the English towns and villages. Bernard was directed to attend Holy Cross School for his lessons. There, he met a young lady, Mary Saunders who was a former student of Holy Cross School. She was volunteering as a teacher for the many displaced persons in the camp. For him, it was love at first sight. For Mary, it was initially her role in the British program established in 1947. The agenda was created by the Committee for the Education of Poles in Great Britain to teach English to Polish soldiers, and to further their education in other courses. In addition the program supported sixteen nursery schools and thirty-four primary schools. It even established housing and educational facilities for more than 2,000 orphaned children. When Mary failed to show up one day, Bernard enquired until he got his answer. His heart had decided. His determination was focused.

Leon Pawlowski 1935

King George V and General Anders on the battlefield

Victory, May 18, 1944

(Taken by an unknown solider in the Polish II Corps)

3rd Carpathian Rifle Division

Bernard 1946

Wedding Day – November 27, 1947

Toronto, 1952

Brothers United: Bernard, Ryszard and Andrzej, 1975

Medals: Warsaw Parade 1992

Monte Cassino Medal

Chapter Twelve
The Final Journey

Iodine could not hide the scars, but love did! Bernard and Mary, after a summer of alluring bliss, were married on November 27, 1947, the day before her twenty-second birthday. Married life meant Bernard had to leave the camp. All he could take was his cap and his badge. His parents-in-law welcomed the couple briefly into their home. Then the newly-weds acquired a home in Chalfont St. Giles. The house was a nineteenth century structure with small and convenient rooms. The firm roof was covered in thatch. An expansive vegetable garden filled the rear with trees at the far end. The blossoms of the cherry tree were always the first to greet the spring. These were happy times in spite of the food shortage that pervaded the British Isles. Events in 1948 decided their future.

The Marshall Plan was introduced by the United States in April, 1948. Also known as the European Recovery Program, the American government pledged thirteen billion dollars to rebuild the industry and economies of devastated countries. From the outset the main goal of the plan was to avoid the repeat of a destitute Germany following the first war. The offer of assistance to the Soviet satellite nations was refused. Residents of Italy barely saw a dime, compelling many to seek a future in the Americas. As for Britain, it did not receive any meaningful support. The country that caused and lost the war was the beneficiary.

The United States also made overtures to the Polish troops opening its ports to residents in the British camps. However, there was for some a catch. Bernard would have to enlist in the American Army. South East Asia was mentioned. He had already fought enough. He had lost more than he could have ever imagined. The United States was no longer an option.

During these first years of marriage, on many occasions Bernard and Mary returned to Hodgemoor Woods for gatherings and festivities. Mary embraced the entire Polish culture and how important it was for her husband to continue to enjoy his traditions. The entire region had become home to many Poles, so it was easy to be drawn into the various celebrations. However whatever pleasantries the Polish camp may have offered, there still remained hellish images in his mind. The sound of artillery, the fire of machine gun volleys, the screams of dying soldiers, the stench of decaying bodies, the soldiers risking their lives to remove and bury the dead, the demoralized spirits, the chaplain who had no more words, and the terror of Plaszow Camp: all these continued to permeate sleepless nights. And then, there was his family. The memories of the last morning together never left his mind searching for something meaningful from his youth. These issues so many would never discuss at camp. They lay buried in the souls of the anguished and devastated.

Discussions at the camp affirmed the aspirations of many of the soldiers. Canada was becoming the first choice. As a member of the Commonwealth with a parliamentary system of government, the country offered all the best of British society and even more – opportunities. Mary filed their application for emigration, shortly after their wedding.

While awaiting word from Canada House, their son, Michael, was born in May 1949. The first grandchild brought joy to the entire family. Bernard was obviously elated, but couldn't avoid thinking of his own father, "He'd be a grandfather." But, with every such thought, the question always echoed, "Is he still alive?" Bernard's ability in the English language improved significantly. Mary realized there was a major hurdle for her husband learning this language. Every Pole spoke and understood at least three languages. And now, her husband was being asked to develop fluency in his fifth language.

However, there was no choice. The family goal was Canada, and English was required. Conditions in England were deteriorating rapidly. Their child did not taste most fruit. A banana or orange, he never saw in England. Family meals contained mainly starch. Soups were the regular evening repast. A small chunk of meat had to last a week. Bones for their marrow were a delicacy. Chicken wings were never discarded. A vegetable garden was essential. Fridges of course were not in existence. Ice was rare excepted on the coldest days in winter. Coal was also becoming in short supply with talk that it was going to be rationed.

One of Mary's brothers was the first in the family to settle in Canada. His income and life style in the new country encouraged their parents, Arthur and Carol Saunders, to emigrate. Bernard was consistently appreciative for the opportunities they extended in England. Now with the parents already in Canada and there to provide sponsorship if required, Mary and

Bernard's application received that extra impetus. On April 1, 1952, the young family arrived by ship at Halifax. A train trip brought the family to Toronto.

Enough could never be said about the immediate influence and assistance of the Polish Legion in west-end Toronto. The Polish II Corps and the Polish Armed Forces in the West may have been disbanded, but the individual soldiers and commissioned officers never forgot each other. A family's need was everyone's concern. The residences in Toronto were many. The first was in the city core. After more than a year in leased dwelling, they moved west to a rented home near High Park. By early 1955 they were renting the basement of a house in Downsview.

Mary encountered considerable difficulty obtaining employment. There was no preference for an English-speaking person from England. One in six Canadians was looking for work. Plus, employment opportunities in any country for women were truly scarce. Ultimately Mary did find a job with an English insurance company. Thankfully, English insurance companies were moderately receptive to English-speaking persons from England. In that profession, in fact with the same company, she remained employed for thirty-three years.

Bernard was stonewalled in his attempts to obtain employment as a machinist in spite of his skills and his experience in Czechoslovakia and Italy. Ben's main hurdle was the English language. Several employers turned aside his application because he was not totally fluent. Whether the reasons were prejudiced or a safety issue was never known. There were many evenings spent on the verge of tears. Finally, his father-in-law visited one employer after it had rejected Bernard's application.

"Machines don't speak English." The assertion was direct. The next day in early 1953 Bernard began employment.

Good fortune rarely shines for long when you're an immigrant. The employer obtained a very significant government contract building aircraft. The weekly salary that started at $70 was over $100 per week within three years. In the 1950s that was a massive increase. With their good economic fortune it was time to consider the purchase of a house.

It was then that wartime events in Europe again covered their dreams in black clouds. Bernard and Mary with their son Michael had high hopes to have their first home by late 1955. Then they confronted the devastating presence of another 'Pawlowski family'. Two weeks prior to their own arrival at Halifax, this other 'Pawlowski family' landed at Halifax. Their parents' names were Michael and Mary. Their son was named Bogdan. Due to that Michael's disturbing past and the family's desire to keep his identity hidden, when the family secured a bank loan, they did so in the names of Mary and Bogdan, eschewing Michael's name. Shortly thereafter they were avoiding their mortgage payments. Without pause the bank foreclosed on them.

So when Bernard and Mary applied for a mortgage, they were immediately rejected because it was concluded that they were the same as Bogdan and Mary.

The name of that other Michael Pawlowski with his infamous past would be flashed across the press thirty years later when he was arrested for war crimes involving mass exterminations.

It seemed to take forever to get the lending institutions to accept that one Pawlowski family was not the same as another. Ultimately that happened, and in May 1956, Bernard and Mary moved into their own home in the north-end of Toronto. Four years later, they provided shelter for Mary's parents. The grandparents lived with Bernard's family until they passed to eternity.

The backyard provided ample opportunity for gardening. Besides the vegetables and flowering shrubs, Bernard planted his trees – cherry, apple and pear – to relive the memories of their home in Chalfont St. Giles.

Willowdale was a small, well-organized community in the larger constituency of North York. Amenities exceeded the norm. Their parish church was an essential ingredient in their lives, a place to share and to worship, and a community home to express gratitude. Italian priests had been assigned to serve the parish because of the number of Italian immigrants in the area and north of the city. Bernard quickly discovered how small the world was when he met several Italian gentlemen who had fought with the Allies in the Italian Republican Army. The priests and the congregation worked well together in so many plans and activities. The first priority was moving out of an entertainment hall for Sunday Mass and having the parish build its own church. Bernard was one of several on a planning and construction committees. The church grounds provided a large field for sports: mainly baseball and soccer. Ben joined the Holy Name Society. When asked, he coached one of the hockey teams for two winters. Mary joined the Catholic Woman's League and with her sister-in-law performed parish secretarial duties. There were so many families in need. Food baskets were required throughout the year. The parish had three rehabilitation centres.

Bernard and Mary volunteered to visit the elderly and infirm. Their son became an altar boy. The opportunities were many to do much.

Bernard was intrigued with the political system. Having lived through the violence and influence of two dictatorships, he was almost thrilled with the idea he could vote and had an influence on the outcome. In fact 74% of eligible Canadians voted in that election of 1957. The Progressive Conservative Party of John Diefenbaker won, but with a minority government having only 112 of the 265 seats. "Only four parties," Bernard expressed on more than one occasion. That government did not last long, and within the year another election was held. That entire concept baffled Bernard in light of events before and during the war. His mother-in-law was actively involved in both campaigns, as she had been in Britain. Bernard readily responded by driving several enthusiastic seniors to all of their political campaign meetings.

Life's bliss suddenly ended in February 1959 when the government ended the construction project of the Avro plane. The decision closed the factory, and Bernard was unemployed. Labour discussions followed, but with no quick resolution for those who remained out of work. Unemployment Benefits were limited both in amount and duration. Times were again tight.

Eventually a permanent position became available at York Gears. As a machinist then as a lead-hand Bernard applied his skills. The requested overtime hours were always completed. The marketing department had secured sufficient contracts to guarantee years of production. Then seven years later, good fortune again shined. Spar Aerospace purchased the firm.

Throughout this time Bernard continued to attend the Polish Legion and complete the visits to the seniors' home. Time with his son was always available. And for his father-in-law time too was made for regular outings to the racetrack. Every third weekend from April to October, Bernard took his son and father-in-law fishing. The catch was plentiful in an era before water pollution.

In August, 1960, the members of the Polish Legion proudly marched in the Warrior's Day Parade at the Canadian National Exhibition. At that time, the emphasis was still on expressing gratitude to the World War I Veterans from the Battles at Ypres, the Somme, and Passchendaele.

1967 was truly a memorable year with so many extremes.

Michael was attending high school in Grade 12 in April 1967. As usual, he'd be home by four o'clock to do some chores or start his homework. His grandparents had already retired. His mom, who was still working would get home about six o'clock. His dad was on the afternoon shift that week, so he wasn't expected home. On entering the house, Michael discovered his father lying on the ground crying. He was prone and quite unable to control himself. Moments, became minutes. The grandmother entered the room and panicked. Bernard was clutching an envelope with its letter. Some photographs lay face down on the rug. The son bent down trying to ascertain the reason for his father's situation. Eventually, he mumbled through the tears, "Here." Michael looked at the envelope. It was all in Polish. He didn't understand a word. The grandmother picked up the photographs, looked at them; and then passed them to her grandson with a shocked expression on her face.

The priest's vestments were black, the casket dark, the followers many. Bernard's mother never stopped looking for her son. For more than twenty years after the war she searched, eventually being given a list of potential addresses in Canada. Her written enquiries begot a possible result. She wrote the letter, describing everything and everyone, and provided her tribute to her husband by sending pictures of Leon Pawlowski's funeral to her son.

After discovering his mother was still alive, and that he had one sister, two brothers and many nieces and nephews; Bernard realized how precious his Polish family was. There were more tears on many more occasions, whenever he regretted not doing more to find his family. He had tried for more than five years – in England and in Canada – through governments and government agencies. There was never a reply, except, 'I'm sorry." After each regretful reply, Bernard conceded that perhaps he was best not to know if the family never survived the initial onslaught. So many comrades had related such stories. "How could they still be alive?" he had often asked himself.

Proud to be Canadians, Bernard, Mary and Michael attended several Centennial events including the Expo in Montreal.

In July, the family returned to England for a three week vacation, visiting the sights that were so important for them. Hodgemoor Camp was no longer there, having closed in 1962. Just a plaque remained. Being in Britain, brought Bernard and Mary closer to Poland but there was still the Iron Curtain preventing permission to visit the country of his birth. English history became very much alive for their son.

Also that summer, the family purchased land for a cottage about seventy miles north of the city. It was basically a wooded lot. The lake fed into others, and then into Georgian Bay. A cottage would be built four years later.

In early autumn following a meeting at the Legion Hall, Bernard was invited to visit a farm north of Toronto. The farm owner, unknown to Ben, had been a comrade in the Polish Corps. The acreage produced vegetables and fruit, but mainly livestock. The slaughtered animals were taken directly to the butchers. Bernard envied his comrade's entrepreneurial and farming skills and the good fortune. The gentleman farmer never relinquished his military skills. On the farm he had placed a series of targets; small foot wide targets on the trunks of old trees. From more than one hundred yards, they shot at the target. Laughter continued almost till midnight. Meeting a fellow Carpathian in such a setting was an incredible experience.

Following that visit to the farm, and bearing in mind all that happened within the last year, Bernard opened his heart regarding the war. Doing so was so rare, as most victims of the war and holocaust era tended to be silent about the tragic events. While driving to the cottage, Bernard started the story. The ongoing saga continued providing the details, the impact, and the consequences of each action, and every decision. The invasion, the concentration camps, the escape, the flight, Syria, Egypt, Italy, Monte Cassino, Piedimonte, Ancona, Bologna, and Hodgemoor all became very real once more.

Bernard's ongoing attempts to return to Poland took eight years. Someone at the Legion suggested it was because of Bernard's involvement in the Polish II Corps. Communist Leaders still had no respect for those soldiers. Efforts by the Canadian Government were not able to hurry the process.

Relief and exhilaration met at the Warsaw airport in 1975 when his mother and two of his siblings greeted him. In Poland they attended Mass celebrated by a Polish Cardinal who three years later became Pope. At Jasna Gora, they prayed fervently to Our Lady of Czestochowa, thanking the Blessed Virgin Mary for caring for his mother for those many years within those very walls. Even on their return to Canada the smiles and joy did not stop. Bernard returned to Poland three more times in the next eight years. Then in 1992 he marched with fellow members of the Polish II Corps in Warsaw.

Poland ceased to be Communist as a result of Pope John Paul II's discussion with General Secretary Mikael Gorbachev. The Pope asked the Soviet Leader to promise to not have Soviet troops intervene in Poland during strikes or demonstrations. Mr. Gorbachev agreed and the Communist Government of Poland, without the support of the USSR, was not able to thwart the will of the people.

In 1984 the Pope visited Canada. Bernard and Mary were there at the Martyr's Shrine and at the special assembly of more than fifty thousand Polish people who greeted their fellow countryman.

While a considerable portion of his time in those years was directed to everything Polish and Papal, Bernard had other reasons to celebrate. His grandchildren were born. And at work, those to whom he had provided the initial instruction on the operation of specific machinery, had subsequently put their minds and skills together and produced the Canada Arm.

Unfortunately, life reminded Bernard once again never to be too happy about everything. In 1984, his father-in-law passed away. Four years later, his mother-in-law died.

The trips to the cottage continued with even more stories that were so important from a mind becoming frail with age. Polish and English were now his only languages. In spite of any fragility, monthly attendance at the Legion Hall, and visits to the seniors' home continued with the consistent level of commitment. There remained always time for God and Sunday Mass.

The first hint of any major health issue occurred in the spring of 1987. Bernard suddenly collapsed after trying to hide the discomfort of internal pains. The blockage in his bladder had been caused by scar tissue as a result of being kicked by a horse in the abdomen during the war. Everything settled down and the energetic spirit returned.

Then in the summer of 1997 just after his 72nd birthday, internal pains became bleeding. They responded to rest and medication; however, weakness continued. The success of his grandchildren meant so much inspiring him to do more and struggle beyond physical limits.

In late April, 1999, stomach cancer was diagnosed with the prognosis that he had a month to live. Driving him one final time to the Legion Hall and to Mass meant so much both to Bernard and to his son. The expressions of satisfaction never dimmed his wrinkled expression.

Michael, then working in Toronto while living out of town, stayed the night on April 28, 1999. He awoke early to prepare breakfast, and to spend precious moments before work to converse with his dying father. Michael didn't have a chance to cook the meal, spill the orange juice or burn the toast. The breakfast was already done; and his father, though dying, was carrying a tray with the food into his son's room. It was time to shed tears.

After work, Michael called his father to make plans to visit on the weekend. Bernard told him not to come, and that he should take his daughter golfing instead. "Just for me," was his last expression.

With all of the visits by continuing care, arrangements were made that Michael would stay over on the evening of May 4th and thereafter.

At lunch on May 4th, his son purchased a standing-crucifix for his father's hospital bed. Having to eventually go into hospital seemed unavoidable. On the way back to the office, Michael stopped by a philatelic shop. His father had real pleasure reading old letters and postcards. Postage stamps bearing the image of the Pope would be especially well received. Several postcards were purchased. One in particular had the stamp of the previous Pope – John Paul I. Ben would surely appreciate the rarity of such an item.

Back at the office while still on lunch, Michael started reading the letters and postcards. The Vatican postcard, with the prior Pope's stamp, attracted his interest. It was dated "5.VI.80" The greetings began, "Blessed Daughter in the Spirit." He stopped immediately after reading the script upon viewing the signature. Disbelief was total. He reread the script, and then whispered, "He won't believe it." The postcard was signed "Johannes Paulus PP II."

Seconds later the office phone rang. His mother was on the line. "Your father's dead."

Countless were the people attending the funeral parlour: from our parish, and neighbours, and those we had never before met. Then as the ultimate tribute after the Rosary, the band and flag bearers from the Polish Canadian Legion attended to present arms, to sing together the national anthems, and to chant their songs of tribute to fallen soldiers. Their rendition of the Last Post brought many to tears. Incredible was the number who volunteered to be pallbearers.

In Holy Cross Cemetery Bernard Pawlowski rests, with his spouse and his parents-in-law. During the funeral service the Italian Priest, being well aware of the efforts of the Allies in Italy, offered the final tribute.

Rest in eternity, for you fought the good fight. You climbed the hill. Your hurt became our freedom.

BIBLIOGRAPHY

Anders, Wladyslaw. Memoirs 1939 – 1946, Paris: La Jeune Parque. (1948) OCLC 724739

Anders, Wladislaw. An Army in Exile. The Story of the Second Polish Corps. London: MacMillan & Co. (1949) ISBN 9780898390438.

Applebaum, Anne. Gulag, A History. New York: Doubleday. (2003) ISBN 0767900561.

Atkinson, Rick. Army at Dawn: War in North Africa. New York: Henry Holt (2002)

ISBN 0805087249.

Atkinson, Rick. The Day of Battle: War in Sicily and Italy. New York: Henry Holt (2007) ISBN 9780805062892.

Axelrod, Alan. Real History of World War II. New York: Sterling Publishing. (2008) ISBN 9781402740909.

Baluk, Stefan and Terry Tegnazian. Sikorski, No Simple Soldier: A Visual History of World War II's Unsong Allied Leader. Los Angeles: Aquila Polonica (2004) ISBN 978-1607720119.

Bauer, Eddy. The History of World War II. UK: Silverdale Publishing. (1984) ISBN 9781856055529.

Bellamy, Chris. Absolute War: Soviet Russia in Second World War. New York: Alfred Knopf & Random House. (2007) ISBN 9780375410864.

Biesiadka, Jacek et al., Twierdza Poznan Poznan: Wydawnictwo Rawelin. (2006) ISBN 8391534022.

Blaxland, Gregory. Alexander's Generals: Italian Campaign. London: William Kimber. (1979) ISBN 0718303865.

Block, Herbert. The Bombardment of Monte Cassino. Italy: Monte Cassino Abbey. (1979)

Blumenson, Martin. Salerno to Cassino. Washington: Office of Military History. (1969) OCLC 22107.

Caddick-Adams, Peter. Monte Cassino: Ten Armies in Hell, London: Cornerstone Publishing. (2013) ISBN 0199974640.

Chicago Tribune. Daily Newspapers (May, 1944)

Churchill, Winston. Memoirs of the Second World War. London: Houghton Mifflin Co. (1986) ISBN 139780395416853.

Cienciala, Anna et al. Katyn: A Crime without Punishment. Yale University Press. (2008) ISBN 9780300108514.

Conquest, Robert. Stalin, Breaker of Nations. New York: Viking-Penguin. (1991) ISBN 0670840890.

Cooper, Matthew. The German Army 1939–1945: Its Political and Military Failure. New York: Stein and Day. (1978) ISBN 0812824687.

Chodakiewicz, Marek Jan. Between Nazis and Soviets: Occupation Politics in Poland, 1939–1947. Kentucky: Lexington Books. (2004) ISBN 0739104845.

Clark, General Mark W. Calculated Risk, The War Memoirs of a Great American General. New York: Enigma Books. (2007) ISBN 9781929631599.

d'Este, Carlo. Fatal Decision: Anzio and the Battle for Rome. New York: Harper. (1991) ISBN 0060158905.

Dzikiewicz, Bronisław. Monte Cassino. Warsaw: Wydawn. Ministerstwa Obrony Narodowej. (1984) ISBN 9788311070431.

Ellis, John. A Statistical Survey: Essential Facts and Figures. New York: Facts on File (1993) ISBN 9781854102546.

Evans, Bradford, The Bombing of Monte Cassino. Self published. (1988) ASIN: B0007BJDRI.

Fest, Joachim. The Face of the Third Reich: Portraits of the Nazi Leadership. New York: Da Capo Press. (1970) ISBN 9780306809156.

Forty, George. Battle for Monte Cassino. London: Ian Allan Publishing. (2004) ISBN 0711030243.

Garlinski, Jozef. Poland in the Second World War. London: Palgrave Macmillan. (1985) ISBN 0333392582.

Gerwarth, Robert. Hitler's Hangman: The Life of Heydrich. Connecticut: Yale University Press. (2011) ISBN 9780300115758.

Gilbert, Martin. The Second World War, A Complete History. New York: Henry Holt (2004) ISBN 9780805076233.

Glantz, David M. & Jonathan House. When Titans Clashed: How the Red Army Stopped Hitler. Kansas: University Press of Kansas, (1995) ISBN 0700608990.

Goldman, Stuart D. The Red Army's Victory That Shaped World War II. Naval Institute Press. (2012) ISBN 9781612510989.

Hamilton, Nigel. Monty: Master of the Battlefield. London: Hamish Hamilton Ltd. (1984) ISBN 9780241111048.

Hapgood, David & David Richardson. Monte Cassino: The Story of the Most Controversial Battle of World War II. Cambridge MA: Da Capo. (1984) ISBN 0306811219.

Harper, Glyn & John Tonkin-Covell, Battle of Monte Cassino – Campaign and its Controversies, Australia: Allen & Unwin. (2013) ISBN 101741148790

Hassel, Sven, Monte Cassino. London: Orion Publishing. (2014) ISBN 101780228171.

Haugen, Brenda. Benito Mussolini: Fascist Italian Dictator. Minnesota: Compass Point Books. (2007) ISBN 0-756519888.

Andrew Hempel. Poland in World War II: An Illustrated Military History. New York: Hippocrene (2005) ISBN 978-0-7818-1004-3.

Heydrich, Lina. Life with a War Criminal. Pfaffenhofen: Ludwig Verlag. (1976) ISBN 978-3778710258.

Raul Hilberg. The Warsaw diary of Adam Czerniakow: Prelude to Doom New York: Stein & Day. (1979). ISBN-13: 9781566632300.

Hosch, William L. World War II: People, Politics, and Power. New York: Rosen Publishing Group. (2009) ISBN 161530046-5.

Jankowski, Eric. Da Montecassino a Piedimonte S. Germano. Italy: Marco Marzelli. (2007)

Katz, Robert. The Battle for Rome. New York: Simon & Schuster. (2003) ISBN 9780743216425.

Keegan, John. Churchill's Generals. London: Cassell (2005) ISBN 0-304-36712-5.

Kershaw, Ian (2000). Hitler: 1936–1945: Nemesis. London: Penguin Books. ISBN 9780140272390.

Kesselring, Albert. The Memoirs of Field Marshal Kesselring. London: Greenhill Books.(1953) ISBN 9781853677281

Kennedy, Robert M. The German Campaign in Poland . Germany: Zenger. (1980) ISBN 0892010649.

Kenneth Koskodan. No Greater Ally: The Untold Story of Poland's Forces in World War II. Oxford: Osprey Publishing. (2009) ISBN 9781846033650.

Knight, Amy. Beria: Stalin's First Lieutenant. New Jersey: Princeton University Press. (1995) ISBN 9780691010939.

Krząstek, Tadeusz. Battle of Monte Cassino, 1944. Polish Interpress Agency. (1984)

Kresy Siberia Virtual Museum: Western Exile's Dilemma. (Updated March, 2015)

Kubica, Jerry. Footprints on Monte Cassino. Create Space Independent, (2014) ISBN-13: 9781495201974.

Kwiatkowski, Bohdan. The Polish Home Army. London: Bellona (1949)

London Times. Various Daily Newspapers. (1943 & 1944)

Lukas, Richard C. Forgotten Holocaust: The Poles Under German Occupation. New York: Hippocrene Books. (2001) ISBN 0781809010.

Manchester, William and Paul Reid. The Last Lion, Winston Spencer Churchill: Defender of the Realm. Boston: Little, Brown. (2012) ISBN 0316547700.

Mead, Richard. Churchill's Lions: A biographical guide to the key British generals, UK: Spellmount. (2007) ISBN 9781862274310.

Merridale, Catherine. Ivan's War: Life and Death in the Red Army, 1939–1945, New York: Macmillan. (2006) ISBN 9780805074550 .

Michulec, Robert. Fall of Monte Cassino. Hong Kong: Concord Pub. (2007) ISBN 9623611536.

Mikolajczyk, Stanislaw. The Rape of Poland, the Pattern of Soviet Domination. London: Sampson Low, Marston & Co (1948)

Montreal Gazette. Daily newspapers. (May, 1944)

Olszewski, Marian. Fort VII w Poznaniu. Poznan: Wydawnictwo Poznańskie (1974)

Ostrowski, Dr.Mark. To Return To Poland Or Not To Return. Thesis to London University College (1996)

Overy, R.J. The Dictators: Hitler's Germany and Stalin's Russia. New York: WW Norton, (2004) ISBN 9780393020304.

Paldiel, Mordecai: Churches and the Holocaust. KTAV New Jersey: Publishing House Inc. (2006) ISBN 9780881259087.

Parker, Matthew (2004). Monte Cassino: The Hardest-Fought Battle of World War II. Doubleday. ISBN 0385509855.

Parkinson, Curtis. Dominic's War. Toronto: Tundra Books, (2006) ISBN 9780887767517.

Paul, Allen. Katyn: Stalin's massacre and the seeds of Polish Resurrection. Annapolis, Md.: Naval Institute Press. (1996) ISBN 9781557506702.

Peszke, Michael. Poland's Navy, 1918–1945. New York: Hippocrene Books. (1999) ISBN 9780781806725.

Peszke, Michael. The Polish Underground Army. North Carolina: McFarland & Company, (2005) ISBN 078642009X.

Phillips, N.C. Official History of New Zealand in the Second World War 1939–45. New Zealand: War History Branch, Department of Internal Affairs (1957)

Piekalkiewicz, Janusz. Cassino: Anatomy of the Battle. Historical Times. (1987) ISBN 0918678323.

Piesakowski, Tomasz. The Fate of Poles in the USSR. London: Gryf Publications (1990) ISBN 0901342246

Pleszak, Frank. Two Years in a Gulag. London: Amberley Publishing (2013) ISBN 9781445601779.

Plowman, Jeffrey & Perry Rowe, Battles for Monte Cassino. UK: Hobbs Cross House. (2011) ISBN13: 9781870067737

Emmanuel Ringelblum. Notes from the Warsaw Ghetto, New York: I-books. (2006) ISBN 1596873310.

Sanford, George. Katyn and the Soviet Massacre of 1940: Truth, Justice and Memory. London, New York: Routledge. (2005) ISBN 0415338735.

Sarner, Harvey. General Anders and the Soldiers of the Second Polish Corps. California: Brunswick Press. (1997) ISBN 1888521139.

Scott, Harriet & William Scott, The Armed Forces of the USSR. Colourado: Westview, (1984) ISBN 0865317925.

Sebag-Montefiore, Simon. Stalin: The Court of the Red Tsar. Toronto: Vintage Books. (2005) ISBN 1400076781.

Service, Robert. Stalin: A Biography. London: Macmillan. (2004) ISBN 9780333726273.

Śląski, Jerzy. Under the Star of David. Warszawa: Panstwowe Wydawnictwo Naukowe. (1988) ISBN 8301049464.

Smith, E. D. The Battles For Monte Cassino. London: Ian Allan. (1975) ISBN 0715394215.

Strachura, Peter. The Poles in Britain, 1940-2000: From Betrayal to Assimilation. UK: Psychology Press. (2004) ISBN 9780714655628.

Stefancic, David. Armies in exile. New York: Columbia University Press. (2005) ISBN 0880335653.

Stewart, Adrian. Early Battles of the Eighth Army. Barnsley, England: Pen & Sword. (2002) ISBN 9780850528510.

Bodie Thoene, Warsaw Requiem; The Zion Covenant, Tyndale House Publishing, 2001, ISBN 9781414301129.

TIME (weekly magazine). Report on British Foreign Secretary. (May, 1945)

Turkiewicz, Zygmunt. Monte Cassino: Sketches of the Battle Fought by 2nd Polish Corps.
Rome: Novissima, (1944)

Wankowicz, Melchior. Bitwa o Monte Cassino. Warsaw: Wydawnictwa. (1989) ISBN 8311076510.

Wankowicz, Melchior. Monte Cassino. Warsaw: Instytut Wydawniczy Pax. (1990) ISBN 8321113885.

Wawer, Z. Monte Cassino 1944. Warsaw: Bellona. (1994) ISBN 8311083118.

Wette, Wolfram. The Wehrmacht: History, Myth and Reality. Harvard University Press (2007) ISBN 9780674025776

Wiesenthal, Simon. Justice Not Vengeance. London: Weidenfeld & Nicolson. (1989) ISBN 9780297796831.

Wizgier, Henry. Hodgemoor Polish Camp near Amersham, 1946-62. Buckinghamshire, UK: Amersham News & Views.

Zabeth, Hyder R. Landmarks of Mashhad. Mashhad. Iran: Islamic Research Foundation. (1999) ISBN 9644442210.

Zaloga, Steven & Richard Hook, The Polish Army 1939-45, Oxford: Osprey Publishing, (1982) ISBN 0850454174.

ACKNOWLEDGEMENTS

Appreciation must be extended to the many persons who provided information pertinent to the struggles and tribulations of so many. Their personal stories make the characters become truly alive.

Bernard Pawlowski, soldier in 3rd Carpathian Rifle Division

Mary (nee Saunders) Pawlowski, spouse of Bernard

Ryszard Pawlowskibrother of Bernard

Arthur Saunders, father-in-law of Bernard

Maud (nee Martin) Saunders, mother-in-law of Bernard

James Saunders, English brother-in-law of Bernard

Margaret (nee Saunders) Crockett, English sister-in-law of Bernard

Franck Serenicky, soldier in 3rd Carpathian Rifle Division

Eduard Przyszbilski, soldier in 3rd Carpathian Rifle Division

Piotr Uzanofski, soldier in 3rd Carpathian Rifle Division

Tomasc Walewicz, soldier in 5th Kresowa Division

Edward Orzel, Q.C. resident of Krakow

Polish Canadian Legion, various members with war experience

Place Polonaise, various persons with war experience

George Rose, soldier in British 8th Army

David Boyd, soldier in British 8th Army

Vito Ladisa, sergeant in Italian Republic Army

John Agro, Q.C., soldier in Italian Republic Army

Rev. Raffaele Villella, resident of Calabria

Benedetto Pacitto, resident of Naples

Robert Griffiths, historian on Soviet history

John Berns, historian on American history

Special Appreciation

Gratitude is express to Wikipedia for its many articles providing research, information and incites confirming details obtained from others.